ONCE AND AGAIN

It was a gentleman's kiss. Light and soft. Quick. Unsatisfying. And he had every intention of leaving it that way.

"I think perhaps it's time to say good night."

"No." She tugged on his neck.

He resisted with a groan. "You're making it most difficult for me to act the gentleman," he said.

Matty looked up at him. Once they left the ship she would no longer be just Matty Maxwell. As Lady Matilda, she might never have a chance to be alone with him again. She did not want to live the rest of her life regretting her last opportunity lost.

"Good," she said, her voice breathy and husky. "Don't be a gentleman. Please. Kiss me again."

Preston could not deny her.

<u>BOOK YOUR PLACE ON OUR WEBSITE</u>
<u>AND MAKE THE</u>
<u>READING CONNECTION!</u>

We've created a customized website just for our very special readers, where you can get the inside scoop on everything that's going on with Zebra, Pinnacle and Kensington books.

When you come online, you'll have the exciting opportunity to:

- View covers of upcoming books
- Read sample chapters
- Learn about our future publishing schedule (listed by publication month *and author*)
- Find out when your favorite authors will be visiting a city near you
- Search for and order backlist books from our online catalog
- Check out author bios and background information
- Send e-mail to your favorite authors
- Meet the Kensington staff online
- Join us in weekly chats with authors, readers and other guests
- Get writing guidelines
- AND MUCH MORE!

Visit our website at
http://www.kensingtonbooks.com

The Christmas Wedding

Laurie Brown

ZEBRA BOOKS
KENSINGTON PUBLISHING CORP.
www.kensingtonbooks.com

Chapter 1

Davies Preston, Viscount Bathers, rolled his brandy glass slowly between his palms. "I agreed to deliver the gold. Nothing else."

Lord Marsfield gave him a stern look, ever the mentor even though Preston had been on his own as an agent for a number of years. Working for the Agency, a secret part of Whitehall, had taken him around the world, given him some interesting experiences, and gotten him into more than a few dangerous scrapes. But never had he been asked to play nursemaid.

Preston sipped his drink, blaming his ennui on the sultry weather. London was always tedious in early September. He should have gone grouse hunting in Scotland. Even Ripley's country party would have been better than this. Egad, no one stayed in the city before the Season started.

Marsfield sat back in his leather chair. Surrounded by the books and fine artwork of his library, Marsfield was the picture of success. He had a loving wife and two children, a comfortable town home, an expansive country estate, and the respect of his peers and the queen. All the things Preston lacked.

Preston suppressed a twinge of envy. He'd chosen

his life and would never regret turning his back on the expectations of his family.

"Why is the queen interested in this American chit?" he asked.

Marsfield unlocked a desk drawer and removed a packet of papers he passed across the desk to Preston. "Matilda Maxwell is the granddaughter of the Duke of Norbundshire."

"Old Norbie procreated?"

"The duke," Marsfield said, emphasizing the title, "disinherited his daughter Cecelia when she moved to New York and married an American named Blake Maxwell. After Cecelia died in a carriage accident, Maxwell left their four-year-old daughter with his aged aunt who had a small farm near a place called Turn-about, Tennessee. Maxwell took to drink and gambled heavily. He held a variety of posts—patent medicine salesman, piano player on a riverboat—anything to fund his next big game."

"I take it he wasn't a successful gambler," Preston said, flipping through the papers.

"When Matilda was seven, the aunt died," Marsfield continued, ignoring his comment. "For his daughter's sake, Maxwell reformed, took over the struggling farm, and for several years was even the town sheriff. But he succumbed to his old habits, and when he hit the road, he took Matilda with him. For a number of years they ran successful scams and made it all the way to San Francisco. Then the money ran out and he became ill. Maxwell died shortly after they returned to the farm."

"And now Old Norbie regrets his actions and wants to make amends to his granddaughter. I'll drink to his tardy noble sentiments. But why the secrecy? Why are we involved?"

"Norbundshire is the queen's cousin and she'd like to help him without creating a scandal."

Preston would bet his last farthing there was more to the story, but he also knew Marsfield would tell him only what he needed to know. He tossed the papers back on the desk. "This seems like a case for your friend Mr. Pinkerton."

"Where do you think I got all that information? Burke has volunteered the use of his new steamship, the *Helene*."

"I thought he had contracted the ship to the Diplomatic Corps for transporting ambassadors and the like."

"The *Helene* needs some time at sea to make sure everything is working properly. You can ride along on her sea trials. She's ready to leave at any time. May I suggest tomorrow?"

"Who's leaving?" Anne Marsfield asked as she swept into the library with a swish of light green silk.

Preston's heart lurched at the first sight of her, a small, familiar reminder she'd been his first love. Unrequited, of course, but never totally forgotten.

"Preston is leaving," Marsfield answered, rising as manners dictated.

"No one is leaving," Preston said at the same time. He also stood and he bowed over Anne's hand. "You look as lovely and refreshing as a cool breeze, my dear. Brings to mind the lawn party at Drusilla Frampton's last May."

Anne smiled before turning to her husband. "You see, others do notice and remember what people wear. I'll need to see my dressmaker to have something made for the dedication of the new orphanage dormitory."

Marsfield groaned and patted his pockets. "You'll make a pauper of me yet."

Preston dismissed the good-natured banter for just

that. He knew the man wouldn't deny his wife his last tuppence, though that was far, far, from happening. Marsfield and he had several investments in common that were doing quite well.

"And you can't send Preston away," Anne continued. "He promised to escort me to the ceremony because we both know how much you hate those long speeches."

"Don't fret," Preston said. "I'm sure Mr. Pinkerton can perform the necessary task for your husband. I shall be here for the dedication and to escort you to the Fuller's soiree Friday night."

Or was that the problem? Was Marsfield looking for an excuse to send him away? Surely he didn't think Preston still carried a torch for Anne. He'd gotten past that long ago. In fact, he was grateful to Anne for teaching him that love hurt. The lesson had saved him from allowing his heart to be broken again. Not that he was a stranger to relationships with women, but he had kept his emotions under control. Although he enjoyed Anne's company and often accompanied her when her husband was busy, the man had no reason to mistrust either his wife or his friend.

Marsfield crossed his arms over his chest. "Don't you think I tried Pinkerton first? Miss Maxwell didn't believe the Pinkerton agent and ran him off her land at gunpoint."

"I see you've decided to send Preston after Norbie's granddaughter," Anne said as she sat on the brocade sofa.

Both men returned to their seats. Preston wasn't surprised to learn Anne was aware of the mission. She had often assisted her husband, and he relied on her for insight and advice.

"That's logical, considering he has already said he would take the gold."

Preston had volunteered for that job so his best friend Burke could stay home with Cordelia, his pregnant wife. Cordelia and her grandmother, Vivian, had received some Confederate gold intended for illegal purposes and had decided it rightfully should be used to help victims of slavery and the war.

"Couldn't this wait?" Anne asked.

"Until the war is over?" Marsfield responded. "Who knows how long that will be?"

Preston had known for some time he would be taking the gold to America and had done his research accordingly. "Despite the fact both sides predict a swift victory, the war could drag on for years."

"I suppose you'll head for New York or Boston and then travel overland to that place in Tennessee," Anne said.

Preston shook his head. "The distance is too great. It could take months, what with both sides tearing up the train tracks. The roads will likely be impossible, even if I could purchase a decent carriage. No, I'll stick to the waterways. Don't forget my first errand is to deliver the gold to Savannah."

"Then you'll have to run the blockade?" she asked with a frown.

"Don't worry. The blockade runners enter and leave most ports with impunity because there's too much coastline for the limited number of Union ships to patrol effectively. Until their navy increases, it's more a matter of luck when they do capture a ship. There is some risk, but if I wait, the odds will likely change for the worse."

"We hear every day about battles and—"

"I'm sure Preston is touched by your concern, my

sweet; however, he's not inexperienced in subterfuge. I hardly think he'll be in any danger he can't handle," Marsfield assured his wife, although he'd never flinched at sending Preston into life-threatening situations before.

"Miss Maxwell ran off the last messenger at gunpoint," Anne pointed out.

"With Preston's particular talents I don't expect him to have any difficulty with the young woman."

"My talents? You want me to challenge her to a duel? Pistols at twenty paces? Engage her in a game of whist? No, we would need a third and a fourth. Fisticuffs? Although it has been a few years since I was in the ring with a woman . . ." Preston said, referring to the time Marsfield had tried to teach Anne to box. Of course, he had thought her a boy when he'd put gloves on her and pushed her into the ring with Preston. That jibe earned a stifled guffaw from Anne.

"Enough. You know bloody well I'm referring to your talent for charming women. All women. From age eight to eighty they fall all over themselves to do your bidding."

"Nonsense. My reputation—"

"As a womanizer is stuff and nonsense," Anne said. "You're too discriminating to deserve that appellation." She cocked her head to one side and put her finger on her chin. "However, most women do seem to think you understand them."

Marsfield threw his hands up. "How, is beyond me."

Preston lifted one shoulder. "I adore women. I like looking at them, dancing, conversing. I like the sound of their voices. If there is a secret, it's that I'm naturally attracted to passion."

"Isn't every man?" Marsfield asked.

"For the most part men skip directly to their own interests, and they expect women to be fascinated as they posture and expound unimaginatively on ordinary subjects. But every woman is passionate about something. It may be fashion—"

Marsfield groaned.

"Or music, gardening, horses, food, painting, sculpture, books, religion, politics—just about anything. Women are more intelligent than men credit—"

"Hear! Hear!" Anne interjected.

"When a woman converses on a subject she's passionate about, she blooms like an exotic flower. Regardless of her physical appearance, she becomes beautiful. I simply listen, learn, and enjoy."

"But do you really understand women?" Marsfield asked. "The way they think?"

"Really, we're not all that complicated."

"Oh, yes, you are," Preston said. "And it's the mystery that makes women so endlessly fascinating." He smiled. "Along with their other more obvious attributes."

That comment earned him a stern look from Anne.

"To women," Marsfield said, shaking his head ruefully and raising his snifter in a toast.

Preston returned the salute and drained his glass. "And if Miss Maxwell isn't susceptible to my charms?"

The only responses were snorts of laughter.

Preston wasn't about to list the women in his life who did not find him witty and charming, starting with his mother. In that particular woman's eyes, he could do nothing right. Egad, just the fact he'd allowed her to creep into his thoughts was a signal to leave London, even if it meant playing nursemaid to Old Norbie's descendant. "What if Miss Maxwell doesn't cooperate?" he asked Marsfield. "Am I supposed to tie her up and drag her back kicking and screaming?"

"Really, Preston. What a horrible notion," Anne said.

"Your mission is to get the duke's granddaughter safely to London," Marsfield said. "How you accomplish that is up to you."

Any other questions he might have had were put aside as Marsfield and Anne's children returned from their outing in the park and demanded their favorite honorary uncle's attention. Preston proceeded to ruin the knees of a perfectly fine pair of buff trousers by giving four-year-old Stephen horsey rides. Then his boots suffered abuse when he gave six-year-old Andrea her first dancing lesson by allowing her to stand on his toes as he stepped off the waltz to Anne's enthusiastic piano playing, which made the tempo more that of a polka. Somehow a wet, sticky peppermint wound up in one of his pockets. And even though Kelso, his valet, would have a fit of apoplexy, Preston enjoyed the frolic with the joie de vivre he'd never been allowed as a child.

When Marsfield called a halt to their parade through the parlors, Preston gave up his soup ladle and cooking pot drum with the same reluctance as Stephen and Andrea.

"It's time for a quiet activity," Marsfield said.

"Not as much fun," Preston mumbled, taking off his newspaper hat. "Spoilsport."

"Maybe so; however, after you wind them up like tops, you go off to your club or wherever, and we're left to deal with cranky children who can't settle down and go to sleep as they should."

"Now, Marsfield, I'm as much to blame as Preston," Anne said. "I've enjoyed the playtime, too."

"A bit of responsible adult supervision would not go

unappreciated," Marsfield said, with a stern look that reminded Preston far too much of his father.

"Yes, sir," Anne said with a mock salute.

Preston replaced his hat, clicked his heels, and offered his own crisp salute.

Marsfield rolled his eyes as the children copied their actions.

"Sir, if the general will dismiss his troops, sir, we will retire to the nursery for the recommended supper of porridge and warm milk and the reading of appropriately soothing bedtime stories, sir." Preston held his wooden expression in spite of several sets of giggles to his right.

"Go along with you then," Marsfield said. He gave Anne a warning glare but smiled at the children. "I'll be up shortly to wish you good night."

Preston called "right face!" and counted cadence as they marched up the stairs, Andrea in the lead, followed by Stephen and Anne. Because Preston brought up the rear, he saw Anne turn and stick out her tongue at her husband.

Preston raised an eyebrow at her.

"I'll pay for that later," she said with a grin.

From the sparkle in her eye, and the little jig to her step, he knew she anticipated her comeuppance with something far, far different from dread.

Preston suppressed another twinge of jealousy.

Only much later, when the ship's crossing allowed him leisure to review the conversation he'd had concerning Miss Maxwell, did Preston wonder why Marsfield had seemed to put an undue emphasis on one particular word when he'd said his mission was to get her *safely* to London?

Savannah, Georgia

Preston tapped on the door of the nondescript facade of an ordinary town house a few blocks from the heart of the city. When no one answered, he set down his heavy satchel and double checked his directions. Impatient to be done with his errand, he knocked again, a bit louder. The door opened mere inches.

"Madame Lavonne isn't accepting visitors," a girl's voice said in a no-nonsense tone. "Good day to you."

Preston stuck out his foot to prevent her from closing the door in his face. He held out his card just into the opening so she would have to open the door to take it.

A young black woman wearing a maid's apron and a colorful turban peeked out.

He smiled at her. "Are you the mistress of the house?"

She looked him up and down with bold eyes. Then she straightened her neckerchief, tipped her head, and simpered up at him, "La, no. I'm just the kitchen . . . um, the ladies' maid."

"Would you do a favor for me? If it's not too much trouble, that is."

She twisted her head to the other side and brushed her hands down the front of her apron. "That depends on what kind a favor you be wanting."

"Please tell Madame Lavonne I have letters from her friends in England, from Archangel."

The woman's eyes grew wide as teacups, making her look even younger. With an unintelligible squeak she disappeared from view, leaving the door half open and Preston standing on the stoop. He waited for a few moments, fidgeting and looking around. Then he picked up his satchel and nudged the door farther open.

"Hello," he said, stepping to the threshold. "Is anyone home?" He peered inside. Knickknacks, bric-a-brac, and objets d'art packed the small entrance hall. Stuffed animals and birds, African ceremonial masks, bones and skulls of assorted sizes, strings of glass beads, primitive paintings of nightmare scenes, human figurines made of every material from cornhusks to fur, and an incongruous five-foot-tall Chinese vase crowded every available inch of wall space and most of the floor area except for a narrow winding path. Every which way he looked, blank eyes stared back at him.

"Mr. Preston?"

"Hello?" He whirled around and for a moment it seemed as if the voice had come from a stuffed grizzly bear. Then a statuesque woman stepped into the hallway. Elegantly dressed, she had a timeless beauty, graceful and poised.

"Madame Lavonne?"

She shook her head. "I'll take you to my aunt." She turned and walked away as if daring him to follow her deeper into the strange establishment.

Down another similarly decorated hall, past several darkened rooms, he kept pace with her silent steps. At the far end, she motioned for him to proceed through a set of open French doors. He stepped into a courtyard sheltered by the branches of a massive oak, as if the house had been built around the tree. Indeed it must have been so because the oak had to be hundreds of years old. Throughout its branches bits of tin and glass had been tied with ribbons of every color, giving it a festive appearance. Even the slight breeze that was present created the tinkling of a hundred tiny bells.

At the base of the tree, among an assortment of statues and altars with offerings of food, whiskey, and coins, sat a wizened black woman in an overstuffed chair. In front of her a small wooden table held a candle, a deck of cards, a bowl of salt, and a glass of whiskey.

"Madame Lavonne?"

She nodded as she lit the candle.

He held out another of his calling cards. "My name is—"

She motioned him to silence. "I do not need your card when mine tell me so much more. Be seated, *s'il vous plaît*. This will only take a moment."

Preston looked around, but the only chair was a low stool made from some kind of tree root. He sat, folding his legs into an uncomfortable pretzel.

Madame Lavonne sprinkled salt in the four cardinal directions, then followed each with a splash of whiskey, all the while mumbling under her breath. She picked up the deck and dealt several cards on the table, face up.

Preston peered over the edge of the table, but the pictures on the cards were not like any he'd ever seen.

"These are tarot cards," she said, answering his unspoken question as she slowly added one on top of another, creating a starburst design on the table. "They tell me the past, the present, and the future."

He watched for a few minutes, but his uncomfortable position caused him to twist this way and that.

"Stop fidgeting, Lord Bathers."

Startled, he looked around the courtyard. The voice had sounded exactly like his childhood tutor, Mr. Christian. Preston hadn't thought of him in years. Again, he peered left and right. Yet he was alone with Madame Lavonne. He looked at her more closely, but she gave no indication she had either spoken or heard the voice. She seemed totally absorbed in her task.

Finally, she looked up. "I see you are a nonbeliever," she said, motioning to the pattern of tarot cards.

"I believe in what I can see and touch."

"And what of religion?"

"An excuse for the sanctimonious to feel righteous."

"Hope? Faith?"

"Sops for the unfortunate."

"Love? Do you not believe in the power of *l'amour?*"

Preston laughed. "Love is the decorative trapping society puts on lust to make it palatable. And lust is only powerful until it is slacked."

"I have much knowledge to share with you; *maintenant*, it will do no good unless you are willing to listen. Perhaps if I tell you the scar above your eye is the result of a sword fight with a friend, then you will open your mind."

Preston lifted his hand to the spot beneath his left eyebrow where the wound had healed in a thin white line. Burke had accidentally whacked him in the head with a wooden sword when they were boys. How could she know? Then he realized Cordelia, Burke's new wife, had probably heard the story and written to Madame Lavonne.

"I'm afraid you'll have to do better than that." He smiled his most charming, can-I-have-another-cookie smile, the one that had never failed to get another sweet from Cook, but Madame met it with a solemn glare.

"The cards say you are about to take a journey."

"I've traveled here; therefore, it doesn't take a leap of imagination to predict I'm likely to go home."

"This card," she said, tapping one with her gnarled finger, "says you'll meet a stranger, a woman with light hair."

He laughed. "Everyone here is a stranger, half of

them women, and I'm sure quite a number of them with light hair. Your prediction may well happen within minutes of my leaving this place."

Madame Lavonne slammed her hands down on the table, making the cards dance and the candle wobble. "Merde! I'm trying to help you because you aided my friends." She picked up a card and shook it under his nose. "You are stubborn, so pigheaded."

With a bit of difficulty she stood. Preston jumped up to offer her an elbow, but she refused his help.

"I warn you, monsieur, the past is not what you think, the present is not as you wish, and the future is not as you plan." With that she turned and stomped from the courtyard with an energy that belied her age.

For a moment he stood, stunned by what had just happened. And he still had the satchel full of gold sovereigns. Cordelia and Vivian had insisted Madame Lavonne would be the one to fairly distribute the largesse.

Should he just leave the satchel under the oak tree?

Then the niece returned. She indicated he should leave the satchel by the courtyard entrance and led him to the front door in silence. As he stepped out onto the front stoop, she laid her hand on his arm, so lightly he barely felt it. He paused.

"My aunt sends her apologies for losing her temper. She . . . she has been under a lot of stress lately."

"Please relay my apologies for my behavior. I baited her shamefully. I can only offer a tedious voyage and an appalling fondness for a good argument as an inadequate excuse."

They said good day.

"Good luck," she called after him as he walked down the street. "You're going to need it."

At that Preston turned back, but no one stood at the

nondescript door. Shaking off a feeling of unease, he set his mind on his second task. Compared to this interview, convincing Miss Maxwell to return to England with him and accept her inheritance should be as easy as a gallop through Hyde Park.

Chapter 2

Westgate Farm, Tennessee

Matty Maxwell jerked awake. Had she heard something? Everything was quiet. She heaved a sigh that stretched into an open-mouthed yawn. With Bessie getting her two-year-old molars, neither of them had slept through the night for what seemed like ages. When that child cried, they could hear her in the next county. Even eight-year-old Nathan, who usually slept like a stone, had been waking up nearly every night.

Standing and stretching, Matty worked the kinks out of her back and shoulders. She'd fallen asleep in the rocking chair again. She should've known better than to sit down before her chores were done.

She looked up at the ormolu clock on the mantel, the only item of her mother's she had managed to save. Two o'clock in the morning was no time to bake, but if she didn't do it now, the loaves she'd proofed earlier would be ruined and there would be no bread tomorrow. She stirred the fire, regretting the necessity for adding yet more heat to the still-stuffy room. The heat of summer had held on. This was good for the cotton farmers, but she longed for cooler weather. Next year she'd find a way to build an outdoor oven like her father had promised.

Matty set the covered pot of dough in the center of the fireplace grate and shoveled the hot coals over and around the Dutch oven.

Running the farm on her own was proving more difficult than she'd expected. Every day she slipped a bit further behind, left a chore unfinished. Yet she would not admit defeat. This was her home, her dream of putting down roots and staying in one place, the only real home either she or the children had ever known. Nathan had been traveling with a band of Indians when she had traded a horse and a blanket for the silent five-year-old. And Bessie had been a newborn infant when someone had left her on Matty's doorstep.

Wiping the sweat from her brow with her sleeve, she grabbed the empty water bucket and headed out to the pump.

The night air caressed her cheek and she wished she had time to untwist her coronet of braids and let the breeze massage her scalp. Instead she pulled her father's old hat more firmly on her head. Fanciful notions would not get the laundry done or the chickens fed. She pulled a bandana from the pocket of her overalls and wrapped it around her neck.

The smell of smoke wafted past her. She hesitated and looked around. It couldn't be from her chimney because the breeze came from the west. She scanned the horizon and spotted an orange glow near the watering hole where her small herd was corralled. Not the wide-reaching burn of a wildfire, and not the small cooking flame a traveler would make to heat his can of beans. No, that fire was meant to burn hot, the sort of fire cattle rustlers needed to heat the irons they used to overbrand.

"Damn thieving Delaney brothers."

They were not going to steal her cattle. She whirled

and ran back into the house for her rifle. Lazy bums didn't even go after the big herds like any self-respecting rustlers would. The Delaneys snuck onto their neighbor's property, placed their brand over the brand they found, then showed up a week or so later to claim their stock that had supposedly wandered off. Well, she'd worked too hard to let them walk off with her property.

She didn't need a lantern to light the familiar path to the watering hole. Although her first instinct was to rush them screaming and yelling, with the old Henry rifle blazing, she forced herself to use caution. She didn't know how many of the brothers there would be and she wanted to get the drop on all of them.

When she peeked through the surrounding bushes, her breath caught in her throat.

Only one man. And he was buck naked.

His back was to her and he stood hip deep in the water. Several of the Delaneys had dark hair but she couldn't reconcile his broad shoulders and lean, tapered waist with the weasel chests and glutton guts of the other brothers. Then again, there were so many; perhaps she hadn't met them all.

She watched as he leaned and twisted, mesmerized by the play of his wet, sleek muscles in the golden glow of the firelight. Her face warmed as if she stood near the flames. Forcing her gaze away, she scanned the area for his brothers. Wolves always traveled in packs.

Then she spotted her six head of cattle tied to a lead line staked near the roaring fire. Her blood chilled to an icy river. Damn Delaney was taking every cow she owned.

She whipped the Henry into position, sighted down the long barrel, and pulled the trigger. Even with the stock jammed tight against her shoulder, the kick from the old rifle staggered her backward. An act of will kept her on her feet and kept the rifle at the ready. Yet when the smoke cleared she wasn't confronted by an angry rustler, but by an empty pond.

She remembered a splash. But she hadn't missed. Not at this distance. A load of buckshot in the arse would make him remember every time he went to sit down for the next few weeks. Painful, but not fatal. If he didn't come up for air soon, he would drown. She stepped closer. Could he have hit his head?

"Damnation and dagnabbit." She set the rifle against a bush and waded in to the spot where he had stood. No body. The water came up to her waist, so she felt around the bottom with her feet. "Come on, Delaney. A few cows aren't worth drowning."

He burst up from the water with a giant roar like a sea monster from the deep. Water slapped her in the face and she turned and fled, her awkward progress slowed by the heavy wet denim of her overalls. She staggered to shore and reached for the rifle.

He tackled her from behind, knocking her flat. She lost her grip on the gun but managed to roll sideways to escape being pinned by his weight. He lunged. She kicked. He pushed. She got in an elbow shot to his ribs. For several minutes they rolled around in the dirt and mud grunting and growling like starving dogs scrapping over the last bone. She kneed him in the hip. He wrapped an arm around her and his hand molded over her breast.

He let go and jumped away from her. "You're a woman."

She scooted back crab-like, using her elbows and heels. "And you're trespassing on my land."

Two facts popped into his brain in quick succession.

This was the very woman he was supposed to charm into doing the queen's bidding, and here he was standing in front of her stark naked. He wasn't sure which gave him the most distress.

As the *esprit de guerre* drained from his system, the pain in his rear became more difficult to ignore. She pointed the rifle at him again and he raised both hands in the air. As she squinted up at him and her focus wandered from his face to his chest and lower, he could not suppress an ironic smile. With the firelight at his back, she wasn't seeing as much as she wanted to see. Then he noted the barrel of the rifle followed the direction of her gaze. "Please don't shoot," he said.

Her attention snapped back to his face. Then she smiled. Despite the mud and dirt, the sweet expression transformed her. He would never have thought her a boy if he'd seen her smiling. That was his last coherent thought before a sharp pain pierced the back of his head and darkness claimed him.

Matilda scrambled over to him. "Is he dead?" she asked her friend Joseph Two Feathers as she knelt next to the inert body.

"No. I am an old man. I can still walk silently but I can only hit hard enough to make him sleep. Maybe give him a big headache."

She tried to roll the man over. "Help me."

"First you shoot him, then you fuss over him," the old Indian grumbled as he lent a hand. "Make up your mind."

"I wanted to scare him away, not kill him." She brushed the dirt from his face. "I can't see much in this light, but he doesn't have the look of the Delaneys."

"This one is from far away."

She looked up at the Indian. When the other members of his tribe had left Nathan behind, Joseph had stayed. She'd come to depend on his help and trust his advice. Sometimes he seemed to have a mystical air, knowledge beyond the normal ken.

He snorted and motioned to the horses tied near her cattle. "A strong packhorse with a light load is the sign of long journey's end."

"He's not a rustler?"

"Can't tell. Only know he's not stealing tonight."

"Why did he tie up my cattle?"

Joseph shrugged. "Maybe he didn't want to bathe with nosy cows."

Matty sat back on her heels. "I'm afraid I've done this poor traveler a severe disservice." She stood and took one of the man's arms. "Help me get him back to the house."

He shook his head. "You go. Clean up and get bandages. Better I make travois. Bring him and horses."

She nodded and headed for home, wondering who the man was, and why he'd come to off-the-beaten-path Turnabout, Tennessee. Why had he chosen her particular watering hole to bathe? Unlike some, Matty didn't believe in coincidence.

Consciousness returned slowly to Preston as he floated prone on a fluffy cloud. Raising his head and peeling one sandpaper eyelid open, he spied a cherub inches from his face. Just like in Michelangelo's paintings, round face, pink cheeks, wispy blond hair, rosebud mouth, blue eyes. He was sure he'd died and gone to heaven until the erstwhile cherub let out a keening howl and ran away. Then he knew he'd landed in Hades, for that high-pitched, ear-splitting torture could only be one of the punishments of the damned.

With a groan he propped himself up on one elbow

and surveyed his surroundings from his awkward position lying crossways on a bed. Not exactly what he'd been led to expect in decor á la the Prince of Darkness. Oh, the bright light was decidedly unpleasant, but the rest of the room hardly bespoke the fire and brimstone Vicar Worthy had so vehemently promised Preston was his due. It seemed a normal bedroom. A bit on the spartan side for his taste, what with bare bedstead, worn quilted coverlet, and plain four-drawer dresser.

A knock reverberated through his skull with the resonance of Big Ben. He pried his other eye open and located the door near the end of the bed. When he saw Matilda Maxwell standing in the doorway, the events of the previous night came rushing back, including the ignominious fact someone had gotten behind him and knocked him out. He remembered bits and pieces of being hauled over a bumpy trail and dumped onto a bed, this bed he assumed. Then she'd sadistically picked buckshot out of his rear with what must have been blacksmith pincers while he'd had only the sparse comfort of rotgut whiskey. Judging from the condition of his head, he'd drunk the entire bottle.

"I see you're finally awake."

"No need to shout." He carefully laid his aching head back on the coverlet and closed his eyes. Where was his valet Kelso and his miraculous morning-after remedy when he needed them? Oh, yes, Kelso had remained behind in New Orleans to see to the issue of transportation.

"I have coffee left over from breakfast, and we'll be sitting down to the noon meal in fifteen minutes. Your clothes are on the chair, and there's warm water in the pitcher."

Preston mumbled something, hoping she would take

it as agreement and leave. He had no idea what chair she spoke of and refused to open his eyes to look.

"I apologized last night, but I'm not sure you were in any condition to understand. You see, I mistook you for—"

"Perhaps we could talk later."

"Well, yes, but I want you to know—"

"If you want me to accept your apology with a modicum of grace, you could at least wait until I'm able to listen without wincing at the sound of your voice."

"Of course."

Her tone clearly told him he'd hurt her feelings, and she shut the door with unnecessary firmness. He covered his head with a pillow. So much for his friend's exaggerated opinion of his abilities. Thus far his demeanor had been less than charming—in fact, less than polite. But what else could be expected? He challenged any man to behave his best in such circumstances. Still, he had the terrible feeling he'd just made his job much more difficult.

When Preston woke again, a small lantern with a low wick lit the room. He rolled to his side, scooted across the bed, and suppressed a moan as he stood. He adjusted the light and noticed several items on the dresser. Picking up the small daguerreotype of a man wearing a badge on his leather vest, he decided the large mustache did not hide Blake Maxwell's weak chin. He replaced the frame next to the worn deck of cards, handcuffs, gold-plated tie clasp, and empty bottle of whiskey that formed a veritable shrine to Matilda's father's life.

His stomach growled, so he made haste washing in the cold water. He could use another shave, last night's having disappeared beneath a mask of dark stubble, but without his saddlebags he would have to settle for finger-combing his overlong hair. Also missing were his guns and the two knives he generally wore secreted beneath his apparel.

He found his rough cotton shirt and denim trousers neatly folded on a chair at the other side of the bed. He had recently purchased the clothing to blend in with the locals. Just as he had worn a *galabayya* in the Sahara, and *hakama* pants in the Far East. Considering the temperatures in the area, either of those choices would make more sense than the tight-fitting style and thick fabric of his current garb. Americans seemed to value durability over comfort. He eased the Levi's over his bandaged posterior and awkwardly managed to don his socks and step into his boots.

Exhausted by the simple tasks, he considered resting his pounding head rather than confronting his hostess, but decided the sooner the unpleasant chore was started the sooner it would be completed. Pasting a pleasant smile on his face he exited the bedroom.

In the adjoining room a stone fireplace took up most of one wall, and Matilda dozed in a rocking chair set in front of the hearth. Although she still wore an oversized plaid shirt and bib coveralls, he couldn't imagine why he'd mistaken her for a boy.

Delicate was the word that came to mind. A few wispy, light blond curls had escaped her coronet of braids to caress her porcelain skin. Her lashes, several shades darker gold, laid like petals on her cheeks that had been kissed blush by the sun. Lush rose lips over a slightly pointed chin gave her face a heart-shaped appearance. In her lap, her hands lay idle atop some sewing, her fingers tapered and elegant despite her short nails and the rough redness that gave evidence to the drudgery of her life. Her hands disturbed him, that and the fact he rarely waxed into poetic drivel when describing a woman. He directed his attention elsewhere.

The room obviously served as both dining and main living room. The far corner held a dry sink and open shelves with assorted pots, pans, mismatched dishes, canisters, and cans of food. A plank table and four slat-back chairs took up the space under the single window. On the other side of the hearth a bench had been made from half a large log. Although the furnishings were spare and simple, everything was neat and tidy. Here and there a few touches such as a braided rag rug and a tin cup of wildflowers relieved the plainness.

The ornate clock on the mantel, incongruous in its splendor, chimed *Greensleeves* to mark half past ten. Matilda stirred. She looked up at him with sleepy eyes, deep blue like an alpine lake in midsummer. When she gave him a gentle smile, he felt a burning ache in his chest. He dismissed it as indigestion, the result of twenty-four hours without food.

Matty looked up at the darkly handsome man. This was the best dream she'd ever had. Tall, well over six foot, his presence seemed to command the very air in the small room, leaving her breathless and lightheaded. Although nothing about him was displeasing, his eyes drew her attention. The color of deep, rich chocolate, his gaze seemed to promise mysteries and pleasures the likes of which were beyond anything she'd ever imagined before. Matty shivered.

Then she realized he was real and she jerked fully awake, stabbing herself in the knuckle with her mending needle in the process. She stuck the side of her index finger in her mouth. She not only remembered who he was, she remembered how aggravated he'd been. Not that she blamed him. What with her shooting him in the derriere and . . . and well, everything.

She jumped up and rushed to put some distance, or at least a piece of furniture, between them. She tripped on the mending that had slipped unnoticed from her lap. Then she stumbled over her sewing basket, formerly handy by her feet. Four awkward steps to disentangle herself, to avoid sprawling across the bench, and to regain her balance, and she managed by a hair to not fall directly into his outspread arms. With a huff of satisfaction, she straightened to her full five-foot-two-inch height.

"Good evening, Mr. Preston."

Raising one eyebrow, he responded, "Miss Maxwell."

He dropped his arms slowly, almost as if he regretted not having to catch her to stop her headlong flight across the room.

"Since you missed supper, I saved you a plate." She stepped to the side and motioned for him to proceed to the table.

He crossed his arms over his chest. "I don't remember introducing myself."

"Yes, well . . ." She sidled past him, lit the kerosene lamp on the table, and busied herself setting out utensils and food. "Your saddlebags, over there," she said, nodding to the corner by the door leading to the porch. "Bessie, you remember her, don't you? You met, or rather—you heard—her earlier."

He nodded with a grimace.

"Yes, well, while I was outside doing laundry this afternoon she woke from her nap and instead of looking for me as she usually does, she busied herself emptying your saddlebags. She's very curious. In her defense, she was probably just looking for a sweet.

When Reverend Henshaw comes to visit he always has peppermints in his saddlebags."

Matty paused and looked at Preston but he hadn't moved or changed expression.

"While I was cleaning up the mess, I noticed my name on a piece of paper."

"And you decided that entitled you to snoop through the rest of my belongings."

She also crossed her arms and glared at him. "I already told that other Pinkerton man—"

"I'm not a Pinkerton agent."

"And I'm not the granddaughter of a duke. You can eat," she said, nodding to the lone place setting on the table, "then Joseph will saddle your horse. I want you off my land before the hour is out."

"Joseph is . . . your husband?"

"My friend and helper."

"Ah, the one who snuck up behind me—"

"He's a Chickasaw Indian and—"

"The one who blackjacked me?"

"He was protecting us."

Preston moved to the table and sat, then in the same movement stood again. He doubted he'd be able to sit comfortably for some time. "Perhaps I'll just eat standing up."

The guilty flush on her face gave him an idea. He rolled the plan around as he took a bite of the bland stew. To buy the time he needed, he would have to play on her guilt despite it meaning he'd be acting the cad. "Cruel of you to expect me to sit a horse after you callously wounded me."

"You were trespassing."

"I was bathing and washing my clothes in preparation for presenting myself formally at a more reasonable hour."

"And if you had, I would have run you off."

"You shot me."

"I thought you were a cattle thief."

Preston forced a laugh. "I should have thought the fact I was naked would have given you a clue otherwise," he said, taking satisfaction when she blushed.

"You had staked my cattle to keep them from escaping, and had built a roaring fire hot enough to heat branding irons."

"I do have certain minimal standards even in the wilderness, and I definitely draw the line at bathing with animals. Your cows would not stay out of the water and kept trying to lick me." He shuddered.

"The salt in your sweat. They need a new salt lick."

"And the fire was to heat my shaving water. I'll admit it might have been larger than necessary, but it also was my only source of light."

"You should have waited for dawn."

"Well, I chose not to and the fact remains, I am disabled due to your actions. The least you can do is offer your hospitality until I am capable of leaving without inflicting additional pain and suffering, and possibly permanent damage to my . . . self."

He held his breath and could practically see the workings of her brain as the expressions flashed across her face, changing from guilt to resignation with lightning speed. He carefully blew out a sigh so it would go unnoticed. Then a look of resolve hardened her gaze and he knew he'd stopped worrying too soon.

"Okay, you can stay, but on two conditions. You do not mention this business of the duke in front of the children."

Children? As in more than one? He glanced toward the twin door to the one that led to the bedroom. They must be sleeping in the third room. Marsfield's research had said nothing about children. And yet she still answered to Miss Maxwell. Curious.

"And the second condition?"

"I would have you sleep in the barn but it burned down last year, and the lean-to where Joseph sleeps is already overcrowded with two extra horses. Therefore, you can continue to sleep in my room if you agree to be handcuffed to the bedstead."

He raised his eyebrows.

"I couldn't sleep easy if I was worried about you wandering around the house in the middle of the night."

"You have my word—"

"I don't know you well enough to trust your word."

"As a gentleman—"

"Save your breath. Most of the so-called gentlemen I've known were not worth spit."

"Perhaps—"

"On Sunday we'll take the wagon into town and you can ride in the back. We'll drop you off on our way to church. You can finish your recuperation at the Turnabout Hotel. Not luxurious, but grand by comparison to here. Agreed?"

That gave him only two days to convince her of the benefits of returning to England with him. Not much time, but what choice did he have?

"Agreed," he said, although he had the uneasy feeling he'd just made a pact the devil himself would approve.

Chapter 3

Matty put the kettle on to reheat and set about making tea, confident she had protected herself while at the same time atoning adequately for the small disservice she'd done her guest. After all, a little buckshot wasn't exactly a mortal wound. Now all she had to do was endure two days, three nights, and a long wagon ride to town without making a fool of herself as she'd done earlier when she practically fell into his arms. It wasn't like she'd never seen a handsome man before.

She'd met her share of men, all right—gamblers and card sharks and men out to make a quick buck. While working with her father she'd felt sorry for a few of the marks, but Blackie Maxwell had always said a successful scam depended on someone who wanted something for nothing. Hardworking, honest people expected to pay a reasonable price for what they got. Well, she was willing to pay for her mistake. She just wasn't going to pay more than was fair.

She poured the steaming water into the teapot. While the tea steeped, Matty got out two mugs. She poured without ceremony and sat one on the table near her guest. He ate his late supper slowly and deliberately as if he wasn't thrilled with the taste but knew there was nothing else to be had.

And there wasn't. Store-bought spices were one of

the first luxuries she'd cut. The children and Joseph didn't mind simple fare but for some reason she would have liked to impress Mr. Preston. Especially since the paperwork she'd read named him as Lord Something-or-other and he was probably used to better.

Of course, those same papers had named her as Lady Matilda and she knew that couldn't possibly be true.

"Thank you," he said, setting down his empty plate. "I've been eating my own cooking far too long. I'd forgotten how good a meal could taste."

The almost-a-compliment warmed her more than its content merited. Yet she refused to analyze why.

"Are you really a lord?" she asked instead.

He didn't respond right away.

"Never mind." She stood, gathered up the dishes, carried them to the sink, and dumped them in a bucket half full of soapy water. "I was pretty sure you weren't." She added hot water from the kettle to the bucket. "You're just another flimflam man. Your papers are good, though, first-class work. Almost fooled me."

"I beg your pardon?"

She turned and faced him. "You don't really look like a Lord . . . What was the name?"

"Bathers."

"That's it." She shook her head and returned to her chore. "I picture Lord Bathers as pasty-faced and thin, with an umbrella or a cane. If there's one thing I learned from my father, dress and attitude are important."

"And how would a real lord behave?"

"Oh, you know. Look-down-your-nose, supercilious, arrogant, condescending, pompous, disdainful."

Preston covered his laugh with a cough. She'd accurately described several peers he could name, though fortunately not most.

"You should try wearing spectacles, maybe a monocle. And do take the time to find a decent tailor. If you don't invest properly up front, your scam has no chance of succeeding."

Her mistake about his identity and her subsequent advice gave him another idea. If she thought he was running a scam, why not let her?

"Then that so-called Pinkerton man was one of your cohorts," she said. "Why did you think you'd succeed where he failed?"

If Preston was going to pull off his plan, it would be best to stick as close to the truth as possible. "Actually, he was a real Pinkerton. I took a calculated risk to see if my papers could pass muster with the famous detective. And if you had cooperated, it would have saved me a long, tedious journey. That alone would have been worth the gamble."

"Well, you're barking up the wrong tree. Even if you had fooled me, I don't have any money to purchase the papers."

"You will when you return with me to England."

"And help you defraud an old man?" She gave him a sour look. "Why me? Surely you could have found someone closer to home to masquerade as the daughter."

"Probably." He wasn't sure where all the lies were coming from because he was making the story up out of whole cloth as he went along. He decided to press his hunch and bet the pot, go all in. "Although to be fair, the original scheme was your father's idea. We'd planned to work together."

Her back stiffened and she froze in place. "When did that happen?"

He mentally reviewed the full set of Pinkerton reports that he'd left back on the ship, and picked a reasonable time. "April. Four years ago. San Francisco. That's why your name is on all the papers. Your father was sure you could pull it off."

Yet he didn't want to appear too eager. Preston looked her up and down as if measuring the merit of a racehorse. "I however have my doubts. You don't look like a duke's granddaughter." He flashed a smile to soften the insult. She ignored both.

Matty turned, walked back to the table, and braced her hands on a chair back. "Why didn't I know about this?"

Preston shrugged. "I have no idea. Maybe he didn't want to say anything until he was sure I could complete my part."

"Find another woman."

"I can't. This has been years in the execution, and those papers cost me dear."

"Get new ones."

"There's no time. The Duke of Norbundshire is quite aged. You could make an old man happy before he dies."

"Don't try to play on my sympathies like I'm one of your marks. I'm too savvy to fall for that ploy."

Preston suppressed a grin. He was actually enjoying trying to outwit her. Not an easy task, he admitted, if only to himself. He tried another tack, pasting a worried frown on his face. "A lot of money has already been invested. And that's not even counting the seven thousand five hundred dollars I paid your father."

"You paid Blackie Maxwell? Why?"

"Only at his insistence, believe me. He said it was to ensure I wouldn't take his brilliant scheme, run it on my own, and cut the two of you out of the deal."

She dropped her head. "We were living pretty high

on the hog that spring. He told me he'd won a small fortune playing poker with some rich cattlemen."

"I've upheld my end of the bargain."

"I can't help it that you made a bad deal, and I won't help you with your scam. My life is here and I intend to stay put."

Preston was afraid he'd overplayed his hand, bluffed and lost.

She sighed. "However, I'm the one who spent most of the money. My father took sick that May and I insisted on the doctors and the trip back here." She straightened her shoulders. "This is a good farm and it will be profitable in a few years. I'll pay back the money you gave Blackie. Someday. Somehow."

Preston decided to let the matter lay for a while. He sensed pushing her now would only cause her to dig in her heels. "I thank you for the thought at least." Then he was at a loss what to do next.

Matty started when the clock chimed eleven. "I guess we should call it a night."

She didn't look at him, and he surely wanted to know what she was thinking. He walked over, picked up his saddlebags, and said as he rummaged through them, "I'm not at all sleepy, which is quite understandable." He pulled out a book and held it up. "I'll just read for a while." With an apologetic smile he headed toward the empty rocking chair.

"But . . . But you can't sit there."

"Oh? Oh, yes, I see what you mean. I'll put another pillow on the seat."

"No, you can't stay out here. You'll have to read in the bedroom."

"The light is less—"

"You can take the lamp from the kitchen."

He couldn't understand why she was so agitated.

Then he remembered the condition she'd set. He held out his wrists in a gesture of submission. "You can handcuff me to the chair, although it will make turning the pages a bit awkward."

"That's not—"

"Oh, I see. The chair isn't enough security. I could easily pick it up. Perhaps you have leg shackles somewhere?"

"I only have the handcuffs because my father—"

"Used to be the sheriff. I know."

"You do?"

"I'm not a stranger to your father."

Before she could respond there was a tap on the door. She went to open it with a sense of relief because, at this time of night, it could be only Joseph. She introduced the two men. They shook hands even though both seemed wary.

"You're talking so much I can't hear the night wind," Joseph said. "How am I supposed to get news of my tribe if the song reaches the moon unheard?"

"We were just discussing retiring," she said.

"And not retiring," Preston added.

Joseph nodded. "I know the problem. And the answer."

He reached out onto the porch and picked up a board, a good seven feet long and at least twelve inches wide.

"What are you . . ." She hesitated in order to duck as he swung the board around and headed for the bedroom. "Wait a minute."

She followed him. "Stop," she said as Joseph placed the board on its side down the middle of the bed. "What do you think you're doing?" she demanded, grabbing his arm.

"I don't know what name to call it, but it's been stored—"

"It's called a bundling board and we do not need it because we are not sleeping in the same bed."

Joseph glanced at her but continued to jockey the board into position. "No space for you in the children's room."

"Don't you worry about me, I can—"

"You work too hard to sleep in the chair. Not good rest. Makes you walk like an old woman until sun is over trees."

"I'll make a pallet on the floor—"

"No, you won't," Preston said as he also entered the room. "I'm a bloody fool for not seeing this before. As a gentleman I cannot put you out of your bed. I'll take the chair."

Joseph looked at him and grinned. "Okay by me."

"You can't," she said to Preston, though she spared a warning glare in Joseph's direction. "It would aggravate your wound. I'll sleep in the chair. It won't be the first time."

"Then, I'll take the pallet on the—"

"There isn't enough empty floor space to accommodate you," she said. "You're too tall. I'll—"

"I'll move the furniture."

"This is best answer," Joseph said as he tapped the board firmly into grooves that had been made on both the headboard and footboard for just such use. "Now you both get bed, both sleep good." He turned and left the bedroom.

Matty and Preston stared at each other for a long moment.

Again he held out his hands.

She motioned him toward the head of the bed with a quick jerk of her head. He sat on the edge of the mat-

tress and she fastened the handcuffs to his right wrist
and the bedpost. After she stepped back, she pulled a
pearl-handled derringer out of her pocket, checked the
magazine so he would know it was loaded, and then
laid it on the chair by her side of the bed.

"Come one inch across that board and you'll be
missing a few important body parts."

"I wouldn't think of it." He settled down on the bed
as best he could, on his right side, his back to the board
and his hand tucked under the pillow. "Not only am I a
gentleman—and I mean that in the best sense of the
word—but even if there were no divider, you would be
safe." He closed his eyes. "You aren't exactly my type."

She spun from the room. Just what did he mean by
that? She banked the fire and blew out the lights, all
the while fuming over his words. She stomped back
into the bedroom, not bothering to be quiet, and
stretched out on her side of the bed fully clothed. For
several minutes she listened to his even breathing.
Eventually she couldn't stand it any longer. She sat up
and leaned over the board.

"What did you mean, I'm not your type?"

A noisy snore was her only response.

She plopped back down on the bed and crossed her
arms.

Preston allowed a smile of satisfaction to curl his
lips as he waited for her to fall into a deep sleep.

Once her breathing had settled into a slow, steady
rhythm, he eased from the bed—moving a bare inch at
a time—and stood up. Stretching both arms, he took a
few small steps. Then he picked up the key she had
tossed onto the dresser. Because her reach would have
come nowhere near accomplishing the task, it obviously had not occurred to her that his would. He

unlocked one half of the handcuffs, leaving the other half secure around the bedpost.

Rubbing his wrist, he tiptoed into the main room. Because his eyes were well adjusted to the dark, he needed only the ambient light and his excellent memory to find his way to the fireplace. His weapons were on the mantel.

He stuck the larger hunting knife inside his right boot and slid the long, thin stiletto into the special sheath that hung down from his neck along his spine. He was willing to leave the guns where she'd put them, but he felt naked without his knives.

Then he took his saddlebags to the table to make what use he could of the pale moonlight struggling through the small, wavy panes of glass. He had already checked, using the ruse of fetching the book, and knew all his belongings had been restored, neatly, if not in his usual precise order. Selecting the left bag, he set aside the packet of papers, his shaving case, some spare clothes, some ammunition, and his money pouch. He ran his hand along the back seam.

To his intense relief, the contents of the secret pocket had not been disturbed. She'd found only the papers prepared for him to present to her. Even though their first meeting had not gone as planned, at least all had not been revealed. He removed a small, oilskin-wrapped packet and tucked it inside his shirt.

After repacking, he set the saddlebags back in the corner and returned to the bedroom. He didn't look forward to spending the remainder of the night with his hand shackled over his head. If he passed on the handcuffs and yet behaved as she wished, would she then view him as trustworthy in the morning? He paused beside the bed.

She sprawled with abandon across the available

space. Her braids had come unwound, one hanging off the side of the bed. The other followed the curve of her throat, decorating the plain neckline of her overalls and ending like a golden question mark over her breast. It struck him that he had never watched a woman sleep before and he was surprised to find her breathy, little snores endearing. What did she dream?

Relaxed, her lips seemed fuller, the bottom one almost a pout and quite kissable. He reined in his wayward thoughts.

Even in sleep a slight worry line marred her delicate forehead. He had noticed earlier the unmistakable signs of overwork and stress. She definitely needed rest more than he did. What if she woke and found him free? Would she then refuse to sleep again?

He knew the answer. If she required him to be restrained in order to feel safe, then he would endure. With a resigned sigh he sat on the bed. The click of the handcuff sounded loud in the serene silence. She stirred. He held his breath for a moment, but she did not wake. After easing into a semi-comfortable position, he dozed off and on out of sheer boredom. Three hours later when she rose from the bed, the slight movement woke him. Wondering what she was up to, he pretended to sleep, picturing her actions from the sounds.

She stirred the fire and set the kettle on to heat. She sat in the rocking chair. He imagined her picking up her sewing or perhaps a book. Why was she up? She needed the rest. Why didn't she just come back to bed? He waited, planning to mark fifteen minutes by the chiming of the small clock on the mantel before calling out to her.

An unfamiliar noise coming from the room next door stopped him. Rather like the fretful whining of a newborn puppy separated from its mother's warmth, only louder, and rapidly gaining in both volume and strength.

Matty heard the first cry, set aside her cup of tea, and rushed to get the child before she woke everyone, as she was quite capable of doing. As soon as Matty picked up the child, the cries subsided to whimpers. But she knew it could well be a short reprieve. She carried Bessie out to the main room, rubbing her back.

"Poor little darling. I know your teeth hurt, but it means you're growing into such a big girl."

Bessie lifted her head from Matty's shoulder and looked up at her with teary eyes as if begging her to take away the pain.

"There's nothing I can do to make it better." She certainly wasn't going to give the child laudanum as the women in town had suggested. "I promise it will go away soon."

That did not seem to suffice because Bess started crying again and worked herself into a real howler. Matty tried walking around, singing, swinging her back and forth, making her rag dolly dance. None of her favorite activities seemed to make a difference.

"Excuse me? Miss Maxwell?" Preston called from the bedroom.

She walked to the door, the crying child on her hip.

"I'm sorry we woke you," she said, "but if you want anything you'll just have to wait. I already have my hands full."

"If you would undo the handcuffs, I think I might be able to help," he said.

"What do you know about babies?"

"Practically nothing," he admitted, sitting up.

Bess crawled up Matty's shoulder as if she was afraid of the stranger and let out a screech directly in her ear. If the man wanted to escape the noise by leaving, she could hardly blame him. She grabbed the keys off the dresser and tossed them to him.

He followed her into the main room and went right for his saddlebags. Well, once he left that would be one less problem for her to handle. She refused to acknowledge the disappointment that lodged in her throat. Instead she sat Bess in the rocking chair, knelt in front of her, and tried to get her to play patty-cake. Out of the corner of her eye she watched Preston.

He didn't leave. From one saddlebag he removed an oblong-shaped packet she remembered but hadn't opened earlier.

"When I traveled with Sir Burton, he taught me to be prepared. This kit is copied from his," he said as he untied the binding and unrolled it. "You can't depend on adequate medical attention while tiger hunting in the jungle or mountain climbing in Tibet, so it's imperative to carry the essentials with you." He selected a small, brown bottle, brought it to her, and held it out. "This may help."

She shook her head. "I will not give this child laudanum. I know—"

"It's not laudanum," he said. "My friend Anne used this with her children. Just rub a drop on the gums."

She looked up at him, skeptical. "Why would you carry medicine for teething?"

"It's oil of cloves." He turned the label so she could read it. "Have you never had a toothache? It's quite effective. Added to tea or brandy it soothes a sore throat. It also—"

"I know what it does," she said and took the bottle. "I just never thought of using it for a teething baby." But when she had a drop of the medicine on her finger,

Bess shut her mouth and turned away every time Matty tried to administer the dose.

"No," Bess said.

Matty tried coaxing and she tried forcing, but it seemed only to make the child squirm more and cry louder.

"No, no, no, no."

"You're going to have to help," she said to Preston as she picked up the child.

"Me?" He wasn't foolish enough to stick his finger in her mouth. Those teeth might be tiny but he'd seen how she clamped her stubborn jaw shut. "I'd rather you—"

Matty handed Bess to him.

For several minutes Preston struggled with the screaming child who suddenly seemed to have a dozen arms and legs. He didn't want to hurt her by holding her too tightly, or drop her by holding too loose. Just like dealing with a woman; either too close or not near enough spelled disaster. What was he supposed to do with a little girl? Words could seduce a woman, but would they calm a two-year-old?

"I have an idea," Preston said, and he motioned for Matty to sit in the rocking chair. He set the child in her lap, then knelt on one knee in front of them.

"No one is going to hurt you," he said, his voice low and smooth. "I promise you."

The child stopped screaming.

Progress at last. Now that he had her attention, what did one say to a girl of such a young age? "When I first saw you, I thought you were an angel. Truly." He left out his second impression.

Bess stared at him, her gaze clearly mistrustful.

"You have expressive eyes. They remind me of an exquisite blue vase I once saw in the raja's palace in

India." And that was the truth. At a loss for anything else to say, he continued on the same tack. "Flecks of gold scattered throughout the lapis lazuli gave the vase an exotic look that transcended its simple design. Overshadowed by the larger bejeweled pieces, others missed the small beauty, but I found it unforgettable." He reached out and wiped the moisture from her cheek. "Shame on the tears that mar such perfection."

Bess leaned toward him, her cries fading to hiccups.

"If I were a poet, I would write a sonnet to your golden curls. If I were a musician, I would sing of your porcelain complexion."

She stared at him, her gaze seeming to reach into his soul.

"But, alas, words fail me when confronted by your unique beauty. I say unique, because even though there are other beautiful girls, none has affected me the same as you have."

"Don't stop," Matty whispered, her voice husky. "It seems to be working"—she cleared her throat—"on her."

Preston nodded without breaking eye contact with the child.

"I hereby pledge to be your champion, to protect you from harm, and to rescue you from distress." He smiled, and Bess smiled back.

"And now my pretty darling, we're going to take care of that old toothache." He touched his knuckle to her bottom lip and she giggled. "I have some medicine to put in your mouth, like this," he said, and demonstrated on himself. He put a drop of the medicine on his finger.

"Now it's your turn, sweetie. Open up for me," he said.

She obliged like a hatchling waiting for a worm.

After he applied the medicine she had a confused expression, but then she smacked her lips a few times and smiled. Without further ado she launched herself into his arms, snuggled her cheek against his shoulder, and promptly fell asleep.

He stood and took a few steps back. Amazing. From screaming tyrant to sweet cherub in the span of minutes. And she'd taken the medicine from him without biting his finger. He looked to Matty expecting praise for a job well done. Instead she stood with her hands on her hips and a frown on her face.

"We did it," he said, his triumph obvious.

"You did it," she countered. "And if I were a gambler, which I'm not, I'd bet you could sweet-talk any woman into, *or out of,* just about anything." She took Bess from him and carried her to her room. Matty paused at the door and turned. "Don't bother trying that on me because it won't work. I'm immune to flattery."

Preston nodded, but he didn't agree. If he'd learned one thing in his life it was that no one, man or woman, was unaffected by a sincere compliment. "I'll remember that."

"See that you do," she called back over her shoulder.

Oh, he would. Matty was stubborn and mistrustful, and changing her mind would be quite a challenge. She had drawn a line he could cross only at his own peril.

Even as a boy he couldn't resist a dare. He returned to the bedroom, lay on the bed, crossed his legs at the ankles, and tucked his hands behind his head. Matching wits with her was the most intriguing mission he'd had in a long time. Smiling to himself, he waited for her to join him.

Chapter 4

Matty needed to get control of herself before she could go back into the bedroom. Where he was. Before she could lie down on the bed. With him. His pretty words had affected her far more than she cared to admit. He wasn't even talking to her, for Pete's sake. But she'd known she was in trouble when he'd said *open up for me* and she'd opened her mouth faster than Bessie when she spied a peppermint candy. Thankfully, he hadn't noticed.

Matty pressed her lips firmly together. She grabbed the broom and started sweeping the plank floor with a vengeance. The last thing she needed in her life was a handsome flimflam man who made her think of the exotic places of her dreams. She'd grown up being dragged from one end of the country to another and she knew the grass was not greener on the other side of the hill. There was no way she would allow him to talk her into his crazy scheme. A bird in the hand was worth two in the English hedge.

She heard a stealthy footstep behind her. She'd forgotten to handcuff him again. Heart in mouth, she spun around.

Her eight-year-old son Nathan stood in the middle of the room, his chestnut hair tousled and a wide yawn on his face.

She took a deep breath. "You startled me." She gave him a smile. "I'm sorry I woke you, sweetie."

He shook his head. He made an exaggerated crying face, pantomimed rubbing his eyes with his fists, and then pointed to the bedroom he shared with his sister.

Matty nodded. Nathan didn't talk much, but he seemed to communicate effectively with expressions and gestures. He and Joseph used Indian sign language, and Matty had learned some of it over the three years Nathan had lived with her.

"You could have come out of your room and met our guest."

The boy shook his head.

Nathan was shy around strangers, around everyone but their little family, she admitted to herself. Whenever they went to town she tried to get him to join other boys in the games they played, but he wouldn't leave her side. She wished she could do something to help him. Nothing had worked so far, but that didn't mean she was going to give up.

"Why don't you come sit at the table and I'll make you a cup of hot milk to help you get back to sleep?"

As he took a seat she noticed he was outgrowing his long johns again. She mentally added another item to her shopping list. They needed all the basic food-stuffs—flour, baking powder, sugar, tea—plus everything they couldn't make or grow, as well as winter grain for the two horses and the milk cow.

Matty rubbed her forehead. At this rate the money in the old cigar box would never last through the winter. She'd sold most of her cattle so she wouldn't have to feed them when the snow came. All except the six seed cows that would start her new herd come spring. If she sold them too, she'd have nothing for the future.

She sighed and set about heating Nathan's milk. Her

father always said to do whatever it took to stay in the game. The cards would eventually turn and the good hands would come, but you had to be in the game to get them.

Nathan tapped on the table to get her attention. With gestures he asked why she was frowning.

She forced a smile to her face. "Oh, I was just thinking about . . ." She couldn't pass her worries on to him. He already saw too much and knew too much. "I was thinking this milk looks kind of tasteless. I say let's add the last of the cocoa and sugar and make hot chocolate."

Nathan clapped his hands.

She stirred in the ingredients, and as she turned back to the table with the pan, she noticed her guest standing in the door of the bedroom. She froze. He moved as quietly as Joseph. How long had Preston been there?

"Do you have enough for one more?" he said, stepping forward. "I can't sleep either."

Nathan scrambled from the table and hid behind Matty, almost causing her to spill the hot milk. She set the pan on the table, and drawing the boy to stand in front of her, she introduced them.

"How do you do?" Preston asked, putting out his hand and waiting without comment for the boy to take it.

Matty's heart swelled when Nathan finally shook his hand.

"So pleased to meet you," Preston said.

And she blessed him for not commenting on Nathan's silence. People who said things like, *What's the matter, boy? Cat got your tongue?* didn't help the situation. "Won't you join us?" she asked, setting another mug on the table.

"Thank you." He fetched the seat cushion from the

rocker and placed it on the chair. Then he sat and, after grimacing, leaned to one side, probably to keep the pressure off his wounds.

Suddenly she was conscious of the fact that she served him from a pan, that she hadn't any cookies or even crackers to serve with the hot chocolate. She twisted her hands in her lap, then jumped up and got napkins for each of them.

Preston took a swallow. "Ah, this is perfect."

Matty had to turn away from the look of bliss on his face.

She noticed Nathan's milk mustache and motioned for him to wipe his face. When he licked his upper lip she said, "Use your napkin."

"And waste that tasty hot chocolate? Nathan has the right of it." Preston took a deep gulp, causing his drink to lap over his lip. He licked the mustache off. "This is the only way to truly enjoy hot chocolate."

Nathan smiled at him and took another big swallow, licking off the remainder with relish.

Preston turned to Matty. "Your turn."

How could she resist the appeal on Nathan's face? She took a sip, allowing the warm liquid to ease up over the top of her lip. She displayed her folly for them to see.

"I think your mother looks good in a mustache, don't you?"

Nathan nodded and clapped his hands.

Matty reached for her napkin.

"Oh, no," Preston said, staying her hand. "You have to lick it off."

She shook her head.

"Watch Nathan. He's the expert. He'll show you how." Preston waved his hand and bowed his head as if presenting Nathan on a grand stage.

The boy sat up straighter in his chair, took his mug in both hands, and added a fresh coat to his mustache. Then he licked it all off with one long swipe.

Preston applauded. "Can I spot an expert? I knew he could do it." He patted the boy on the shoulder. "Good job." He turned to Matty. "Now you do it."

Nathan beamed as if he'd won a solid gold medal. He nodded his encouragement.

How could she not? She couldn't reach all the foam. She tried again, tipping her head back in her effort. Then she settled for quick stabs of her tongue to reach the last bits in the corners of her mouth.

Nathan applauded, but Preston was strangely silent. He cursed himself for a fool.

The childish game had turned into erotic torture when Matty had darted her tongue in and out. Those little moans hadn't helped either. And worst of all, he couldn't get up and leave the table without making his arousal known.

"Preston? Are you all right?"

No. "Yes, of course."

Nathan rapped the table and clapped his hands, looking from Preston to Matty.

"Oh, yes, she did a fine job," Preston said, understanding what the boy meant. "Not as well as you, of course, but she did have rather a small mustache to work with."

Nathan picked up his mother's mug and handed it to her. When she took a swallow, he pushed up on the bottom with his finger. She made a strained noise in complaint, but the result was a marvelous full mustache.

Nathan indicated the two adults should have a contest. Preston's better sense told him to refuse, but when he glanced at Matty she had a superior smile on her face as if she knew the nature of his torture and dared him to continue the game.

He vowed to wipe that smug look off her face. He took a gulp. As she licked her lip he watched her every move and mimicked each nuance. She stared back at him as if mesmerized.

She took another gulp from her mug, as did he. Then he took the lead, alternating long, slow sweeps with quick thrusts. She followed his rhythm, sometimes mimicking, sometimes doing the unexpected. When she bit her bottom lip, he groaned.

He tipped up his mug for another drink, but the chocolate was gone.

She looked into her empty mug and sighed. Then she noticed Nathan had leaned back in his chair and fallen asleep, a smile and a faint, foamy mustache on his upper lip.

Preston held out his mug. "More?"

She shook her head and looked him in the eye. "There is no more," she said.

Was she talking about more than chocolate? He gave himself a mental slap. Of course, she meant there was no more to drink. His physical reaction, due solely to his lack of female companionship for too long, had affected his reasoning. He would have to guard against such a situation happening again. His mission was to get her safely to London, not to seduce her.

"Perhaps that's for the best," he said.

Without speaking, she stood and helped Nathan to his room. He was fast asleep moments after she tucked him in. She sat on the edge of his bed and dropped her head into her hands.

What was the matter with her? She was behaving in ways she'd never thought she would. Not until that man had come into her life. He was dangerous. He made her think of dancing in his arms, of moonlight kisses, of . . . of things she had no business wanting. Not with him. Not with a flimflam man who would always be looking for the next big opportunity. She needed roots and stability, wanted that for her children.

Preston made her want the moon.

She'd thought she could deal with his presence, but tonight had proven her weaker than she'd expected. The only sure way to regain control of herself was to get him out of her house, out of her life. As soon as possible. Why wait for Sunday? If they went to town today, she could do her shopping and leave Preston at the hotel.

She slapped her hands on her knees. She would start the preparations immediately. They would leave at sunrise.

"Why are we stopping?"

Matty tied the reins and set the brake on the wagon, climbed down from the seat, and walked around to the back. "We're about twenty minutes from the edge of town. We usually stop here for breakfast."

Nathan stumbled from the back of the wagon. Matty sent him to the copse of small trees and bushes about twenty yards off the road to look for firewood.

"Watch out for snakes," she called after him.

Preston scooted to the edge of the wagon from the pallet in the back he'd shared with the two children. "I'll help him."

"You can bring that basket over to those blackened rocks," she said, pointing to one and then the other. "There should be enough wood to get the fire started."

"Why a fire? It's cool this morning, but not unpleasant."

"The children need hot porridge to start the day right. And I brought the coffeepot."

"Isn't there a restaurant in town?"

"I refuse to pay fifty cents for Mrs. Barstow's watery porridge and nasty coffee when I can make better myself. At least I would be able to do so if someone would get a fire going."

He bowed from the waist in exaggerated acquiescence and then set about his designated task. At least she wasn't treating him like an invalid any longer. She had refused to let him help load the wagon, harness the horses, or drive. When he'd tried to talk to her during the two-hour trip, she'd only shushed him over her shoulder, warning him not to wake the children.

He soon had a small fire burning. Nathan brought wood and they made coffee and set a pan of water to boil.

Preston returned to the wagon. Matty had dressed Bess even though the girl was still asleep.

"Keep an eye on her for a few minutes, will you? I need to . . . I'm going . . . Oh, just watch her." Matty grabbed a blanket and headed for the bushes and a bit of personal privacy.

He leaned against the wheel, wishing he had a cheroot. Nathan joined him and copied his stance.

"It's quite magnificent," he said, sweeping his arm to take in the rolling hills still covered with mist. He could see why others might be drawn to the wild vista, though he missed the manicured pastures and flower-filled meadows of his home. Not that he spent much time at The Rookery, the seat of the Earl of Stiles, where he was born. But he always knew it was just a few hours away from the bustle and bad air of London. "Not at all what I'm used to."

Nathan looked curious so Preston continued, trying to

think of things that would interest a boy. "I grew up in the country, riding across rolling hills and meadows, fishing the streams and ponds. At least once a week my friend Burke and I climbed the great rock escarpment on the west of the estate to check the progress of the hawks that nested there." He chuckled. "Or just to feel like we stood on top of the world. That was always the first place we went when school let out for the summer."

He felt a tug on his sleeve and looked down.

"S-s-school?"

Preston's throat tightened. So it wasn't that Nathan couldn't talk, he just refused to do so. And Preston empathized. He'd suffered agonizing embarrassment until Mr. Christian gave him the tools and the confidence to overcome his own problem.

"I attended school in London," Preston said. How could he let Nathan know he understood, that help was available? "But not until I was several years older than you. I had a tutor at home who taught basic academic subjects and helped me with my speech impediment."

"D-did you s-s-stutter, t-too?"

"Yes, a bit. I had trouble saying certain sounds and I got so nervous speaking that even what I could say came out wrong."

"N-n-not now."

Preston placed his hand on the boy's shoulder. "I'll give you one of the exercises my teacher gave me." He searched the ground for a smooth stone, too big to swallow accidentally, yet small enough to fit in the boy's mouth. "He had me put a stone like this in my mouth and I practiced saying my lessons around it until I could be understood. Then when I spoke without it, talking seemed much easier." He held the stone in his open palm.

Nathan picked it up as if he were touching the Holy Grail. He then motioned with his chin toward the trees.

"I won't say anything," Preston promised, remembering his own chagrin when his problem was the topic of discussion. His parents had argued fiercely, placing blame and responsibility in each other's lap. From the corner of his eye he noted Nathan put the stone in his pocket.

Matty emerged from the trees and stopped by the fire. She poured a bit of the hot water on a cloth and washed her face and hands. After stirring some ground meal into the pot to make the porridge, she returned to the wagon.

Preston cleared his throat. "Nathan, why don't you go add some wood to the fire."

"That's not necessary," Matty said, but the boy had already jumped to obey. She turned to Preston and crossed her arms. "What are you up to?"

He had to press his luck because time was running out. Since she'd changed her mind about letting him stay in her house, this could well be his last chance to speak to her alone.

"I would very much like for you to reconsider my offer. There are many amenities lacking in your house and on your farm. If you did this, you could afford a new barn and—"

"Stop. I will not leave my land, and nothing you can say will change my mind. Nothing. And that's the end of this conversation." She turned and picked up the still-sleeping child and marched to the fire.

Preston followed at a slower pace. He hated to entertain an alternate plan, but he'd never failed a mission and didn't intend to start now. When he'd asked Marsfield if kidnapping was a viable option, he'd been joking. He hadn't meant to tempt fate.

A glint of sunlight on metal from the far hill caught his eye. Instinct propelled him forward in a flying lunge.

"Get down." He tackled Matty around the waist, rolling as he pulled her to the ground so he didn't land on top of her and the little girl. The bullet whistled by his ear.

Nathan scrambled over, and Bess woke up screaming. The second bullet took out the coffeepot.

"What's happening?" Matty asked as they settled into half-seated, half-lying positions behind the low rocks.

"I'd say someone is shooting at us."

She gave him a look that clearly said his usual levity under fire was not appreciated.

"But why?"

"I'll go ask him," Preston said, crawling on his elbows and knees toward the last rock large enough to hide him.

"No, wait. Don't go."

"We can't stay here, pinned down and waiting for him to finish us off," he explained.

She gathered her children, one under each arm.

"Stay down. I'll be back in a few minutes," he said.

"Wait! Where are you going?"

"At this distance he'll have difficulty hitting a moving target. I'll make my way to the wagon to get your rifle. Hopefully, it's loaded with bullets rather than buckshot."

"It is, but it's quiet now." She sat up about a foot and tried to look over the rocks. "I think he's gone."

"Get down."

A bullet ricocheted off the rock. She plopped down into the dirt.

"We'll wait right here," she said.

"Good idea."

"Please, be careful."

He grinned. "When you're lucky, you don't have to be careful." He gave her a cocky salute and took off, running a zigzag pattern as he raced for the far side of the wagon.

Chapter 5

Preston made it to the wagon without a shot coming near. That meant the shooter had a specific target and it wasn't him. But why would someone want Matty dead? He would have to puzzle that out later. His first order of business was to get her out of danger.

He calmed the nervous horses, hoping they wouldn't bolt when he put his plan into action. He climbed into the wagon bed. Keeping his head down, just in case, he reached through the space under the high wagon seat and retrieved a box of ammunition and the rifle. Then he untied the reins and threaded them under the seat. He gently urged the horses to back up the wagon, getting as close to the fire rocks as possible.

Resetting the brake, he took up a position with the rifle.

"Matty?"

"Are you all right?"

"Yes. Now I want you to listen carefully. I've moved the wagon closer. When I start firing, I want Nathan to run and climb into the back. Matty, I want you to wait until I give you the word, then it will be your turn. Understand?"

"We understand."

"All right. Nathan get ready and . . . run!" Preston fired at the position on the hill where he had seen the flashes of gunfire. He didn't expect to hit the shooter, but his target would be forced to take cover.

Nathan climbed into the wagon.

"That's a brave lad. Now here's what I want you to do." He reloaded the rifle and held it out. "Do you know how to shoot?"

The boy looked terrified, but he nodded and took the gun.

"I'm going to go and help your mother with Bess. When I say so, I want you to fire at that tall pine below the boulder." He pointed out where to aim. "Can you see it?"

Nathan took a deep breath and pointed to the right place.

"Good. Don't worry about trying to hit anything specific; just pump as much lead into that tree as possible."

Preston rubbed the boy's small shoulders and gave him a smile of encouragement. "You can do this."

He slipped from the wagon.

"Preston? What's happening? Where's Nathan? Is he all right? Damnation and dagnabbit, answer me!"

"No need to shout," he said as he slid to the ground beside her.

She screamed, and Bess cried even louder.

"That's so much better," he said, clearing his left ear with his finger.

She punched his shoulder with her free hand. "You scared me. You could have told me you were coming."

"Next time I'll send my card around first." He grinned, relieved she no longer trembled. "Are you ready to leave this soiree? Your carriage awaits."

She gave him a determined nod.

"I'll carry Bess. You'll run faster without her."

"She's very upset. I'm not sure she'll go to . . ."

Her words faded when he held out his hands and Bess jumped into his arms. She stopped crying and wrapped her little arms around his neck, giving Matty a triumphant look.

"I think you've made a conquest."

"I'm her champion, remember? When Nathan starts shooting, I want you to run as fast as you can and jump into the wagon. Don't go in a straight line, but don't stray too far to either side. Understand?"

"Got it."

"I'll be right behind you." He covered Bess's ear with one hand and tucked her head against his shoulder. "Nathan?" he hollered. "Get ready. Fire!"

He boosted Matty up and she took off, feet flying. He gave her a head start of a few yards, then followed, arriving just as she rolled into the wagon bed. He handed her the girl, ran around to the side, and climbed over the wheel. After he took over from Nathan, Matty settled the two children together on the pillows and blankets and crawled forward to his side.

"What can I do to help?" she asked.

"Do you want to shoot or drive?"

She found the reins. Two bullets thudded into the thick, wooden side of the wagon. "The brake is still on," she said, panic edging her voice. "I can't reach it."

Preston turned to stand, but Nathan had already scrambled over the side and climbed toward the front like a monkey. He released the brake and made his way back.

"Go," Preston said.

Matty slapped the reins and whistled to her horses. They took off at a good pace, seemingly as relieved as their owner to be leaving. She didn't slow them until Turnabout was in sight.

She stopped at the first building on the edge of town.

"Sheriff Jones, I want to report an attempted robbery," she said to the potbellied man sitting on the tiny porch in front of a barred window.

Preston kept his own counsel. He didn't believe the motive was robbery. He climbed from the back of the wagon and helped her down.

"That so?" the man said, not bothering to remove either his hat or the toothpick from his mouth. He stood with effort and waddled over to the edge of the porch, where he towered over them. He shot his double chin forward. "Who're you?" he asked Preston.

Matty quickly introduced the two men. "If you leave now, Sheriff, you might have a chance to catch him."

"Ain't seen you around town," he said to Preston.

"He's staying with me," Matty answered. "Can we focus on the important issue?" She planted her hands on her hips. "Someone shot at us. The children might have been hurt." Her voice caught in her throat. "Or even killed."

"Everybody all right?"

"Yes, but—"

"Did you see who done it?"

"No, but—"

The sheriff scratched his belly. "Then I don't see no point in rushing out there. Likely won't find nothing but a lot of empty shell casings."

She glared at him for a moment, then turned on her heel and climbed up into the wagon seat. She had to fish below her knees for the reins, which gave Preston time to join her.

"I'm not sure I like your looks," the sheriff said to Preston. "You say you're staying out at Matty's place? You don't look like no ranch hand."

"I'm not. I'm a—"

The wagon jerked forward and Preston sat down harder than he'd intended.

"Ouch."

"That man is the laziest, most—"

"He's right, you know."

"What?"

"Whoever shot at us is long gone by now."

"Still, he should have done . . . something."

"What would you suggest?"

Her response was a little growl that reminded him of the tiger cub he had rescued and nursed until her broken leg had healed. Even though the cub was totally dependent on him and purred when he scratched her stomach, if angered she had sharp teeth and claws and instinctively knew how to use them. He had several small scars on his right forearm, evidence he'd underestimated her ability to teach him a lesson.

Matty pulled up in front of the emporium. Preston jumped down and gave her a hand. She marched around to the back of the wagon and helped the children down.

"The hotel is across the street," she said as she set the jumble of blankets in the back into a semblance of order. "I'm sure you'll be quite comfortable. Joseph will bring your horses tomorrow and leave them at the livery. We do thank you for the rescue today."

"I'll help you with your errands," he said, unwilling to leave her unprotected.

"Not necessary. I'll leave my list with Mr. Sanders and he'll have everything loaded into the wagon." She picked up her reticule. "Good day to you," she said as she turned to face him.

The tableau that greeted her made her heart ache. Preston, so tall and handsome, waited by the store entrance. He held Bess in one arm, her porcelain doll looks a contrast to his dark eyes and hair. Nathan stood proudly at his side, Preston's arm around his thin shoulders. A picture of what could never be.

"Come," she said, reaching for the little girl.

"No," Bess said, wrapping her arms around his neck. Nathan shook his head and leaned closer to Preston.

"Mutiny?" Matty crossed her arms. "Children who do not mind their mother do not get to pick out a piece of candy."

"Well, well. What have we here?"

She spun around. "Oh, hello, Virginia."

Dagnabbit. Running into the minister's sister was not an uncommon occurrence, but if Matty had been paying attention to her surroundings she would have avoided the woman if at all possible.

"Matty. And how is pretty little Bessie?" Virginia asked as she reached out to pat Bess on the cheek. The girl turned away, leaving the woman facing Preston. "Aren't you going to introduce me?" she asked Matty without bothering to look in her direction.

Virginia smiled and Matty was surprised the woman's face didn't crack with the unusual effort. Unable to politely do anything else, she introduced them.

"Miss Henshaw." Preston managed a creditable bow even though Bess wiggled and hid her face in his shoulder and Nathan tried to hide behind him.

"You're new to our little town. Let me be the first to officially welcome you. I'm sure you'll soon feel right at home. We're a very friendly town."

"I'm—"

Matty poked him in the side. "He's just visiting," she said. "An old friend of the family."

"Really? So you're staying at Matty's? We all worry so about her, all alone out there with only that old Indian for company. Women must be so careful. A woman's reputation is her greatest treasure, and yet it can so easily be made worthless."

"She also has the children," he said.

"Of course. But children are not appropriate chaperones. Vigilant observance of the social rules is the best protection women have against ruination."

"I don't need a chaperone when I have my rifle," Matty said. "I can protect myself."

Virginia ignored her and turned to Preston with a simpering smile. "Perhaps I've said too much. I do tend to go on when speaking of a matter I feel so strongly about," she said, fidgeting with the small cameo broach at her neck. "I hope we'll see you in church on Sunday. My brother, the Reverend Henshaw, is quite well known for his sermons."

"I'm sure I'll find it quite edifying."

"The first service is at eight."

Virginia patted the nape of her neck as if to make sure her hair had not suddenly taken a mind of its own and escaped the severe bonnet.

"Mr. Preston may not be in town that long," Matty said. "He has business elsewhere, don't you?"

"Nothing more pressing than the state of my soul."

Matty hid her snort of disbelief with a cough. She'd tried to save him from his folly, but he'd thrown it back in her face. Well, he was on his own now. She certainly had no interest in his activities.

"Bravo, Mr. Preston. Well said." Virginia folded her hands, closed her eyes, and raised her face heavenward. "I pray more men will see the light as you have."

"I'm sure you're a busy woman, Miss Henshaw, and we have taken quite too much of your time," Preston said with a smile and a step back to leave a clear path on the wooden walkway in front of the emporium. "I do wish you a good day."

"Ah, well, yes. I do have some pressing business to take care of. I suppose I should see to it right away."

Matty took perverse pleasure in seeing Virginia flustered. That woman had been a thorn in her side ever since she had come to Turnabout. And her brother? That was another matter altogether.

"Good day to you, Mr. Preston." She turned to Matty. "Oh, and you, too, dear Matty," Virginia said. "I know I'll see you again soon." She flashed her a smug smile before leaving.

Matty made a face at her back.

"Friend of yours?" Preston asked in a low voice. He looked amused.

She pasted an innocent smile on her face. "I try to be polite to everyone. Even you." She sailed into the emporium, followed by his low chuckle.

She tried to ignore him as she gave the shopkeeper her list and answered his questions concerning quantities. Preston wandered about the store entertaining the children by trying on silly hats and making sock puppets to grab at their noses. Did her children laugh like that with her? Did she ever laugh like that?

Loath to cut their merriment short, she pretended to have an interest in purchasing yard goods, fingering the imported turquoise silk embroidered with tiny butterflies of all colors that caught her fancy.

"That would look lovely on you," Preston said.

She jerked her hand away as if the material had burned her fingers. "Impractical. I can see me feeding the chickens or milking Emmie Lou in a dress made of this. Though the cattle would probably follow me wherever I went."

"I would follow you," he whispered near her ear for her alone to hear.

"Stop it," she muttered under her breath. Yet she

could not deny the thrilling shiver that crept down her spine. She forced her attention back to practical matters, making arrangements with the shopkeeper to pick up her purchases in an hour.

"Come, children. We're going to Mrs. Barstow's for breakfast since ours was ruined."

"Excellent idea," Preston said. "I'm hungry. Aren't you?" he asked Nathan, who nodded his response.

"I don't remember asking you," Matty said to Preston.

"What happened to being polite to me? Would you have me starve? Or simply suffer a lonely meal?"

Nathan tugged on her sleeve, his look begging her to let Preston come along like the man was some sort of stray puppy he wanted to feed. That couldn't be further from the truth. More like a stray wolf that had befriended her children and was using them against her better judgment. If she had difficulty resisting Nathan's plea, she never should have looked at Bess, who seemed ready to cry at a moment's notice, or at Preston.

In the depths of his liquid chocolate eyes she read loneliness and longing. Which she promptly dismissed as a reflection of her own undependable emotions.

"Mr. Preston—"

"Just Preston will do."

"Mr. Preston may join us. But after breakfast, we must finish our errands and he must take care of his own business." She finished her sentence by giving him a warning look. Then she turned and led the way to the restaurant.

The meal went better than she expected. The children and Preston were on their best behavior, and because Mrs. Barstow was under the weather and her daughter Amelia was cooking, the food was delicious and the portions large. The only disagreement came when Preston insisted on paying the bill, but she gave in rather than make a scene as he threatened.

"I'm going to the livery to make arrangements for my horses," Preston said, putting his napkin beside his empty plate. An outright lie, but necessary. His real intention was to search for a telegraph office. He chose the livery for his errand because it was on the far end of town. But he didn't want Matty to leave without him. "Perhaps Nathan would like to accompany me?"

"No," Matty answered.

"P-p-p-please?" Nathan asked.

That the boy would risk being heard by others in the restaurant was a measure of his desire. Matty's heart melted. She agreed with a sigh. Would she never be rid of the man? Leeches were easier to shed.

"We'll meet at the emporium in half an hour," she said. Nathan gave her a hug before they left. Matty picked up Bess, sleepy now that her little tummy was full, and thankfully not insisting on going with the others. When she stood, Amelia Barstow beckoned them into the kitchen.

"I'm so glad to have a chance to talk to you alone," Amelia said.

Matty had always liked the plump woman who was about her own age of twenty-four and also still unmarried. Even though Amelia was a terrible gossip, she didn't have a mean or malicious bone in her body, unlike some Matty could name.

"Come sit with me," Amelia said, leading her to a small table in the corner and pouring a fresh cup of coffee for each of them. "Oh, it feels good to get off my feet."

"I can't stay long," Matty said, sitting and shifting

Bess into her lap. "But it's so nice to see you again. How goes the courtship with Big Jim?"

"That man thinks more of his horses and livery stable than he does of me. But that's neither here nor there. I wanted to warn you. Virginia Henshaw is on the warpath again."

"I can hold my own against the likes of her."

"Not this time. She got a lawyer up at the state capitol to file papers to give legal guardianship of Bess and Nathan to her and her brother."

"What? They can't do that."

"She can, and she has. The story is she's just waiting for the response, which she expects in two weeks."

"Two weeks?"

"And that's not the worst."

Matty's head reeled. What could be worse than losing her children? What was she going to do?

"The worst thing," Amelia continued, "is she's not going to wait for the papers. She's found out you've got a man living in your house and—"

"I do not."

"That Mr. Preston?"

"He's not living with me. He stayed one night because he was wounded."

"One night is more than enough."

"He was handcuffed to the bedpost, for Pete's sake."

Amelia's eyes lit up, but she said, "I don't think I'd let anyone else know that. It's not likely to help your case."

"My behavior in this town has always been above reproach."

"I don't think that's going to matter to Virginia. She's rallying the good women of the town, all her vicious cohorts, to demand the children be removed immediately from your immoral house, your den of iniquity."

"But they know me. Surely they don't think that I—"

"That is one handsome hunk of a man. Broad shoulders, and big, brown, soulful eyes, and that cat-got-the-cream smile. Add to that clean fingernails." She sighed, her ample bosom heaving. "Mighty hard to believe any woman could resist him."

"Well, I can."

"Personally, I can't imagine why you'd want to." Amelia got a dreamy look in her eyes. "I'd let him put his boots under my bed any night."

"What am I going to do about Virginia?"

"If you're asking me what I'd do, first I'd get out of town before that vigilante committee found me. Then I'd go and get me a fancy lawyer and fight for my rights."

"I can't afford a lawyer." Matty felt as if she were sinking in a pit of despair, choking slime closing over her head.

Amelia shook Matty's shoulders and made her look her in the eye. "Those children are yours. They need you to be strong."

But her horrified mind wouldn't focus. "I don't understand. Virginia doesn't even want Nathan," she said, as if that made a difference.

"No, but she'll have to take him in order to get Bess. I heard she has a family up north of here that will adopt him because they need another worker."

"A worker? He's eight years old! He has chores, but he's not capable of doing a man's job." Matty sat up straighter. "I can't let her do this."

"Now you're talking. Do you have a plan?"

"Not yet, but I will. First I need to get them home safe and sound." Matty stood. "Will you help me?"

"Of course I will."

"Go take a look down the street and make sure Virginia isn't still out there. I left my wagon at the emporium."

Amelia went through swinging doors to the sitting area and returned quickly. "There's a group of women on the steps of the church. If you leave by the back way, and stay behind the buildings, you can get close to your wagon without them seeing you."

At the door, Matty gave her friend a hug.

"Good luck. I'll get everyone I can to speak against Virginia doing this," Amelia promised.

A glimmer of hope propelled Matty forward.

She made it to the rear of the emporium without incident. Keeping to the shadows, she sidled to the front. As quickly as possible she settled Bess in the back of the wagon with her blanket and dolly and climbed into the seat. The shopkeeper came out with a package.

"I'm almost done loading, Miss Maxwell," Mr. Sanders said.

"I'll get the rest later."

"But this is for—"

She slapped the reins.

He tossed the package into the wagon bed and stared after her, scratching and shaking his head.

She headed to the livery, grateful it was located away from the church. As she pulled to a stop, she spotted Nathan by the corral. He stood with Preston and Big Jim, a small copy of their stance, chewing on a piece of hay and watching the horses.

She called to get Nathan's attention. "Get in the wagon. We're leaving right now."

Her panic must have been apparent in her voice, because both Nathan and Preston came running.

"What's wrong?" Preston asked.

She didn't have time to explain. "Get in, Nathan. We're going home."

"No, not you," she said when Preston also climbed into the back of the wagon.

"Tell me what's wrong," he said, making his way around the boxes and bags and scrambling onto the seat next to her.

"Please get out."

"Not until you tell me what has happened, because something obviously has."

She wasn't willing to waste valuable time just to be rid of his unwanted presence. She would deal with that later.

"Hold on tight," she called back to Nathan and Bess as she turned the wagon around in the middle of the street. In order to get home she would have to drive past the church. She leaned forward to give the reins some slack and an extra snap as she slapped them on the horses' backs.

"Giddap!" she hollered, and the animals responded as if they were prize stallions rather than poor, old farm horses.

Preston braced his legs and grabbed the edge of the seat. Not because he was afraid, but because he didn't want to fall off and thereby miss the wild ride with Matty.

When she finally slowed, several miles from town, he asked, "Are you going to tell me what happened?"

"Not now," she said, indicating with her head that she didn't want to talk in front of the children.

He accepted that and carried on the bulk of a normal conversation about unimportant things. All the while, he sensed her inattention and tension. He steeled himself to be patient.

Joseph met them at the house, questions about their unexpectedly early return and Preston's presence clearly written on his usually passive face.

Preston shook his head and shrugged to let the other man know he was also clueless. He could only assume—hope—Matty would talk to him sooner rather than later.

Before they finished unloading the supplies from the wagon, a lone horseman rode into the farmyard. Matty told Nathan to take Bess inside and keep her there.

Without any need for communication, Joseph flipped a pistol to Preston and the men took positions leaning casually against the wall on either side of the small porch.

Matty took a stance by the door to await the visitor, her old Henry repeating rifle cradled in her arms.

Chapter 6

"That's far enough, Reverend Henshaw," Matty said when the man was about ten feet away.

"Now, Matilda, I've asked you to call me Horatio," he said with a smile as he dismounted. "I'd like to speak to you. In private," he added with glances at Joseph and Preston.

"Say your piece and be gone," she said.

He began walking toward her until she leveled the rifle in his direction. He stopped and raised his hands.

"I'm not armed. You wouldn't shoot a man of God, would you?"

"I'll shoot anyone who tries to take my children from me."

"I've come to ask you to consider Virginia's actions as a blessing."

"Are you crazy?"

Again he glanced at the other two men, who stood like silent sentinels.

"I am a man of God, but I have seen the wickedness of this world. I understand every woman carries the sins of Eve in her bosom, and I forgive you for succumbing to temptation."

"*You* forgive *me*?" she asked, enunciating each word. Obviously mistaking her incredulous question as encouragement, he continued, "Yes, yes. I forgive you and I want you to marry me."

"What? I never did anything to give you the slightest reason to think I was remotely interested in marrying you."

"That's why this is such a blessing. We can move to a new town, go west. Find a place where no one knows your notorious reputation. Without the encumbrance of children, you can start a new life. I'm willing to give up everything for you, to be with you. And I will save you. I will save your soul."

"What are you going to do, beat the evil out of me?"

"I'm sure that won't be necessary," he replied, though the thought seemed to bring an unholy spark to his eyes.

"And my children? What plans do you have for them?"

He flicked a spot of dust from his coat sleeve. "Virginia wants them. She'll take care of them." He straightened to his full height and raised his hands as if he were in the pulpit. "Repent, Matilda. Come to me with remorse in your heart and I will give you salvation. Shed your lascivious ways." He opened his arms as if to embrace her. "Come to God."

She shot at his feet. He jumped back.

"You are a sanctimonious, self-righteous snake." She shot again, and again, punctuating her words and dancing him back to his horse. "You're a pious prig, a depraved, conceited jackass. I wouldn't marry you if you were the last man on earth. Now get on your horse and skedaddle. If I catch you or your holier-than-thou sister anywhere near my children I will shoot either of you with great relish."

He mounted his horse. "It's not too late. I can save

your children from Virginia. All you have to do is marry me."

"Are you deaf? Shoo. Git. Begone." She released several shots at the horse's feet and in front of its nose. The animal reared in panic and took off running.

"You're going to regret this," he called back to her as he clutched the horse's mane and slipped sideways in the saddle.

She placed a parting shot over his head, not lowering her rifle until he was out of sight. She sank down and sat on the steps, her legs no longer capable of holding her upright.

Joseph and Preston joined her, one on each side.

"I will take care of him," Joseph said, making a slicing motion across his throat. "No one will see me."

She shook her head. "I don't think that will help."

"The woman, too," Joseph offered.

"No," she said, putting her head on his shoulder. "Though I do thank you for the offer, my friend."

"What are you going to do?" Preston asked.

"I'm not sure. I need time to think."

"You and the children can come to England with me."

"Stop it," she said, jumping up and turning to face him, her hands on her hips. "Don't I have enough problems without you badgering me? An old enemy of my father's is trying to kill me. And—"

"Is that who shot at us this morning?"

She threw her hands up in the air. "I don't know, but it's the only thing that makes sense."

So she had deduced the shooter had targeted her. Preston's opinion of her intelligence went up another notch.

"As if anything makes sense anymore." She paced in a tight, little circle. "Reverend Henshaw has gone loco, his sister has a lawyer who's going to give her legal custody of my children—"

"Can she do that?" There must be more to the story than she was telling.

"That mean, vicious woman has the audacity to accuse me of being an unfit mother in order to steal my children. And she's gathering the so-called *good women* of the town to support her cause. And I can't afford to stop her."

Suddenly all the air seemed to leave her body. She forced herself up the steps. When Preston stood to follow, she paused at the door. "I'd appreciate it if you would leave me alone for a while," she said.

She didn't bother to wait for his agreement but went inside and sat at the table. She dropped her head in her hands. What was she going to do? Tears dripped through her fingers.

"M-M-Matty?"

She sat up and wiped her face on her sleeve. When would she learn to carry a handkerchief? She reached out and gathered Nathan into her arms. His little shoulders trembled and he squeezed her with all his strength. He had obviously heard more than she would have liked. "Now, I don't want you to worry," she told him, and sniffed. "I'll figure out some way to take care of everything. You understand?" She pulled the boy away to look into his eyes.

"You are my son. No one is going to take you away from me."

He nodded. "W-what are w-we g-g-going to d-do?"

She had to be honest with him. "I don't know yet," she admitted. "But I promise you I'll do whatever it takes."

He nodded and ducked his head.

She put a finger under his chin and tipped his head up. "What are you thinking?"

"England h-has t-t-teachers for b-boys like m-me."

She gave him a hug and sent him to play with his sister while she did her chores. Yet the children were never out of her mind as she put things away, cleaned, and cooked. The familiar tasks helped clarify her thoughts, and in the end the best option was the biggest gamble.

But she wasn't foolish enough to bet it all on a blind. Wiping her hands on her apron, she went to find Preston. He'd made himself scarce, but she located him in the shed behind the house currying one of his horses. "I have a few questions for you."

"I find this calms me as much as it does the horse."

"What is that supposed to mean?"

"I just thought to save your clothing from destruction."

She looked down. She had twisted her apron into a large knot. After smoothing it out, she took the currycombs from him and stepped into his place.

"What did you want to know?" he asked, sitting on a nearby barrel.

"If, and this is only a theoretical question, if I were to help you with your scam, how much money are we talking about?"

Now that was something he hadn't considered. "Well, let's see." He fingered his chin and squinted upward as if he was adding numbers in his head. He needed a number large enough to pique her interest but not too large or it might scare her off. "I'd say maybe one hundred thousand pounds." Though in truth the duke's income was probably twice that per annum.

"That would be about fifty thousand dollars. That's a lot of money."

"Yes, it is," he agreed. Her pounds-to-dollars conversion was incorrect, very incorrect. But since she'd given him a clue as to her comfort level, he decided not to tell her different. Her father must have been more than a petty thief.

"What's the split?"

"After expenses, seventy-thirty."

She laughed, though he thought it sounded a bit forced.

"Fifty-fifty."

As he saw it, she had no choice, and yet she bargained for a better split as if she had an ace up her sleeve. He had to admire her guts. "Sixty-forty."

She patted the horse and gave Preston the combs. "You pay all expenses up front and we split all profits fifty-fifty."

"You drive a hard bargain, but agreed." He stuck out his hand.

"I haven't agreed to anything yet. I just wanted to know the facts before I make a decision." She turned to leave the lean-to. "Lunch will be ready soon. Don't forget to wash up before you come in."

She stopped at the pump herself, taking a moment to look around her home. Suddenly she saw the place with fresh eyes, as a stranger might, as Preston probably did. A collection of shacks with peeling paint, sagging fences, and failing crops. Three and a half years of her life sunk into this soil and a stiff wind could blow it all down.

After checking on the children and stirring the pot of stew, she walked up the hill to where her father was buried under the big oak. She gathered a few wildflowers and laid them where the headstone would have been set if she'd had the money to have one made. She stood for a moment with her arms wrapped around her waist.

"I hated every dishonest deed you ever did. I hated when you involved me, but I did what you wanted because I loved you."

She sat with her back against the tree and closed her eyes, imagining she sat next to her father. "Somehow I got the idea that the secret to happiness was honest labor, and I've worked very hard. You know I have. And what has it gotten me?"

Only the breeze in the leaves answered her.

"I never gave you enough credit for what you tried to do. Oh, I know you loved the thrill of a big score, but I now realize that in your own way, you were trying to provide for me.

"Mr. Preston wants me to help him pull off your grand scheme. I know you didn't tell me about it because you didn't want to get my hopes up, didn't want me to believe this scam would be big enough to be the last one. The very last one."

She stood and brushed off the seat of her overalls. "Well, Father, I just wanted you to know I understand. If I do help with this scam, I probably won't be coming back here any time soon." She blinked away the tears that threatened. "I've got to go now. My children need me to take care of them, just like you took care of me."

As she walked back to the house, she realized she'd already made up her mind. If she went to England, there was a chance they would fail or get caught and she might still lose her children there. But if she stayed, she would lose them for sure. She'd just have to do everything she could to make sure Preston was successful.

Then there was the matter of Preston himself. She

could scarce believe she was actually going halfway across the world with a man she had known for less time than it took to get to Cincinnati. Not her. Not mistrustful, practical Matty. But she'd been pushed to the edge of a precipice where there was no safe, logical way out.

Her best bet dealing with him was to let him think he held all the winning cards. Never would she make the mistake of trusting him even if she let him think she did. She patted the derringer in her pocket, vowing to keep it handy.

She set out the noon meal before calling everyone to the table. After saying grace and before serving the stew and day-old bread to soak up the gravy, she said, "I have an announcement to make."

Four expectant faces looked back at her.

Bessie banged her spoon on the table, eager for her serving of food. "Foo. My foo."

The tension broken, Matty smiled and served the meal. "I suppose we can talk as we eat. If we're going to England, we have lots of plans to make."

Preston and Nathan cheered.

She turned to Joseph. "I'd like you to come with us."

He gave her a rare smile, but he declined. "I have done the bidding of the great spirit. Now, I return to my people."

Nathan ran to the old man, his hands speaking private words.

Joseph took the boy's hands in his gnarled ones. "I will see you again, little warrior. I will be a very old man by then, but we will meet one more time. I have seen this in a vision, so you know it is true."

Nathan nodded but his tears fell unchecked.

"You have much in here." Joseph touched the boy's chest with his finger. "And here." He touched his head.

"You must learn to let it out here." He touched the boy's mouth. "Only then can you fulfill your destiny."

Nathan dried his eyes and returned to his chair.

Matty didn't know what to say. That was probably the most she'd heard Joseph talk in three years.

"I suggest we leave today," Preston said.

"Impossible," Matty countered. "There's too much to do. I need to pack everything. There's the animals to see to and—"

"And someone trying to kill you."

"No one shot at us on the way back," Matty said, realizing she hadn't even worried about the shooter because she'd had so many other matters on her mind.

"He probably didn't expect you to make the return trip so soon and therefore wasn't watching the road," Preston said.

"Oh. That sounds reasonable."

"So does leaving today. You don't know if the townswomen will come here, or whether Henshaw will return. He seemed bloody determined to marry you."

She spared Preston a scathing look, which only made him grin.

"Just pack what you'll need to get to Memphis. We can buy whatever else you need there," Preston said.

"Memphis?"

"A riverboat will be the fastest mode of transportation."

"Taking the wagon over land would be less expensive. We could take supplies and camp—"

"Traveling east would put us in territory currently under contention by Union and Confederate forces. The war hasn't reached this far west yet, but it's near enough to take into consideration."

"Point taken. However, there's no need to go to

Memphis. The steamboats will stop in Turnabout to pick up passengers if a red flag is run up."

"Do you really want to go back into town?"

Her shoulders sank. "I . . . I . . ."

"It's hard to think of something you've known for a long time in a different light."

She pounded her fist on the table. "This is not fair. Why should we have to leave our home?"

Joseph stood. "The old woman who weaves each of our fates does not ask what design we wish. I will ready the wagon and horses," he said as he left.

Nathan quickly spooned the last of his stew into his mouth and followed.

"We should leave as soon as possible," Preston said. "What can I do to help?"

From a cupboard built into the wall she removed two well-worn portmanteaus. "I never thought I'd have any use for these ever again. I don't even know why I kept them."

"Perhaps for sentimental reasons?"

"No."

"They look as if they've been through their share of adventure."

"I should have burned them."

An hour and a half later, Preston paced beside the wagon. "What can she be getting now?" They had already packed more than they would need. He stomped up the stairs. "Matty? Are you ready to leave?" When she didn't respond he entered the house. He found her with her portable writing desk open on the table.

"Didn't I already put that in the wagon?"

"I took it out. I'm giving Joseph ownership of the

farm animals. I don't want him to have any trouble when he takes them back to his tribe."

"I gave him my horses, too. Perhaps you should include them in your paper."

She looked at him as if he'd done a great deed. And it made him feel strange. His only thought had been that the two animals, not Thoroughbreds by a far measure, weren't worth the trouble of taking them across the ocean.

"I won't be needing them," he explained. "And Joseph has agreed to stick around for a few days, so it will look like we're still here, or maybe just in town. Hopefully, the ruse will fool our long-distance shooter."

She finished writing, blotted her signature, wiped off the pen, and repacked her supplies. "I'll put this back in the wagon."

"Just a moment. Do you own a dress?"

She gave him a funny look. "Yes. Why?"

"It's not due to personal preference. I think you look very . . . practical in that outfit. But when we get to Memphis I'd rather we didn't attract undue attention. Just in case the shooter gets wise and follows us, we should try to blend in with the crowd to make trailing us as difficult as possible."

"Do you really think he'll follow us?"

"I'd rather not take unnecessary risks."

"I thought you were a gambler?" she asked with a smile.

"I am a successful gambler, and that means balancing the risk against the payoff and making smart decisions."

She bristled, but he wasn't sure why her mood changed from playful to serious.

"Fine. I'll wear an uncomfortable, impractical

dress." She picked up her writing box and marched to the door.

"Please bring that basket," she said, nodding to a covered wicker box next to the table. "Put it someplace the children can't get to it."

His curiosity piqued and his imagination ran wild. What sort of things would a woman keep secret? He asked what was in the box before he realized it might be old love letters or fancy lace unmentionables.

"Christmas presents," she whispered, as if the children, who were outside with Joseph saying good-bye to the animals, might hear her.

"It's only November."

"Well, they don't get made overnight. I have to plan ahead in order to have everything ready."

As she left, Preston picked up the basket. He fought the urge to peek inside. The idea of a mother working hours in secret to prepare presents for her children on Christmas morning was as foreign and surprising to him as . . . as finding an elephant in the parlor would be. Oh, he'd had presents on Christmas, lots of them. His mother made an extensive list and handed it to the housekeeper to fulfill. The maids did the wrapping.

He did his own gift giving much the same way, depending on his man Kelso to not only shop but often to know the right choices to make. Kelso kept track of such things as which cigars Marsfield preferred, and which wines persnickety Burke enjoyed. Preston would even bet Kelso knew which modiste his sisters favored this season, and which pieces of jewelry his mother deemed appropriately expensive. Preston knew none of these things because he'd never bothered to find out. He followed Matty outside, a strange hollowness in his chest.

And he nearly ran into her as she dragged one of the portmanteaus back inside.

"If you continue taking things out of the wagon, we'll never be ready to leave."

"You wanted me to wear a dress. My clothes are in here."

They jockeyed around each other, almost like a dance. She shut the door behind him.

"I'll just be a few minutes," she called out. "After you hide that box, get the children into the wagon and we can leave as soon as I come out."

He did as she requested, taking a few minutes to wish Joseph well. Preston gave him the address where he could contact his friends and promised to encourage Nathan to write him letters in care of the Signal Trading Post.

Now that the moment to leave neared, Nathan dragged his feet in the dust as they walked back to the wagon.

Matty waited in the shade of the porch for them.

Whereas the baggy overalls had hidden her figure, the high-necked, long-sleeved style of her dress revealed an hourglass shape while it covered all but her hands and face. Only the scraps of lace at the neck and wrists kept it from looking puritanical. Preston found it strange to be enticed when he had been inured to the displays of creamy shoulders and cleavage currently the rage in London ballrooms. The faded blue color of the dress highlighted her eyes, making them seem brighter by comparison.

She had removed the braids and twisted her golden hair into a simple chignon, the style accenting her delicate cheekbones. The whole effect was demure and wholesome, and yet he had the feeling it was a costume, a facade. His gut told him the overalls, or something equally outrageous, suited her better.

"Don't say a word," she warned him.

As she stomped down the stairs, she plopped an ugly straw bonnet with sad little rosebuds that had seen better days on her head and tied the ribbons under her chin. The wide-brimmed style shielded her face from the sun, and his gaze.

"You look very nice," he said, holding out his arm to help her into the wagon.

She stepped past him, hiked up her skirt, and climbed to the seat unaided, flashing him a good look at the denim trousers she wore underneath her dress.

"I don't know why I'm surprised," he said under his breath.

She tilted her head so she could see him around the side of her bonnet. "I heard that. I'm only being practical."

"Ah, yes, practicality, the missing element of fashion."

"Of women's fashions," she clarified as she settled on the seat he'd previously padded with several blankets. She arranged her skirt to cover her boots. "Men don't sacrifice comfort for the sake of style."

"Obviously, you've never worn a necktie," he mumbled as he climbed up beside her and took the reins. For once, she didn't argue with him about driving the team. For once, he wished she would. Her calm in the face of such a drastic change in her life was unhealthy.

She twisted around in the seat to watch her home get smaller and smaller and finally disappear as he turned the team southward on the main road. When she straightened, she sniffed a few times. He handed her his clean handkerchief.

"I'm not crying." But she took his offering and

ducked her head to dab surreptitiously at her eyes. "I never cry."

"The longest part of a journey is the leaving of the gate."

"Another proverb?"

"No, just something my father always used to say."

"Well, it's silly. This journey will take a lot longer than a few hours." She looked back over her shoulder. "I know I forgot something important. Leaving in such a hurry is crazy. You'd think a posse was after us." She whipped back around to face him. "You're not a wanted man, are you?"

"I assume you're speaking of the authorities? No, my face is not on any reward posters."

"Too bad. I could use the cash."

"I don't want you to worry about expenses. I'm prepared to cover everything needed."

"Out of the take."

"Pardon?"

"All the expenses will come out of the take before we split fifty-fifty, right? That was our deal?"

"Oh, yes, of course."

"Good." She pulled a small notebook and the stub of a pencil from her reticule. "I'll keep track of everything. Besides the insurance money you gave my father, what have you already spent?"

"Don't you trust me?"

She didn't respond, but then he already knew the answer.

Chapter 7

Except for a few short stops to stretch their legs and water the horses, they had traveled steadily south. Matty had played games, sung songs, and read from a worn copy of Hans Christian Andersen's stories to keep Bess and Nathan entertained. But the last half hour, the stupor of travel had settled, punctuated only by the monotonous *clop, clop* of the horses' hooves.

"We should make camp soon," Matty said.

Preston looked past her to where the sun had started its dip behind the distant mountains and the sky had begun to pink. He nodded. He'd been searching for a likely site.

"Look. There's a clearing."

"We'll go a bit farther. See those rocks up ahead?" He'd been eyeing the formation for the last couple of miles. The hill looked as if it had been split in half, leaving a ragged limestone cliff at least a hundred feet tall and a hundred and fifty feet long. One man on the peak would command a good view of both the road and the river.

"Why? There's good grass here and probably a stream over by those willows."

"It would require a battalion of men to defend such a position. We have two rifles, one pistol, and your little toy gun."

"You're expecting . . ." She waved her arms to encompass the peaceful countryside. "Wild Indians? Hordes of Yankees and Rebels?"

"I'm not *expecting* anything, but preparation often averts trouble."

"Better to be safe than sorry. A stitch in time saves nine. I can match you adage for adage. Stop mouthing platitudes and tell me what devious path your suspicious brain has taken."

"I will explain my logical and sensible reasoning. A lone wagon is a prime target of opportunity. With the horses unhitched, we'd have no chance of escaping should road thieves or river pirates decide to use darkness to aid an attack."

"This road is well traveled and safe."

"As evidenced by the great number of wagons and horsemen we've passed on the way?"

"Most people have enough sense to leave early in the morning and arrive at the next town before the day is half gone."

"Exactly my point. The only company we encounter will be up to no good."

"In the four years I've lived in this area, there have been no reports of any robberies or attacks along this road."

"Isn't this the same road, albeit some distance away, where you were shot at this very morning? Should our feeble ruse back at the house not fool the shooter, I would prefer not to make a second chance any easier than necessary."

Matty said nothing as he drove past the clearing.

Preston shifted so the rocks poking him could make a different spot sore. His back, legs, and especially his abused butt protested the inhumane treatment. At least he was in no danger of falling asleep. He scanned the countryside. A week past full, the moon provided sufficient light to see the area around the campsite.

He had sought his perch soon after parking the wagon in the lea of the hillside as close to the cliff as possible, leaving the chores of unhitching the horses and setting camp to Matty and Nathan. He'd wanted to climb the hill before the last of the daylight faded.

Yet he had to admit it was a relief to get away. The hours sitting next to Matty on the narrow seat, smelling her clean soap scent, listening to her melodious reading voice, had been a unique torture. Each bump in the road, each time she turned to face the back of the wagon, her arm rubbed against his arm, her thigh pressed against his thigh. He'd even found her off-key singing endearing rather than irritating because she'd exhibited as much enthusiasm and enjoyment in the silly songs she sang as the children did.

As he watched the quiet scene below, Matty rose from the pallet in the bed of the wagon. She added wood to the three fires he had instructed they build. About twenty-five feet apart, the fires were another ruse to make any passersby think several wagons had camped together and would be, therefore, well defended. A weak subterfuge, to be sure, and only effective from a distance, but he was doing everything he could.

He avoided looking directly at the campfires because that would compromise his night vision for fifteen minutes or more. Yet he was aware of her. Matty sat near the central fire, her shawl wrapped around her hunched shoulders, appearing so alone and defenseless. His gut clenched and he blamed the unfamiliar feeling on the fact that he'd missed supper.

He forced his gaze away, sweeping the trees and the

river, not focusing on anything in particular, letting his instincts pick up any movement or anything out of the ordinary. When he allowed his peripheral vision to stray to the campsite, Matty had returned to her bed.

What was it about the woman that kept drawing his attention back to her? She was nothing like Anne, his measure against which all other women had fallen short. Matty was so different he had no basis for comparison. Anne dressed in the first water of fashion, and Matty wore denim trousers. Anne was accomplished in watercolors, music, and dance. Matty sang silly songs with more volume than finesse. He doubted she painted landscapes or played the pianoforte with the same expertise she'd demonstrated shooting a rifle, cooking over an open campfire, or caring for her cows. He reasoned that he could not get her off his mind because she was his mission. He was responsible for her safety, and therefore must remain aware of her at all times.

Matty couldn't sleep. She was having second thoughts. And third and fourth thoughts. The step she'd taken, which had seemed so imperative and logical in the daylight, loomed rash and imprudent in the night's retrospective. Without Preston around to distract her, she had too much time to worry. His presence bolstered her confidence because he seemed to have no doubts they would succeed.

She stared up at the stars, feeling a bit lost and vulnerable. Would she see the same stars over England? Her attention soon strayed to the dark bulk of the hill to her left. Somewhere up there Preston stood guard, keeping them safe. She might not agree with his career choice, admire his motives, or trust him, but tonight she was thankful for him. Rolling to her side, she placed one hand on Bess's little back and fell into a deep sleep.

Preston's senses alerted him before he consciously saw the movement on the river. Shadows against darkness. He continued scanning, narrowing the parameters. Keeping his focus moving was a technique proven more dependable at night than staring at one spot. Then he saw them.

Two men in a small canoe stopped paddling. The one in the prow pointed to shore. The other raised his paddle and waved it downstream. Preston could almost hear their argument in his head. He held very still, not wanting to inadvertently dislodge a single pebble. His gut told him the one in the rear was in charge. They might be simple travelers curious about the fires. Or they could be scouts for either the Union or the Confederate armies, which were both five—maybe six—days' travel to the east. Or one of the men in the boat could be the man who had shot at Matty earlier.

The second man prevailed, and the boat moved off with the current. Preston breathed a sigh; however, it wasn't in relief. The multiple campfires may have averted a potential disaster, but now they could well have enemies behind them and in front of them.

By the time they had finished a predawn breakfast, traffic on the road was already bustling. Mostly farmers going to market. A few settlers with all their belongings loaded on and strapped to their covered wagons. Some going north. Some going south. Following their dreams or maybe their conscience. A small cadre of Rebel soldiers headed north at full gallop. Matty guided her wagon onto the road behind a dairy farmer and in front of an obliging couple with a load of potatoes and carrots.

The children began the day on the seat beside her so Preston could catch a nap in the wagon bed. Because of the limited space Bess soon climbed into the back to play with her dolly and her basket of ribbon, lace, and material scraps. Matty warned her not to wake Preston. Nathan soon followed so that he could stretch out and read his well-worn copy of *Robinson Crusoe*.

When she looked back some time later, both children were sleeping, one snuggled on each side of Preston. She could not help but smile.

As they approached the city, the noise level increased, and Preston and the children roused. He climbed over into the seat and sat Bess in his lap. Nathan stood behind Matty and looked over her shoulder.

"It's changed so much since I was last here. So many new buildings. I don't seem to recognize a thing."

"Follow these wagons. Markets are usually located near the transportation hubs. I'm guessing that's also where we'll find the riverboats."

She agreed with his plan. And she agreed to wait at the market while he went to purchase berths on a riverboat headed to New Orleans.

Two boats were docked at the pier. Preston bypassed the first because it seemed in ill repair and, judging from the music and clientele, catered to gamblers and drunkards. The second boat was clean and bright, the crew polite and respectful. Definitely the better bet.

From the shipping agent he learned the berths were fully booked. His choices were to take the gambling boat, wait days or maybe a week for another riverboat, or continue on the road. Before committing to a lengthy land journey, he decided to see if there were other boats plying the river that would take on four passengers. Perhaps he could charter a cargo vessel or even a fishing boat. He paused outside the shipping office to get his bearings. Someone hailed him by name.

Surprised, he looked around the busy pier. Who did he know in this place?

"Thank heavens, I found you."

"Kelso?" What was his valet doing here? "You're supposed to be in New Orleans arranging for us to run the blockade."

"Yes, sir." The man looked Preston up and down and then shuddered. "*Where* did you get those hideous clothes? Never mind. I don't think I want to know. If you'll follow me to the hotel, I'll have you properly groomed in no time." He turned to lead the way.

"One moment."

"Milord?"

"Why are you here? Besides worrying about my attire, of course."

"Oh, yes. You received this message from Marsfield." Kelso searched his pockets.

"Just tell me what it said. I assume you read it?"

"Yes, sir, I did. Seeing as you were unavailable and it might be important. And it was." He searched all his pockets a second and third time.

"And it said?"

"Sorry, sir. I seem to have left it at the hotel. Marsfield urges you to make all possible haste. Not that you would tarry in the execution of your duty."

Preston deduced that second bit was from Kelso.

"The Duke of Norbundshire is gravely ill. The queen would like to see him reconciled with his granddaughter before his death."

"So you tracked me here to deliver the message. Good job, Kelso."

"It wasn't that difficult, sir. If you remember, I purchased your passage from New Orleans to Memphis. However, once I got here, I had no idea your method of travel, so I deemed it best to presume you would return using the same itinerary and wait here. I've checked in with the shipping agent several times every day."

"I've always said you were quite resourceful, Kelso. However, we seem to be stuck in this backwater for a while. The only appropriate transportation is booked."

"In anticipation of your need, I've kept up to date on the river traffic. If you'd accept a suggestion, sir?"

"Of course."

"Most of the owners of the larger farms, plantations I believe they're called, use the river as their main method of transportation and have private vessels. One in particular, quite the gambler, is currently in town. I do believe if properly approached he could be persuaded to escort an important personage such as yourself to New Orleans in his new boat, one of the fastest on the river."

In other words, the owner needed cash but would not want it known that he'd stooped to selling the services of his boat. "I understand. And where might I meet this plantation owner?"

"At the hotel. May I suggest you change your clothes and perhaps have a shave first?"

With a hand on his shoulder, Preston turned the man in the opposite direction. "First, we will retrieve Miss Maxwell and her children."

Kelso stopped in his tracks. "Children? But sir . . ."

Preston continued walking, forcing the shorter man to scurry to catch up.

"Milord? You never said there would be children. I

do not like . . . I mean I'm not experienced in caring for—"

"Consider them Lady Matilda's chaperones."

"Yes, sir, but—"

"There is another matter you should be aware of," Preston said as they continued walking.

"At this point it wouldn't surprise me if you'd decided to bring home wild Indians."

Preston looked at him with a raised eyebrow. "Matty's Indian friend didn't want to come." He couldn't suppress a smile when the man grabbed his heart. "Though I must say you would have found Joseph Two Feathers to be less trouble than Nathan and Bess."

"No doubt."

They approached the marketplace, and although he could have taken Kelso aside to explain everything, Preston was anxious to see Matty again. The only reason, of course, was to be assured of her safety.

"I'll fill you in later on all the details. For now, just go along with whatever I say."

"Playacting, sir?"

"Without a script. Ah, here we are."

Matty had been out into the market against his directions. All three of them were finishing some confection and had red jelly smeared around their mouths and on their fingers. Although it occurred to him that kissing the sugar from Matty's mouth would be delightful, instead he handed Nathan his handkerchief. Bess held out her arms to him and he picked her up, noting Kelso cringed when she left little jelly prints on his shirt.

Preston introduced Kelso as his cohort who would be helping them for the rest of the trip.

"You never said there was another partner," Matty said, giving him a stern glare.

She would have looked more intimidating without red jelly on her lips. He forced the idea of raspberry-flavored kisses from his mind.

"I can hardly convince anyone I'm Lord Bathers unless I have a valet," he said.

Matty gave the stranger a skeptical glance.

Preston tried to see his valet from her perspective. Small in stature, dressed to persnickety perfection, a cool, aloof attitude—none of which inspired confidence or gave any indication of Kelso's true worth. "We have worked together for some time, and he'll prove most valuable on the trip."

"If you want him, his take comes out of your share." She crossed her arms.

"Fine. I'll foot his salary and his bonus when we succeed."

"Quite a large bonus, I presume," Kelso muttered.

Preston slapped him on the back and laughed. "Now let's get this lot to the hotel."

"Hotel? I thought you were getting berths on a riverboat? Can't we stay on board until it leaves?"

"There's a bit of a problem with that. I'm still making arrangements for the trip. It may take a day or two."

"There are some campsites south of the market that the farmers use."

"We need to be somewhere the shipping agent can find us when he gets word of another riverboat approaching." At least that sounded logical. He didn't want to tell her the real reasons. Not only did he need to put some distance between them, he wanted her tucked up safe and sound while he hunted down the gambling plantation owner.

She bit her bottom lip. "It's not too expensive, is it?"

"No, quite reasonable," he said without hesitation, although he had no idea of the cost.

Finally she agreed.

"You go along, milord. I've informed the manager of the Hotel Sandovar you may be arriving. I'll see to the . . . ah . . . baggage." He picked up a burlap sack, then put it back. "Perhaps I'll also make a few purchases in the market as long as I'm here."

"Excellent idea, Kelso. Perhaps you'd be good enough to also purchase the items on this list, which we will need for the trip." Preston removed a slip of paper from his pocket and handed it to his valet. Then he held out his free arm for Matty. "Come along, Nathan. We'll escort the ladies."

"Wait." Matty turned back to Kelso. "After you're finished, that potato farmer over there has offered to buy the wagon and the horses."

"As you wish, Lady Matilda."

"You may call me Matty."

Preston stepped in. "That would spoil the illusion, don't you think? Perhaps we'd best begin—"

"As we mean to end," Matty finished for him. She shook her head. "I'll have a hard time getting used to it."

"All the more reason to start today."

Matty luxuriated in the large bathtub. Now *this* she could get used to. Hot water she didn't have to haul and heat herself. Fine-milled, lavender-scented soap. Even a special liquid soap just for her hair. Amazing.

Too bad she didn't have hours to waste. With a regretful sigh she stood and wrapped herself in the soft bath sheet. She twisted another towel around her hair and went into the adjoining bedroom. A tall, plain woman in a severe gray dress, white apron, and white mobcap stood by the bed, laying out clothes.

"Who are you and what are you doing in my room?" Matty tried to judge how long it would take her to get her pistol from the drawer where she had put it.

"My name is Edith Franklin." The woman dipped a curtsy. "Mr. Kelso engaged me as your maid and to help with the children."

"Thank you, but I don't need a maid. And those aren't my clothes."

"Mr. Kelso told me your luggage had been lost and that you had no evening wear appropriate for the dining room." She stepped back so Matty could see what lay across the bed. "A local seamstress made this gown available. Is it not lovely?"

The lemon silk and lace creation wasn't the sort of dress Matty would choose for herself. Too many fussy ribbons and bows and rosettes. But it was beautiful none-the-less, and probably quite expensive with those deep, lace flounces.

"If you would be so kind as to thank the seamstress when you return the dress. I have no need of it. I requested supper served in my room. You may also thank Mr. Kelso for his consideration, but I have no need of a maid either." She walked to the door that led to the next room, a sitting room that connected with a second bedroom. "Nathan? Bess? What are you two doing?"

"Do not worry, Madam. The children are playing with the new toys Mr. Kelso bought for them."

Mr. Kelso was getting on her nerves.

Matty stepped behind the dressing screen and threw on her chemise and ratty old robe. She ran a comb through her hair and went looking for the children.

In the attached bedroom, Bess sat on the floor in the midst of tiny dresses, hats, and shoes. "Mine," she said, holding up a China-faced doll with real hair. "Pretty."

Nathan sprawled on one of the beds, absorbed in a

book of instructions for the building set spread out on the coverlet.

"I would appreciate the opportunity to be of service to you," Edith said, having followed her. "I have quite a number of years' experience." The woman seemed stern and quite forbidding until she looked at the children. "However, I'm especially grateful for this job because I do enjoy caring for children."

"I'm sorry, but I manage quite well on my own."

Edith nodded toward the children and motioned Matty into the sitting room, indicating what she had to say was not for young ears.

"I understand your caution, especially where your children are concerned. Mr. Kelso checked out my references. Except for my last position, they are exceptional."

Matty was not surprised to learn Mr. Kelso was thorough as well as efficient. "It's not that. I don't . . . Why no reference from the last post?"

"My previous employer expected more than the duties for which I was hired." She straightened her shoulders. "He said a woman such as I should be grateful for his attentions and threatened that I would never work in Memphis again if I did not cooperate. I did not. Since then I've prayed for a position which included travel."

Perhaps a hand with the children would be nice. For a little while. Maybe just for the journey wouldn't be too expensive.

A knock on the door interrupted her thoughts. Matty scuttled out of sight and Edith answered. She came into the bedroom carrying a large bouquet of flowers and a note addressed to Lady Matilda.

Matty ripped it open, knowing it could be from only Preston. Despite being handwritten, the invitation to dine with him that evening was very formal. And it was signed *Lord Bathers*.

What was he up to?

Was he trying to run a quick scam before leaving Memphis? Well, she'd agreed to help him with one; why shouldn't he assume she was game for another? She would disabuse him of that notion quickly enough. Using the hotel stationery, she dashed off a note, sealed it with wax, and gave it to Edith to deliver to the bellman who would in turn present it to Lord Bathers' valet.

Preston read the note and laughed out loud.

Kelso paused in his intricate preparations of his lordship's shaving equipment. "Sir?"

"Matty has just wished me to the devil." He put the note in his pocket and leaned back in the chair. "Not in so many words, of course, but suffice it to say I'm free this evening to play cards with the designated plantation owner."

"Very good, sir. I shall make inquiries." With a practiced flick of the wrist, Kelso wrapped a hot towel around Preston's face, leaving only a small opening for his mouth and nose.

"No rush," Preston said, relaxing. This was much better than scraping his own face. "I'm in no rush at all."

So his invitation had shocked Matty. He wished he'd thought to deliver it in person. Then he could have asked her about the servant he'd had Kelso hire. She probably wanted to know who was going to foot her pay. He smiled. Well, he had more surprises up his sleeve. Starting with tomorrow morning. And he couldn't wait to see her face.

Chapter 8

Luxury rotted your brain. Not only had Matty slept well-past dawn, she'd agreed to breakfast in bed after Edith had appeared with Bess already fed and dressed for the day. Along with the tray, the new maid had delivered the information that Lord Bathers had taken Nathan on an excursion to view the boats. Matty sat back against the pillows and sipped her coffee. Just a few more minutes and then she would return to real life.

She must have dozed because noises in the next room caught her by surprise. When she heard Preston's voice, she started and spilled her coffee. Luckily it was already cold. Jumping up from the bed, she used the napkin to clean up as best she could.

Edith entered, announcing she had a caller. She presented Lord Bathers' card. "I'll do that," she said, taking over the cleanup. "I've laid out your clothes, and there's warm water in the washbowl behind the screen."

Matty thanked her and rushed to get dressed. This is what came of being lazy. She hated being caught unprepared. She washed, dressed in her old blue dress in record time, and sat at the dressing table even as she fastened the last of the small buttons at the neckline. A quick brush, a few twists, and a couple of hairpins. She turned to put on her stockings and shoes, but giggles from the other room made her decide slippers would do.

As she rushed into the sitting room, Bess jumped up and down in the middle of the room and clapped her hands. Nathan lay on the settee, holding his sides and laughing. Preston, seated cross-legged on the floor, had the doll's straw hat on his head, a little purple, lace dress on top of his cravat, and one tiny white glove on each tip of his index fingers.

"Pretty, pretty," Bess said. Then she switched the straw boater with a miniature riding hat that had a pink feather.

Despite his position on the floor, Preston looked every inch the English peer: elaborately knotted tie, blue superfine jacket, gold brocaded vest, buff trousers, and knee-high Hessian boots polished to a mirror shine. His hair had been trimmed, and he'd had a close shave. He'd even added a crested ring on his right hand to complete the look. More than handsome, he seemed quite at ease in his elegant attire.

"Very nice," she said, suddenly self-conscious in her old dress and slippers.

"Thank you," he answered. "I've always considered pink feathers quite de rigueur for any true gentleman of style."

Bess replaced the purple dress on his cravat with a green ball gown.

"Excellent choice to go with the riding hat," Preston said to her. "But don't you think Esmerelda is getting chilled without her clothes? I think she wants these." He divested himself of the assorted apparel and handed it to Edith so she could help Bess.

As the child turned her attention to dressing her doll, he looked up at Matty and smiled.

A curl of warmth started low in her stomach, which she could not attribute to the lukewarm coffee. He was so natural playing with Bess and Nathan. Almost as if he'd taken care of children before. Did he have children of his own? Was he married? She really knew nothing about him.

"Good morning, Slugabed."

"Same to you, Mr. Preston."

"Are we back to that? What have I done now?"

"Thank you for the lovely flowers."

"You're welcome."

"However, they were a totally unnecessary expense. I do not approve of extravagance, especially when it costs me."

"I purchased the flowers personally, not as part of our deal."

"And the toys and—"

"Surely you don't begrudge your children a few trinkets that will help entertain them on the long trip."

"Well, no, I suppose not. But the new clothes and—"

"Aren't you the one who said looking the part was necessary for success?"

"Well, yes, but—"

"You'll never convince anyone you're the granddaughter of a duke with that ensemble. The slippers alone would be a giveaway."

"I would never wear . . ." She paused when she saw his grin, clearly claiming victory in their verbal battle. "Arrgh." She threw up her hands. "You're right. New clothes. New shoes. Fancy hotels and servants. Let's spend all the money before we even get it."

He jumped up and wiped imaginary dust off his knees. "No time to shop now. Our transportation to New Orleans awaits." He turned to Edith. "Is everything packed, Miss Franklin?"

"Almost, sir. Mr. Kelso notified me luncheon would be served aboard the vessel. As soon as Lady Matilda is through with her toilette, we can be ready to leave in a matter of minutes."

"Another riverboat docked?" Matty asked. "And you secured berths? Was it too terribly expensive?"

"Not exactly." Preston flashed her a triumphant grin. "We now own a thirty-foot flatboat. Quite well equipped. Nathan and I inspected it this morning."

"You bought a boat? Of all the—"

"I won it. Playing poker."

Matty turned from him. "Edith, why don't you take the children into their room and help them prepare to leave?"

"Yes, milady." Edith helped Nathan and Bess pick up their things and followed them into their room.

Matty gave Preston a hard stare. "I should have known," she said, shaking her head.

"What is that supposed to mean? I had to do something to occupy my time after you wouldn't have dinner with me."

"Don't blame this on me."

"I'm crediting you."

"I don't want anything to do with gambling," Matty said and set her lips in a firm line. Her father's addiction to cards was the reason she never had a real home. The scams were just the means to enter another game. Although she had no idea how deep Preston's pockets were, she did know there was never so much money that it couldn't all be lost when he hit a losing streak. As all gamblers did sooner or later.

"We needed transportation and I provided it," Preston said, his tone a bit huffy.

"And you could have just as easily lost everything." She wrapped her arms around her waist. She and the children could well be stranded right now if his luck had gone differently.

"I've told you before, I am a successful gambler."

"But—"

"And the first rule of being a successful gambler is to never risk more than you can afford to lose."

"You can afford to lose the cost of a thirty-foot boat?"

He leaned forward to whisper, "I can when I'm playing with a marked deck." He grinned like a boy bragging about putting a little girl's pigtails into the inkwell on his school desk.

"You cheated!" From the settee she picked up a small, square pillow with large, gold tassels on the corners and smacked him on the shoulder. "Of all the rotten, low-down, dirty—"

He grabbed the pillow before a tassel caught him in the eye. "Hey, I never said it was *my* marked deck."

She froze. "You mean you out-played someone who tried to cheat you with a marked deck?"

He grinned again. "It wasn't all that difficult once I learned the pattern. The thing about players who use a crooked deck is that they tend to count on the marks and forget about playing good poker. I cleaned him out before midnight."

"Good." She smiled up at him.

When she looked at him like that, like he'd done something wonderful, a little bubble of something that seemed almost like happiness lodged in his chest. Something he was not at all used to feeling.

"If there's one thing I can't stand it's a liar and a cheat," she said.

The realization he'd done nothing but lie to her from practically the moment they met burst that bubble, leaving an acidic burning in its wake.

"Yet that's exactly what you've agreed to do, isn't it?" he said. "What else would you call a scam other than lying and cheating?"

"You needn't remind me." She rubbed her temples with her fingertips. "Doing the wrong thing for the right reasons doesn't make me any less culpable."

He'd lashed out without thinking and instantly regretted his words. Was she thinking about backing out? If she did, completing his mission could become quite unpleasant. He had to diffuse his earlier faux pas.

"No need for a hair shirt. Believe me, the duke will be happier than he's been in years and he'll never miss the money. He's richer than Croesus."

"It's still a lie."

"Everyone lies every day. It's the grease that allows people to rub along together without abrasion. *So glad to meet you. Love your hat. Marvelous party.* Society would crumble if communication were limited to only the absolute truth."

"None of those little white lies involve fifty thousand dollars."

"True, but that's a difference of degree rather than principle."

She threw up her hands. "According to you, scamming the duke is the polite thing to do."

"My insignificant contribution to civilization," he said with a low bow, sweeping one arm wide.

"I'm trying to have a serious discussion and you're . . . you're bantering."

He paused. The temptation to assuage her guilty conscience tormented him. But if he presented her with the truth, she would not only disbelieve him but might well refuse to continue the journey. His best bet was to keep her off balance, at least until he delivered her to Norbundshire. He straightened and struck a pose.

"If you're looking for absolution, perhaps you should have accepted Henshaw's proposal."

She took a step back. "That's a horrid thing to say."

He shrugged and gave her the bored, nonchalant expression he had used effectively at the gambling table. "Either you're in the game or not. There's no whining after the cards are dealt."

"I could wait for a better hand."

"If you fold now, you're done. The game moves on without you."

"I could find another table. I know from experience, there's always another game."

"True. However, the ante elsewhere is rather steep. Are you willing to pay the price?"

Her shoulders slumped. "No. I'm not a gambler but I do have enough sense not to cut off my nose to spite my face."

"If you're in, it's a commitment to the end. I have too much invested and enough other things to handle without worrying you'll back out on me at the last minute."

"I won't back out."

"Well, partner, we should get moving. The boat is waiting and the duke isn't getting any younger."

"One last thing before we go any farther. Partners must depend on each other. I think we should agree never to lie to each other."

"Agreed," he said. "Partners should trust each other."

"I want your word as a gentleman that you won't lie to me."

"That sounds distinctly like you don't trust me."

"About as far as I could throw you. But you seem to place a high value on being a gentleman, so say the words."

She waited, and he could think of no way to escape the challenge. "I give you my word as a gentleman I will not lie to you." And it was the biggest lie of all.

She stuck out her hand. "Shake on it."

Instead of doing that, he leaned over and kissed the back of her hand, not only in a gesture to beg her forgiveness in advance, but also to hide his shame. Although he had often flaunted the gentleman's code, had made fun of it and pushed it to the limit, this was the only time he had ever falsely given his word. The only time he felt unworthy of the name *gentleman*. And worse, despite her previous misgivings, she'd trusted him enough to take his word for the meaning it should have carried.

She snatched her hand back and turned away. "I'll be ready to leave in ten minutes," she called over her shoulder as she left the sitting room.

Matty stumbled into the bedroom and sat on the chair by the dresser. She examined the back of her right hand, looking for a scorch, a burn, a brand. The lingering touch of his lips had surely left a mark. Despite the heat she'd felt, the skin remained unblemished. Yet the warmth had been real, for it stained her cheeks and pooled low in her stomach.

What was wrong with her? How was she going to deal with him if every time he touched her she had this unusual and quite embarrassing reaction? Almost as if she were allergic to his touch, except she didn't break out in a rash. Once, when she was a child, eating strawberries had caused red welts on her chest and arms. She checked under her bodice. Maybe a bit flushed but no sign of hives.

Either the reaction was a milder form of an allergy or it was something else. But what? She'd never felt like this before.

Since she had no one to ask, her best course of action would be to stay as far away from him as possible. Not an easy task when they would be traveling together. Perhaps she would be all right if she was careful not to let his skin touch her skin. Especially his lips. Who could say what would happen if his lips accidentally touched someplace more sensitive than the back of her hand? Like the lobes of her ears? Or the nape of her neck? Or her lips?

No, no, no. She would not allow herself to even think about kissing him. That way led to disaster. They were business partners, nothing else. Once the scam was complete, she would never see him again.

She ignored the hollow feeling caused by that thought, and put on her stockings and shoes. When Edith entered, Matty was nearly finished packing.

"That's my job, Lady Matilda," the maid scolded, and she shooed her away from the wardrobe.

She left the task to Edith, but she would never get used to being referred to as Lady Matilda. No fancy, fraudulent title was going to change the fact she was plain Matty Maxwell from Turnabout, Tennessee. And she'd best remember that, because she would return there when this adventure was over. She'd have a bit of money to fix up the farm and, more importantly, she could afford a lawyer to legally adopt her children, but she would still be the same person.

At least she hoped so. She looked around the room, more spacious and comfortably furnished than any room in her home. Breakfast in bed. A maid to pack for her.

"Lord Bathers said he would meet you in the lobby," Edith said. "Why don't you take the children and go ahead? I'll see to this."

Matty acquiesced and thanked her. As she left the

room, she rubbed the back of her hand. *Don't get spoiled,* she warned herself. All this luxury was only temporary. Just like Preston, it would soon be gone.

Matty stared at the boat as she alighted from the carriage. Although she was familiar with the flat-bottomed, barge-like proportions of local riverboats, she had never seen one quite that elaborate. The cabin, perched in the center of the deck, was constructed in the Greek Revival style, complete with white, fluted columns. The rest of the boat was painted in varying shades of green to resemble rolling, green fields. With her hand on Preston's arm, they paused on the wharf to allow Edith to board ahead of them with several boxes, and Kelso was but a few steps behind her with a luggage cart and several footmen from the hotel to help unload.

Then Preston escorted Matty to the gangplank, carrying Bess in his other arm. Nathan scampered ahead.

"Welcome aboard the *Shangri-La,*" Preston said.

Only after Matty had stepped aboard did she see the detail of the artwork. A mythical forest spread across the inner surfaces of the boat. Centaurs galloped along the port balustrade. Elves danced between the trees that lined the starboard railing. Water sprites frolicked in a stream that ran from prow to stern. Fairies peeked up from between the painted blades of grass below her feet. Bess clapped her hands in delight, but Matty was not as easily entranced. Despite strategically placed leaves or branches, none of the figures wore a stitch of clothing.

She leaned forward to get a closer look at two elves, but Preston took her elbow and swept her toward the rear of the boat.

"There will be plenty of time for that once we're under way."

As they neared the single, small paddle wheel at the back of the boat, her attention focused on an intricate painting designed to make the observer think the painted gnomes were running the boat's propulsion system. Ingenious, and so realistic, she was surprised when a tall black man stepped from behind the engine housing.

Preston introduced Captain Josea Jones.

"Welcome aboard, Miss," he said, removing his cap and bowing.

"Thank you, Captain." She stuck out her hand, and after a moment's hesitation, he shook it. "You have quite a unique boat here."

"Yes, Miss. My apologies for the—"

"Is everything ready to leave?" Preston asked, cutting off whatever else the captain had to say.

"Yes, sir." The man straightened to his full height and his face became impassive. "Our supplies are loaded and steam is up. As soon as your belongings are aboard, we can cast off."

Preston looked over his shoulder to see the hotel employees leaving with their luggage cart. "I do believe we're ready."

"Yes, sir." The captain turned on his heel and attacked the ropes with practiced efficiency.

Then he and two boys not much older than Nathan used long poles to push the boat away from the dock.

"You didn't have to be so rude," Matty whispered to Preston.

"I beg your forbearance. I have reason for wanting to leave as soon as possible." He reached out to cup her elbow, steadying her as the boat lurched into the river's current.

The crew stowed the poles. The captain raced back to pull levers and fiddle with dials on the engine. As the boys finished coiling the ropes, the paddle wheel began to move and quickly picked up speed.

"And that reason would be?" she persisted. Had the shooter followed them? Had Preston seen him about town? If her children were in danger, she had the right to know.

The boat's steam whistle screeched two long blasts, signaling their departure and delaying his answer. Bess didn't like the sound and clung tightly to his neck.

"Would you care for a cup of tea?" Preston asked Matty when the noise had faded to only the deep humming of the engine. "The captain's wife is in charge of the galley. Her name is Tiny and she told me earlier she always has the kettle hot."

"What are you trying to hide? As far as I'm concerned, concealment of the truth is the same as lying, and less than an hour ago you promised never to lie to me."

A high-pitched scream and loud thump sounded.

Chapter 9

After the scream, there was more mysterious thumping and bumping and banging. Almost as if someone was fighting off an attacker. Matty automatically looked for Nathan to be sure he was safe, even as she ran toward the commotion. He sat in the prow with the two boys she had seen earlier and a plethora of fishing gear. She waved for him to stay there. "Edith?" she called as she reached the cabin. "Where are you?"

She pushed on the door, but something soft blocked the way. "Edith? Are you all right?"

Muffled noises were her only response.

Matty pulled out her pearl-handled derringer and pushed harder on the door.

"Wait," Preston said, as he arrived sans Bess. "I'll—"

"You won't fit," Matty said, bracing her back against the jamb for leverage. She slipped through the small opening. The door slammed shut behind her.

The maid lay on the floor of the cabin, struggling to free herself from the collapsed stack of boxes and baskets. Stockings, undergarments, and all sorts of clothing flew every which way.

Matty grabbed a large box and set it aside. "Edith, are you all right? What happened?"

The maid managed to shove a basket off her chest and sit up. "Sorry, milady. I didn't mean to make such a mess." She picked up a piece of yellow muslin. "Oh, dear, I tore your new dress."

"Hang the dress. It's you I'm worried about. What happened?"

"I'm sorry. It was just such a shock and then I slipped. Everything just came tumbling down."

Matty had a hard time following the story, what with Preston slamming into the door with his shoulder in repeated attempts to dislodge it. "Just a minute," she called to him as she helped Edith to her feet and into a chair.

"I'm fine," the maid said as she leaned back and closed her eyes. "I'll clean this up in a moment."

"You just take it easy." Matty patted her hand. Then she waded through clothes and hats and toys and books to the door. Practically everything she and the children owned, and all sorts of things she didn't recognize, was strewn about the floor. Her small store of face powder had dusted much of the clothing and still clogged the air. Her precious bottle of lavender bath oil had broken, and the scent was overwhelming. She moved the box wedged against the end of the bed and had to jump out of the way as Preston broke the door down and came bursting through.

The fierce expression on his face caused her to take another step back. This was a side of Preston she'd never expected. The ferocious warrior primed for battle. The Crusader knight ready for any encounter with the enemy. After looking around the room, he took a deep breath and, with obvious effort, relaxed. Suddenly, the London sophisticate was back. "I must say you have an unusual method of unpacking."

"I would have opened the door for you if you had waited a minute as I asked."

"And I would have preceded you inside had you

waited as I requested." He made his way to the maid's side. "How are you feeling, Miss Franklin?"

"I'm sorry I'm so clumsy to have caused all this. I just wanted to get milady and the children settled. Those inept porters left everything on the bed. Then I saw . . ." She waved weakly around the room. Her hand neared the wall and she pulled it back with a cry. "Shameful, that's what they are," she whispered, leaning forward and pointing to the paintings on the walls without actually looking at them.

"Then what happened?" Preston asked her gently. He was fairly sure by now an intruder was not involved, but he wanted to make sure.

"I must have stepped back too quickly, and I slipped. I grabbed for the bed to get my balance and, the next thing I knew, everything came tumbling down on top of me."

The captain's wife knocked on the doorjamb and offered her assistance. Kelso and the captain stood behind her. Preston helped Edith to her feet. "You go with Tiny and have a nice cup of tea. Here, the captain will give you a hand. Kelso will clean this up." He also directed his valet to fetch cleaning supplies.

He turned to Matty. "We can wait on deck—"

"Where's Bess?" she asked without turning around. She stepped to her left to peruse the next section of the elaborate mural that covered all the walls.

"With Nathan and the captain's sons. I handed her off on my way here. That's why you beat me to the door." He cleared his throat. "About the paintings . . ."

"They're quite well done." She touched a tree with one finger. "Almost three-dimensional. These apples look as if I could reach out and pick one."

"There was no time to have them painted over."

"Now that would have been a crime. This rose

should have a scent. And this fairy could fly away at any moment."

"I'm a bit surprised by your reaction." He could hardly credit she stared at the Bacchanalian scenes and saw apples and flowers and fairies.

"I'm neither blind nor stupid," she said. "You forget I've been in saloons and gambling halls since I was a child. I've seen worse." She took another step to the left, and giggled. "I love that the little gnomes have left their hats on. What have we here?" She leaned closer for a better look at two elves bent backward over a tree stump. "Oh my. Is that even possible?"

"Matty."

"Well, is it? It seems quite realistic, but terribly uncomfortable." She moved on to the next scene without waiting for his answer. "Look at these skin tones. Magnificent. I swear they must be breathing."

"Heavy breathing," Preston muttered, rubbing the back of his neck. Of all the responses he'd envisioned—horror, disgust, refusal to sail on such a boat—interest and appreciation were not even on the list of reactions he'd expected. Again she'd surprised him. Despite her lack of innocence, made obvious by two children, he'd expected a woman of her breeding to be shocked. "Are you a painter?" he asked as the sudden inspiration popped into his head.

"Not really. But I did study with a master for several months in preparation for a certain scam my father designed. I was supposed to be a child prodigy, and this rich woman paid to send me to study in Paris."

"I didn't know you lived in France."

She flashed him a quick, disgruntled look over her shoulder. "You're missing the point. It was a scam. She *paid* for me to go; I didn't actually do it."

"Of course."

"I did finish the portrait of her I'd started while Blackie worked the scam. I sent it to her but never heard if she liked it or not. No return address, you know."

"Naturally. So then you do paint?"

She shook her head, yet still did not turn to look at him. "I used to dabble when I had the time. No real talent. I talk about painting better than I actually do it. Look at these brush strokes. Pure genius the way the artist captured the light on this centaur's leg. At least I think it's his leg. It's hard to tell in that position. Maybe it's not." She tipped her head to the side. "Oh my."

Although he was inured to erotic artwork by dint of exposure, Matty in her little puritan dress with her hair in its tight little bun commenting on the various body parts and positions was having a decided effect upon him. He grabbed her by the shoulders and spun her toward the door. "Enough art appreciation for one day."

They nearly collided with Kelso, who had returned with a bucket of soapy water, a mop, and an armful of rags. Matty slipped by and disappeared around the side of the cabin.

"I thought I told you to hang some sheets or something over these paintings," he said to Kelso.

"That you did, sir. And I was going to see to it as soon as I got your wardrobe shipshape." Kelso started cleaning with jerky motions. "I figured Miss Franklin would be busy with the children for quite some time."

"May I presume you will take care of the task immediately?"

"Yes, sir," Kelso said, his tone a bit on the sour side. "Just as soon as I finish with this mess."

Preston realized his attitude had been sterner than the circumstances called for. His valet had only been doing his job as he had seen it best. "Thank you. I do appreciate that this trip has called upon you to rise above and beyond your normal duties."

Kelso bowed to him in quite a formal manner. "The cook says luncheon will be served within the hour, though she flatly refused to divulge the menu to me."

Preston hid a relieved smile. So that was the reason for Kelso's pique. He made a mental note to smooth things over later. Even a short trip of three days could prove unpleasant if the servants were feuding.

He turned away and decided to find Matty. Not for any particular reason other than he wanted to see her. But he couldn't tell her that. He left the room, trying to think up a reasonable excuse for seeking her out.

Matty made her way toward the front of the boat, the cool breeze a welcome relief against her flaming cheeks. She could only hope Preston had not seen her unavoidable reaction to the paintings. Her interest had not been feigned, nor her appreciation of the artist's technique, but the subject matter had been shocking.

Her father had been careful to shelter her from the baser aspects of his chosen profession by arranging for her to stay with friends or at respectable establishments. She had been in a saloon and three gambling halls, but only to fetch her father for one reason or another, and she had waited near the door while someone else found him and brought him to her.

She wanted Preston to think of her as a woman of the world so he would have confidence she could carry off the scam. She refused to analyze her motives beyond that. And she hadn't lied to him. Not exactly. She had simply behaved in a certain manner. He would come to his own conclusions, and if those happened to be false and to her advantage, then he was the one at fault for believing the worst of her.

Her relationship with Preston was getting more complicated by the day. Needing a simple hug, she sought out her children and found Nathan and the other two boys hanging fishing poles over the side of the boat. Bess sat safely ensconced in the middle of a large coil of thick rope, intently watching a worm crawl over its ridges.

Matty sat on the bench beside Nathan. "Are you having fun?" she asked, but she needn't have because the look on his face told her he was happy.

"M-my n-n-new f-friends," he said, nodding toward the other boys.

"Hello," she said. "What are your names?"

"Jebidiah Jones," the taller one said as he snatched off his cap with one hand and bowed without letting go of his pole. He elbowed his brother, who then copied him.

"Obadiah," the younger one said.

"Catch anything yet?" she asked.

"Nah," Jebidiah said. "I told 'em it's too late in the day for fish to be feeding. I told 'em we should get up early in the morning. That's the time to fish."

"Sometimes we get lucky," the other boy said. "Besides, it's fun."

Nathan grinned and gave his pole a jiggle.

She checked on Bess, who seemed about ready to nod off in her little cocoon. Matty settled back on the bench to enjoy the peaceful landscape sliding by.

"Jeb? Obie?" their mother called. "Time to wash up so you can set the table."

The boys handed their fishing poles to Matty.

"We got chores but we'll be back lickety-split," Jeb said. He ran after his brother, who was already halfway toward the back of the boat.

"What am I supposed to do with these?" she called after the boys.

"Just don't let 'em fall overboard," Jeb called back.

Matty juggled the two cane poles, finally wedging the end of one under the bench cushion and the other between two boxes. After a few minutes, the end of Nathan's pole dipped.

"I got s-something," he said. "W-what do I do?"

"I don't know," she said. There weren't any fish in their pond at home, so she had never been fishing before. She looked around for help and saw Preston standing stock-still beside the cabin, his knees flexed and arms out as if poised to pounce.

"Don't move," he said, urgency coloring his voice.

"I won't," Nathan said, his full attention on his fish.

But Matty followed Preston's line of sight and spied what caused him to behave so strangely. A long, black snake slithered across the deck, perilously close to where Bess sprawled asleep, her little arm hanging outside the coiled rope, her little hand within the snake's path. If she jerked in her sleep and startled the animal, it might well strike.

Matty leaned forward to stand.

"Just sit tight," Preston said.

"I am," Nathan said. He struggled to hang on to the pole, oblivious to the drama behind his back.

"I know why they call them cottonmouths," Matty whispered. "Because that's what your mouth feels like when you see one."

"Poisonous?"

"Very."

Nathan turned, and Matty put her hand on his shoulder to keep him in place and calm.

"Just another inch and I'll have a shot," Preston said.

"You're not going to shoot that close to Bess!" Matty cried.

"Not exactly," he answered, drawing out his words and not shifting his gaze.

Then he moved, so quickly, she barely saw it as it happened. In one smooth, lightning-fast motion, Preston reached behind his neck, drew a knife, and threw it at the snake, pinning its head to the deck.

Matty jumped up and, even though the animal still writhed in its death throes, she leaped over it, snatched up Bess, and scurried to the other side of the deck.

Now that the danger was over, Matty started to shake, and tears poured down her cheeks. She held Bess so tightly the child woke, and she began to wail either in protest or from the tension around her. Preston put his arm around Matty's shoulders, and she leaned into his strength, thankful for his presence. What would have happened if he hadn't been there? She shuddered.

"It's all right now," he whispered into her hair.

But if he hadn't been there? Then she remembered that if he hadn't shown up at her door, she would still be safe at home. She pulled away from him.

"L-l-look at the s-snake," Nathan called as he climbed up on the bench for a better view.

Matty did not even have a chance to tell him to get down before a jerk on his fishing pole flipped Nathan over the side of the boat.

She screamed. With two, long steps, Preston launched himself into the water after the boy. Matty ran the length of the boat.

"Help! Stop the engines! Man overboard! Boy overboard! Help! Stop!"

The captain threw a lever, and the sudden silence was ominous. He tossed the anchor over the side.

"Nathan? Preston?" She couldn't see behind the boat due to the size of the paddle wheel housing. "Nathan?"

All the other people on the boat came rushing up. Edith took Bess, and Kelso helped the captain launch a small dinghy. Although Matty wanted to go with them in the rescue boat, she could see the space was limited and would be needed to bring back Preston and Nathan. She prayed they would need the space.

Waiting for their return, waiting with no way to help was the worst. She paced the deck. Tiny tried to get her to drink some tea, but she refused. She paced some more. Edith suggested a glass of sherry to calm her nerves. Matty refused. What was taking so long? Surely they hadn't traveled that far before the engines had been cut.

She leaned so far over the side, trying to see what was happening, she was in danger of falling herself. Then she heard rhythmic splashing. The sound of oars?

"Preston? Is that you? Where's Nathan? Answer me, dagnabbit."

"Nathan's fine," he finally replied. "Just a bit wet and exhausted. And determined to learn to swim at the first opportunity."

His voice sounded close, and the small boat soon pulled up next to the railing. Her poor, bedraggled son struggled aboard. Thankfully Tiny had thought to have blankets handy, so Matty wrapped one around Nathan and gave him a squeeze.

"Don't you ever scare me like that again," she scolded.

He shook his head. She knew he was uncomfortable being the center of attention, but she wanted to make sure he was all right before letting him go with Edith to fetch dry clothes.

Matty stood and turned to Preston. He leaned against the railing, a blanket draped over his shoulders, and sipped a glass of brandy. Everyone else seemed to have drifted away to attend to their duties, so they were alone.

"Thank you for saving Nathan's life. And for saving Bess earlier. Although mere words hardly seem sufficient."

She looked at him in that special way again, the one that made him feel ten-feet tall. Only this time he could not turn away from the temptation. He held out his hand. "Come here."

For a long, unbearable moment she hesitated; then she stepped forward and put her hand in his. He drew her closer.

"I seem to remember reading it is customary for a fair maiden to reward a heroic deed with a kiss."

"I suppose that means you expect two?"

He smiled down at her. "I will graciously endure any reward you wish to bestow."

She raised one eyebrow. "Endure?"

"Since we've never kissed, I have no basis for a positive comment," he said with a shrug.

She stood on her tiptoes and planted her lips squarely on his. He required all his hard-learned self-control to refrain from sweeping her into his arms, to let her end the kiss.

The easy, bantering words he had planned turned to sawdust in his mouth. Shook by the honesty in her sweet kiss, he stepped back. He hung his head so she would not see the shame he felt for manipulating her. "Thank you," he said. "You may consider your duty as fair maiden well done."

"Was my kiss that poor?" she whispered, tears in her voice. She turned and ran.

"No. It's not that." He followed her, catching up with her before she ducked inside the cabin. She twisted to get away from him, but he backed her against the wall, blocking her escape with an arm on either side. "Please let me explain."

She stilled.

With a thumb and finger he tipped her chin up so she looked him in the eye. "I've learned, quite recently as a matter of fact, that I don't like obligatory kisses. It's like biting into fruit made from wax when I wanted marzipan. Duty kisses are another form of social lying. When you kiss me, I want it to be because you want to, not because you feel obligated to do so by some silly convention."

"You're the one who brought it up."

"Yes, I was. And I was wrong. I'm sorry." He stepped back and bowed low. "Please accept my apologies for taking advantage of the situation."

She tapped him on the shoulder. "Arise, Sir Sadly Mistaken."

"Pardon?"

"I'm not party to your gentleman's code, or your fair maiden's code, or whatever you call it. I would never kiss you out of some absurd, abstract sense of obligation."

"Then why . . ."

"For the simplest of reasons. I was curious what you tasted like."

"And . . ."

"River water," she said with a grimace. She slipped into the cabin and propped the door in place behind her. "Not terribly appealing," she added.

He laughed and set out with a jaunty step to find Kelso and a hot bath. River water, indeed. Bloody good thing that condition was only temporary. The next time she kissed him would be a very different matter. He couldn't wait to get her alone again.

Matty leaned against the door panel. She'd lied to

him. Straight-out, out-and-out lied. And after she had made such a big fuss about him telling her the truth.

His kiss had not tasted of river water. He had tasted of brandy and those peppermints he'd bought for himself and Nathan. And he'd tasted of forbidden passion. A unique flavor she could easily become addicted to.

There could be no more kisses.

She had seen firsthand how the craving for something a person couldn't have destroyed one's life, and the lives of those who loved and depended on him. Preston's presence was temporary.

There would be no more kisses.

Chapter 10

Every port in the world had its own distinct odor. New Orleans smelled like overripe vegetables and rotting fish with just a hint of honeysuckle and sea salt. Preston stood in the prow of the boat as it made its way toward a docking space at the mouth of the river, his mood as sour as the air around him.

He had not had a single opportunity to speak to Matty alone. For the last seventy-two hours she had shielded herself behind the presence of the children or that self-appointed guardian of female virtue, Edith. Why had he ever thought Matty needed a maid? The idea had been to hire someone to help with the children so he would have more time with Matty.

Not that he didn't care for children in general; and her two were fine specimens, smart and lively. He had to admit he quite enjoyed their presence. In small doses, of course. He preferred adult conversation and activities. Adult female companionship, to be more particular. Matty's company, to be specific.

And that bothered him more than he cared to admit. Not since his youthful crush on Anne had he been so bedeviled by a woman. He'd decided long ago getting over Anne had been difficult solely because his love was unrequited. His interest in other women had faded soon after he'd bedded them, hence his disinterest in a permanent liaison.

Neither Marsfield nor Burke seemed to have the same problem. Both of their relationships had improved, surprisingly so, with familiarity and commitment. The circumstances of Preston's birth must have left him lacking something essential for marital bliss.

But not for bliss of the conjugal variety.

The best way to get Matty out of his system was to spend more time with her. Let familiarity breed contempt. Or at least disinterest. Yet, she was purposely avoiding him.

He had a plan to change that, but first he had to get the whole group to the Bahamas where Burke's ship awaited them. As the afternoon slipped away, their slow progress through the river traffic was almost as frustrating as a certain woman he could name.

According to Kelso, the blockade runners would be leaving port over the next three nights to take advantage of the dark moon. Preston needed to book passage immediately or waste a month in New Orleans waiting for another opportunity.

As if his thoughts had the power to summon his valet, Kelso arrived with a steaming cup of tea.

"We will dock in approximately ten minutes," he announced. "Everything is prepared for a speedy debarkation."

"Thank you. Have you informed Lady Matilda?"

"I go there directly. Miss Franklin is aware of our requirement for haste, and her charges will be ready. The captain says hacks are always available on the quay."

"Do you trust the blockade runner will be waiting?"

Kelso shrugged. "A man motivated by greed is usually dependable when additional funds are forthcoming. My worry is the contract I arranged was for three persons, and we are now double that number."

"I'm sure we can reach an agreement. Time is more important than money." Preston noted the change in the engines and the boat slowing even more and deduced they were near their destination. "One more thing. Please ask the captain to see me as soon as he has a spare moment."

Kelso bowed and went about his errands.

While Kelso shepherded children and luggage off the boat and into a carriage, Preston met with Captain Jones.

"We wish you fair the rest of your journey," Jones said.

"Thank you." Preston handed the man a packet of papers. "This boat now belongs to you."

"But, sir—"

"And I thank you for taking it off my hands, as I no longer have need of it. I don't have the time to arrange for a sale and would hate to see it sit and rot for lack of use."

"You do not understand. A slave cannot own property. This will revert to my master, who will be most happy to have his boat back, so I thank you for him."

"Actually, until I handed you those papers, I was your master. I won your family's services along with the boat. As I find the idea of human bondage distasteful, I included your manumission papers along with the name and address of a woman in Savannah who can help you make the most of your future."

The captain fell to his knees. "Sir, I haven't the words to thank you—"

"Then don't." This was precisely why Preston had

waited until the last minute to tell the captain the news. If he'd had the time to handle the matter anonymously through an agent he would have preferred to do it that way. "Get up, man. You're embarrassing me."

"I could kiss your feet."

"And ruin the shine on my boots? Heaven forbid." Preston grabbed him by the arms and hauled him up. "You must now stand on your own two feet. Good or bad you reap the consequences of your own decisions just like any other man."

The captain straightened his shoulders and stood tall. "My family thanks you for your generosity. I will find a way to repay you."

Preston put his hand on the other man's shoulder. "The only repayment I would have is to know your sons are grown into fine, strong men."

The captain nodded.

"Now, please return to your duties, and not a word about this to anyone until we have left."

Once more the captain seemed to want to say something, so Preston held up his hand and shook his head. Captain Jones bowed low. As he walked away, Preston imagined a new confidence to the captain's step, and smiled.

When he turned, Matty stood just beyond the corner of the cabin, that look on her face.

"How long have you been there?" he asked.

"Long enough." She looked down at her hands and bit her bottom lip. "That was very noble of you. I'm grateful you thought of it."

Damnation, he didn't want her bloody gratitude. He wanted her to desire him as he desired her. He wanted her naked and panting beneath him, begging him to do the very things he wanted most to do. Preston brought a halt to those thoughts.

He could never allow things to get out of hand and go that far. Spending time with her should be enough to foster a return to his normal state of mind. This was Matty, after all. With her denim trousers and two children and none of the social skills he had learned to admire. Matty, who had an annoying penchant for getting under his skin. Especially when she looked at him that way. He pitied the poor man who would have to live up to the shining expectation in those eyes. Thankfully, he had always been lucky, and it wouldn't be him.

He rubbed his chest. Bloody tea gave him indigestion again.

"Don't get all mushy and dewy-eyed," he said. "I was only being practical. We haven't time for anything else."

"Still, you thought of it."

"What? No complaint about the money? We could have sold the boat for a tidy profit."

She shrugged. "You got what you paid for it. You're even."

He tried another tack. "Eavesdropping is not an admirable activity for a lady."

She stomped her foot. "I never said I was a lady, so I don't know why you expect me to do everything the way a *lady* should," she said, practically spitting out the title.

He'd finally succeeded. That adoring look was gone.

"A lady does not stomp."

She crossed her arms.

"Or stand like that. Or pout."

"Where do you get all these inane rules? Are you making them up as you go along, or is there a book, a manual of silly regulations for a lady to follow?" Matty assumed a pose, holding an imaginary looking glass between her thumb and two fingers, her pinkie pointed skyward. "A lady never looks to the left, only to the right," she said in a haughty tone worthy of an Almack's matron. "A lady begins walking on her right foot, never the left. A lady never eats crispy crackers because the noise of chewing, even if audible only to herself, would offend her delicate sensibilities."

Preston stifled a smile. Just wait until she learned some of the real rules. Her parody was not far off the mark. He hoped he was in the room when she met her first London dandy and encountered her first society maven. Sparks would surely fly. But if he let that happen, he would have done a disservice to Norbundshire, the queen, and to Matty herself.

"Bravo. Mocking what you don't understand is a time-honored method of bringing the enemy down to size."

"I'm not totally ignorant. I know enough not to drink out of the finger bowl."

"No need to get your dander up. Your manners are quite acceptable by American standards."

She tapped her foot. "How kind of you to say so."

"But there is great difference between what you think you know and court etiquette. This goes beyond which fork to use. For instance, what is the proper address for a duke?"

"My lord?"

"No. Your Grace. Or, if you're meeting two earls, which one should have precedence?"

"The one standing nearest."

"No. The one with the oldest title. Some peers can trace their pedigree back dozens of generations." His father, for instance. "Other titles were granted more recently, and therefore are of less precedence."

"Did you say pedigree? You mean like that mean, little, bug-eyed dog No-Nose Gertie had imported from China after her husband Shorty struck bonanza gold and they moved into the big mansion on the hill in San Francisco? He had a pedigree a yard long."

"Shorty?"

She smiled. "The dog. His Highness Chew Fat."

"Something like that. Perhaps less interesting."

"Are you beginning to think I can't carry this off, pretending to be a duke's granddaughter and all?"

"I'm sure you'll do fine with some preparation. Never fear. Your lessons in how to act like a duchess begin as soon as we board the *Helene,* which is waiting for us in the Bahamas. You'll have approximately three weeks to practice before we reach London."

"I thought it took months to cross the Atlantic."

"It's the age of steam, my dear. The *Helene* is the most advanced ship afloat. Truly a marvel of modern engineering."

"Did you win it in a poker game, too? Or did you steal it?"

"I'm not a bloody pirate."

"So, where did you get such a ship?"

"I borrowed it from the owner. He owed me a favor."

"Big favor, I'd say. What did you do?"

"No time to discuss that now. I see Kelso signaling frantically for us to rescue him from the formidable presence of Miss Franklin and your children."

Matty spun around and scurried toward the gangplank. "Poor dears have been cooped up in the carriage all this time."

Preston could only hope the distance to the blockade runner would be blessedly short. If wishes were horses he could ride along outside.

* * *

"That one can go," the blockade captain said, nodding toward Nathan. Captain Markham flicked a crumb from his full mustache. Their arrival had apparently interrupted his supper.

"But not that one," he said, pointing to Bess with his chin.

Matty hugged the girl and turned her away from the captain's gaze. She didn't have to tell Preston she would not leave without one of her children.

"Captain Markham, let's talk terms," Preston said. He fingered the message that had been left in the shipping office. Again Marsfield urged all speed regardless of expense. Preston had already agreed to fares more than the dilapidated scow appeared to be worth, but he trusted Kelso's opinion the ship was the best choice. "Perhaps an additional bonus would change your mind."

The captain shook his head. "A baby's cry can be heard for miles across open water. Too risky. I don't intend to hang as a traitor."

"Every trip is risky."

"But the odds are better'n fifty-fifty. When they get worse than that, I'll retire and take up me old job on the ferry. No worries other than the occasional drunkard puking up his guts or falling overboard."

"The good life," Preston said.

"You got the right of it, mate. And I intend to get back to it. No ankle-biters. Not at any price."

Matty spun on her heel and marched back to the carriage, dragging Nathan and Edith with her. Preston motioned with his head for his valet to follow them, knowing Kelso would understand it also meant for him to keep an eye on everyone's safety. Preston stayed and encouraged the captain to return to his meal, agreeing to join him in a drink while he ate.

When a greedy man said, *not at any price,* what he really meant was, *this is going to cost you your grandmother's eyeteeth.*

Matty bounced Bess on her lap in a vain attempt to stop her crying. What was taking Preston so long? The carriage was stuffy and crowded with bits and bobs from their travels. Edith's usually neat hair stuck out in all directions as she leaned back and pinched the bridge of her nose to alleviate a headache. Nathan sulked in the corner because she wouldn't let him get out and run around the carriage. Kelso had retreated to sit on top with the patient driver, ostensibly to better protect them.

Matty tapped on the roof with the handle of her umbrella.

Kelso opened the trap. "Five minutes later than the last time you asked me," he answered, before she even had a chance to ask the question.

"That wasn't what I was going to ask," she lied. "We would like to get something cool to drink. We're all quite parched."

"This isn't a neighborhood where you want to be wandering around after dark."

Matty lifted the shade and, sure enough, darkness had fallen. Even from her narrow view, she could see Kelso was right. "Perhaps you would be so good as to fetch something for us."

"There's not a lemonade stand nearby, just your basic waterfront dives, bars, and saloons. Your choices of beverage are rotgut whiskey, rotgut rye, or rotgut rum. All served in a dirty glass."

"Thank you. We'll pass."

Before he could close the trap completely, she said, "Oh. Kelso?"

"Yes, miss?" His craggy face filled the square opening in the roof.

"What time is it?" she asked with a sweet smile.

"Arrgh." The lid slammed shut.

What seemed like hours later, Preston opened the carriage door.

"Come along," he said. "We can stay aboard until we leave tomorrow night."

Nathan bounded out, and Preston reached for Bess.

"Where have you been? What made the captain change his mind?" A sudden thought occurred to Matty. "You didn't gamble with him and win the ship, did you?"

"No. I told him we would give Bess laudanum to keep her quiet."

Matty snatched the girl back into her arms. "I will not drug her. That could kill a child her age."

"I never said I told him the truth." He looked her in the eye. "I lied to him, Matty. You never said I couldn't lie to anyone else."

She handed Bess to him, quickly gathered up their belongings, and followed. "But what if she does cry?"

"She won't. I'll hold her the entire time, and she never cries when I hold her."

"But what if she does?" Matty scrambled to keep up with his long-legged stride. "If her teeth start hurting, or she gets scared, or for no reason at all? What will the captain do then?"

He took her elbow with his free hand and guided her across the gangplank.

"At sea, the captain is like a demigod," she said in a low voice. "Answerable to no man. I'm scared."

"The captain is answerable to me."

"Because you paid the fare? I don't think that's enough. I don't trust him."

They stepped aboard and a one-eyed sailor rushed forward to help Kelso with the baggage.

"Welcome aboard, sir," the old tar said with a nearly toothless grin. "It's always lucky to have the owner aboard." He pulled his forelock and scurried away.

"You bought this scum bucket?" Matty looked around. "I'm no expert on ships, but whatever you paid, you were hoodwinked."

"Purely a matter of expediency. Now, let's all go below and get settled in our cabins."

She stood firm. "How much did you pay?"

"Looks aren't important. She's solid in the deck, quick to the helm, and runs well before the wind. Seaworthy. That's what counts."

"Can you get the money back?"

Preston heaved a sigh. "It won't come out of your share of the take."

"If we don't get there, I won't have a share," she muttered under her breath.

"You're just going to have to trust me," he said.

Chapter 11

Matty ran her hand along the smoothly polished mahogany railing. The *Helene* was a world apart from the ship that had brought them to the Bahamas, fortunately without incident, although not without worry. And now they were on their way to yet another world, London.

From the moment they'd stepped aboard the *Helene,* she and the children had been treated like royalty. The smartly uniformed crew was excruciatingly polite, going out of their way to be of service. Preston's friend must be both rich and powerful.

Matty left the private balcony and returned inside. Her suite of rooms was more luxurious than anything she had ever known or dreamed. Lavender velvet drapes surrounded a bed made up in snowy silk sheets. In the sitting area, brocade chairs of a similar shade of lavender flanked a self-contained stove that could be used to warm the room when the weather became chilly, as it soon would. An elegant desk took advantage of the light from one of the two large square windows.

In the separate bathing chamber, hot water—pumped from below decks—emerged from golden taps into a marble bath large enough for several people. The very thought made her blush. A second stove would warm that room and the adjoining dressing area where the mirrored table contained every imaginable cosmetic. The closet alone was bigger than her bedroom at home.

On the other side of the bedroom were the smaller rooms for the children and Edith, and in between, a large solarium where they spent most of their time.

Preston's suite was across the hall, and she could only assume his quarters were as luxurious as hers, yet he seemed to take it all in stride. Even Kelso seemed quite at home. Not once had she heard him comment, as Edith constantly did, on the clever use of space or the ingenious storage. Of course, they had traveled from England to the Bahamas on the same ship, but still, she would think some comment on the luxury would have been made by one of them. Unless this was the manner in which they were used to living.

The more Preston seemed in his element, the more she fretted about the part she was to play in their venture.

Then again, since she had known him, Preston had not commented on the poverty of any of their other surroundings. Perhaps he was too polite. In retrospect, she cringed at what he must have thought of her tiny house with its crude plank floor, rough log walls, and makeshift furniture. Yet, she would give up all this to be done with the scam and to be back there, secure in the knowledge she was in her very own home and no one could take it or her children away from her.

Edith burst into the room, her face uncommonly flushed. "Come, milady. Come quick."

"What is it?" Matty asked, even as she rose to comply. But she spoke to an empty doorway. Had one of the children been hurt? She'd heard no cry. Had they broken something? She'd warned Nathan not to play with his new ball inside, but then she'd heard no crash either. She entered the solarium with confused trepidation.

Along the far wall, beneath the bank of windows that allowed in the bright sunlight, the sofa was covered with bolts of silk of every imaginable hue. Vibrant jewel tones and the palest pastels, embroidered with flowers and birds and patterns, all jumbled together with swaths of lace and yards of ribbons.

"I hope you can sew," Preston said with a shy smile.

"I can," Edith said, fingering a pink silk. "My mother was a seamstress, but she never had material as nice as this to work with."

"Excellent. There is also a trunk of assorted paraphernalia for a fashionable young woman—hats, shoes, gloves, undergarments, and the like. Perhaps you can help Lady Matilda ready some ensembles prior to our arrival." He motioned to the pile of material. "Although I expect we'll have to hire a seamstress or two once we arrive to complete everything needed."

"Where did all this come from?" Matty feared he'd raided the coffers of the ship's owner.

"I spent near the whole day in New Orleans's stores. Despite the blockade I found everything we should need."

Kelso had said his master was shopping, but she had thought he was covering for Preston while he went gambling.

Edith sank beside the sofa and reverently lifted a length of turquoise-blue silk embroidered with tiny butterflies of all colors. "Isn't this the prettiest thing you've ever seen?"

"Yes." In fact, Matty recognized it as the fabric she had lingered over at the emporium back home. The very expensive fabric.

She pulled Preston aside and whispered, "How much did all this cost?"

"Can't you, for once, accept a gift without asking the cost?"

"Would your mythical paragon of propriety from the Land of All Things Virtuous accept petticoats and stockings from a man who was not a relation? I see by your expression, it's as I suspected." She marched back and began folding the material. "I cannot accept your gift."

Edith groaned and hugged pieces of chartreuse silk and Battenburg lace to her breast.

Preston took Matty by the arm and led her to the windows. He crossed his arms and looked down his nose at her. "A proper wardrobe is a necessity."

"I agree," Matty said.

"That's a first," he mumbled.

"And since it is essential to our success," she continued without giving him the satisfaction of knowing she'd heard him, "the cost should be included in the expenses portion of our agreement."

"You are one stubborn woman."

"I accept your compliment whether you meant it as one or not. Do we have a deal?"

He bowed. "I will have Kelso locate the receipts."

"Thank you," she said, returning his bow.

They returned to where Edith, with a loving pat, laid each piece of fabric into the box they had come in.

"We will keep the material and other items," Matty announced.

"Oh, thank you, Lady Matilda."

"I don't know why you're thanking me. It will mean more work for us both to get all this sewing done in time."

"But it will be such an honor and so much fun to work with such lovely fabric."

Matty could only shake her head, not understanding the older woman at all. How anyone could consider sewing to be fun was beyond her.

"Now, the pièce de résistance." Preston picked up an oblong box that had been reserved on the side and flipped it open with a grand gesture. "Voilà! The latest fashion patterns from Paris."

Edith and Bess both squealed and clapped in delight at the assortment of dolls dressed in miniature ball gowns, a riding habit, and every sort of dress needed by a lady of fashion during her busy day. They both rushed to Preston, arriving at the same time due to the fact Edith was slowed by the need to rise without disturbing any of the precious material. Each grabbed one end of the box from his arms. The box slipped to the floor, and both scrambled to scoop up as many dolls as they could hold. Edith had the advantage but, judging from the vocalizations, she was equally as covetous of the ones she did not hold.

"I'll meet you in the salon," he said, speaking sotto voce as he backed toward the door. "I do believe now would be an auspicious time to begin your lessons."

"Coward," she said under her breath as he drew even with her.

He paused long enough to whisper in her ear, "A man who stands between a woman and the thing she desires most is brave. A man who stands between two women who desire the same thing is an idiot."

"Damnation." Matty threw the fork onto the table.

"Ladies do not curse," Preston said.

"Dagnabbit, then."

"Don't say *dagnabbit,* either."

"Then what am I supposed to say?"

He blinked several times. "Why, nothing, I suppose."

She looked up at the painted ceiling of the salon and counted to ten for patience. "I have to have something to say, or *damnation* will pop out before I can stop it."

"Very well. We'll find some innocuous word for you to use, but later. Right now, let's concentrate on formal dining etiquette."

"All these rules are so silly. Speak to the man on your left when the hostess speaks to the man on her left. Speak to the man on your right when the hostess turns her head."

"Turns the table."

"Whatever you want to call it. What if the man on my right is drop-dead boring?"

"He probably will be."

Preston flashed her a grin and she relaxed.

"But that's no excuse to be rude," he added. "Now. You likely will only have to suffer through a few dinner parties. The duke is not socially active, so he will probably only want to introduce you to a few of his old friends. If you know what to expect, you'll feel more comfortable."

"I doubt that," she mumbled.

"The footman will hold the serving dish to your left. You glance at the food and nod slightly, like so, if you want some. Or you shake your head ever so slightly if you do not. After that, you don't look at him again, or it seems as if you're uncertain he will do his job properly, thus insulting the hostess. You do not watch the food as it travels to your plate, or someone might think you're starved."

"And ladies don't get hungry?"

"Never."

"Then why bother eating?"

"A lady gives the impression she came to the table for the conversation and socialization. She acts as if she is tasting a bit of this and a nibble of that as a courtesy to her hostess."

"So I should eat a decent meal *before* I go out to dinner?"

"Perhaps that would be best," he said with a sigh.

"Hey, I'm just being practical." Then before he could jump in, she added, "I know, ladies don't say *hey.*"

He nodded. "Now, pick up your fork in your left hand, tines down—"

"I don't see why I have to use my left hand."

"Because that is the proper hand."

"You might as well have me wear one of Bess's bibs, because I'm going to spill everything down the front of my clothes." She tried to hold the fork with the easy grace Preston exemplified, and failed. "Learning to eat with chopsticks was easier."

He gave her a quizzical look.

"We had a Chinese cook for a while when we lived in San Francisco."

"You like Chinese food?"

"I love it. Chin Li made this marvelous dish he called Imperial Chicken. I've tried to make it, but it's just not as good."

"When we get to London, I'll have to take you to this little family-owned place on Water Street. Not exactly a restaurant, it's mainly a working man's lunch counter—a bowl of rice with a few pieces of meat and vegetable for tuppence. But there are a few tables in the back, and if you give the Changs three days' notice, the grandfather will make his Celestial Duck. It's as tasty as anything I ate in the emperor's palace itself."

"You went to China? When?"

"I spent five of the last seven years traveling. We spent the better part of eight months in China."

"What do you wish you'd brought back?"

He sat back in his chair. "You know, I've been asked many different questions about my journey, but you're the first to ask that." He looked thoughtful for a moment. "I guess I'd have to say nothing."

"Nothing at all? Not jade statues or antiques or artwork?"

"I do have a number of pieces, but I bought them all in London. I think people want souvenirs because they never intend to return. I have every intention of going back someday, and I want it all to be there just as I remember it so I can share what I experienced with my . . . companion." He cleared his throat. "But I digress," he said, and then frowned. "And you regress."

She followed the direction of his gaze and realized that, while listening to him, she'd propped her elbows on the table to make a comfortable cradle for her chin. She slapped her hands into her lap.

"Once more, take your fork in your left hand and your knife in your right. Pretend to cut a tiny piece of, say, beef cutlet. Return the knife to a position along the side of your plate, and put the portion into your mouth, opening your lips only wide enough to slip in that morsel."

She tried to do as he instructed. Halfway to her mouth with the empty fork, her stomach growled, loudly. "If we have to practice eating, why can't we do this with real food?"

"Because at meals, you're busy reminding Nathan to sit up straight and use his napkin, and preventing Bess from feeding her peas to her doll or from throwing partially masticated meat on the floor."

Was that all she did during dinner, harangue her children about their manners and food intake? She hadn't realized before how others might see their somewhat-hectic family meals. The truth hit close to the bone. She ducked her head. "It's hard for Bess to chew right now," she said.

"I understand, and you should pay attention to the children. However, this is important, too, and you need to be able to concentrate because we have a lot to cover, and limited time. Of course, real food would be helpful, as would someone to serve, but we will do our best with what we have."

"Edith and I could feed the children in the solarium, and then I could join you for supper later."

"That sounds terribly civilized. Are you sure?"

"As long as I'm there to read a story and tuck them in, I don't think they'll even miss me. They have so many new toys, thanks to you."

"I'll notify the steward." He laid his utensils precisely across the top of the plate so the tips crossed.

She tried to copy his action, but her knife and fork refused to balance and slipped haphazardly into the middle of her plate.

"Shall we move on to the next lesson?" He tapped his lips with his napkin as if they'd actually eaten, and laid it beside his plate. Then he stood, held her chair for her, and led her to the center of the room.

She hoped they were going to practice the waltz. She'd always longed to have someone sweep her around a ballroom, like a flower floating in a stream of whirlpools and eddies. To have Preston take her in his arms would be beyond anything she had ever dreamed. She shivered in anticipation.

"Can you curtsy?" he asked.

"Of course I can," she said, hiding her disappointment by demonstrating. She held out her skirt to either side, and bobbed down and back up. "Milord," she added for extra measure.

He cringed. "Appropriate for a parlor maid or possibly the waitress in a pub."

His comment bruised her feelings and she lashed back. "If you wanted to know if I could curtsy like a duchess, then you should have been more specific with your question. Because if you had asked the appropriate question, I would have answered we do not have dukes and earls and whatnot in America, and therefore I was not taught to kowtow in the appropriate manner."

"My sincere apologies for the thoughtless remark. In the future I will try to remember this is as much of a cultural change for you as it was for me when I went to China or India or Egypt. I was grateful to have a mentor to guide my steps, and I shall endeavor to do the same for you with the same forbearance and understanding shown me."

"You went to Egypt? Did you see the pyramids and that big head out in the middle of nowhere? I read about that. What is it called?"

"The Sphinx."

"That's it. I read an article in the *Scientific American Journal* by this fascinating woman archeologist who is an expert on Egyptian hieroglyphics. She said there is a lion's body attached to the giant head, and she wants to raise money for the monumental task of digging it out. She thinks there's a temple underneath the body. Oh, what was her name?"

"That could only be Emily Weston Dandridge."

"Yes! Did you read the same article?"

"Not that particular one, but I've read others, and I attended the session when her crackpot theory was presented to the Royal Society."

"I thought her hypothesis quite logical, and it is backed by her extensive research."

"Sir Mariette excavated the area in front of the statue and found nothing of significance. The sand has since covered it over. Dr. Jamison, who has much more experience, predicts that if she persists in her ill-considered plan, the head will topple over on its nose. If Emily isn't careful, the Society will rescind her husband's grant, and she won't be digging anywhere but in her vegetable garden."

"My, my. Don't tell me you're one of those men who thinks a woman can't have an intelligent thought or two."

"Not at all. Quite simply, my friend Burke is married to her sister, Cordelia, and any negativity Emily stirs up will reflect on him."

"You're claiming to know Emily Weston Dandridge?"

"I warned Burke marrying into that family would cause him no end of problems. He's not bothered by the possibility, but I'm concerned for him."

Matty leaned back, crossed her arms, and gave him an assessing stare. "You're really good. I don't know how you can use that story to flimflam any money, but I was buying the whole thing, lock, stock, and barrel. Up to the point when you said you personally knew her. That was just a tad bit too much."

Preston raised one eyebrow and returned her gaze with a steady one of his own. "And if I told you it was the truth?"

"Then I would say shame on you because we agreed not to lie to each other," she said, calling herself a hypocrite with her next breath. She hadn't been totally honest with him about a number of things, that well-remembered kiss, for one. Even the memory of which had the power to heat her cheeks.

She turned her face away and noticed the clock on the wall. "Oh dear, I seem to have lost track of time. I should check on the children. Poor Edith is probably frazzled by now."

"I will not count the day wasted if we at least get through a lesson on curtsying."

"Will it take long?" she asked.

"The basics are easy, but you will have to practice many, many times to make it seem effortless and graceful."

"Oh, goody," she muttered.

"Pardon?"

"Nothing, nothing. Effortless and graceful. I've got it. Carry on, my good man. Curtsy away, and all that rot."

"If you're trying to mimic me, I never say either *my good man* or *all that rot.*"

She gave him an innocent smile. "Too prosaic?"

"I will ignore that remark. Now, to the lesson." He looked around the room, then returned to the table and snatched the snow-white cloth from beneath the dishes in one smooth motion.

"How did you do that?" she asked, amazed the fine china plates and crystal glasses did not land in a shattered heap on the floor.

"I did a stint with a magician and I . . . No, you won't detour me again. We've wasted too much time on tangents as is."

"Your tangents are more interesting than your lessons."

"When you first meet Norbundshire, you will curtsy thus." He wrapped the tablecloth around his waist and used it to demonstrate a low curtsy. "Back straight, arms slightly curved, elbows down, slide your right foot back behind your left as you bend your knees. Eyes down, head bent slightly forward. Hold the position until you are recognized by the duke. He will probably take your hand and raise you up as he says some words of welcome. Now you try," he said as he stood.

"Do I have to wear the tablecloth?"

"Will you please try to be serious?"

"Killjoy."

"If you don't think you can handle this, we can call off the whole scam. If I instruct the captain to turn around immediately, you can be back in your own house within a month."

As much as she wanted to return, the problems that had sent her packing would be waiting for her if she did. "My apologies." She did her best to imitate his graceful curtsy.

"Back straight," he barked at her. "Do it again. Don't bob your head. Again, and this time pretend you're floating. No, don't raise your arms like you're trying to fly. Again."

She lost count of how many times she curtsied and how many ways she did it wrong. The muscles in her thighs and derriere protested the unaccustomed strain.

"We're making progress. Now I'll pretend to be the duke. You walk up, curtsy, and I'll take your hand as he would."

She backed up a few feet as he took his position near the settee and struck a pose as if he were speaking to another person. Taking small steps so as not to aggravate her sore legs, she approached and sank into a deep curtsy. "Your Grace," she said, raising her right hand palm down.

"My dear granddaughter," Preston said in a gruff

voice. He put his hand under her outstretched one and bent over to pass his lips near her knuckles. "I am so pleased to finally meet you."

As he straightened, he gave a slight upward pressure to her hand, her signal to rise. But she couldn't. The overworked muscle in her right thigh twitched in a painful spasm. She gripped his hand like a vise and hauled herself up.

To his credit, he managed the unexpected maneuver by leaning back to counterbalance her weight. That would have worked, except her feet tangled together as she tried to relieve the painful pressure on her right leg as quickly as possible. She stumbled forward, pitching directly into his chest. Because he was already leaning back, he could not regain his equilibrium, and both of them tumbled backward onto the settee.

He grunted as she plopped on top of him, but he had the presence of mind to wrap his arms around her so she didn't tumble from her awkward landing spot onto the floor.

"Sorry. I'm so sorry," she muttered as she scrambled to stand. But the pain in her right leg brought tears to her eyes as she tried to straighten it. She rolled to her left side, curled her knee up to her chest, and rubbed the muscle.

"It is I who should apologize. I should have known not to overdo it on the first day."

"Did I hurt you?"

"Not at all," he said, looking down at her with a strange smile. "Can I be of service? I know several rather effective massage techniques."

"I'll bet you do," she muttered. "I'll be fine in a minute." She scooted to one side a few inches, but stopped when he took in a sharp breath. "You are hurt," she accused.

"No, but if you continue to wiggle like that, you may unman me yet."

"Oh."

He maneuvered his legs free of her skirts; then as he sat up, he lifted her and pulled her forward until she was curled in his lap.

Her muscle cramp wasn't much better, but she noticed it a lot less.

"I know exactly what you need," he said as he stood, carrying her with him as he did.

"What are you doing?" she shrieked, and wrapped her arms around his neck.

He paced toward the door.

"Put me down before someone sees us."

"No one is here." He strode down the hall. "And if they were, I could bloody well care less."

Chapter 12

"Put me down before you drop me." She tried to stretch her legs toward the floor, and succeeded only in causing herself more pain. She tried to stifle her whimper by tucking her head into his shoulder.

"I won't drop you if you stop squirming."

He carried her down the short hall and kicked open the door to her suite. He marched into the bathroom, set her into the deep marble tub, and then turned on the hot-water tap full force.

"What are you doing?" she cried, pulling herself to the edge with her arms. "Help me out of here. You'll ruin my clothes."

He pushed her back down with a hand on her shoulder. "If you'd prefer, I could take them off."

She crossed her arms over her breasts and glared at him.

"I see not," he said, sitting on the edge of the tub and adjusting the water temperature to his liking. "A hot soak is the second-best cure for sore muscles."

"I take it I don't want to know the best cure."

He grinned. "A massage would be a lot more fun. For both of us."

She forced her lips into a thin line to keep from returning his smile. And she refused to let her mind wander to where his apparently already was. "While I appreciate your concern for my well-being, I do believe I could have—"

"You would have dithered around, checking on the children and who knows what all before you took care of yourself. Oh, don't look at me as if I had only your comfort in mind. We still have a lot of work to do, and you can't afford to take even a few days off."

The water was up to her waist, and the heat seeped into her muscles. She relaxed against the curved back of the tub and closed her eyes with a sigh. "Thank you," she said. "This does help."

In the silence that followed, she tried not to think about the intimate setting or how close he sat to her. A warm flush suffused her body, and she decided it must be the steam from the water that made her feel so languorous and dreamy.

"You should soak for at least an hour," he said over his shoulder as he turned the tap off. Then he stood. "Don't move; I'll be right back."

She forced herself to sit up straighter, which was difficult, considering that the weight of her wet clothing dragged her down. "I don't think I could get out even if I wanted to."

He returned with a decanter of brandy and a small snifter. He poured several fingers and handed it to her.

"I've never imbibed strong spirits," she said, not taking the glass. Probably due to her father having such a fondness for the drink.

"This little bit won't hurt you; it will only help you relax." He set down the bottle and reached out to curve her hand around the glass.

She took a tiny sip and shuddered. "Yuck." She tried to give it to him but he pushed her hand back toward her mouth.

"Think of it as medicine," he said.

She held her nose and knocked it back in one gulp. As she gasped for air, the brandy burned its way to her stomach, leaving a not unpleasant warmth in its wake. "The aftertaste isn't so bad," she rasped.

"I should think not. That's forty-year-old Napoleon brandy you're slugging back like a thirsty longshoreman. It's the finest brandy in the world."

He handed her his handkerchief.

"God only knows what the worst tastes like," she said, dabbing at her eyes.

"I think a cup of tea might have been a better idea. I'll ring for one."

"Perhaps you should fetch Edith." Matty unbuttoned the top two buttons of her high neckline. "I could use her help getting out of these wet clothes."

As he left once more, she relaxed, a tingling warmth reaching her fingers and toes.

Preston ordered tea from a sailor serving as footman. Then as he set about the rest of his errand, he cursed himself for a fool. Who would have thought a woman in a bathtub, fully clothed, mind you, would have such an effect on him? Now if she'd been naked, parts of her luscious body playing peekaboo with foamy suds, his reaction would have been expected. He shook the image of Matty, all rosy and slick from the warm water, out of his head.

With a sense of relief, he located Edith in the solarium with the children. However, she was sound asleep in the rocking chair with little Bess in her lap. According to Nathan, they had not been asleep long. The boy begged him in broken whispers not to awaken Bess because she'd been whiny and cranky and thoroughly unbearable all day.

He agreed, realizing that meant he would have to serve Matty her tea. When he returned to her suite, he found the footman had set up the tea tray near the twin chairs. Preston prepared a cup and carried it to the bathing chamber, steeling himself to remain calm and unaffected. Yet he was unprepared for what he found, and it rocked him back on his heels.

Preston leaned against the doorjamb, a bit to catch his breath and a bit for support as the surprise sight caught him in the knees. And a few other places he refused to acknowledge.

In the short time he'd been gone, Matty had completely unbuttoned her dress and had managed to slip it off so her shoulders and arms were bare, and only a thin chemise made practically transparent by the water plastered her full breasts like a second skin.

"Oh, Napoleon likes his brandy," she sang, low and off-key, as she poked at the air bubbles floating under her wet skirt. "And so do I, so do I."

A quick glance told him she had helped herself to another dose or two of the medicine. Not a good idea. The effects of the brandy could be magnified by the temperature of the water, especially if one wasn't used to it.

She spotted him and smiled. "I was just wishing you were here, and there you are." She giggled. "It's nice to have a wish granted, and so quickly, too." She waved toward her feet. "Now I wish for more hot water. It's getting a bit chilly and the taps seem so very far away."

But he decided it would be a better idea to get her out of the water. He returned to the suite, fired up the stove, and threw a blanket over one of the chairs, setting it close to the flames.

"Why do you keep disappearing?" she asked when he returned. "I look up and, poof, you're gone." She smiled. "But I wished you back again, didn't I?"

"Let's get you out of there," he said, removing his

coat and throwing a large towel over his shoulder. He grabbed her under her arms and hauled her to a standing position. "Good grief, you weigh a ton," he said with a grunt.

"I am a rock," she admitted, flopping her arms over his shoulders and nuzzling his neck. "You smell like brandy."

"No, that would be you." He braced her with an arm around her waist while he pushed the heavy dress and petticoats over her hips. He then lifted her, leaving most of her clothes behind in the tub. As he carried her to the chair he'd prepared, she spread her arms wide.

"I am a bird," she sang.

He lowered her into the chair, and wrapped the blanket around her. He went down on one knee and removed her shoes and stockings, tucking the blanket over and around her feet.

"I wish for you to kiss me," she said.

He looked up at her, the soft, dewy look in her eyes almost irresistible. "I never take advantage of women who have had too much to drink."

"Don't you want to kiss me?"

She blinked as if fighting tears, and it nearly undid him. He moved to kneel at the side of the chair and turned her to face him with a finger under her chin.

"I very much want to kiss you. When I do, I would prefer for you to be totally in control of your faculties. More than a prelude to lovemaking, kissing is an art unto itself, with many subtle nuances. When we kiss, I want to feel your every reaction, read your thoughts through your lips, breathe in your response."

"Yes," she whispered, leaning toward him.

He cleared his throat and stood, stepping back a pace. "And that only works when both parties are capable of paying complete attention."

"Hey, I was paying attention," she said, her tone indignant. She struggled to free herself from the blanket.

He pushed her back into the chair by the shoulders, and then he braced his arms on either side of the chair, straddling her legs with his own.

"You, my dear, are to stay put. Understand? Good. Now, I'll pour you a fresh cup of tea and then—"

"Why won't you kiss me?"

"Because you are sozzled. And though the experience might be enjoyable, it would only be a fraction of what it could be."

She looked up at him.

And he made the mistake of gazing deep into her eyes, of seeing her hurt wrapped in a tattered cloak of dignity. His undoing.

"Oh, bloody hell." He leaned down and kissed her, meaning for it to be a quick peck to end the argument.

And yet he lingered, her lips a magnet drawing him back, again and again. The familiar taste of brandy he expected, but the true enticement was the earthy undertone of passion countered by an elusive high note of sweetness. Distilled Matty. Mere brandy had never been so intoxicating.

Only their lips touched, but his body was as aware of hers as if they were lying naked together.

A warning bell went off in his head. He was becoming drunk on her kisses. Entranced. Addicted. He pulled away. She followed, straining upward to maintain contact. She freed her arms from the blanket and wrapped them around his neck, whether to pull him to her or herself to him he didn't know, and it unfortunately didn't matter. Either way, it made it more difficult for him to undo his mistake.

"Easy, darling," he said, holding her arms and slipping his head beneath them. "You need to rest." He crossed her hands in her lap, crisscrossed the ends of the blanket over her, and tucked it tightly around her sides.

"I'm not tired," she said around a yawn. Her head lolled back against the cushion. "Not tired," she mumbled as her eyes closed.

"Liar," he whispered. He kissed her forehead. "Sweet dreams."

Preston leaned his forearms on the ship's railing. With a flick of his finger he sent his unfinished cheroot into the wake of the large, steam-driven paddle wheels. The churning water echoed his chaotic thoughts, his mind a maelstrom of visions of Matty. In her boy's clothing, and toting the Henry rifle nearly as big as her. Matty with a foamy milk mustache. Wearing her ugly, bedraggled bonnet and singing off-key. Her smile. Her lips dewy from his kiss. Images of Matty swirled and roiled.

Matty giving him that look that made him wish he was deserving of her admiration. He wasn't. He'd lied to her and uprooted her, all in the name of completing his mission. All to appease some old man's conscience before he died.

And Preston had been sorely tempted. The duke would already need all his considerable influence to have Matty accepted. Preston's attentions would only complicate matters. Not that London's matrons would be of much concern to Matty once she returned to America with her children as she intended to do.

He looked down at the brandy snifter in his left hand and swished the contents around and around. Taking a sip, he grimaced. The liquid tasted flat, as if missing something essential. Would he forever relate brandy to

the taste of Matty's kisses? With a growl he flung the
drink, glass and all, overboard.

"Shall I get you another year, milord?"

"No, thank you," Preston said, recognizing Kelso's
voice even though he hadn't heard his approach over
the noise of the wheels and water. He also recognized
something else in the servant's very proper tone.

"The steward has responded to your note."

Preston turned. As he expected, Kelso was turned
out in the armor of his position, starched shirtfront beneath the proper tails for serving after six. He held his
silver tray on the tips of his gloved fingers, and his
right hand was tucked behind his waist. His posture as
stiff as his collar and cuffs, Kelso stared straight ahead,
not directly at him but at some spot over his shoulder.

All this meant his valet disapproved of something.
The last time he had acted thus was because Preston
had purchased a red wool vest Kelso had deemed in-
appropriate. Their relationship, an odd mixture of
friend and traveling companion, coworkers for the
agency, and longtime servant and master, had been
quite strained for a number of weeks until Preston tired
of the vest and allowed its disposal. What sartorial mistake had upset the man this time? Preston had no clue.
But he was sure to find out sooner or later. Until then
he could only respond with the same tiresome formality.

With a sigh of resignation, Preston took the envelope
and read the note. The steward would be able to fulfill
his request for a formal setting for the evening meal.

"Will there be a reply, milord?"

"None is necessary, thank you." He tossed the open
note toward the tray, knowing Kelso would read it, if
he hadn't already, and would have his evening attire

prepared in a timely manner. "Please notify Lady Matilda we will be dining at eight."

"Very good. Will that be all, milord?" Kelso asked with a step back and a low bow, which he managed to complete without tipping the tray one degree off horizontal.

Preston leaned back against the railing, deliberately assuming a casual pose with his elbows propped on either side.

"There is the matter of your behavior," he said, and was rewarded by the sight of the valet's prominent Adam's apple bobbing up and down as he swallowed his improper response. "Come on. Out with it, man. I have no intention of mincing around for the next month of Sundays until I learn what's bothering you."

"My opinions are of no interest to you. And that is how it should be."

"Rubbish. What is it this time? Is it the denim trousers?"

"It is not my place to comment on your behavior, milord."

"So, it's something I've done." Preston racked his brain and couldn't think of anything he'd done lately that would cause Kelso to get a poker up his ass, at least nothing his valet was aware of him doing. Preston shrugged and said, "You'll just have to tell me, because I'm not coming up with any possibilities."

Kelso glared at him. Then the valet set his tray aside, took off his glove, and slapped Preston on the cheek with it.

"You're challenging me to a duel?" Preston asked, unbelieving the man's actions even though his face stung.

"Seeing as Lady Matilda has no one to stand up for her honor, it behooves me to take that place."

"On what basis?"

"On the fact she's a fine young woman who deserves to be treated with respect."

"No, I mean on what basis do you judge she's been dishonored?"

"I may have tolerated your amorous assignations in the past, even helped with more than a few, but when I saw you sneaking out of Matty's bedroom with your coat in your hand, I could not turn a blind eye. I can add two and two. Shame on you."

"I'm afraid you've added wrong and come up with five," Preston said, interrupting Kelso's tut-tutting.

"Then what were you doing in her room?"

"She fell and pulled a muscle while practicing her curtsy. I simply made sure she was comfortable."

Kelso looked down his nose at him, which wasn't easy considering the difference in their heights, and gave him the stare the valet usually reserved to vendors of dubious-quality goods. "Comfortable, you say? You didn't—"

"No, I did not," Preston interrupted, knowing he was on shaky ground, and wanting to get his denial in before the valet completed the question. His behavior may not have been completely innocent and honorable, but with a bit of discretion her reputation was undamaged.

"Did she—"

"That's enough." Preston pulled himself to military attention and assumed a haughty expression that would have made his father proud. "I requested your comment on my behavior; however that does not give you leave to discuss the Lady's actions in any way or to anyone. If I hear you've been gossiping about her, I will skip the formality of a challenge and simply run you through. No one, I repeat, no one, will besmirch her name. Are we clear on that?"

"Yes, sir." Kelso's quizzical expression turned into a broad grin. "Yes sir!"

With that, the little man turned and trotted back along the deck toward the cabins, stopping midway to jump up and click his heels. Preston shook his head. His valet had always been a bit unconventional, which suited him just fine, but he grew stranger and odder by the year.

"I'm afraid this dress won't be dry in time," Edith said, readjusting the fabric so a different part of the skirt faced the stove. "I don't know what possessed you to wash it today of all days."

When Matty had woke from her nap, she had set the room to rights and spread her dress in front of the fire to dry. But she had needed some explanation for the wet clothes. Edith may have questioned her sanity, but she didn't disbelieve her story.

Matty looked up from the fashion dolls to which Edith had attached bits of material and trim that she wanted to use for each. "Never mind. I'll simply send word I'm indisposed and dine in the solar with you and the children."

Edith looked as if she was about to argue, so Matty distracted her.

"These are all so lovely," she lied. Matty wasn't thrilled with any of the fashions because they were all designed for a tall, willowy woman. She had no misconceptions about her own figure. Short, a bit on the stocky side, shoulders too wide, arms too muscular, no waist to speak of, and bosoms unfashionably full. The cinched waists and large puffed sleeves of the Paris designs would serve only to accent her faults. The huge hats would make her look like a mushroom. "I can't decide which I like best."

Edith stopped fussing with the old blue dress and scurried across the room to the desk. "I thought we could start with this day dress. Just right for receiving callers. Perhaps out of the turquoise with the butterfly embroidery."

"No," Matty nearly shouted; then she moderated her tone. "No, I think the rose moiré would suit better."

"Don't you like the butterflies?" Edith asked in a sad voice as if her feelings had been hurt.

"Of course, I do." That particular fabric held memories of home, of the day in the emporium. "I'm just not sure it's right for any of these designs."

"We could use it to make you a new dressing gown," Edith said, eyeing Matty's well-worn, barely still-pink robe. "That way you could wear it every day."

"I like that idea."

"Good. I was afraid there for a minute I wasn't going to get a chance to work on the material. I think it's my favorite."

"Mine, too," Matty said, and patted the other woman's hand. "Now, what are the children up to? Isn't it almost time for their supper?" She moved to the dressing table to brush and braid her hair. "We should hurry up if we intend to join them."

"Oh, don't worry about the children. Mr. Kelso has taken care of everything."

Kelso again. "He has?"

Edith came up behind her and took the brush from her hand. Matty closed her eyes and relaxed. The luxury of having someone else brush her hair was something she would miss when she returned home. Edith seemed to enjoy the chore and chatted away as she made sure each strand received one hundred brush strokes.

"Yes. The cabin boy is teaching Nathan how to play Chinese checkers, and Mr. Kelso made arrangements for that nice, young Lieutenant Harvey to write his letters and read in the solar. He'll keep an eye on the boys so they don't get too rowdy. Can you believe he already has three children of his own? He looks barely out of the nursery himself." She chuckled to herself. "That's a sure sign I'm getting old when I look at handsome young men in uniform and see boys playing dress up."

"And Bess?"

"Quite the little socialite, our Bess is. We've been on several walks on deck to take in the fresh air and she smiles and waves to everyone. She's already the darling of the crew. The cook made ginger cookies for a nice little tea party. The ship's carpenter made her a cart to hold her dollies. She pushed them around and around the solar, babbling a mile a minute as if they understand her and talk back. A bit of porridge and a story, and the exhausted dearie is already out like a light. She'll sleep through the night for sure."

"Nathan knows to listen in case she wakes?"

"That boy is the soul of responsibility. Never says much, but seems to have eyes in the back of his head. And smart? Once he sees a word, he remembers it. Why, he's already reading books quite beyond his years."

Matty hadn't known that. Suddenly, she felt a distance from her children. She supposed it was inevitable once they left their insular little world of the farm, but she wasn't prepared for it and didn't like it. True, part of her guilt stemmed from the fact she'd been with Preston and not with them. Her children, it seemed, had managed quite well without her. She wasn't prepared for that either. She definitely didn't like it.

"If Nathan is reading beyond his years, I should like to monitor his choice of books."

"Mr. Kelso has already thought of that, and with Lieutenant Harvey's assistance has put together a whole shelf of books appropriate for Nathan to read. Classics, adventure stories, fables, even some of those new books called science fiction. The boy is like a child in a candy store. That Mr. Kelso seemed to know exactly what was needed."

"There doesn't seem to be anything that man doesn't know." Matty said it, but she certainly hoped it wasn't true.

"Yes," Edith said with a sigh. "I do admire efficiency."

Matty glanced at the maid's reflection in the mirror. The woman looked positively lovesick at the mention of Kelso's name. Rather incongruous considering she was a good head taller than the bandy-legged valet. Matty hoped Kelso wasn't taking advantage of Edith's tender heart just because they were thrown together on this journey. Shipboard romances rarely lasted beyond the final port of call.

A fact Matty would do well to remember.

In addition, Edith had not been taken into their confidence and believed they were who they represented themselves to be. She had no idea Preston was a flimflam man, or that Kelso and Matty were his cohort and co-conspirator.

"Things are not always as they seem," Matty said, trying to warn Edith, and wondering if she should tell her the truth.

"La, I know that." Edith parted Matty's hair down the middle and twisted the bulk into a chignon. "I wasn't born yesterday."

"I shouldn't like for us to become too dependent on

Mr. Kelso. Although Lord Bathers has been most generous, soon after we reach London I'm sure they'll be about their own business. We must be prepared to see to ourselves."

Matty decided to ask Edith to accompany her back to America, and if she chose not to continue the relationship after finding out the truth, then to settle a sum on her that would allow her to retire from service, maybe open a little dressmaking business of her own.

Edith stuck in one last hairpin and stood back to admire her handiwork. "I take each day as it comes. Worry never puts a dollar in your pocket, and fretting about the future only puts frown lines on your forehead."

Matty leaned closer to the mirror. Nothing as yet, but by the time this matter was over, she was bound to have several deep lines.

Meanwhile, Edith laid out the yellow dress from New Orleans.

"I thought you returned that to the dressmaker?"

"Mr. Kelso said there was no time, and I couldn't just leave it behind." She straightened a lace flounce. "Your blue dress isn't dry, and you simply cannot wear your overalls, so this one will have to do."

Matty walked to the bed and eyed the pile of lace ruffles, bows, ribbon roses, furbelows, and gewgaws that masqueraded as an evening dress. "My overalls will be sufficient for dining with the children."

"Nonsense. According to Mr. Kelso, his lordship has gone to a great deal of effort preparing for this evening. Also the cook and the steward. Seems a bit selfish of you to disappoint them just because you don't want to wear a particular dress." Edith turned her by the shoulders and gave her a push toward the dressing screen.

Matty resigned herself to attending the supper,

which was in fact yet another lesson in decorum. The dress wasn't the real problem. She would have to face Preston for the first time after, well, after what had happened. What was she going to say? What did a proper lady say after she had gotten drunk and thrown herself at a man? She doubted any of the etiquette books covered the situation. Of course not. A proper lady would never be in such a dilemma.

Her best course would be to say nothing, to pretend it had never happened. Yes, that was her plan. Now she only had to worry about being able to pull it off.

She put her hand to her forehead and could almost feel the frown lines forming.

Chapter 13

Preston retied his tie for the third time. And for the third time, Kelso slapped his hands away and tied the tie again.

"If you will only leave it alone, sir."

"It's too tight. Are you trying to strangle me?"

"Not yet," the valet muttered.

"A person should not have to be uncomfortable for the sake of fashion."

"What idiot said that?" Kelso asked as he pulled and arranged the white silk to his satisfaction. "The very willingness to endure sets the fashionable apart from the hoi polloi." He stepped back to admire his handiwork. "Perfect. Now you must hurry or the lady will arrive before you." He held his master's coat. "Any discomfort should serve as a reminder that you are a gentleman."

Preston shrugged into his favorite maroon evening jacket and turned to the mirror. Kelso had arranged the tie in the classic and complicated waterfall knot. The man was an artist.

Preston ripped out the fanciful knot, complaining, "I can't breathe." He retied it in a simple floppy bow à la Byron. "That's better."

Kelso blocked the exit with his body spread-eagled

across the door. "I won't let you leave looking like a . . . a tradesman."

Preston glanced back at the full-length mirror. Well-cut coat, gold brocade vest, knife-pressed trousers, and shoes buffed to a bright sheen. "I hardly think I resemble the corner butcher. In fact, I rather like the style."

"Please, milord, consider my reputation."

"Cease the melodramatic posturing. It's not as if the ton will be attending en masse. Now, step aside. As you pointed out, it's getting late."

"On one condition, milord. Please promise me this is a temporary aberration brought on by the sea air."

He readily agreed. In fact, he decided, the excuse could well come in handy if Matty questioned him about her actions that afternoon. Would she even remember? Preston walked down the hall to the salon, softly whistling the sea chantey, "What Do You Do with a Drunken Sailor?" He wasn't likely to forget.

Matty paused with her hand on the doorknob. She was not the sort to put off unpleasant tasks in the hope it would make them go away. She took a deep breath. A brisk knock made her jump back. Not wanting Preston to think her too eager, she rushed to sit at the small desk and waved for Edith to answer the door.

"Good evening," the maid said. "My, my, don't you look grand. Bright and shiny as a newly minted penny."

Matty leaned to the right in an effort to see around the half-open door, and nearly fell off the chair. She righted herself just as Edith made way for Kelso to enter. The valet was dressed in the full formal livery of a footman, including a red coat with gold epaulets, a braid, brass buttons, knee britches, and a powdered wig.

He bowed low and said in a surprisingly sonorous voice, "Lord Bathers requests the honor of Lady Matilda's presence for supper in the salon."

"Where did you get that outfit?" Edith asked as she circled around the man, touching a bit of braid here and there.

"Ease off, Edie," he said out of the side of his mouth. "T'weren't my idea."

"I think you look marvelous," Edith said. "I never would have suspected you had such adorable dimples in your knees. Really, where did you get the clothes? Surely this isn't your uniform?"

"Please, speak up," Matty said, rising and stepping forward. "I would be interested in hearing your answer, too."

Kelso swallowed, his Adam's apple jumping. "We cobbled it together from bits and bobs the crew had on board. Finley used to be in the Royal Band. Yardley does some theatricals in his off time."

"I see," Matty said, even though she'd not met the sailors he named. "And why would you go to such great lengths to dress up? Surely not for my benefit."

"Yes, milady. Lord Bathers wanted this evening to be as formal as possible so that you might get a taste of what to expect when you arrived in London."

"Oh, he did, did he?" There had to be more to his scheme than that.

"I think the knee britches are quite fetching on you," Edith whispered sotto voce.

Kelso's cheeks flamed.

Matty turned her back so he wouldn't see her amusement at his expense. So that was how Preston was going to play out his hand. He intended to intimidate her. As if he hadn't already done a thorough job of that earlier.

Oh, Preston was good. She'd known that, but she hadn't seen just how good until now. Shame on her for being a fool and succumbing to his charm. But what was his game? Did he intend to take all the money and leave her stranded in London? Did he intend for her to take the fall? Damn him for putting her children at risk.

A small flame of anger began to burn, and she fanned it to life. She might not know how to address the seventeenth earl of Whatsis with his dog-eared pedigree, or how to curtsy with elegant grace while wearing a tablecloth, but she had learned the art of the scam at the knee of a master.

She was Blackie Maxwell's daughter.

She would find out Preston's game and protect her children, and she would proceed with her part in the way she knew best—her own way.

"Milady? Are you all right?" Edith asked.

Matty spun around. By the concerned expressions on both servants' faces, she must have spent too much time ruminating. "I'm fine. In fact, I'm better than fine."

She didn't have a full-fledged plan yet, but she had a few ideas. The first step was to take control of her schedule, thus limiting her exposure to Preston and giving herself time to plan and prepare.

"If you will wait in the hall," she said, pushing Kelso toward the door. "I'll be ready in a few minutes." She gave him a sweet smile and shut the door in his face.

Then she turned to face Edith. "Get your scissors."

The woman stared at her as if she'd lost her mind. Maybe she had, but Blackie had always said, *Never forget who you are. No matter what character you play,*

if you retain your own identity the ruse will ring true.
The hideous dress she was wearing did not portray her
as she wanted to be seen.

"Hurry up," she said to Edith, and ripped off two
large satin bows from the shoulders of the gown.

"Wait," Edith said, finally appearing to understand
and running to get her sewing basket. "Wait, you'll tear
the material."

"Leave the lace," Matty directed as she watched in
the mirror as Edith worked.

Rosettes, more bows, and gewgaws fell to the floor.
Within minutes, the simple lines of the dress were vis-
ible. Without the extra padding, the sleeves skimmed
Matty's arms. The five-inch-deep lace ruffle around the
neck and over the shoulders camouflaged several faults
and flattered her waist. The fabric draped smoothly to
the hem. They left a few of the decorations that pulled
up the skirt material and displayed the lace flounce underneath, providing interest and thereby lengthening
the look and making her appear taller. Finally, Edith
stepped back.

Matty smoothed her elbow-length gloves and patted the hair ornament Edith had made from a few white
feathers and flowers found among the supplies Preston
had bought.

"Much better," Matty said with a nod of satisfaction.
"Too bad we can't do anything about the color." Yellow
had never been her favorite, and it made her complexion appear sallow. She pinched her cheeks. A bit of
face powder would help, but hers had been spilled on
the boat in New Orleans.

Edith's eyes lit up, and she dug in a dresser drawer
and pulled out a colorful shawl. The pattern of red,
pink, purple, and yellow was a perfect complement,

Take A Trip Into A Timeless World of Passion and Adventure with Kensington Choice Historical Romances!
—Absolutely FREE!

Enjoy the passion and adventure of another time with Kensington Choice Historical Romances. They are the finest novels of their kind, written by today's best-selling romance authors. Each Kensington Choice Historical Romance transports you to distant lands in a bygone age. Experience the adventure and share the delight as proud men and spirited women discover the wonder and passion of true love.

Get 4 FREE Books!

We created our convenient Home Subscription Service so you'll be sure to have the hottest new romances delivered each month right to your doorstep—usually before they are available in book stores. Just to show you how convenient the Zebra Home Subscription Service is, we would like to send you 4 FREE Kensington Choice Historical Romances. The books are worth up to $24.96, but you only pay $1.99 for shipping and handling. There's no obligation to buy additional books—ever!

Save Up To 30% With Home Delivery!

Accept your FREE books and each month we'll deliver 4 brand new titles as soon as they are published. They'll be yours to examine FREE for 10 days. Then if you decide to keep the books, you'll pay the preferred subscriber's price (up to 30% off the cover price!), plus shipping and handling. Remember, you are under no obligation to buy any of these books at any time! If you are not delighted with them, simply return them and owe nothing. But if you enjoy Kensington Choice Historical Romances as much as we think you will, pay the special preferred subscriber rate and save over $8.00 off the cover price!

We have 4 FREE BOOKS for you as your introduction to

KENSINGTON CHOICE!

To get your FREE BOOKS, worth up to $24.96, mail the card below or call TOLL-FREE 1-800-770-1963. Visit our website at www.kensingtonbooks.com.

Get 4 FREE Kensington Choice Historical Romances!

♥ **YES!** Please send me my 4 FREE KENSINGTON CHOICE HISTORICAL ROMANCES (without obligation to purchase other books). I only pay $1.99 for shipping and handling. Unless you hear from me after I receive my 4 FREE BOOKS, you may send me 4 new novels—as soon as they are published—to preview each month FREE for 10 days. If I am not satisfied, I may return them and owe nothing. Otherwise, I will pay the money-saving preferred subscriber's price (over $8.00 off the cover price), plus shipping and handling. I may return any shipment within 10 days and owe nothing, and I may cancel any time I wish. In any case the 4 FREE books will be mine to keep.

Name _____

Address _____ Apt.____

City _____ State _____ Zip _____

Telephone (____) _____

Signature _____

(If under 18, parent or guardian must sign)

Offer limited to one per household and not to current subscribers. Terms, offer and prices subject to change. Orders subject to acceptance by Kensington Book Club. Offer Valid in the U.S. only.

KNHL4A

and the exotic flowers livened up the outfit, to Matty's delight. She draped the shawl over her shoulders.

"It's amazing," Edith said with a smile. "The very same dress and yet it's so much more flattering."

"A well-dressed woman once told me, the secret is in the details. If you choose only the latest details that flatter, it will always appear as if the newest fashions were made just for you." Matty refrained from telling Edith the fashion advice came from one of the highest-paid courtesans in San Francisco. When her father had introduced her to Chantrelle, he hadn't expected Matty to recognize the name. He also hadn't known the woman and the young girl had become friends of a sort, meeting for tea and advice. Chantrelle had taken up painting, and Matty had taken up shopping. That was when they were living high, before her father had gotten sick.

Matty shook off her memories. "Now, let's see about you."

"Me?"

"You'll need gloves. What else? I know." Matty retrieved a white brocade shawl and handed it to Edith.

Edith refused to take it and stepped back. "I can't go with you."

"You can, and you are," she said, shaking the shawl. "Take this." When the maid did as she was told, Matty proceeded to find a pair of gloves and a piece of lace to pin in Edith's hair.

"But the children need—"

"You said they were well taken care of."

"My sewing. I was—"

"We'll work on that tomorrow."

"But I've not been invited, and I don't know how to act!" Edith wailed.

"Neither do I. This is supposed to be a lesson in

decorum, not a supper for two. And what could be more decorous than for a maid to accompany a lady?"

"But what will I do?"

"You'll pay attention and help me remember everything. We'll learn together."

"I suppose I could sit in the corner and work on my embroidery. I'm making a little smock for Bess."

Matty was willing to accept any level of participation. Anything so she wasn't alone with Preston. "Excellent." She picked up her reticule and fan.

Kelso knocked on the door again.

"You go ahead," Edith said. "I'll get my hoop and thread and meet you in the salon."

She nodded to Edith, who then opened the door.

Kelso stood at attention as if he'd been waiting in that position the entire time. He bowed, and then offered his arm. "May I escort you to the salon, Lady Matilda?"

Matty took his arm with a gracious nod that, to be honest, she copied from Preston.

As they paced slowly down the short hall, Kelso said, "May I be so bold as to compliment you on your appearance, milady?"

She gave him a genuine smile. "Thank you."

When they reached the door to the salon, he said, "If you will wait just a moment, I will announce you." He paused with his hands on the twin doorknobs. "Can you whistle, milady?"

"Yes," she answered slowly, confused by his question.

"Very good. I'm only a whistle away." He cleared his throat. "Should you need my assistance . . . or . . ."

"Or what?"

"If you need anything, anything at all, whistle and

I'll interrupt . . . I'll help . . . come to your aid . . . Oh, blast it. Just remember, if you whistle, I'll respond."

"Thank you, Mr. Kelso. That is a welcome assurance." What else was she to say? However, it must have been the correct response because the little man nodded, straightened his waistcoat, and flung the double doors of the salon wide.

"Lady Matilda Maxwell," he announced in a voice loud enough to have carried across a crowded ballroom.

She assumed a haughty expression, the very face employed by Mrs. Herbert Carlisle III on the occasion of their meeting when Matty was but a child. Though, to be truthful, she had earned the woman's disdain by asking if that meant she was the third Mrs. Carlisle. Matty realized she was stalling.

She took a deep breath and straightened her shoulders. Attitude formed perception, and perception was everything. She stepped forward just as Edith skidded to a halt behind her.

"Miss Edith Franklin," Kelso announced loudly.

Preston froze halfway to a standing position, a dumbfounded expression on his face.

"That'll put a knot in his knickers," Kelso muttered under his breath as he turned to shut the doors to the salon.

Matty smoothed an invisible wrinkle from the left side of her skirt, using the motion to peek over her shoulder at Kelso. The valet had assumed an impassive mask, and if not for the sparkle in his eyes, she might have believed she'd imagined his comment. When she faced Preston, he also looked as if nothing untoward had happened.

He was smooth, all right, but she treasured the shocked look she'd seen on his face. Hopefully, her plan, whatever it was when she came up with one, would put the same expression there. And it would last more than a few seconds. And she would have the pleasure of seeing it.

That was a lot to ask. She would have to plot and scheme carefully. But later. Right now she needed to pay attention, to learn. With Edith and Kelso present there would not be any interesting forays, either conversational or otherwise, into areas unrelated to the matter at hand.

Preston recovered his equilibrium with a bit of difficulty. Not because Matty exhibited the temerity to include her maid in the invitation, but because the other woman's presence brought to the fore a dashed hope he had not even been aware he'd harbored. He had anticipated an intimate tête-à-tête with Matty.

His disappointment was the surprise that had rocked him on his heels.

Falling back on the social skills ingrained in him since childhood, Preston welcomed the women as if both had been expected. With an ease he didn't feel, he transitioned into an explanation of the formal dining table, set for fourteen, the ideal size for a dinner party.

In reality, the lessons were unnecessary. Her grandfather knew she'd been raised in an environment that did not include court etiquette, and he could care less. If it had mattered to him, he would have dictated a course of remedial decorum. Hell's bells, she would likely set a new style. The insipid ton would probably find her refreshing and unique.

Just as he had.

All the preparation, the whole pretense of lessons, had been an elaborate excuse for him to spend time alone with Matty. Pulling the wool over someone else's eyes was one thing; being so foolish as to deceive one-self was quite another.

Preston faced the fact his motives were not altruistic. But the question remained, why had he felt the ruse necessary?

He would have to puzzle that out later. Moving to stand at the head of the table, he explained the care to be taken in seating guests according to precedence. "The highest-ranking woman to the right of the host, and the highest-ranking man to the right of the hostess. Second-highest to the left, and so forth, alternating man, woman, man, woman toward the center of the table, ranging from high to low."

All the while he droned on and on, both women paying rapt attention to his every boring word, a picture formed in his mind of Matty yelling "Supper's ready!" and of the jewel-encrusted members of court stampeding into the dining room and scrambling for places at the table.

"What are you smiling about?" Matty asked. "Even you can't find this subject remotely interesting."

"Just a random, unconnected thought. Nothing really."

"Oh, do share with us. A little levity would not be remiss."

"Are you implying I'm boring you?"

"Implying? In that case, I shall endeavor to make myself more clear in the future."

Edith had the kindness to hide her snicker behind her handkerchief, but Kelso chortled out loud.

Oh, ho! He could play that game, too. Preston bowed his head toward her, signaling he recognized her challenge. She smiled and nodded back, a gesture accepting his entry into the verbal foray.

He seated the ladies at the table and rang the tiny silver bell beside his plate. "This would normally be the duty of the hostess, but with your forbearance I will assume the role."

"I'm sure you'll make a wonderful hostess," Matty responded with a sweet smile. "Will you forgo your after-dinner cigar and play the pianoforte for us instead?"

"Actually, I was thinking you might join me for a cigar. And a brandy."

Kelso nearly dropped the tureen of turtle soup he was serving. They both ignored the clunk of the dish onto the table, but her smile faded a bit at the corners. Touché.

"No brandy, thank you," she said. "I've never enjoyed the effects of strong spirits."

He allowed himself the smallest of smug smiles.

"But a good cigar sounds wonderful," she added.

Was she serious? Or had she simply meant to shock him?

Edith choked and dropped her spoon into the bowl, splashing hot soup everywhere. She couldn't seem to catch her breath. Everyone jumped up, Matty yelled for him to do something, and Kelso yelled at Edith to breathe as he patted her on the back. Preston hauled her to a standing position and, bracing her against the back of the chair, he whacked her between the shoulder blades. A morsel of meat flew across the table, and she wheezed in a breath.

"She'll be fine in a minute," Preston said as he helped her back into her seat.

"Are you sure?" Matty asked, kneeling beside the chair and patting Edith's hand.

Edith nodded her agreement.

Matty moved aside as Kelso brought her a glass of water and insisted she take small sips.

Then Matty turned to Preston. After thanking him for his timely assistance, she added, "Perhaps we should call a truce until after the meal."

"Pax?" He held out his hand.

"Pax," she said, shaking on the agreement. "Until after the meal," she added.

Threat or promise, he wasn't sure.

But then it didn't really matter, did it? Either way was equally enticing.

Chapter 14

Matty laid her fork across the top of her plate. She had nibbled her way through dinner per Preston's previous instructions, and his advice had been correct. There had been so many different dishes, if she'd eaten a full serving of anything, she wouldn't have survived to the last course without bursting.

Despite an inauspicious beginning, the rest of the dinner had proceeded without incident. Preston took the lead, explaining as he progressed, and Matty and Edith faithfully copied his actions. He'd made the whole process entertaining with anecdotes and stories of faux pas made by the rich and famous. Contrary to her expectations, she'd had a marvelous time.

"Normally, no one rises from the table until the hostess gives the signal," he said.

"What sort of signal?" Matty asked, refraining from making a cheeky remark about waving semaphore flags or sending up puffs of smoke. After all, the peace treaty was still nominally in effect.

"Oh, usually something quite obvious." He shook out his large napkin and wrapped it around his head turban style, explaining that particular headgear was very popular among the matrons of society. "If the ladies will join me in the parlor for tea and cakes," he said in falsetto tones. He stood and stepped away from the table, motioning for the others to do the same. Whipping off the turban, he added in his normal voice, "Or in this case . . ."

He made a bow, sweeping his arm toward the wall opposite the entrance. The green velvet drapes opened, courtesy of Kelso's impeccable timing, to reveal a balcony. The valet opened the French doors that led to a small table set for three, coffee service, and a plate of assorted pastries, petits fours, and candied fruit.

It must have been prearranged, for when the doors opened, at that moment, a string quartet on the deck below began playing. Edith applauded.

The evocative strains of a waltz wafted up on the balmy night breeze. Moonlight gave a glow to the white tablecloth so it seemed to float in midair. The silver coffee service gleamed, reflecting back the exotic flowers of her shawl. The effect was magical and seductive. Matty walked onto the balcony as if in a trance.

She gripped the railing, the cool solid wood a reassurance she wasn't dreaming.

"May I have this dance?"

She turned. Edith had stayed inside to chat with Kelso, but Preston had followed her. He held out his hand.

"Perhaps some other time," she said, thankful her tone held a note of polite regret without sounding wistful.

He waited. And raised one eyebrow, his question obvious though unspoken.

"I've never had the chance to learn the waltz," she said, ducking her head. She'd been to a few barn raisings and frontier hoedowns, but the Virginia Reel and Turkey Trot were as out of place here as lumps of coal in a jeweled necklace.

"Then this is your lucky night. I happen to be an experienced dance master."

"Another scam?"

"Come. We won't have many nights such as this as we head north into winter weather. The moonlight and music should not be wasted."

He hadn't responded to her question. And that was answer enough. Yet, he was right. She would never have another night like this, so she might as well make the most of it.

She put her hand in his, and he led her down the curving stairway. The deck had been cleared and the dark wood polished to a mirrored sheen. Pausing in the center of the temporary dance floor, he bowed to the crew members-cum-musicians. She curtsied. The music drew to a close and the quartet returned the salute. Preston then bowed to her, and she curtsied again.

"Much improved," he said, then immediately launched into an explanation of the basic box step.

Swallowing the smart remark she would have made, she instead paid attention. She was going to dance the waltz. With Preston.

"Step forward with your right foot, slide your left foot up and to the side, shift your weight to your left, and close with your right," he said as he demonstrated. "That's half of the box. Then you'll step back with your left, slide and step with your right, and close with the left, thus completing the box and ready to begin again. Let's walk through it together."

Standing next to each other, they stepped off the box several times.

"Right, slide, close—and head up, back straight, don't look down—and left, slide, close. Again. Right, slide—"

"I've got it. I've got it. Stop distracting me."

"Then let's put it to music." He stepped in front of her, placed her left hand on his upper arm close to his shoulder, and put his right hand on her back halfway between her neck and waist. Strangely, the warmth of his hand sent shivers up her spine. He held out his left hand, and she rested her free hand on his. Then he nodded to the musicians.

For eight bars they stood still, like porcelain figurines on a mantelpiece, as the violin set the lilting theme. The other instruments joined in, and he led her in the steps.

One, two, three, she counted in her head, but she soon lost herself in the rhythm of the music and no longer needed to keep track of her steps.

He added sedate turns and made following him easy by putting mild pressure on her back and slightly pushing or pulling on her hand. She tipped her head back. The stars, like diamonds scattered across black velvet, seemed close enough for her to reach out and gather them by the handful.

The music built, and he turned tighter, whirling her in thrilling wide sweeps. The world spun around her, faster and faster. She closed her eyes.

"If you look at me, you won't get dizzy."

She blinked, and focused on his face, his eyes.

"I take it you like the dance," he said with a chuckle.

She couldn't find the words to describe her feelings, so she just nodded and grinned.

The music rose to a crescendo, and the last bars drifted out to sea. He swung her under his arm and outward, ending in a bow. She sank into a curtsy that was neither elegant nor graceful because she was breathless and laughing. Still, it elicited applause from Edith and Kelso watching from the balcony.

She blew kisses to the servants and to the musicians.

"And me?" he asked.

"Thank you."

"It has been my honor. I'm told a woman never forgets her first waltz."

"Not just for the dance. The night. The moon. Everything is magical."

"I can't take credit for the weather or for the moon."

"The music. The dinner. Thank you for a wonderful evening."

She flung her arms wide. Breathing deep, she turned slowly in a circle. Then she wound her arms around her shoulders.

"What are you doing?"

"When I was a little girl and didn't want to leave someplace or didn't want to forget something, my father would tell me to take it all in my arms—the sights, the sounds, the smells—and wrap everything up and put it in my heart. Then I would never really leave any place behind because I would always have it with me."

"I have a better way of making a memory." He nodded to the musicians and swept her into another dance.

"And does a woman always remember her second waltz?" she asked. She flashed him a coquettish smile.

Preston looked down at the woman in his arms. Whether Matty knew it or not, she was ripe for the plucking. The watchdogs on the balcony were only a minor hindrance. A few of the right phrases whispered in her ear, a few stolen kisses in the moonlight, and he could waltz her directly to his bed.

He nearly missed a step when he realized he had planned the evening in an attempt to seduce her. Why? Had he simply played the scene so often it had become second nature?

Seducing Matty didn't feel right. No. It did feel

right, more than right. His body responded to her as it hadn't to any other woman in more years than he cared to admit. It just didn't feel *honorable,* and that was the mystery. He had long ago rejected society's narrow vision of what was proper when a willing woman was in his arms.

Oh, he had played the honorable gentleman with Anne because she loved his friend and he, her, but it had been difficult and painful. And he had regretted it for quite some time.

But he had moved past that disappointment, and what did Anne have to do with Matty? They were so dissimilar, polar opposites in many ways. Where Anne was cool and elegant, Matty was sunshine and stubbornness.

He swung her in a wide arc, and her joyous, uninhibited laughter reverberated in his chest.

Matty was going to sweep through the stuffy London parlors like a sudden spring storm. As the granddaughter of a duke, and one who would have a sizable income of her own—not to mention her inevitable inheritance—she'd soon be considered the most eligible woman in town. A few snotty matrons would be outraged and shun her, but heritage and riches would win out over personal history. She'd have her pick of invitations, and her pick of suitors.

Why would she want him? A bastard in all but name.

Preston brought the dance to a close in time to the music. When society learned the truth about Matty's blood lines, they would embrace her with open arms. If they ever learned the truth about him, they would turn up their noses as if to avoid the stench, and collectively turn their backs.

The best he could do for Matty was to complete his mission as stated. Bring her safely to London. And that included keeping her safe from his base inclinations. Was that what Marsfield had meant?

"What's wrong?" she asked, a tiny frown marring her forehead.

"Nothing. Why would you ask that?"

"You look like you just sucked on a lemon. I didn't step on your toes, did I?"

His mission was going to be harder to complete than he'd thought. For both their sakes he needed to put some distance between them. Physically and otherwise. Her lessons, once a ruse to spend time with her and to make friends with her, could be used for the opposite purpose as well.

"No, you did not step on my toes, but if you're ready for a critique—"

She groaned dramatically. "Can't we just enjoy the evening?" Her shoulders sagged as she gazed skyward.

"You're the one who said dress and attitude made all the difference. You do want this scam to be successful, don't you?"

"Yes." She crossed her hands primly at her waist like a penitent schoolgirl. Yet her eyes sparkled and she fairly bounced up and down on her toes.

He found her natural exuberance and playfulness irresistible. And that would never do.

He proceeded to wipe the smile from her face by listing every minute detail of her mistakes, and it felt as if he were stabbing himself in the gut. Hara-kiri. Seppuku. Thrust in with the *wakizashi,* the traditional short sword of the samurai. Draw it across and up. Withstand the agony to achieve an honorable ending.

What hurt most was seeing the light within Matty diminish before his eyes, and knowing he had caused her pain. But she would thank him someday.

"Are you ready to continue the lesson?" he asked, motioning with his arm toward the dance floor.

"No. I believe I've had enough for one evening," she said, her voice cold and flat. "In fact, I think the fish must have been tainted, because I'm not feeling well."

Wishing him a quick good night, she climbed up the stairs without waiting for him to escort her and disappeared beyond the curtains, followed by a scowling Edith.

He had taken several steps in her wake before he realized what he was doing, and forced himself to halt.

Preston dismissed the musicians and strolled to the railing, pulling a cheroot from his breast pocket. But before he could light it, he suddenly and violently lost his dinner over the side.

"Bloody honor," he muttered, wiping his mouth with his handkerchief.

"Milord?" Kelso asked.

How long had the man been standing behind him?

Preston turned. "I think the fish at dinner was tainted," he said, glad Matty had provided a convenient excuse, because his brain was not functioning to form.

"I'll take that up with the cook. Is there anything I can get you? Perhaps a brandy?"

"Hell, no," Preston said. The last thing he needed was any reminder of Matty's kisses. However, when the force of his reply caused the shorter man to take a step back, Preston moderated his tone to say, "I'm simply taking the air for a bit before retiring for the night."

"But, milord, it's not half past ten?"

"Since when am I not allowed to go to bed at a decent hour?"

"Never, sir. It's just so unusual that I was surprised. I will ready your chamber immediately."

"Thank you. And see if you can locate a hot water bottle."

Kelso looked at him as if he had asked for flannel pajamas and a hot milk toddy to go with it.

"Dammit, man. Can't you see I'm ill?" Preston bellowed.

"Of course, milord. I can see you're quite affected," Kelso said in a calm voice as he bowed in response. "And it's not the fish," he muttered as he turned away.

Matty pounded her pillow, then flipped over and plopped her head onto it. Damn that man. He had her turned inside out and upside down with his blow-hot, blow-cold tactics. One minute she thought he liked her; the next he seemed to despise her. He looked at her as if she were a bonbon and he was starving; then he turned away in distaste. How was she supposed to know what to think?

She could not get comfortable in the over-large, luxurious bed. "Dagnabbit," she said, throwing the comforter and half a dozen of the fluffy pillows to the floor.

She was supposed to be concentrating on making the scam successful and protecting herself and her children, not worrying about what he thought of her.

After more than an hour of tossing and turning, she rose and lit the lamp on the desk. Taking out pen, ink, and paper, she sought to put some order to the jumbled quagmire of her thoughts. She started with a clear statement of her goals. To earn—no, scratch that— *acquire* sufficient funds to legally adopt her children, and to provide them with a comfortable and safe home.

Anything else, including girlish dreams and impossible fantasies involving Preston, must be forgotten.

A tear fell onto her paper. The lamp must not have been trimmed properly, causing smoke to get in her eyes as she worked. Matty found a handkerchief to wipe her moist cheeks.

Once she had her priorities straight, everything else she needed to do fell neatly into place. She would spend more time with her children, thus allowing Edith freedom to complete the necessary sewing. Matty had noticed a number of books on agriculture and animal husbandry in the ship's well-stocked collection. She would study each day so that she was better prepared to make her farm a success. And she would learn everything she could from Preston, but would limit her exposure to him to a mere two hours per day.

So far she had not questioned him regarding how the scam would run, and that was an error she intended to correct. The more she knew, the better chance she had of protecting herself from being duped. Until she knew more, she could not formulate a plan for what she would do after they reached London. She wrote down a final goal, which was to find out as much as she could about Preston and his scheme.

She heaved a sigh. She should finally be able to sleep. Looking up, she found it had gone past two o'clock. Perhaps she should check on the children before she lay down. She donned her old robe, picked up the lamp, and padded barefoot to the other room.

Preston sat in the chair nearest the door to the hall, ostensibly because it was the most comfortable— which it was not—but he'd told Kelso so. A book lay open on his lap. He was not reading *One Thousand Fascinating Facts About Larvae*. It had simply been the first volume handy. And while his valet had been bustling about the room, he had pretended intense interest.

He was also not drinking the mulled wine set on the side table, or smoking the cigar, trimmed and ready to light. He had, however, left the door to the hall open to relieve the stuffiness in the room.

Although he could not hear her movements, he knew Matty's late-night habit of reading or sewing, and of wandering about to check on the children. She would probably check on her cows in the middle of the night, too, if they had brought them along. He watched the light under her door. Knew when she moved through the solar and returned some minutes later. Finally, the light went out.

Preston stood and stretched his cramped back muscles. He yawned and decided it was time to seek his rest. He would need to be on his toes tomorrow and every day until they reached London and he could deposit Matty on her grandfather's doorstep.

Perhaps once he'd completed this mission he would look into the possibility of an extended trip to the Orient. Perhaps for several years. Travel had been the balm that had soothed Anne from his system, so surely it would work again.

Not that there was any comparison between the two women; after all, he was not in love with Matty. It was just that he would prefer not to encounter her at a soiree or musical with her new husband, the undeserving wretch who would value her purse more than the unique person she was. If that happened, Preston would be forced to make polite chitchat when he would prefer to drive his fist through the man's teeth.

Strange, in the picture that came to mind, the other man looked a lot like him. Only without the stance of bored indifference, the attitude of soul-weary ennui. Her husband seemed relaxed and content. Damn him.

Better for Preston to be on the other side of the world so he would not dream of the man's hands on Matty, his lips on hers. Touching her silken skin. Tasting her brandy kisses.

Strange, when he'd dreamed of Anne she had always been with Marsfield. And she had always been fully clothed.

He picked up the glass and chugged the wine, hoping it would help him to dreamless sleep.

Chapter 15

"It's hard to believe we're anchored only a few hundred yards from the city," Edith said as she folded Bess's little dresses and put them in the trunk.

"Yes, yes it is." Matty nodded. Having become inured to the maid's near-constant chatter, she listened with only half an ear.

"Amazing to cross an entire ocean in a mere three weeks."

"Twenty days." The longest twenty days of Matty's life.

"We were up on the deck this afternoon watching the sights through the spyglass Mr. Kelso gave Nathan. I do hope he's all right."

"Who? Nathan? What's wrong—"

"No. Mr. Kelso. He went ashore with the captain and a few of the men in one of those rowboats. Something about seeing the harbor master and making arrangements. All I know is he didn't come back with the others, and he still hasn't returned. I do hope he's all right." Edith walked to the window and looked out, wringing her hands.

"It's late. I'm sure he's waiting for morning."

"There are so many dangers in the city. Robbers and footpads and pickpockets. Press-gangs. White slavers! Oh, the poor little man."

Matty hid a smile. She refrained from saying she was sure Kelso was safe from the white slavers. "Didn't you tell me he was born and raised in London?" Edith and Kelso had become quite chummy during the voyage, and Matty had gleaned a lot of knowledge about the valet and his boss secondhand. She just hoped garrulous Edith had listened more than she'd talked. A faint hope, but then the maid really knew very little about Matty or her life before they met.

"The city is so big."

"I'm sure he knows his way around. I've always had the impression Kelso can take care of himself."

Edith sighed, but she agreed.

"Why don't you call it a night?" Matty said. "It's my understanding we'll have plenty of time in the morning to finish, because even though the ship will enter the docking area in the morning, we won't disembark until noon."

"You should get some sleep, too. Tomorrow will be a long day."

"I'll just read until I finish my peppermint tea."

"Very well, but I'm sure I won't sleep a wink."

After Edith left, Matty tried to pay attention to the *Burke's Peerage* Preston had given her. Too dry. Too boring. Who cared if the sixth Baronet of Pippinshire was named Wilberforce Thumpton? She set the book on the table and picked up *DeBrett's*. Same thing. She tossed it aside.

Nerves. They always made her restless the night before setting a scam in motion. All the planning, all the setting up, would be for naught if the first few minutes went badly.

What she needed was physical activity. If she were at home, she would take a brisk ride, or chop wood, or

clean house. She looked around the room. Other than
a few stray bits and bobs, the place was immaculate.

A walk around the deck? Too cold. After the tropics,
the December weather seemed bitter indeed.

Yet, no floors needed scrubbing. No rugs needed beating. A blessing, and yet, as crazy as it sounded, she
would have appreciated a washboard and a pile of dirty
laundry to work off the energy thrumming beneath her
skin.

If there was no other option, then a walk it would be.
She would just have to bundle up.

Preston stood outside her door, his hand raised to
knock. He hesitated. If he told her the truth now, would
she refuse to see her grandfather?

Preston had not come so far to fail at the finish line.

Yet he had the misguided notion he should be the one
to tell her, that he should confess his lies. Then what did
he expect her to do? Grant him absolution? Bestow forgiveness? He shook his head. And lowered his arm.

More likely, she would shoot him.

And he couldn't blame her.

Was it cowardly to delay the inevitable? Maybe? No.
Once the mission was complete, he would take his
punishment, whatever she thought he deserved.
Bloody hell, he would welcome it. Maybe then he
could get her out of his system.

He returned to his room.

Nothing she could concoct could be worse than the
agony he faced nightly in his dreams.

Matty stood in the middle of the deserted deck, every
vestige of the magical evening they had once spent

there—gone. The space where the musicians had sat was full of nautical equipment. The floor was under an inch of snow, the balcony empty, the drapes drawn tight. Even the moon seemed to have abandoned her. Only the stars remained. And they seemed cold and distant.

Tomorrow her world would change completely. She would leave the ship behind, most likely never to see it again. Even if she did return to America on the same ship, it would be without Preston. A few more days and he would be gone. Forever.

She would survive, just as she had survived all the other good-byes and leave-takings. She would survive because she had the memories.

So few memories to last her the rest of her life.

Now she regretted not making a few more. Something warm and cozy to pull out on a sleepless night. Smiles to remember when she was sad. Kisses for when she was lonely. Too bad she and Preston had not made love. Surely that would have been memory enough to survive the long, cold winters ahead.

Was it too late?

If she knocked on his door, would he turn her away?

She didn't know. And that about summed up her relationship with him. She didn't know what he would do if she showed up uninvited in his bed, ready and willing. Would he initiate her into the rights of womanhood with gentle caring? Or would he ravish her with wild, uncontrollable passion? Maybe a bit of both?

She should be so lucky. He would probably kick her out on her naked butt with a list of everything she'd done wrong in her woefully inadequate attempt at seduction.

That she would not survive. Her fear of rejection was stronger than her need, and that was saying a lot.

The memories she had would have to do. Like the

night of her first waltz. She wrapped her arms around her body and closed her eyes. Then flinging her arms wide, as she had done as a little girl, she spread the memory all around her. The summer-like scent of the sea air, the moonlight, the music. And Preston.

As if it were real, he smiled at her and took her in his arms. Together they waltzed around the deck, just as before.

She kept her eyes closed, the memory so vivid her feet seemed to leave the deck on the wide turns.

"Shame on you for dancing alone, when I long to be your partner."

She skidded to a halt and opened her eyes.

Winter returned with a vengeance, and yet Preston was still there. That had never happened before. As if she'd wished him there.

Except he was wearing wool gloves and an overcoat she'd never seen, so he couldn't be a figment of her memory. Snowflakes clung to his rich dark hair, giving her a preview of the still-devilish good looks he would have when he was older.

He moved to take her in his arms and continue the dance, but she held her ground.

"There's no music," she said.

"Yes, there is. It's here." He took her hand and laid it over his heart.

Whether real or imagined, she felt the beat of his heart.

With both hands on her waist, they danced, and he swung her higher and faster until she clung to his neck. He slowly came to a stop and slid her to her feet. Though she never thought to remove her arms. They stood there for a long moment, their steamy breaths making clouds.

Suddenly nervous, she asked him, "Do you remember your first waltz?"

"Not fondly."

"Now you will have to explain that," she said, flashing him a smile. She refused to examine the jealous pleasure his statement gave her.

"I'd rather not."

"You must."

"It's not as interesting as you seem to think. My sisters are adamant—the duties of an older brother include having his feet trodden upon repeatedly and at regular intervals. And they desired to waltz. Therefore, I was forced to learn, and squired each of them about the floor in turn."

"You never mentioned you had sisters. How many? Do they live in London?"

Preston realized his mistake too late.

"I knew I should have made up a more interesting story. Would you believe me if I told you my first waltz was really with the daughter of a notorious courtesan?" he asked in an attempt to distract her.

"Will I meet them?"

"The courtesan and her daughter? I should say not. However, I can introduce you to a woman who has two monkeys as pets. Would you like that?"

"Yes, very much. And will I meet your sisters?"

"Not if my luck holds. We should go inside and get something warm to drink before you freeze. Tea or hot cocoa?"

"How many sisters do you have? What are their names? How old are they?"

He groaned. "Matty, please."

"Why don't you want to talk about your family?"

He did not have a ready answer.

Although he no longer considered his sisters the

bane of his existence, he tried to avoid his parents whenever possible. His mother, nicknamed The Dragon by his friend Burke, required Preston's presence for certain social events in order to keep up appearances. In addition, he saw the Earl of Stiles annually for the compulsory state-of-the-estate meeting, which always ended with his father lamenting Preston's lack of interest in the title and the responsibilities that went with it.

He'd never told his parents he knew their secret, knew he would never inherit. When the truth became known, he was prepared to walk away and leave everything to the rightful heirs without a backward glance.

Matty would never be satisfied with flippant, easy answers, not with the way she felt about family. And explaining it all to her would open an old wound he had spent years healing. Nor would she be easily distracted.

He looked down at her, standing in the circle of his arms, with snowflakes tipping her eyelashes, and her cheeks flushed. Talking about his family was the last thing he wanted to do.

A dozen flowery phrases came to mind. Well-practiced compliments and witty tributes. Flattery and guile guaranteed to coax a woman into the mood for seduction. None seemed right for Matty. Not that her features did not deserve poetic adulation, but she had demanded honesty from him. The artful words stuck in his throat.

"We should go inside," he finally said. "Your nose is turning red."

She buried her face in the front of his coat. He wrapped one arm around her and felt her shoulders shaking. Damn. Now he had made her cry. That's what bloody honesty did.

"I'm sorry, Matty. I didn't mean to hurt your feelings."

She looked up at him, a wide smile wreathing her face.

"You're laughing?"

"Not at you." She took several steps back. "I was laughing at myself."

His arms fell to his sides, bereft as well as empty. "Why?"

"It's embarrassing," she said, shaking her head.

He was too intrigued to let the matter drop. "You tell me why you were laughing and I'll tell you about my sisters. Deal?"

She tipped her head to the side and narrowed her gaze. "You'll answer all my questions?"

"That could take all night. Six questions."

"Twelve."

"Eight, and that's final."

"Dagnabbit, I knew I should have started higher."

"Too late. Do we have a deal?"

After a moment's hesitation she agreed.

"Good. You first," he said.

"Why me?"

"Someone has to go first, and I called it."

She gave him a quick glare. "Very well." She bit her bottom lip for a moment, then mumbled something very fast.

"Say again. I couldn't hear you." He leaned forward.

"Your hearing difficulties are not of consequence to our deal. Your turn."

"There is nothing wrong with my hearing. You're cheating. Now say it again." He took a step closer.

She mumbled faster and lower than before.

"Again." He put his ear inches from her mouth.

"I thought you were going to kiss me!" she yelled.

He jumped back, whether from the volume or the surprising content of her confession, he would never know. "What?"

"I know you heard me that time."

"They heard you in Trafalgar Square." He crossed his arms over his chest. "I don't see why you found that amusing?"

"It just struck me as funny. You know, I'm thinking you're going to kiss me, and instead, you tell me my nose is red. Different. Not what I expected. That's why I was laughing." Matty shook her head. "Never mind. It's not important." She turned away from him. "Forget it."

But it was important. Her explanation had revealed more than she'd meant to expose. She had *wanted* him to kiss her.

"I won't even hold you to our deal." She headed toward the stairs. "It's cold. I'm going in."

"Matty, wait."

"No, it's too cold," she called back over her shoulder. "Good night."

He knew in his gut if he let her walk away now she would agonize over her perceived faux pas and conclude he didn't want to kiss her. Then she would convince herself it didn't matter because it was only a momentary aberration brought on by the waltz. And she would decide never to dance with him again.

All for the best. The silver lining. The first step toward disentangling her from his life.

He should definitely let her walk away.

He marched after her.

Up the stairs, tugging on the fingers of his glove. Crossing the balcony, he tossed one glove over his shoulder. He heard her little squeak of surprise when he stuck his foot in the way of the French door so it could not latch. He shouldered the door open as she scurried across the salon.

He followed her into the hall, his long strides easily gaining on her running steps. He tossed away his other glove and stopped her at the door to her room with a hand on her elbow.

"Matty, I—"

"Thank you for the dance," she said, resisting the pressure on her elbow and refusing to face him. "Good night."

He grasped her shoulders and turned her around. He tipped her face up and then gently cupped it in both hands. With his thumbs he wiped the moisture from her chilled cheeks.

"I wasn't crying," she said. "It was the wind, and the—"

He shushed her, gentle as a whisper.

With a slowness that defied his pounding heartbeat, he leaned forward. He breathed in her scent, crisp winter and peppermint tea. He smiled. Who would have thought the odor of wet wool could be erotic? Closer. Her perfume a mixture of honeysuckle and lilac.

He kissed the tip of her nose, still chilled from the night air.

"My apologies for any insult," he whispered.

Then he kissed her lips. An under-the-mistletoe kiss. A gentleman's kiss. Light and soft. Quick. Unsatisfying. And he had every intention of leaving it that way.

But as he slowly pulled his lips away she raised up on her toes to press into his kiss. She swayed, and he caught her to him with an arm around her waist.

A warning bell went off in his head, and he pulled back. "I think perhaps it's time to say good night."

"No." She tugged on his neck.

He resisted with a groan. "You're making it most difficult for me to act the gentleman," he said.

Matty looked up at him. Once they left the ship she would no longer be just Matty Maxwell. As Lady Matilda, she might never have a chance to be alone with him again. She did not want to live the rest of her life regretting her last opportunity lost.

"Good," she said, her voice breathy and husky. "Don't be a gentleman. Please. Kiss me again."

Preston could not deny her. Just one more kiss.

He might have resisted the feel of her leather-clad fingers on his neck. He might even have been able to control himself after she slanted her head to one side to deepen the kiss, and pulled his head toward her. But her little moan of pleasurable need was irresistible.

He gave in to the desire to taste her lips. She responded in kind—exploring, and dueling, and caressing. Long-banked fires burst into raging flames.

She ripped off her kid gloves and threaded her fingers in his hair.

He pressed her against the door, wanting to feel her body against his length, but their bulky clothing frustrated him. The door latch gave, and they stumbled into her room. He used the momentary separation to shed his overcoat, as did she, not breaking contact with his lips.

Trailing kisses along her chin, he reached the sensitive lobe of her ear. She arched into his kiss, and he clutched her closer, yet not close enough. Never close enough. He nipped and kissed a path down her shoulder, breathing out her name, telling her all the things he wanted to do in languages she would not understand, things no proper gentleman would ever say to a lady.

Matty did not need to understand the words. The

need resonated within her, echoed her yearning. The longing beneath the words inflamed her passion. Whatever he desired, she wanted to give. Whatever he offered, she craved.

"Yes," she whispered.

What was he doing? Preston reminded himself that this was Matty in his arms. Slaking his lust may well have the outcome of purging her from his system, but it would be doing her a grave disservice. She was not the sort to give herself lightly.

He cursed the man whose existence he had tried to ignore, the man who had taken advantage of her giving, passionate nature and left her with children to raise alone. Preston would not do the same. Not even if it meant his own suffering. Using all his hard-earned self-control, he gentled his kisses.

"Now it really is time to say good night," he said, kissing her on the forehead.

Then quickly, before he could change his mind, before his baser instincts took over, he set her aside and exited the room.

"Damnation and dagnabbit," she said as he closed the door behind him.

He took a deep breath and headed for the brandy bottle.

Matty stomped her foot. How dare he kiss her like that and then just walk away. Those kisses had promised . . . something. And she wanted it, wanted what all the gibberish was about.

She kicked his coat.

She wasn't totally ignorant. After all, she had grown up on a farm, and had known women who talked frankly about men. But she had never experienced it for herself, had never wanted to, before meeting Preston.

Now she would never know.

She didn't think she would ever feel this way about someone else, couldn't imagine ever wanting another man the way she wanted him.

She made ready for bed and straightened up the room so Edith would see nothing amiss. Finally, nothing remained except his coat, lying crumpled where he had dropped it, a constant reminder of his deceit.

Damn him for making promises with his kisses and then walking away.

She decided to throw his coat out in the hall. Let him worry about an explanation. He was so good with glib excuses and fluid lies. She picked it up. The scent of his cologne wafted up. She smoothed her hand over the soft wool, remembering how it had felt against her cheek when he had held her, caressed her.

"Dagnabbit."

Without further deliberation, she whirled around and went to get her pistol.

Chapter 16

Preston paced his bedroom, unable to settle down, unable to even enjoy his brandy.

Perhaps he should write Matty a note. No, he owed her an apology in person. In the morning. He tried out several scenarios in his head, yet none was satisfactory. There did not seem to be polite words for leaving a woman sexually frustrated, and citing his own agony hardly seemed appropriate.

He slouched into an easy chair and propped his slippered feet on the footstool. He sipped his brandy without pleasure. Perhaps he should wait until afternoon when he could obtain flowers. Apologies always went better with bouquets. And gifts. Perhaps he should purchase some trinket or two. Jewelry was always effective.

No. Matty was not like other women he'd known. She would not be softened by baubles or blossoms. Only a bloody-honest baring of his soul would do for her. And that would be the most difficult of all.

A sharp knock on his door caused him to sit up. Who the bloody hell could that be? It was past midnight.

"One moment," he said, setting his glass aside.

The door burst open before he had a chance to stand and answer it.

"Don't bother to get up," Matty said as she marched into his room. "You forgot your coat." She stopped next to his chair and dropped his overcoat on the floor. Then he could see the derringer that she had hidden beneath its folds.

"I could have gotten it in the morning," he said calmly. Despite his previous experience to the opposite, he had no fear she would shoot him. Not in cold blood. Yet he was deliciously curious as to what else she did intend to do.

"I'm very angry with you."

"I can see that. In fact, I was just thinking of an appropriate apology."

"Were you?"

"Yes, just before you . . . arrived."

"Hmm. I see. Well, I don't think an apology is sufficient."

"No? I had considered flowers or jewelry. Is that what you had in mind?"

She shook her head. "Not at all." But this was pretty much as far along as she had thought through her plan, and she wasn't sure what to do next.

"If you're here to challenge me to a duel, it's not customary for the woman to defend her own honor. Perhaps the captain would serve as your second."

"I want you to make love to me," she blurted out.

"At gunpoint? Not very romantic."

She had come this far and was not going to back down. "Stand up and take your clothes off."

"Matty—"

"I'm serious," she said, leaning over and waving the gun under his nose. "Do it."

With a move so fast she wasn't even sure she saw it, he knocked the gun from her hand, grabbed her arm, and twisted it in such a way she fell into his lap. She struggled to stand.

He wrapped both arms around her, holding her firmly, yet not hurting her.

"Calm down," he said, his voice brooking no argument.

She stilled, and he loosened his hold.

She bit her lip. She had tried and failed. Now the only thing available to do was to get out with whatever shred of dignity she had left.

"Just relax for a minute," he said, rubbing her back.

She leaned against him. "I'm—"

"Shush. No words yet. You can't relax if you're talking." He pressed her head to his chest and caught her legs under the knees to curl them to one side.

He hummed a simple melody, low-pitched and soft, and she heard the bass notes rumble in his chest. He rubbed small, warm circles on her back. The tension left her body, and she slumped against him.

"Sweet Matty," he said, kissing the top of her head. "The pistol was unnecessary. If you had only asked, I would have obliged."

She popped her head up. "Really? In that case—"

He pressed her head back down. "Not yet. Please let me finish. I apologize for leaving you so abruptly earlier. Not for leaving, itself, because that was the honorable thing to do, but for not explaining why."

He took a deep breath, knowing that to be honest with her, he had to be honest with himself. Maybe for the first time.

"The chase is what has always fascinated me about women. The wooing and the courting are exciting and challenging. Once I've succeeded, I've usually lost interest rather quickly."

"Is this a warning?"

He chuckled ruefully. "Quite possibly so."

"Noted. It doesn't change my mind."

"I'm not even sure that's what I'm trying to do. I want you more than I've ever wanted a woman before. I'm torn because I'm not sure if I want to get you out of my system. And I don't know what I'll do if it doesn't work like it has in the past."

She sat up and twisted around in his lap so she could look him in the eye. "Say that part again."

"I don't know if I want to get you out—"

"No, no. The part about wanting me more than any other woman. Say that again."

He smiled. Looking her straight in the eye, he said, "Matty Maxwell, I have never met anyone like you before, and I have never wanted a woman the way I desire you."

"That's good enough for me," she said, jumping up to stand beside the chair.

Of all the reactions to his confession he might have expected, that was not one of them.

"So stand up and take off your clothes," she said. "Times a-wasting."

She truly was unique, and against his better judgment, he was in danger of falling in love with her. Even knowing she would soon despise him for all his lies, he could not resist her now. Even if he rotted in the hell her inevitable hatred would cause him, he had not the will to turn down the gift of one night with her.

She untied the belt on her dressing gown. He stood and stayed her hand. She flashed him a confused look.

"Let me," he said. He slowly undid the sash and peeled the silk wrapper away, kissing each bit of skin he bared. "I remember this material. I knew it would suit you perfectly."

Matty fought to remain standing on her weak knees. She had never expected him to undress her. All her information about sex, which wasn't actually all that much, had come from women in the profession, women whose goal was to complete the transaction as quickly as possible. They had obviously never met Preston. He was in no hurry. Which left her with the dilemma of what to do. She decided to copy his actions as she'd done with her earlier lessons in decorum.

When she reached for the sash of his paisley smoking jacket, he sucked in his breath. So he felt much as she did. The realization empowered her to boldness. She ran her hands up the black satin lapels and slid the garment off his shoulders.

She needed no direction to caress his chest and arms; his skin was invitation enough. She ran her fingers through the light furring on his chest—not too much, but not bare like a boy. Following the arrow of hair, she ran her hands lower and lower.

His erection strained against the black satin of his loose pajama bottoms. Although not a surprise, it was a bit larger than she had been led to expect. Curious, she ran her hand along the satin-covered length, measuring the width with her fingers. No way was that going to fit inside her. Her only hope was that there was some sort of padding inside his pants. She reached for the tie that held the material in place.

Again he stopped her hands.

"Easy, darling. You don't want me to come in your hand, do you?"

She had no idea what he was talking about, but from the format of the question she guessed it wasn't something he wanted to happen, so she shook her head.

"My turn," he said, reaching for the high lace neck of her white cotton nightgown.

Whereas she would have ripped the buttons off, he undid each tiny pearl with care. Slow. Too slow. Hands at her sides, she gathered the loose material in her fists, finally stepping back to flip the gown over her head.

Only her lacy chemise was left.

"Women wear too many clothes to bed," he said, reaching for the ribbon ties.

"What do you wear?"

"When I'm with a beautiful woman, nothing at all."

He took her in his arms, lifting her, holding her high on his chest for a moment, kissing the swells of her breasts, cupping her derriere to him.

When she wrapped her legs around him, he nearly staggered in surprise. But then he remembered she was no innocent, and her response made sense. She arched into his kiss. Her breasts strained against the thin chemise. He took the material in his teeth and freed one nipple and then the other.

He laved the already-tight buds, blew gently on her nipple, then licked and sucked and teased with his tongue, circling and flicking the tip. When he moved to the other nipple, she moaned and arched deeper into his mouth. He liked a woman who knew what she wanted and could communicate her needs.

Matty nearly swooned with the unexpected pleasure. So many new experiences, new feelings, she could not fully comprehend one before another washed over her. She'd melted with his first kiss. Smoldered with the second. Shivered. Soared when he'd lifted her into his arms. Then fearful she might fly apart, she'd anchored herself by wrapping her legs around his waist.

Then he kissed her breasts. And she wanted something she couldn't name. She just knew she wanted more. She squeezed her legs, and his answering moan resonated into her breast and blew her inner coals into flames. More. She threaded her fingers into the silken hair at the back of his neck and pulled him closer still.

She knew there was more, and she wanted it all. She wanted him to do everything he could do. Everything he had done to other women, and more. She wanted him to touch her everywhere, all her secret places. She wanted to give him whatever he would have, everything. More. All of herself.

Preston delighted in Matty's participation in their lovemaking, giving and taking with fervor equal to his. He did not want her to ever regret making love with him, much as she might regret ever meeting him. He wanted this night to be special. A night she would never forget.

He slowed the pace of his kisses. She would not have it, and ground her hips against him.

Steeling himself against his own raging needs, he walked to the high bed, leaned over, and laid her on the soft sheets he had turned down earlier when he had actually contemplated sleeping.

"Let go of me for just a moment," he said.

She shook her head and tightened her grip.

"I'm only going to make us more comfortable."

"*More* is my new favorite word," she mumbled, flopping back onto the pillows and stretching like a cat.

He dropped the bed curtains for warmth, then kicked off his slippers and climbed beside her into the big bed.

"Mmmm," she said, snuggling into his arms. "I wished for you, and here you are."

"What else do you wish?"

"For you to kiss me."

She seemed suddenly shy. Had he misjudged her? Very little of the light seeped into the cozy cave of the large bed, and he focused on her expression. "Is that all? More kisses?"

His reticence confused her. She had been led to believe once a man was aroused, nothing would stop him.

Perhaps he needed encouragement? No, she could not conceive of him as timid. Yet, she knew in her woman's heart he'd been aroused, so what was holding him back? Why didn't he just do it? He seemed to prefer her to be bold. Her cheeks heated. Bold? She'd been brazen. So be it.

She pushed him to his back and knelt beside him. She untied her chemise. He tucked his hands behind his head and crossed his legs at the ankles, perfectly at ease.

Then she raised the chemise, the sparkle in his eyes encouraging her and yet causing her to draw out the moment. Once over her head, she tossed the garment aside.

If she kept up this torture he would lose his resolve to go slowly.

She waited for him to make a move, worrying her lower lip with her teeth. He merely stared at her. She licked her dry lips.

Her teasing was torment—delicious—and more than he deserved. He opened his arms, and she slid into his embrace with a tiny moan, raining hot little kisses over his face. He rolled her to her back with a long, wet kiss, drawing out her tongue and stealing her breath.

Instead of settling between her legs, as he so wanted to do, he positioned himself on his side, next to her. He traced her moist lips with his fingertip, rededicating himself to his purpose. "I would like to give you a woman's pleasure, first."

She looked up at him, her confusion obvious. Was it possible no man had pleasured her in such a manner? "Perhaps you know it by another name? I'm sure you'll understand once we start. That is, if you wish it?"

Matty hadn't the slightest idea what he was talking about. But Preston obviously knew more about matters of lovemaking than she. He had given her nothing but pleasure—oh, so much pleasure. Whatever he wanted to do was sure to be an adventure she would enjoy. "I wish for you to give me a woman's pleasure," she said, crossing her fingers that she was right to trust him.

"Lie back and relax. Close your eyes," he instructed. "This is about touch."

She wiggled into position, arms at her side, knees and ankles together, eyes closed. Straight as a stick and just as pliant.

"I'm ready," she said.

So the little minx wanted him to work for her reward? He accepted the challenge with a chuckle. Her eyes flew open.

"What? Have we started?"

"Not yet. Believe me, there will be no doubt when we actually start. But first," he said, pausing long enough to come to his knees, flip her over on her stomach, and straddle her derriere with one swift move. "You need to relax."

"Didn't we already do that?" she said, her voice muffled.

He leaned forward, removed the pillow, and stretched her arms so her hands rested beside her hips. He pinned her there for a moment with the weight of his body and whispered in her ear, "Not quite like this. All you have to do is enjoy."

He placed his hands on her back between her shoulder blades. He felt her entire body tense beneath him as if she prepared to buck him off. Unconcerned, he began slowly, rubbing in small circles, following the contours of her muscles.

"That's not bad," she mumbled.

But the words were unnecessary. Her body had already told him she'd decided not to flee. He kneaded the muscles of her shoulders and upper arms. She was firm and well defined. Probably from all the farm work she'd done. He worked each section until it was soft and supple.

"Actually quite nice."

"Hush," he said. "No talking."

He worked his thumbs down her spine, rubbing in tiny circles, allowing a portion of his weight to add to the pressure.

Her groan of pleasure made him smile.

"Sorry," she said. "I'll try harder to be quiet."

He scooted lower on the bed to reach her tailbone. "Noises are fine; just no words." He worked his way down to her toes, accompanied by her groans. On his way back up, he added his mouth to the massage, licking and kissing and nipping as he rubbed and kneaded and smoothed, encouraged by her moans and purrs of pleasure.

With an arm braced on either side of her head, he leaned forward to nuzzle the delicate skin behind her ear. Beneath him, she spun to her back and pulled him to her, locking her lips to his. Her body strained to reach his. She was definitely ready for the next phase.

"I'm not done yet," he said against her lips as he detached her arms from around his neck.

She plopped back to the mattress. "There's more?" She blinked up at him.

Although her incredulity pleased him, he credited it more to her lack of this particular experience than his prowess. After all, she must know she had not reached her peak. Perhaps she did not expect this to give her that pleasure. He reaffirmed his determination.

His own eagerness to continue surprised him. Not that he hadn't enjoyed such pleasures in the past, but he'd never sought it as a means unto itself. He now saw it as a technique to be employed for its own unique satisfaction, a pleasure to be taken by giving, a singular gratification earned by her response, which could be fully savored.

And he was keen to elicit her responses and to savor them fully. He needed to safeguard his self-control. If she grabbed his penis again, his body might well betray his best intentions.

He spied what he needed, and scooted her to the center of the bed. He raised her arms so she could grasp two carved rosettes in the ornate headboard, and folded her hands around the wooden knobs. She gave him a quizzical look.

"As long as you hold on to the rosettes, I will continue. If you let go, I'll stop."

"Is this a game?" she asked.

"No, it's a test of will." But whether it would be a test of hers or his, he wasn't sure.

If Matty had doubts whether or not she should continue, she quickly squashed them. She had wanted it all, and now she would have her wish. She settled her shoulders and arms into a comfortable position, gripped the rosettes, and closed her eyes. "I'm ready when you are."

"I would prefer it if you looked a bit less like a vestal virgin prepared for sacrifice," he said as he stretched out beside her.

She fluttered her eyes open. How could she not look like a virgin when that's exactly what she was?

"What have you got against vestal virgins?"

"Nothing, as long as they stay in the vestal where they can sigh over love poems, moon over a handful of flowers, and whisper inane protestations of undying love to their hearts' content. Give me an experienced woman with a realistic, no-nonsense, no-strings-attached appreciation of sex over a shy, teary-eyed twit-of-a-virgin any day."

And what had made him think she was an experienced woman?

Perhaps her wanton behavior, a little voice inside her head answered. A blush heated her cheeks as she remembered what she had done, and how enthusiastically she'd responded to him, enjoyed his intimate touch. A warm flush suffused her entire body.

"That's what I want to see," he said. "That look says, *kiss me and be quick about it.*"

It did? How had she managed that?

Then he kissed her, and she forgot all about pretending to look experienced, for she was lost in the glorious reality of his lips on her lips, of his tongue as it jousted with hers. He nipped her lower lip, then blew on it, sucked it, and laved it. Then he moved to do the same to her earlobe, her shoulder. He kissed along her collarbone to the small indent at the base of her throat, then traveled lower at an agonizingly slow pace.

Too slow. She wanted to grab his head and push it into position over her breast. Her arms twitched.

"Shall I stop?" he asked, each word punctuated by a kiss.

"Not if you want to live," she said, the words a surprise to herself, the husky tone nearly unrecognizable as her own. She squirmed upward to relieve the pressure on her arms.

"That's what I adore," he said with a chuckle.

What had she done? How could she do it again if she didn't know what it was? If she asked, would he realize she was really naive and turn away in disgust?

He cupped her breasts. "Hello, sweet lovelies. I see you both were expecting me."

What? She raised her head. He had moved until he

lay half across her stomach, and the man was talking to her breasts. Was he crazy? He peeked up at her and winked, as if to let her know he was aware of her watching him.

"See how nicely you both fit into my hands."

His tan, elegant fingers contrasted sharply against the paleness of skin untouched by the sun.

"And see how eagerly you respond to my touch."

He ran his thumbs around each nipple. She not only felt her nipples *ruche* into tight buds; she watched it happen. Then he wet one finger in his mouth, and ran it around the hardened tips. The fascination of seeing what he was doing warred with the need to press her breasts into his hands, his mouth. She could not do both and retain her hold on the rosettes, so she fought the urge, watching as he lowered his head.

"Anticipation," he whispered, his breath delicious on her wet nipple. "Yours and mine."

He paused with his mouth an inch from her breast. Then he flicked the bud with the tip of his tongue.

She couldn't wait any longer. Slamming her head back into the mattress, she arched her back, pushing her breast into his mouth. If he was surprised by the violence of her reaction, it didn't show, for he immediately wrapped his arm under her.

Using his lips and tongue, he lavished one breast while kneading and tweaking the other with his free hand.

She moaned and thrashed, wanting, needing, yet not knowing what she sought. As he lowered her to the bed, she dug in her heels, feeling a coil of need deep inside.

"Tell me what you want," he said, his voice rough and breathless.

She didn't know! How could she tell him when she didn't know? "More," she whispered.

"What? Tell me again." He rolled her nipple between his teeth, while at the same time he lightly pinched the other breast.

"More!" she shouted, but it came out as a guttural rasp. "You know damn well what I want. Do it."

"Ah, Matty, always direct and to the point."

He realized he liked her lack of artifice. She certainly wasn't faking her intense response to his touch. Nor could he deny his physical reaction. He was rock hard and throbbing.

When he stopped kissing her breasts, Matty nearly cried out in dismay. But she bit her lip. So far he had delivered nothing but pleasure, and if there was more, she wanted to experience it. She wasn't totally ignorant of the mechanics of coupling, but so far this encounter had shared little resemblance to barnyard rutting. Perhaps she knew even less than she thought she did. As he smoothed her stomach with the palm of his hand and kissed even lower, a vague uneasiness warred with the delightful anticipation. What was he doing?

She gulped her words of protest, determined not to reveal her naivete, determined to trust him. But it was not easy. Her arms trembled with the effort it took to keep from letting go, the rosettes her anchor to earth while the rest of her body soared in a warm summer sky, wisps of gossamer clouds tingling her skin.

Preston laid his head in the cradle of her rib cage. The staccato of her heartbeat urged him to hurry, but he resisted. He rubbed his cheek against her skin and breathed in her scent. Yet his hands were not idle, ever exploring, seeking new territory to discover, spreading her thighs, touching everywhere but the one spot.

He rolled to a position between her legs. She rocked

her hips against his length and breathed out in little moans.

Why shouldn't he seek his release? In a moment's work he could be inside her. He groaned aloud at the thought. But he had promised, and her woman's pleasure came first.

He slid lower, molding her hips with his hands. He laid claim to her with his mouth, and rode her bucking hips upward without breaking contact.

Matty cried out in surprise, the *no's* of her *oh no no* lost in her panting gasps, sounding more like *oh oh oh*. Then she dissolved into the sensation, coherent thoughts left behind as she shot past the moon and into the heavens, the stars leaving trails of sparks as they grazed against her skin.

Preston slowed his assault, easing her away from her peak, intending to let her enjoy the climb to fulfillment several times. She dug her heels into the mattress to lift her hips, and he smiled at her eagerness.

He slid his arms under her knees and brought her legs to his shoulders. Then he renewed his assault with his tongue and his fingers, using every trick he knew, giving no quarter, and allowing her no respite.

Matty soared higher, faster, the very stars detonating around her. She cried out Preston's name and reached for him, knowing he would anchor her, protect her. She curled her body upward, finding his embrace before exploding into the unknown void.

Chapter 17

When Matty woke, she lay in the curve of Preston's arm. Though he was next to her, the bed covers separated them and had been tucked securely around her.

"How long have I been asleep?" she whispered, her throat dry as if she had been running.

"A minute, maybe two. Is this the first time this has happened to you?"

She supposed there was no point dissembling now. He probably already knew she was a virgin, *had been* a virgin. She ducked her head and nodded.

He smoothed her hair back off her forehead and chuckled. "It's nothing to be ashamed of."

She lifted her chin. "I'm not ashamed. I'm . . ." What could she say? Shocked by what he did? By what she did? "I guess I was a bit surprised, that's all."

Again he chuckled. "Many women never experience it, and others only rarely."

Even though her head was clearing, his conversation seemed to be going in circles, confusing her again. Never? Rare? "What are you talking about?"

"What happened to you. The French call it *le petit mort.*"

"The little death? What an awful name for losing one's virginity."

He sat up straight and stared at her with narrowed eyes.

"What do you mean? Losing one's virginity?"

She rolled her eyes. "Well, I think that's obvious."

"Are you saying you're a virgin?"

"*Was* a virgin. Until a few minutes ago."

"But you have two children?"

Had he lost his mind? "They're adopted." He still looked at her as if she had two heads. "That's why I agreed to help you with your scam." No sign of comprehension. "So I could afford a lawyer to make the adoption official, and then Virginia Henshaw couldn't take them away from me. Strike any memory bells yet?"

"You did *not* tell me your children were adopted."

"Well, if I didn't mention the fact, it was probably because I didn't think it was any of your business." Suddenly it dawned on her. He thought she'd had the children out of wedlock. He thought she was a . . . a woman of loose morals. And just what had she done to disabuse him of the notion, the nasty little voice in her head asked. She didn't want to face the answer. But even if it was well and justly deserved, the insult stung.

Preston scooted off the bed and stood uncertainly by its side. A virgin. The thought staggered him. It was one thing to enjoy an experienced woman regardless of her rank, and quite another to dishonor the virgin granddaughter of a duke.

"This puts making love in a rather different light," he said.

"It's a little late for that now." She grabbed the covers and pulled them up around her neck. She turned her face away. "Please hand me my clothes and turn your back."

"There's no call for dramatics. I'm the soul of discretion."

No reaction from her.

"It's not as if you're ruined," he added. "No one in society will know this happened."

She would still be able to land a titled and wealthy husband, and none would be the wiser. Somehow, the thought gave him little comfort; in fact, quite the opposite. Perhaps that's why his next sentence came out rougher than he intended.

"Stop pouting, Matty. It's not that important."

She turned to him, her eyes shooting daggers even as tears ran down her cheeks. "Maybe to you it's nothing. You probably deflower virgins on a regular basis. One before dinner every Tuesday and Thursday, and two on even-numbered Saturdays. But this is the first and only time I've lost my virginity, and ... and ... Stop laughing. Stop this very instant."

But he could not. He tried to catch his breath to tell her of her mistake, but when she hit him with the pillow, he wound up doubled over and holding his sides. He fell onto the bed and then covered his head with his arms as she pummeled him. Finally, he managed to cry uncle. She stopped.

He uncovered his head hesitantly. She stood on the bed in a fighting stance, a miniature Valkyrie warrior, her weapon raised in one hand, her naked breasts peeking from between strands of wild blond hair. He stared at her as feathers floated down and settled like snow. Only he wasn't the least bit cold. In fact, it was quite warm and close inside the drawn bed curtains.

He cleared his throat. "If you were a virgin this morning . . ."

She raised the now-useless pillow higher. He noted a second reason for being glad she wore no clothes when he remembered she usually carried her derringer in her pocket. Instead, it was safely tucked beside the cushion of the chair. He held up his hand in a halting gesture.

"If you were a virgin this morning, then you are still a virgin now," he said.

"But, we—"

"No. We did not."

She propped one hand on her hip. "I distinctly remember you and I—"

"What you remember is known as a 'woman's pleasure.' Because I didn't physically enter your vagina, your hymen remains as it was, and therefore, the state of your virginity is maintained." He leaned back on his elbows and flashed her a smile. "However, with you standing over me like you are, I am more than ready to remedy that situation."

She threw the pillow at his head and dove for the covers.

His instincts rolled him out of the path, and he extended the motion, propelling his body to a standing position. Whatever she was—virgin, or siren, or both—if he aspired to make sense of anything, it wouldn't happen lying next to her in bed. Especially knowing she was naked. Especially when her scent filled the confined space. Self-control had not been an issue for a number of years. If he couldn't restrain his wayward thoughts, or the reaction of his body to her nearness, then the next best option was to exit the situation.

And yet he hesitated.

"Are you all right?" he asked.

She pulled the covers off her head. "I'm fine. It's back to the vestal for me, undamaged, and a bit the wiser."

"Matty, I—"

"Not now." She managed to keep her chin up. "I

would prefer for you to leave the room for a few minutes."

"Is there anything I can—"

"No, thank you. I believe you've done enough."

He gave her a formal bow, and he backed up several steps. The bed curtains parted, and then, in an instant, fell closed, and it was as if he'd disappeared. She held her breath until she heard the click of the door latch. She threw another pillow in that direction, then sprang from the bed.

How could he act as if nothing had happened? As if changing her world had meant nothing to him. As if she had been a diversion, relief from the stifling boredom of an evening at sea. Perhaps less exciting than a rousing game of chess with the captain, but more thrilling than their pedantic lessons.

To give the devil his due, he had warned her. Once the challenge was over, he'd lost interest quickly. And to a man like Preston, who could have any woman he desired simply by crooking his pinkie and smiling his devastating smile, plain Matilda Maxwell had presented little challenge. Shamefully minute challenge. She certainly would never compare to the desirable, well-dressed, and well-bred women of London's social whirl.

Matty dressed in her robe, wanting to leave as quickly as possible. She threw her nightgown and chemise over her arm. She looked around, but she didn't see her derringer.

She'd only been making a glib comment when she'd said she was a bit the wiser, but perhaps the truth had sprung from her lips. If knowledge preceded wisdom, she'd learned more about herself and her body in one night than in any day prior to this, including the time she'd begun her menses and kind-hearted Belle of MayBelle's Card Parlor and Social Club had taken a

terrified little girl aside and explained the facts of life
to her. That day Matty had learned what it was to be female; today she'd learned what it meant to be a woman.

Almost.

Matty crossed the hall and collapsed in the chair by
the stove. The difference was inside her. Although, according to Preston, she was still technically a virgin,
she didn't feel particularly virginal. She was changed,
and the transformation, albeit incomplete, could not be
reversed.

Preston gave Matty ten minutes to set herself to
rights before returning to his bedroom. She was gone.

He resisted the urge to go after her.

He should feel relief. He'd been saved from making
a huge mistake. Yet, he was not relieved. He was worried about Matty. The cold, controlled woman he'd left
in his bed wasn't the woman he'd come to know. If
she'd yelled at him, raged at him—hell, shot at him—
that would be different.

He was afraid he'd hurt her.

"Bloody hell."

He stomped across the hall and knocked lightly on
the door.

"Matty?"

"Go away."

"We need to talk."

"I'm sleeping."

"Open the door."

He waited impatiently, then raised his hand to knock
again.

The door flew open. She stood a few feet from him,
her eyes flashing, her naked breasts heaving beneath

the thin silk wrapper. So much for his worry she would be crying her eyes out.

"If you're feeling guilty for not taking my virginity," she said, "please don't concern yourself. I'm sure I can find someone in London in the next day or two to complete the job you started."

She slammed the door in his face.

He grinned. Now that was the Matty he knew and loved.

The last thought staggered him. He was no longer in danger of falling in love; it had happened.

"Matty."

"Go away."

"We've already had that conversation."

"And it's over. I'm not listening to you."

"Either open this door or I'll bust it down!" he yelled.

She whipped the door open. "Hush. You'll wake the children."

"Then let me in and I'll talk in a normal voice."

"No. Edith could wake and find you here." She looked him up and down. "In your pajamas. And by the way, your pants are on inside out."

He grabbed her arm and pulled her across the hall to his room, shut the door behind him, and blocked it with his body.

"What are you doing?" She tried to push him away, but her size was no match for him.

"I want more," he said.

"What?"

He took a step toward her, and she backed up a step.

"Are you drunk or crazy?"

"Neither," he said, taking another step. "I'm hungry. Greedy. Unsatisfied. I want more. I want you."

She turned and ran, climbing on the bed in order to

circle around to the now-unprotected door. Feathers stirred, and before they settled, he sidestepped, blocking her path.

"Is this what you call rapidly losing interest?" she asked. She stood in the middle of the bed, wary, ready to counter if he lunged at her, ready to run in any direction the minute she saw an opening.

But he did not lunge. He sat in the chair and pulled out her pistol that had been tucked beside the cushion. He pointed it at her. "If you don't want to talk, then take off your clothes."

"That's not fair."

"Turnabout is fair play."

"Not very original." She crossed her arms over her breasts.

"I'm serious."

"You wouldn't shoot me."

"No? You shot me. Again, turnabout is fair play."

"Are you trying to scare me?"

"No, just trying to get you to listen to me. Preferably naked."

"Why naked?"

"Because then you're less likely to run away should I take my eyes off you for a moment. Of course, if you're naked, it's not likely I'll look away for any reason. Not even if the ship was under attack and on fire."

"Really?"

She sounded pleased.

Finally he'd managed to say something right.

"On one condition," she said. "You take off your clothes, too."

His incredulity must have shown on his face because she added, "I don't want to be the only naked person in the room."

That meant he would have to put down the gun. If

he'd read her wrong, and he was never quite sure how to read her, then she would have the chance to get away. With but a moment's hesitation he chucked the derringer across the room and shucked his clothing.

When he looked up again, she was not only naked but she was kicking the feathers to make a clear place on the bed.

"Here," he said, holding out his hand.

She walked to him, and to his surprise, jumped, wrapping her arms around his neck and her legs around his waist. He grabbed her with one arm, and with the other, swept the coverlet and all the feathers aside. She shifted her weight, and the movement nearly unbalanced him. With a little squeal, she grabbed for the bedpost. That move caused the tip of his penis to rub against her, already hot and wet and ready for him.

She moaned with pleasure and sought his mouth in a searing kiss.

Although he would have taken her differently the first time, her body demanded immediate entry. Bracing his back against the post, he pushed the tip of his penis inside her. She moved her legs, pinning him tightly against the smooth wood. He ducked his head to take her nipple into his mouth, rolling the bud against his tongue and teeth. She arched back, holding on to his biceps for an anchor.

With one hand on each hip, he drove into her, breaking past her hymen quickly to spare her as much pain as possible. She took in a sharp breath, but he held her firmly against him. He cautioned himself to remain still. As a virgin, she would need a few minutes to get used to him inside her.

She blinked. And he was afraid he'd hurt her.

"I'm sorry I hurt you."

"No, it's not that."

She wiggled her derriere a bit, and he groaned with the sensation.

"I think you like that," she said, wiggling a bit more.

He clamped her hips firmly in place.

"Be still or I won't . . ."

"Won't what?"

"Are you in pain?"

She thought about it for a moment. "No. Is this supposed to be painful? Because I can tell you right now—"

"It's only painful the first time."

"Nope, no pain. A little uncomfortable, kind of a full feeling, but definitely not painful. Actually rather pleasant."

"Then why were you crying?"

"I wasn't crying."

"I saw you blinking away tears."

She looked confused; then, as if she suddenly remembered, she inexplicably smiled.

"Oh that. I'd thought earlier when I first touched you that there was no way you would fit inside me, not as big as you are, and yet you did. I was surprised, that's all."

He laughed and held her close.

"You are a wonder, Matty Maxwell."

In more ways than one. He had never carried on a conversation while inside a woman before. He had never laughed while making love. But then again, Matty was not just any woman.

His deep laughter had caused his body to move, which in turn caused Matty's eyes to widen and her mouth to make a little *oh* of surprise. Perfect for kissing. A perfect opening. He kissed her, sliding his tongue in and out, mimicking the movement with gentle motions of his hips.

Matty quickly caught the rhythm and soon added little variations of her own, a side-to-side motion and an offbeat hesitation that drove him wild. He would not last much longer, and he wanted her to come before him.

He pulled her hands free of the post and laid her on the bed driving in deep and hard.

Matty gasped. She tried to pay attention to what he was doing so she could respond in kind, but her thoughts kept scattering, lost in the wonderful sensations of his hands and his mouth and the feeling of him inside her. She gave in and let her body function on instinct, matching his thrusts. He covered her belly with one hand, and his thumb found a magic spot that sent her flying among the clouds, to the stars.

She cried out his name. He drove into her. Harder. Faster. Harder. Pumping the stars into explosive fireworks.

She wrapped her legs around his waist. He leaned back, holding his weight off her, surging into her. He growled, a deep animal sound, a primal call that spoke to her in a way no words could. Another thrust. And he arched his back, filling her as deep as possible. He held that position, and warmth flooded her. She zoomed back to the stars once more.

When she came to her senses, she lay in his arms.

"Try to sleep," he said, tucking the blanket around her.

"Can we do it again?"

He chuckled. "Not right away. I need a bit of time to recover."

She snuggled against his chest. "Wake me when you're ready."

"You should wait a few days after your first time. You may be sore in some places."

She popped her head up and smiled at him. "I feel wonderful."

"Do you remember the first time you rode a horse on a long, extended gallop?"

"Yes, it was glorious."

"And do you remember the next day?"

"Oh." She laid her head back on his chest. "So how long do we have to wait?"

"We'll see. Now try to sleep." By tomorrow she would know the truth. That he had tricked her and lied to her.

"I'm not a bit sleepy," she said around a huge yawn.

He knew he should get her back to her room, and yet the precious moments of holding her in his arms were numbered. By tomorrow she would know the truth and she would hate him.

Preston watched the dawn from the railing of the ship and therefore was among the first to see the small boat rowing out to their anchorage. Kelso alighted with a message from Marsfield.

Preston ripped open the seal. After reading it, he slapped it against his hand. "Did you read this?"

"Yes, sir. Lord Marsfield allowed me to read it yesterday afternoon before he sealed it because I would have so many errands to run."

"Why does he want me to put Lady Matilda up at Stiles Manor? I thought I was to drop her off at Norbundshire's."

"I'm sure I don't know, milord."

"Good God, doesn't he realize my mother could well be in residence for the holidays? She positively hates the country in winter. Surely, he doesn't expect me to subject Matty to The Dragon."

He paced the deck. What could Marsfield be thinking? What was going on with Norbundshire? Then it
occurred to Preston the old man might have died. He
inquired, but again Kelso admitted to knowing nothing.
Preston paced some more. If Norbundshire was dead,
he couldn't just leave Matty on his doorstep as he had
expected to do. And yet, Preston didn't have enough information to make another plan.

He would not take Matty to Stiles Manor, though,
and that was final.

"I'll leave immediately to meet with Marsfield and
find out what's going on. You stay here. I should return
in a few hours, but if I'm not back by the time you disembark, settle them in a nice hotel."

"Sir, I have taken the liberty of—"

But Preston wasn't listening. He was already focused on the upcoming meeting with Marsfield.
"Leave word of their location at the town house. I'll
check back there as soon as possible."

"But, sir, I—"

"No time to argue." Preston did not even have
enough time to go back and tell Matty good-bye, as the
lighter that had brought his valet was preparing to
leave. In truth, he could probably request that the boat
wait for him, but he had no idea what to say to Matty.
And not because of the previous night.

Something about this matter was very wrong.

If he was going to be the one to have the unpleasant
task of telling her the truth, he would wait until he
knew the whole story.

Chapter 18

Matty woke and rolled over, reaching for Preston, but only cool sheets met her touch. Then she heard Edith moving about the room, enough warning to cover her eyes as the maid opened the bed curtains.

"Rise and shine," Edith said, her tone much too chipper. "The children are dressed and fed and making the rounds with Mr. Kelso, saying their proper good-byes. Mr. Kelso says we're to be ready to leave within the hour."

Matty sat up and pushed her hair out of her face. So that was the reason Edith was singing like a morning lark. The ubiquitous Kelso had returned.

The maid sat a breakfast tray on Matty's lap.

"You'd better eat-up quick. You forgot to braid your hair before bed and, from the looks of it, you had a restless night. It's going to take a good twenty minutes just to brush it out."

Matty hid a secret smile behind her coffee cup. Restless, indeed.

"Is there any word from Preston?" she asked, making her tone casual and indifferent.

"Oh, he was gone before dawn," Edith chattered as she laid out a rose-colored dress for Matty to wear. "Off to run some errand or other. Sometimes I don't know what to make of that man. Oh, I know he's helped you and all, but I can't say I'd trust him over-much. Here one minute and gone the next. Mr. Kelso would only say that Lord Bathers had to see a friend. Sounds fishy to me. I mean, what kind of friend does one call on before breakfast?"

Matty set aside her tray, no longer hungry. Not only had Preston not left her a note, he'd left without so much as a word of when he would return. Or even if he would return. She rose from the bed, and winced in pain.

"Is something wrong? What is it?"

"I think I sprained my ankle," she lied. "Perhaps I should wrap it in gauze for support." She gave Edith a brave smile. The places Matty hurt, no bandage could help.

Preston paced a circuit around the parlor, impatiently stopping at the door each time to look up at the empty staircase. Finally, Marsfield appeared, as tousled as Preston had ever seen the usually impeccably dressed man.

"You're a mess," Preston said.

Marsfield glared at him and motioned for the butler to serve the coffee. "Any man uncivilized enough to call at this ungodly hour doesn't merit the courtesy of grooming."

"Your note did say as soon as possible."

"Damn it, man. I didn't mean it literally."

Preston took the coffee cup from the butler and added a dollop of whiskey to it before handing it to Marsfield. "A bit of the hair of the dog that bit you. I take it you had a late night?"

Marsfield gulped his drink, then closed his eyes for a long minute. "Another one of Anne's bloody charity balls. Boring as all hell, but she couldn't leave until the very end because she was one of the hostesses." He put his hand to his head. "I think I drank too much. I remember leaving to play cards with Wilbur, but not much after that."

Preston accepted a cup of coffee. Curious. Not at all like his friend to overindulge.

After Marsfield dismissed the butler, and the man had closed the parlor door, Preston turned to his friend.

All vestiges of a drunken night were gone. Marsfield dumped his coffee into a nearby planter, and he refilled his cup. "Hair of the dog, bah!" He set his cup on the table next to him, ran his fingers through his hair, and straightened his dressing jacket.

Preston raised an eyebrow.

"I met with a contact last night. The ball was a good cover until I was held over by circumstances and needed a reason for returning so late."

"Does this have anything to do with Lady Matilda?"

"Why would you ask that?"

"A gut feeling. Does it?"

"Not directly."

"Even if it's indirectly, I'd like to know."

Marsfield gave him an assessing look. "Why?"

Preston did have a gut feeling, and it wasn't a pleasant one. "No particular reason. Matty, rather, Lady Matilda, is currently my responsibility, and I should know of anything that affects her."

"I'll think on it."

Preston knew from experience he would get no more information until Marsfield deemed it appropriate. In the past, he would have waited, albeit impatiently. But this time the matter involved Matty.

"Be quick about it. I'm not leaving until I know everything you do concerning Lady Matilda."

Marsfield raised an eyebrow.

"Please," Preston added.

"I should think you would want to call on Norbundshire and have the matter concluded as soon as possible. Then I have an assignment for you in India. Quite an interesting—"

"Hang bloody India. I'm . . . Wait a minute. Why should I call on Norbie? Shouldn't Lady Matilda pay the call?"

"Might be a bit of a shock to the old man, and the reception could be a bit sticky since he's not expecting her. Might refuse to see her."

Preston jumped up so fast his empty coffee cup slipped off the saucer and fairly flew across the room. "You sent me halfway round the world to fetch her, and Norbundshire doesn't even know she's coming? Whose crazy idea was this?"

"The queen's."

Preston sank into the chair. Now what was he going to do?

"Her Majesty feels strongly about the importance of family," Marsfield continued. "She wants the duke to reconcile with his granddaughter and decided that if the woman was nearby she could be produced at the first sign Norbundshire might change his mind."

"Strike while the iron is lukewarm?"

"Er, yes, you could say that."

"And which fool has been chosen for the task of convincing the old curmudgeon to relent?"

"Why, you, of course."

Preston leaned back and closed his eyes. "Why did I know that would be the answer?"

"Then it was superfluous to ask the question."

"Call it wishful thinking." Convincing a cantankerous old man of something he'd set his mind against harked back to Preston's unpleasant meetings with his father. He'd never had much success at that either. There had to be someone else. He sat forward and propped his elbows on his knees. "This is just the sort of diplomatic imbroglio Burke would find fascinating. He would do a much better—"

"He does not know the woman as you do."

And never would! Despite the outlandish surge of jealousy, Preston managed to keep his face impassive.

"You, on the other hand, will be able to present the woman's good qualities. She does have some?"

"Of course. She's—"

"Save it for the duke. I personally don't care if she has two heads and a tattoo on her left hip. That's just in case you thought about volunteering me for the job."

"With all due respect—"

"Her Majesty is confident you will perform your duty with the keenness and creativity you have demonstrated in the past. Those are her words, not mine."

Preston groaned. If the queen was aware he'd been assigned, there was no way out except to fail. And this time, more than his reputation was at stake. Matty's future depended upon his success. They were both doomed.

"I concur with her opinion," Marsfield added. "I have every confidence in your abilities."

Preston had no choice. "I'll call upon Norbundshire this afternoon." He didn't bother keeping the defeatism from his voice.

"He's at his country estate."

"Damn." He couldn't catch a lucky break. Norbundshire was a day's ride on horseback in good weather, and at this time of year, the country lanes would be no better than muck. A carriage, while more comfortable, would add another day, minimum, and that was predicated on the roads being passable. Not a good bet. He resigned himself to a long, cold, miserable trip.

"And the other matter?" He hated to ask, somehow knowing it would be more bad news. "The one indirectly connected to Matty?"

"I've been doing a little investigating into Edgar Walmsley."

Preston had attended Eton at the same time as Walmsley. At least until "Wormsy" had been sent down for cheating on his Latin conjugation exam, though rumor had had him guilty of torturing the headmaster's cat. Since then they'd run into each other now and again at the gaming tables. Never the same table. Preston had enough sense not to sit down with a poor player who was also a poor loser. By repute, Walmsley had some nasty habits. Needless to say, they didn't move in the same circles.

"What's Wormsy up to these days? Opium? Slavery? Reviving the Hellfire Club?"

"He's Norbundshire's heir. A distant connection, but since Chauncey Smythe was lost at sea, and Matthew Carleton and his brother Merton were killed in that carriage accident, Walmsley's next in line to inherit."

"That's not good." Hard to believe Matty could be related to such a worthless human being, no matter how distant the connection.

"The man seems to have turned over a new leaf," Marsfield said with a shrug. "Since being named heir, his behavior has been exemplary."

"An apple may look perfect on the outside, but cut deep enough and you'll find the rot, and the worm."

"Or you may simply find the apple core."

"You think he could change that much?" Preston didn't believe it for a minute.

"I can't condemn a man without evidence." Marsfield stood, indicating the meeting was over. "However, I will say my investigation is ongoing."

"I presume you'll keep me posted." He also stood and shook the other man's hand.

"Good luck with Norbundshire."

"Thank you," Preston said. He was going to need it.

Matty hesitated on the doorstep, looking around as she wiped her boots more than necessary. When Kelso had said he was taking them to Preston's town house, she hadn't expected anything so grand. One of six attached houses, the white curving facade of the building faced a round central park flanked by two more buildings of the same graceful design.

The weather seemed much milder than it had the past two weeks at sea, but she had no other reference point to compare. In the park, five children bundled up to their eyeballs played kick ball under the watchful attention of two governesses, a uniformed nanny pushed a pram, and under an arbor, an elderly couple sat on one of the decorative wrought-iron benches. She noticed Nathan gazing longingly at the play area and pushed him ahead of her inside the door.

"First things first. Unpack, and then play."

The entry hall was decorated with simple elegance. The intricate wallpaper depicted a Far Eastern flower garden with bridges and waterfalls and fantastically dressed people strolling the white shell paths. Trees, stately pagodas, and magnificent temples rose to the tall ceiling where colorful birds flew overhead.

In the center of the entrance, a round glass and gilt table held a large Oriental vase of mostly blues and greens that echoed the hues in the checkered marble floor. Instead of the usual flowers in the vase, an arrangement of tall peacock and ostrich feathers drew her eye toward the elaborately carved staircase. Along that wall, an imperial procession, including regal litters, mounted warriors, and elephants, climbed toward the stately palace depicted on the landing.

Matty looked closer and saw that the lanterns that would light the hall at night were designed to fit into the artwork so perfectly it would look as if the miniature people had lit their lamps. She felt like a giant who had stepped into a strange and wonderful world.

"It's amazing," she said. Was this his real home or just something rented for the scam?

"His Lordship commissioned it when we were in Japan a few years back." Kelso bowed and motioned her toward the stairs. "It depicts the emperor's estate in Hokkaido." He motioned to the landing with his chin. "A small country house."

"You mean it's a real place?" She stepped closer. Bess reached out for one of the women figures as if she would have another doll. Matty pulled her hand back, not wanting her to leave messy fingerprints.

"And real people," Kelso said. "The emperor, his family, and his entourage. That's Colonel Hempstaid having tea, and Sir Burton conferring with the elders in the temple. Preston is up there in the litter with Princess Sakura." He snorted. "The artist, Kazuhiro Fujiwara, liked to think he had a sense of humor. None of us ever got anywhere near the princess, much less talked to her. Although we did see her from afar several times."

"And are you in the picture?"

Kelso snorted again. "Yes, but Fujiwara didn't like me any more than I liked him."

Edith went from figure to figure. "I can't find you." The valet sighed and shook his head as if giving in

to the inevitable. "I'm the one walking behind the elephant with the big shovel."

Matty struggled to keep a straight face, but Edith
failed to cover her mouth quickly enough and a giggle
escaped.

Obviously this was Preston's home. He must be
doing quite well at his chosen profession.

"I thought I heard someone out here." A slim, gray-
haired woman entered from the rear of the house,
wiping her hands on an oversize apron.

Kelso introduced the housekeeper, Mrs. Toni Manor.

"Welcome. I hope you'll soon feel at home."

Matty doubted it, but she returned the woman's
friendly smile. "Thank you." She introduced Edith and
the children.

"You will excuse all the hubbub, won't you? It's always sixes and sevens when His Lordship shows up.
Never gives us any warning, does he?"

Matty nodded and shook her head and didn't get a
word in edgewise. Mrs. Manor obviously didn't expect
an answer to her questions. Edith had a rival in the say-
as-many-words-in-one-breath-as-possible department.

"We've opened all the rooms. Lady Marsfield is upstairs supervising the last of preparations. Gone
through this house like a whirlwind, she has. Her and
that Miss Mayberry she brought along to help with the
children's rooms? She's a wonder, that woman. Don't
you think so?"

Matty nodded, but she wasn't sure whom the housekeeper referred to.

"Why, we've had a parade of tradesmen in and out
since early this morning. Carting in furniture and
boxes. Airing the drapes and beating the carpets. Insisted I hire two chambermaids and a footman to help.
Can you imagine that?"

Matty shook her head, imagining burly tradesmen airing out drapes.

Mrs. Manor turned to Kelso. "You won't recognize the upstairs," she said, giving him a warning look.

"She wouldn't dare change anything in his private rooms."

"No. At least I don't think so. But nothing else in the house has been left untouched."

The valet slid open double pocket doors whose presence had been hidden within the wallpaper design. "His Lordship is not going to like this."

Matty peeked over his shoulder. She didn't know what she expected, but she could see nothing amiss in the lovely green and gold parlor.

"And that's not all she did," Mrs. Manor said in a conspiratorial whisper. "She got into an argument with Henri and she fired—"

"I'm sure the rest of your litany can wait until your guests have at least removed their hats and coats," said a well-modulated voice from midway down the stairs.

Matty looked up to see a tall, beautiful woman in a stylish green dress seemingly float down the rest of the steps.

Mrs. Manor curtsied and apologized at the same time.

"You must be Lady Matilda," the woman said.

Kelso did the honors.

"Call me Matty," she said, still unused to her role.

"And I'm Anne. I'm sure we're going to be friends."

Matty doubted that would happen in the few days she'd be in London, but she smiled in response.

"Kelso, please get the footman and see to the luggage," Anne said, taking charge. "Mrs. Manor, if you would show everyone upstairs, Miss Mayberry can help Miss Franklin and the children get settled. Lady

Matilda and I will have tea in the parlor. I'm sure she can use a pick-me-up, and I'm positively parched." She hooked her arm through Matty's and turned her to the left. "We can get acquainted, and you can tell me all about your adventures with Preston."

"Pardon?" Matty said, blinking. Just how much did Anne already know? She certainly was free with ordering his servants about, and if what Mrs. Manor had said was true, also quite free with his money. Was Anne party to the scam? Another accomplice necessary to making everything look right? Possibly an unwitting accomplice? Until Matty knew more, she would simply play along and reveal as little as possible.

"Oh, I've known him for years," Anne said. "Being with Preston is always an adventure."

"Do you think so? Actually, the trip was quite tedious," Matty said, taking a seat on the green brocade settee.

Anne flashed her a quizzical look; then she smiled. "He is very handsome."

"If you like the dark, brooding type."

"I've heard Preston described in many ways, some quite colorful, but *brooding* was never one of them."

Matty was saved a reply by the entrance of a young maid staggering under the weight of a large, silver tray. The ladies confined their talk to the subject of children while the maid set out the tea things.

"Shall I pour?" Anne asked.

"Please do." Matty smiled, but the other woman's ease stepping into the role of hostess did not please her. It bespoke a familiarity beyond acquaintance. Anne was just the sort of woman a man like Preston should have—beautiful, elegant, and sophisticated. Everything Matty was not.

Anne dismissed the maid and then asked, "Cream or lemon?" as she filled a delicate china cup.

"Sugar. Two, please." Matty watched the other woman's every move in the futile hope she would one day be capable of such effortless grace.

"For the record, I do like dark, brooding types. When you meet Lord Marsfield, you'll see why," she said, her lips curling up at the corners in a cat-got-the-cream smile. "Biscuit?"

She noted the way Anne's eyes sparkled when she mentioned her husband, and Matty suddenly felt much more friendly toward the other woman. "Yes, please. I do believe I will have one."

"Have you heard from Preston? I quite expected him to be here by now."

Matty stiffened. He had not left her so much as a note, and yet this woman seemed to know of his plans.

Anne seemed to read her thoughts because she leaned over and patted Matty's hand. "Marsfield expected Preston to call on him this morning," she explained. "I simply surmised this would be the first place he would come after his appointment." She smiled. "Especially since you are already here."

"What Preston does with his time is of no concern to me." Since Matty hardly sounded convincing to herself, she wouldn't be surprised if Anne didn't believe her. "I have better things to do with my time than worry about his whereabouts."

"I see. And I do understand. With children and the holidays, there is always so much to do. Why, the decorating alone is a job in itself. I haven't done anything along those lines because I thought you might have some ideas, some family traditions or such that you'd want to incorporate."

Matty looked around. Her whole house would fit inside the one large room. "Not really," she said in a small voice, overwhelmed by the thought of the task. Preston hadn't said she would be expected to do anything like that. "Anything you want to do is fine with me."

"Wonderful," Anne said, clapping her hands. "I do love to decorate, and I've always thought this would be a perfect room for a Christmas party."

She proceeded to regale Matty with descriptions of evergreen swags over the mantels of the twin fireplaces, holly and mistletoe balls, and some newfangled idea that Prince Albert had brought from his homeland of putting a whole tree in the room and lighting it with candles. Anne fairly danced around the room, describing what would go where.

Matty shook her head. "That seems like a lot of trouble to go through for—"

"But it will be fun."

Fun? Matty felt the wide gulf that separated her from a woman like Anne. An ocean of difference. So much work and expense, for what? Christmas was less than a week away, and she and the children could well be opening their presents on a ship returning home. Again she shook her head. "I can't—"

"The children will love it. My two will show them how to make paper chains. We already have yards and yards of them at my house. And we'll ask Cook to make gingerbread men."

Anne continued her listing, and Matty began to see her point. In truth, her children would adore all the activity. How could she deny them after upsetting their lives and dragging them halfway around the world? Even if they had to leave London in a precipitous manner at least they would have enjoyable occupation in the meantime.

"All right," Matty said, throwing up her hands in surrender. "But I have no idea where to even start."

"Don't worry. I'll handle everything." Anne rubbed her hands together. "I was so afraid this would be a boring holiday. You see, my sister Letty usually comes with her brood, and that always creates excitement of one sort or another. But this year they're visiting his relatives. And my brother, Robert, he's such a dear that you'll love him on sight; he's on his honeymoon and doing the grand tour he didn't get a chance to do when he was younger, so they won't be back until spring."

Matty nodded, pretending an interest in people she would never have the chance to meet. A tiny kernel of regret burned in her breast.

"Listen to me babble. It's just that I'm so excited. We should start—"

A loud thump interrupted her. It sounded as if something had fallen against the wall. Something big. Both women jumped up.

"Damn it, man."

She recognized Preston's voice.

"Be careful with that bloody thing." Another bump sounded against the wall, not as loud. "What the hell is going on?"

Chapter 19

Matty stood with Anne in the parlor doorway and stared at Preston. He held the Oriental vase under one arm, the feathers inside of it forming an exotic fan across his chest. A workman carrying a ladder tried to maneuver his ladder around to take it out the back door, but he tangled it with another ladder that another workman was bringing down the stairs.

"This'll only take a minute, Guv'nor."

"Just take it out the front door," Preston said.

"Can't do that, Guv'nor. Wouldn't be right." The workman finally jockeyed his ladder free and carried it down the hall toward the rear of the house. The second man followed.

Preston seemed to sense their watchful presence and spun around. "Matty. What are you—"

"I don't know what you're so upset about," Anne said. "They're only doing their job."

"He nearly knocked me over, and then he nearly broke this," Preston said, pointing to the vase. "Yuan Dynasty. Fourteenth century. Irreplaceable."

"Then perhaps you should store it away while there are children staying in the house," Anne said.

A footman ducked under the ladder and took the vase; then he too disappeared toward the back of the house.

Preston had handed over his prize without a second glance. "There aren't . . ." He stopped and did a double take. "Just a minute. You there." When the young man didn't reappear, he turned to Anne. "Who was that?"

"Who?"

"The footman," he said, pointing in the direction the young man dressed in green had taken.

"That was Giles. The footman."

"I don't have a footman. And why was he wearing Stiles livery?"

"I could hardly ask him to perform his duties naked."

"Anne," he said in a warning tone, and glared at her.

"My tea is getting cold," she replied with a sweet smile. With a graceful sweep of her skirts, she returned to the parlor.

He looked around the hall before he said to Matty in an urgent whisper, "What are you doing here? I told Kelso to take you to a hotel."

So now he spoke to her. After Anne left. He had never intended for her and the children to stay in his house. How could he treat her so callously after last night?

She had no one to blame but herself. She had initiated their lovemaking, thrown herself at him in a most wanton manner. He had simply complied with her wishes. Still, it hurt to mean so little that she wasn't even worthy of being a guest in his house.

Of course, she did mean something to him. As his business partner, she held the key to a vault of riches. He couldn't pull off the scam without her. She straightened her shoulders. She wasn't going to let him uproot her and the children again. Whether he liked it or not, she would play out the rest of the hand he'd dealt—from his house, and on her own timetable. She was not going to leave until after Christmas.

"I do not like hotels," she said, spinning on her heel. She resumed her seat in the parlor.

"Kelso!" he yelled up the stairs.

"More tea, please?" she asked Anne.

"Certainly."

"Kelso!" he bellowed even louder.

"And another biscuit, I think." Matty ignored the sound of Preston stomping up the stairs. Not only would he never harm the children, Edith would protect them with her life. Kelso might not fare so well under Preston's ire, but Edith would protect him as well, if needed. She turned her attention to Anne, her newest ally. "You were saying about the decorations . . ."

Preston pulled up his collar against the mean drizzle as his horse plodded along through the unending mud. Perhaps he should have used the carriage. It could hardly have been any slower going, and if he had to travel into the country in order to see Norbundshire, at least he would have been comfortable.

But no, he hadn't wanted to wait for the carriage to be brought out, and the horses to be hitched. He'd been in too much of a hurry to leave.

Oh, Kelso claimed he had tried to tell him Lady Marsfield had learned of their arrival through no fault of his, of course. Kelso also vowed he'd had no knowledge of her plans, other than her insistence Lady Matilda could not properly stay in a hotel. Since when had Anne become an arbiter of propriety? And if she was so concerned about Matty's reputation, why didn't she put her up at Marsfield House? They had room. If she had set out to upset his life on purpose, she couldn't have done better.

He took another sip of brandy from his flask, pacing

his drinks so he wouldn't arrive on Old Norbie's doorstep dead drunk. Hell with that. He took a deep slug.

Damn the brandy for reminding him of Matty's kisses. But he would not think about that. Better to hold on to his anger.

Then, to top it off, Anne had insisted he could not stay in his own house. His own house! He could go to a hotel, or stay with Burke, or go to his club. Or to Hades, her tone had said, and his valet had handed him a bag, already packed. All to protect little Matty's precious reputation. Her steadfast champions. Guardians of her virtue.

Hah! If they only knew.

He took another drink. Matty. The woman who had demanded at gunpoint that he strip off his clothes. The woman who had jumped into his arms, naked and oh-so-willing. A wildcat with a purr as big as her heart.

His friends would succeed where he had failed. They would protect her from him.

That was the real crux of his anger. Being with her had not sated his appetite, only whetted it for more. How was he ever going to bypass the determined defenders of morality and be alone with her again? How was he to survive if he could not?

Perhaps it was for the best. Matty would certainly be better off without him. As soon as he brought this mission to a close, he would take the India job Marsfield had mentioned. Maybe from the other side of the world he could forget her.

Preston doubted it would work, but it was his only choice.

But first he would have to insure Matty's future by convincing Norbundshire to accept his granddaughter. Preston capped the flask and put it away.

* * *

"I'm here to see Lord Norbundshire," Preston said, handing the butler his card even though the door had opened a mere six inches.

"One moment." The butler, a skeleton of a man with a hangdog expression, closed the door.

Preston bristled at the discourtesy. Making him wait on the stoop was sheer insolence. Especially in such inclement weather. And where was the stable boy for his horse? The poor animal deserved a good rubdown and a bucket of oats for his service.

He tapped his foot and counted to ten, then rapped with the brass knocker again. The same man opened the door in the same manner, sticking out his bony hand to hand back the calling card.

"The duke is not at home."

When the butler started to shut the door again, Preston stuck his foot in the way. Enough rudeness. Even if the duke was not at home to callers, the decent thing to do would be to offer a bit of hospitality to a weary traveler. A hot drink and a few minutes in front of the fire would not only be appreciated; it was the minimum to be expected.

Preston strong-armed the door open and strode into the foyer as the butler stumbled back, hanging on to the door handle. He turned, flipped off his wet cloak and hat, and held them out. The butler ignored him, staring past his shoulder.

"Never mind, Stanford. I'll see to Lord Bathers."

Preston recognized the oily voice.

The butler bowed and, as he stood, Preston thrust his cloak and hat into the man's hands. "Please see these are dried and brushed," he said before turning away.

"Hello, Walmsley. Imagine meeting you here. I hadn't heard they'd closed every hellhole in London."

Walmsley ignored his comment and spoke to the butler instead. "Be quick about it. Lord Bathers won't be staying long." He waved the servant away with orders to bring tea to the library.

"I wouldn't know about London," Walmsley continued as he motioned for Preston to precede him through a door on the right side of the foyer. "I've reformed my wicked ways—"

"The whores must be in mourning."

"And I've dedicated myself to making the last days of the duke's as comfortable as possible." His expression conveyed a mixture of sadness and sanctimoniousness.

"I'm here to see His Grace."

"So I gathered. My great uncle is unwell and not receiving unexpected visitors."

"He's not your great uncle."

"Well, great-uncle-three-times-removed is such an unwieldy mouthful," Walmsley said, motioning to an uncomfortable-looking chair covered in black horsehair. "The meaning is much the same."

In other words, he was the heir to the title, and that was all that counted. Preston took the maroon velvet-covered chair nearest the meager fire. "Stanford did not bother to present my card."

"Why do you say that?"

"Unless he's a world-class sprinter, which I seriously doubt, he could have hardly made it to the duke's chamber and back to the door so quickly."

"How do you know the duke is in his chamber?"

"You said he was unwell."

"Stanford was simply trying to save himself steps when he knew the inevitable answer. All the servants are aware the duke is dying and at home to only his oldest friends. Even they are a strain on his delicate condition, and I would forbid them, too, if I could."

Preston kept his face impassive despite his recognition of the slight slip of the tongue. Walmsley was the one who had decided Norbundshire would not see him.

The butler arrived, and Preston accepted a cup of weak tea. At least it was hot.

"I'll tell you what," Walmsley said. "I'll present your card to my great uncle myself while you drink your tea."

Preston handed over a card, and Walmsley scurried off.

After a long moment, the man seated in the corner shadows finally spoke. "You won't get in to see him, you know."

Preston had noticed the man right away and had been curious why Walmsley had neither spoken to him nor introduced him. "I surmised as much earlier."

He leaned forward. "Then why—"

"So I could drink my tea without the irritant of Walmsley's presence."

The man sank back into his seat.

"And so I could speak to you. Who are you and why are you here?"

"My name's Collins, James Arthur Collins. I've been the duke's man of business for six months, ever since my father passed on. I've been here every day for two weeks, and that great nephew, or whatever he is, won't let me see the duke. I don't like Walmsley. He scares me."

The man rose and took the seat on the opposite side of the fireplace. Preston was a bit surprised the man was well past middle age. His father must have been ancient. Collins was pale and portly. Obviously spent a lot of time hunched over his books.

"My business with the duke is quite urgent, sir. If you could help me in any way to see him—"

"Exactly what is the nature of your business?"

The man sat back with an affronted expression. "I cannot disclose private information."

"Thank you, Mr. Collins. You've just told me all I need to know." He stood and placed his empty teacup on a nearby table.

"I've told you nothing."

"You've told me you're an honest man," Preston said, taking the other man under the arm and hauling him to a standing position. "Come along, Mr. Collins."

"Wh-where are we going?"

"We're going to see Norbundshire."

Collins broke free of Preston's grasp, and he stumbled back to his original seat to retrieve his leather satchel. "Thank you, sir."

"Stay close. We make a bigger target that way."

"I beg your pardon?"

"Nothing. Just a bit of battlefield humor."

"I'm sure I wouldn't understand."

Preston gave the man an encouraging pat on the shoulder, and then threw open the library door. He strode right past Walmsley, who was returning, and Collins scurried in his wake.

"Where do you think you're going?" his host called after him.

"I don't think I'm going; I am going. I came all this way to see Norbundshire, and that's exactly what I intend to do."

"I'm with him," Collins mumbled, so close behind Preston they could have kept warm with the same cloak.

"Come back here. Just who do you think you are?"

"I don't think I am—I know I am—Davies Preston,

Viscount Bathers." He didn't slow his pace, but he didn't rush either. Mr. Collins puffed behind him like a steam engine. "Really, Walmsley, I know you failed grammar, but you could at least try to better your speech once a mistake is pointed out."

They had almost arrived at the main landing where the stairs split to reach the two wings of the house, and Preston had no idea which way to turn.

"To the right, Lord Bathers."

"Thank you, Mr. Collins."

"Come back!" Walmsley yelled. "I'll call the constable!"

"I would be pleased to meet him," Preston called back. "Everyone is so friendly in this part of the country."

When they were out of sight of the foyer, Preston put his arm under the older man's and hurried him along.

"The door at the end of the hall," he said, huffing and puffing.

"Mr. Collins, it's my educated guess Walmsley is now searching for a weapon, and will soon be after us. Probably a dueling pistol, but that's pure conjecture."

"Oh, dear. What are we going to do?"

"We're going to run," Preston said, putting his words into action and fairly dragging poor Mr. Collins down the long hall. Though to give the man his due, he tried. He'd probably never run so fast in all his life. Then again, he'd probably never been chased by a man with a gun.

Matty shook her head. "I like the holly wreath better."

"But the bay leaves smell so nice," Anne said from

her position standing on a chair. She was so tall she could reach all but the highest points from the floor.

"Except no one is going to be climbing on top of the fireplace like you are. If we put the bay wreath on the table, we can arrange some candles inside."

"Great idea," Anne said, hopping down. "Yum, I smell gingerbread. I'm starved. Let's go to the kitchen and see how the children are doing."

"You're always hungry," Matty said with a laugh.

"A temporary condition."

"You're ill?"

Anne laughed. "I'm never ill." She cupped her belly and turned to the side. "What do you think?"

Now that she pointed it out, Anne did look more rounded than flat. "You're pregnant?"

"I'm so glad you guessed. Marsfield thinks it's bad luck to tell anyone, so I have to wait until someone figures it out before I can talk about it."

"Congratulations. That's wonderful. When is the baby due?"

"Late spring. You're the only one who knows, besides Marsfield of course, so you can't tell a soul."

"I won't. And you won't do anymore climbing on chairs."

"Oh, pshaw."

"She's right, you know," a strange female voice said. Matty turned toward the door.

"Climbing will wrap the baby's cord around his neck," said a plump, elderly woman dressed in a myriad of bright colors like a peacock. She and a very-pregnant, very-pretty girl stood on the threshold.

"Vivian. And Cordelia." Anne rushed to meet them. Cordelia looked very sweet in her robin's egg–blue day dress with an overlarge pinafore-like overdress to accommodate her large belly. Anne introduced everyone as she helped her friend waddle to a chair.

"I'll ring for more tea," Matty said, delighted to have more company. London was turning into such fun.

"Sorry to barge in like this," Cordelia said. "I was going bonkers cooped up in the house with Burke hovering over me like I could spit these babies out at any minute."

"Twins?" Matty asked.

"Girls," Vivian said.

"Granny," Cordelia said with a note of warning in her voice. "You don't know that for sure."

Vivian cackled in response.

"I just had to get out," Cordelia continued. "I don't care if women aren't supposed to be seen in public after they start showing. For me that would have been six months. I wish I were tall and could carry a baby like Anne does. She could probably go to the country for the weekend and come back, voilà, with a baby."

Anne laughed. "How long have you known my secret, and why didn't you tell me you knew?"

"Oh, Granny says it's not polite to say anything to the mother-to-be until she mentions it first, but she told me you were having a boy ages ago. I think she knows before it happens."

Matty's knees suddenly weakened. She hadn't thought of that possibility. Could she be carrying Preston's child? While Anne and Cordelia continued to chat, Matty sat beside the older woman. She didn't even have to ask. Vivian shook her head and gave her a sad smile.

"Not this time, dearie," Vivian whispered. She put a small bundle of calico and yarn in Matty's hand. "Put this charm under your pillow, and maybe next time."

Matty had to swallow before she could choke out her thanks. There would not be a next time.

Fresh tea arrived, and by the time Mrs. Manor had set everything out, the subject had changed to the holiday and their planned festivities.

"I think Matty should give a party here," Anne said.

"Oh, no," Matty said even as the others agreed. "I couldn't."

"Of course, you can. The house looks wonderful."

"It's too short notice," Matty insisted, shaking her head. "And so much to do to put a party together. I couldn't—"

"I know," Anne said. "I'll cancel my Christmas Eve party, and you can have it here. Just a small gathering of friends. And the children will have such a good time. I always hire someone to play Father Christmas and hand out gifts."

"I heard you hired Mrs. Donafry for your cook," Vivian said.

"Anne did," Matty said weakly.

"Such a coup," Vivian said. "Especially this time of year. Her puddings are famous."

"You don't suppose she would have some ready today?" Cordelia asked. "I am eating for three, you know."

"You're going to turn into a pudding," Anne said, smiling at the younger woman and patting her hand. "Let's finish planning the party, and then we'll eat."

"I still don't think this is such a good idea," Matty said. But the other three women were a runaway team. There was no stopping them. If Preston was unhappy with her staying in his house, when he found out about the party he was going to bust a gut.

Then again, what could he do? If he threw her out, she would refuse to help him with the scam. A niggling kernel of doubt crept into her thinking. She'd never met a flimflam man with so many wonderful friends.

Preston and Mr. Collins burst through the door of Norbundshire's bedchamber.

"Who the hell are you, and what are you doing?" the man in the bed shouted.

Preston helped Collins to a chair, then rushed back and locked the door. For good measure, he pushed a heavy table in front of it.

Preston approached and made formal leg. "Your Grace."

"Yes, yes, yes. Get to the point, man. Can't you see I'm busy dying?" Although he lay in a fine example of Louis XIV overblown gilded luxury, the huge bed in no way dwarfed the man. Broad of shoulder and wide of girth, with a mane of wild gray hair, the duke had a commanding presence despite the fact he was dressed in a red and white striped nightshirt and a high-pointed nightcap.

Preston introduced himself and requested a private audience.

Norbundshire looked around the room. Two more elderly gentlemen sat at a table on the other side of the bed playing cards.

"If you're not trying to keep us in, who is it you're trying to keep out?" Norbundshire asked.

"Walmsley, sir."

"In that case, you'd better lock the door to the dressing room, too."

As Preston did so, there was a pounding and rattling on the bedchamber door.

"Go away and let me die in peace!" Norbundshire hollered.

"Uncle, there is a lunatic loose in the neighborhood. I'm concerned for your safety."

"Him I know," Norbundshire said, nodding toward Mr. Collins. "Are you the lunatic?"

"I've been called worse," Preston said, folding his arms over his chest and returning the old man's steady gaze.

"You're Stiles' boy, aren't you?"

"Like I said, I've been called worse."

"Go away, Walmsley," Norbundshire called toward the door. "The only lunatics in here are the ones who are supposed to be here."

Preston opened his mouth, but Norbundshire hushed him with a motion and pointed toward the dressing room. Within seconds, they heard the rattling of that door.

"He, he, he," the old man cackled. "Told you so. Now what was so all-fired important that you had to disturb a dying man?"

"You don't sound like you're dying," Preston said.

"Don't be impertinent. Of course, I'm dying. Heard that damn doctor with his nasty potions tell my so-called nephew it would only be a matter of days now. Days! You hear me?" Norbundshire fell back on his pillows. "Days," he echoed weakly, and closed his eyes.

One of the other elderly men stood up and walked over to the bed to peer intently at the duke. Norbundshire opened his eyes, and the other man jumped back.

"Sit down, Lothario," Norbundshire said. "I ain't dead yet. No, wait, Loth. Fix these pillows so I can sit up."

"Sure thing, Shaky," Lothario said.

"Lothario?" Preston asked before he could stop the name from coming out of his mouth.

"A nickname. He's quite the one with the ladies, you know. Ever since Eton. We've been friends for more'n sixty years."

Preston watched Lothario toddle back to his chair. Tiny wisps of neatly combed gray hair covered his head. The man had to be eighty, yet his clothes were stylish and of the latest cut.

"Lothario doesn't talk much, on account of he's got no teeth to speak of." Norbundshire reached over to the bedside table and picked up a hand mirror. He smoothed back his still-abundant white hair. "I could use a haircut. And a trim," he added, stroking his full beard. "I don't look so bad for a corpse."

"You want that on your tombstone?" Lothario asked.

Norbundshire grinned into the mirror. "Maybe it should say I still got all my teeth. Rub 'em with salt every night. Remember that, boy."

"I will, sir. I—"

"That other good fellow is Wiggy. So called because he was the first of us to get a powdered wig. Wore the damn thing everywhere. Shame they went out of style, though. Never had to wash or comb your hair back then," he added in a conspiratorial whisper. "But then again, they were always getting bugs in them," he continued. "The wigs. Itched like crazy, too, especially in the summer. And the powder was a mess. Everyone always looked like they'd been out in the snow."

"Sir—"

"Can't hear a word we're saying, Wiggy can't. Deaf as a stone without his ear horn, but still sharp as a tack at cards. Say, you wouldn't want to play a few hands of whist, would you? Pound a point."

Preston shook his head. He knew when he was being suckered. If those three men had been playing cards together for fifty years, they probably knew tricks that weren't even *in* the book.

"Come on. Make a dying old man happy."

"You mean make him richer."

Norbundshire chuckled. "Teach you a thing or two, we would."

"Maybe later," Preston said. If it meant he could speak to the duke alone, he was willing to be skinned at whist. At least for a few hands. "After we take care of some business."

"Fine. Fine. Out with it." Norbundshire rubbed his chin. "Are you here with the other carrion-eaters? What is it you want? My wine? The artwork? No. I'll bet you want to purchase some of the family jewels for a lady."

"Not exactly."

"Carrion-eaters. All of them. Someone even wanted to buy the statues out of my garden. The minute I die, they'll pick this place clean. And Walmsley will stand by and take the cash."

"Perhaps Mr. Collins should conclude his business first. Then we can speak privately."

Collins clutched his satchel to his chest. "My business is private."

"It's all right, Collins," Norbundshire said. "I know why you're here." He turned to Preston and explained. "I only make my will good for a year. Keeps everyone on their toes that way. Remember that, boy."

"If you have no changes, Your Grace, I've made three fair copies of the old one with new dates. All you have to do is sign them and ask two of these gentlemen to witness your signature."

Norbundshire glared at him from beneath his bushy eyebrows. "You know there have to be changes, Collins."

"Yes, sir. Simply cross out her name, insert another, and initial the change. All perfectly legal."

Norbundshire waved for Collins to bring forth his papers, and he started digging in his satchel. Lothario and Wiggy continued playing cards as if nothing else was going on.

Preston had come representing Matty's interests, and it sounded to him as if Norbie was cutting someone out of his will. Surely he didn't mean her. If so, that would make Matty dependent upon Preston, which had certain advantages.

Yet if that was the case and he'd done nothing to prevent it, he would not be able to live with himself.

"Does this have anything to do with your granddaughter?" Preston asked.

All sound and motion stopped. All three spectators stared at him with mouths agape, then in unison turned toward the duke.

"What do you know about my granddaughter?"

"She's the reason I'm here."

"Out. Out. All of you out." Norbundshire pointed to Preston. "Except for you. You sit right there." He indicated a chair near his bed.

Collins looked around as if lost, but the other two men had obviously been through the drill before. They picked up their small table and slowly carried it to the dressing room without so much as disturbing the hand. Collins followed and shut the door.

When Preston turned back, Norbundshire had a large, wicked, old-fashioned black-powder pistol pointed at his chest.

Chapter 20

"Don't let the age of this weapon fool you, boy."

Preston looked down the long barrel of the flintlock pistol Norbundshire had pointed at his chest.

"It's loaded and primed," the old man said. "The way I figure it, at this distance it can blow a hole in your chest big enough for me to put my foot through."

"I don't doubt it, sir," Preston said, sitting back in his chair.

"My hand might not be as firm as it once was, but I can hardly miss."

"Seems steady enough to me. I'm sure you wouldn't miss," Preston answered, giving the man a relaxed smile.

"You're not scared. Maybe you really are one o' them lunatics."

"The way I figure it," Preston said, copying the duke's manner of speech, "is that you want to know what I know. Therefore you won't shoot me. At least not until I've had my say."

Norbundshire dropped the gun to his lap.

"And besides that, you don't have a wick in the touchhole. That thing would never fire."

The old man laughed and set the pistol aside. "Know your firearms, do you?"

"My father has a similar one in his collection. I

snuck it out and shot it for the first time when I was eight years old. Blew the back out of one of my mother's dining room chairs. That's when my father decided I should have lessons."

"He teach you how to hunt?"

"No, but he hired one of the best shots in England to do it for him."

"I always thought a father should be the one to teach his son."

"I agree."

Norbundshire cleared his throat. "Well, now what is this about my granddaughter? Did you know her?"

"Yes," Preston said with a bit of hesitation. Norbie had asked the question in a strange manner.

"Blast it, man. Did you or did you not know my granddaughter?"

"I've just returned from America and brought Matty back with—"

Norbundshire clutched his heart. "Who put you up to this cruel joke? My granddaughter is dead."

"No, she's—"

"No no no. Don't torment me."

Preston was making a cake of it. Best to start at the beginning. "The queen—"

"Must it always be the members of my own family who torture me?" Norbundshire groaned, lay back, and rolled to his side, facing away from Preston. "Go away," he said in a pitiful voice. "I need a few minutes alone. To collect myself."

Preston stood and walked to the door. He opened it, but instead of entering the dressing room, he simply motioned for the others to remain seated. He closed the door and, without making a sound, slipped to the side of the room where the shadows would conceal his presence.

Within minutes, Norbundshire sat up, as dry-eyed as you please. He took out a big fat cigar, clipped the end, and lit it with a lucifer, puffing on it with obvious enjoyment.

"I can see you're all broken up," Preston said, stepping forward.

Norbundshire jumped so high the cigar flew out of his hand, scattering ashes across the bed. The linens began to smolder in several places. The old man crawled across the bed patting the burning spots out with his bare hands. "For God's sake, help me before the bed goes up in flames."

"I shouldn't," Preston said as he sauntered toward the water pitcher on the washstand by the dressing room door. "You deserve a taste of your ultimate fate." He poured water over the bed.

"What'd you do that for? Now I'll catch my death of a cold sleeping in a wet bed."

Preston gave him a sardonic smile and returned to his seat.

Norbundshire picked up the soggy cigar, frowned, and tossed it over his shoulder. He crawled off the bed, wrapped himself in a red brocade dressing gown, and switched his linen nightcap for a black Persian lamb toque. He stirred the coals in the stove. "Damn Walmsley. Cheap bastard won't even give a dying man sufficient coal to heat his room." He removed another cigar from the humidor on the bedside table and lit it. "How did you know?"

"Do you mean besides your decided flair for the dramatic?"

Norbundshire bowed low in Preston's direction before taking a seat by the stove.

"When you pulled the gun, I figured out *Shaky*

didn't refer to any sort of palsy; therefore, it must be short for *Shakespeare*."

"I once considered the stage my destiny. Until my father disabused me of the notion by cutting off my allowance and threatening to disinherit me."

"Is that why you——"

"Before you say anything else," Norbundshire whispered, "you might want to check the door."

"The door?"

"Quietly." He waved Preston onward.

He opened the door cautiously, finding only two round imprints in the deep pile of the carpeting.

"I'm surprised Walmsley hasn't worn out the knees of all his trousers," Norbundshire said.

"Is that why you spoke so loudly and kept distracting me with tangents?"

The old man took a bottle out of his pocket and sprayed some liquid into his throat. "It's hell on the pipes, but I didn't want him to miss a single word of my sterling performances."

"You're not dying, are you?"

"Hell, boy. We're all dying from the day we're born. 'So shalt thou feed on Death, that feeds on men, And Death once dead, there's no more dying then.' Sonnet one hundred forty-six."

"I would have guessed Shakespeare even though I'm not familiar with the line."

"How about this one? 'After your death, you were better have a bad epitaph than their ill report while you live.'"

"We can——"

"*Hamlet.* How about——"

"We can play guessing games later, Your Grace. We have some serious business to discuss."

"I'll bet you're a lot of fun at parties."

"Not often."

"I was being sarcastic."

"So was I." Preston smiled. He actually liked the old curmudgeon. "Why are you pretending to be dying?"

"I wasn't acting at first. I think Walmsley was poisoning me. Him and that doctor of his. The more I took his medicine, the worse I felt. So I started spitting it out as soon as his back was turned."

"Why didn't you just leave?"

"Easy for you to say, boy. How far do you think I'd get without help? Even if I managed a horse, I'd never last in the saddle for long. Lothario and Wiggy are as much prisoners as me. Once they came to visit me, Walmsley didn't dare let them leave."

"Your servants—"

"Bah! Don't you think he thought of that? The first time when I was really sick, he fired them all and hired new ones of his own. And not too many of those. The fewer to have to keep quiet. That creepy butler and some slatternly cook. We're not sure if the food is making us sick because it's so bad, or if he's putting the poison in it now."

Norbundshire patted his ample belly. "None of us are eating enough to keep a bird alive. I'm a mere shadow of my former self."

"Still a pretty big shadow."

"Well," Norbundshire said, with a chuckle. "Must admit I feel ten years younger." He looked out the window and then at the clock, with a frown. "Speaking of eating, Stanford should have been here with our supper by now. Punctuality was his one good quality."

Preston stood.

"You don't think he's decided to starve us to death, do you?"

"No."

Norbundshire dropped back into his seat. "Whew. I can't think of a worse way to go."

Preston retrieved Collins from the dressing room. "We're going downstairs to reconnoiter the situation," he said, tossing him the old flintlock pistol.

Collins dropped his satchel to catch the gun, then juggled it from hand to hand. "I . . . I don't know anything about firearms."

"That's all right." Preston had only given it to him to help him with his nerves. "Just keep it pointed away from you. And me."

As they crept downstairs, the house had a deserted air. Not that it had been warm and welcoming to start with, but now the silence was oppressive. They found no one in any of the main rooms that were growing chillier as the fires died down. They headed down the servants' stairway.

In the kitchen, a slab of meat on the fire spit burned black on the bottom while still raw on the top. A large bowl on the table sat empty, a number of ingredients at the ready. A door to the outside banged open and shut in syncopation with the gusting wind. Looked like everyone had left in a hurry.

There was a movement to his left. Preston whipped around, changing his aim at the last second as a boy stood up from behind a table. The knife Preston had thrown imbedded itself six inches above the boy's head.

"Who are you?" Preston demanded. "What are you doing here?"

"Fenwick, sir." The boy stood frozen against the wall. "I be the one that comes from the village for the slops."

"You're a brave boy," Preston said. Many a grown man would have soiled himself in the same situation.

"And mighty glad to be a short one," Fenwick said.

Preston retrieved his knife and returned it to the sheath behind his neck.

"Can I see your knife?"

"No." Preston turned to see to Collins, who had fainted. As he hauled the man from under the table by his feet, Fenwick hovered over his neck.

"What do you keep it in? Can I see it? Can I try it on?"

"No." With a bit of searching, Preston found a pitcher of water and wet his handkerchief. Fenwick followed him around the kitchen.

"Do ya think I could learn to throw a knife like that?"

"No." Preston laid the wet handkerchief across Collins' brow, and the man blinked his eyes.

"Am I dead?"

Preston helped him to sit, and propped him against the sturdy table leg. "You're fine." He handed him the handkerchief that had fallen to the floor. "Keep this on your head for a few minutes."

Then Preston turned to Fenwick. "You say you're from the village. Are there any still there who used to work for the duke?"

"Sure, lots. Most got no place else to go. Been a real hardship since that Walmsley come." Fenwick spat after saying the name.

Preston flipped the boy a coin. "Go and tell them all they've got their jobs back. Starting immediately. Tell them the duke needs them right away to get this place in order."

"Yes, sir." The boy gave him a snappy salute.

"And tell them we need supplies." Preston looked around. Most of the kitchen shelves were bare. "Food. Tell the baker we need bread. Meat from the butcher.

And we need coal." He thought about his poor horse that had probably fared worse than the humans here. "Hay and oats, too. Right away."

The boy started for the door.

"And Fenwick, see me when you're done, and I'll have another coin for you."

"Yes, sir." He saluted once more and disappeared into the night.

Collins pulled himself up using a chair, and then plopped into it. "Where do you suppose Walmsley and the others went?"

"To the devil, for all I bloody care."

"But—"

"Why don't you sit here for a few minutes? I'm going to report to the duke and then find my coat and check on my horse."

Collins stood. "I'd rather go with you. To report to the duke. I'd rather not stay down here alone. What if they come back?"

"I truly doubt that will happen. Not tonight, anyway." But Preston schooled himself to patience as he helped the other man up the stairs and down the long hall.

Matty hugged her pillow, unable to sleep. Although the sounds of the city were muffled, she longed for the quiet of her rural home. The crackling of a fragrant cedar wood fire instead of the hissing coal stove. The gentle plopping of snow falling from branches instead of the bitter wind rattling the glass windowpanes.

And where had Preston gone? He was out there in the city somewhere but had not bothered to send her a single word. Kelso said Preston would be staying at his club. What did that mean?

She pictured Preston at MayBelle's Card Parlor and

Social Club. High-stakes gambling, lively music, flowing whiskey. And women. Lots of scantily clad women. Painted up to look beautiful. Women draping their bare arms around his shoulders and whispering naughty suggestions in his ear as he smoked his cigar and played cards.

Matty punched her pillow. Again and again.

Preston smoked his cigar and played cards. With three old men who had just about cleaned him out of all the cash he had on his person. He threw down his hand and pushed his chair back. "That's it for me, boys."

"Come on. One more hand," Norbundshire said. "It's the shank of the evening."

"It's gone past two o'clock."

"Like I said." Norbundshire shook his head. "Young people these days," he said to Lothario. "Got no stamina. It's the modern conveniences to blame. Makes them soft."

Given a decent meal and adequate heating, it seemed as if these fellows could go all night. Except for Collins, who had nodded off in the chair by the parlor fire hours ago.

Preston gave an exaggerated yawn and stretched his arms. "I know when I'm outclassed." He still wanted to make a circuit around the house and check the guards he'd set before he sought his bed.

Norbundshire stood. He woke Collins and sent him upstairs with Lothario and Wiggy, requesting Preston stay behind for a minute. The duke poured them both a drink and settled into the chair Collins had warmed. Preston sat opposite him.

"Now that we're alone, tell me about my granddaughter. How is her little farm doing? And the children, Nathan and Bess? Bet they're growing like weeds." He chuckled. "Did you meet the Indian, Joseph? I'd like to meet a real Indian someday."

"How do you know—"

Norbundshire laid a finger aside of his nose. "I have a correspondent who keeps track of her for me. My little secret."

"You said you thought she was dead."

"Pish-tosh. That was for Walmsley's benefit. He's got some papers that say so, but they'll never stand up in court. Collins has everything he needs. When I do die, Matilda will inherit everything I own, right down to the garden statuary. Except the bloody title. Can't do anything about that. Walmsley will be the next Duke of Norbundshire. Fat lot of good it will do him without a penny to his name. I've seen to that."

Preston was flabbergasted. He hardly knew what to say. He'd spent the entire day pussyfooting around the duke so as not to shock the man into heart failure, fake or real, and had planned on speaking to him tomorrow after he'd had a good night's rest. Then it turned out the old man had known about his granddaughter all along.

"Yessiree," the duke said, leaning back with a self-satisfied smile. "I've outwitted them all." He gave Preston an assessing look. "My granddaughter will be rich one of these days. And she's available. Are you married?"

"No, but I'm the last person you'd want Matty to marry. Well, maybe not the very last. Walmsley and the Reverend Henshaw would be directly behind me in that line."

Norbundshire sat forward, and he grabbed Preston's collar with a speed and force that belied his age. "What do you know about Henshaw? Why would you put him in company with that weasel Walmsley?"

Preston gently removed the other man's hand, and he proceeded to tell him of Henshaw's determination to marry Matty against her will, and of his machinations to force her into an untenable situation.

"Damn. I thought I could trust a bloody man of the cloth." Norbundshire clasped his hands together. "You've got to go back to America. You've got to save her."

"That won't be necessary, sir. The reason I came to see you is to tell you I've brought her to London."

"She's here?"

"In London. Staying at my town house." Preston sat back, ready to receive the old curmudgeon's delighted thanks.

"You bloody fool," Norbundshire said, rising to his feet. "That's the first place he'll look."

"Who?"

"Walmsley. Don't you see? That's why he left. He must have heard enough to realize she's alive. If he kills me now, he's ruined. He has to make sure she's dead first."

Preston was already headed toward the door.

"Wait. It's the middle of the night." Norbundshire followed him into the foyer. "You can't go now."

"The hell I can't." Matty could be in danger, and that's all that was important. He woke up the footman and ordered his horse saddled and brought around immediately, sooner if possible.

Without waiting for the footman's return, Preston found the coat closet under the stairs and donned his cloak and gloves.

"It's snowing and frigid cold. At least wait until daylight."

"By then I'll be a quarter of the way there."

"The roads are icy and—"

"Don't worry, sir." Preston put his hand on the older man's shoulder. "I'll protect her."

He only hoped he wouldn't be too late.

The stable hand arrived with the horse. Preston mounted and kicked the horse's flanks.

"Don't let that horse slip and throw you. You'll freeze to death before someone finds you. Fat lot of good you'll be to my granddaughter then," Norbundshire called after him.

Matty came down the stairs after getting Bess settled for her afternoon nap. The little girl didn't want to miss any of the excitement. With all the activity and comings and goings, her sleep schedule had been hard to keep and, as a result, she was cranky. Matty had given Edith a break and rocked Bess while the others ate luncheon.

It had been so peaceful in the nursery. She'd missed her quiet time with her children. Forgetting the rest of the world for a bit, she had continued to hold and rock Bess even after she had fallen asleep. Since she hadn't slept much the night before, Matty had nodded off for about an hour herself.

At the door, Giles argued with a gentleman. "I told you Lady Matilda is not at home."

Matty just didn't understand the practice of not being *at home* when she obviously was there. She'd met so many nice friends of Preston's that she looked forward to meeting more.

"That's all right, Giles. Please come in," she said to the gentleman, directing him into the parlor. "May I offer you a refreshment? Perhaps something warm? Tea?"

"No, thank you."

She dismissed Giles and sat on the settee. "Are you a friend of Preston's?"

"Actually, I'm a friend of yours."

"Really?" Something in the man's ingratiating tone didn't set quite right. "I wasn't aware I had any friends in London."

"My name is Edgar Walmsley and, to be more precise, I'm a friend of your grandfather's."

The man set her teeth on edge. She wished she hadn't been so quick to dismiss Giles.

"He's quite anxious to meet you, and sent me to fetch you."

"Perhaps some other time," she said, not thrilled about going anywhere with him.

"It's quite urgent we leave right away. He's dying, you know."

"I'm not going anywhere before I have my tea," she said, standing. She reached for the bellpull to summon a servant. Any servant's presence would be welcome.

"Not so fast," he said, pulling out a pistol and pointing it at her.

Her hand hovered inches away from the bellpull.

"Step back," he said.

She did as she was told, hoping to buy some time to think of a way to call for help.

"That's better," he said with a nasty grin. "Now we're going to—"

There was a light tapping on the door.

"Get rid of whoever it is, and be quick about it." He hid the gun underneath the flap of his coat, but it was still aimed at her.

Nathan opened the door. He pantomimed eating, telling her that her meal was waiting.

"Maybe later, sweetie," she said. "Please tell the cook I'll dine after I've finished with my guest." Matty hoped Nathan would catch her subtle hint that something was wrong and go for help. She'd learned a little of the Indian sign language the boy and Joseph had used, and she made what she thought was the hand motion for *enemy*. She couldn't do much else without making Walmsley suspicious.

The boy nodded, and he closed the door without giving her any hint she'd been understood. Had she been too subtle? Had she given the wrong sign?

"My carriage is waiting. We're going to take a little trip. Just you and me."

She crossed her arms over her breasts and set her mouth in a mutinous frown. "I'm not going anywhere with you."

"You will cooperate, Lady Matilda. Do not think I will hesitate to use this."

"If you shoot me, the entire household will come down on your head. Even you can't be that stupid."

"You're right. I'm not. But if you refuse to cooperate, we'll just sit here until someone else comes along, and I'll shoot you and him. Perhaps that boy will return."

What if Nathan hadn't understood her clues and came back to see what was taking her so long? What if he had understood and brought help, but he led the way? Would Walmsley really shoot a child? Somehow she knew the answer was yes.

She stood up. "I'll get my things."

He tucked the gun under his jacket again. "No quick moves. Anyone who gets in my way winds up dead, understood?"

She nodded. But no one was around as she retrieved her coat and hat, left the house, and climbed into the waiting carriage.

Once she'd made sure her son was out of danger, Matty settled back against the squabs of the carriage seat and waited for her chance to escape.

Chapter 21

Preston dismounted and raced up the front steps of his town house. He stumbled on the threshold, his gait a bit unsteady after so many hours in the saddle, and he lurched into the entrance hall.

"Ho, there," Marsfield called from a chair in the parlor. "Seems our Preston has had quite—"

Preston leaned against the doorjamb. "Where's Matty?"

Burke shook his head. "We just arrived minutes ago to fetch our wives. What seems to be the problem?"

Preston turned away without answering. Nathan appeared at his side and tugged on his coat. He tousled the boy's hair and said, "Not now, son. I have to find Matty."

Preston started up the stairs, meeting the footman on his way down. He grabbed the young man by the shoulders. "Where's Lady Matilda?"

"I don't know," Giles said, his eyes wide. "Upstairs?" he said, his tone indicating it was a wild guess.

"You just came from there. Was Matty upstairs?"

"Not that I saw, but I wasn't looking for her; I was—"

Preston set the footman aside, causing Giles to grab the railing for balance as Preston pushed past him. Most of the rooms upstairs were empty, but a crowd gathered in his former storeroom, now apparently a play area.

Anne and her two children sat with their backs to him, at a table covered with colored papers and pots of paint and glue. Cordelia sat next to Bess, trying to prevent the child from pasting a strip of pink paper to her head. He caught Edith's eye and motioned her over, not wanting to upset the children.

"Welcome back, sir. We're—"

"Where's Matty?"

"Why, I'm not sure. I—"

"When did you see her last?"

"Let's see." Edith scratched the bun at the back of her neck. "She put Bess down for her nap."

"When was that?" he asked.

"Oh, a good two hours ago."

Preston groaned.

"There's so much to do for the party, she's probably downstairs with the cook."

"Henri? He never lets anyone in his kitchen."

"No? Mrs. Donafry. Who's Henri?"

Preston shook his head. Nothing made any sense, but then, nothing was important until he found Matty.

Nathan tugged on his coat again.

"There you are," Edith said. "You're missing all the fun. Come on. We're making Christmas decorations."

Nathan shook his head. He looked up at Preston.

"Sh-sh-she's g-gone. M-m-matty's g-gone."

"What?" Preston knelt down and took the boy by his slim shoulders. "Do you know where she is?"

"I t-tried to tell, b-b-but n-nobody would listen to me."

Preston felt as if he'd been kicked in the gut. He of all people should have known better than to ignore the boy. Pulling Nathan into a hug, he apologized. Then he looked the boy in the eye. "Matty is in danger, isn't she?"

Nathan nodded.

Through a series of hand gestures, expressions, and halting sentences, Preston finally learned Nathan's story. He'd been suspicious and had hidden on the landing, where he'd watched the man take Matty out of the house at gunpoint. Then he'd followed the carriage to the end of the block, had jumped on the boot, and had ridden all the way to its destination. Unable to get into the house where she was, he'd run home for help.

"Then she can't be far away."

Nathan nodded. He pantomimed directions, indicating four blocks east, seven blocks north, and then another five blocks east.

"That would be Harding Street," Marsfield said.

His friends had come up the stairs behind him and had heard the news. Preston blessed Marsfield's encyclopedic knowledge of the city.

"I think Norbundshire has a grand mansion on Harding Street," Burke added. "I seem to remember attending a reception for the Turkish ambassador. But Norbundshire hasn't been in residence there for years. Keeps a smaller place nearer the House of Lords."

Preston stood. "Can you remember the number? Do you remember anything about the layout of the house?"

Burke shook his head. "Not with any surety."

"We'll figure out a plan on the way," Marsfield said. "My carriage is in the street since I wasn't expecting to be left cooling my heels in the parlor."

"Let's go," Preston said, turning. The boy tugged on his coat again, and he forced himself to pause. "Don't worry, son. We'll bring her home safe."

"I'm g-going with you," Nathan said, standing tall. "I know which house it is."

Preston could have insisted the boy describe the house and then leave him at home, but he doubted

Nathan would stay behind. Better to have him with them where they could keep an eye on him.

"Come along then," he said.

Kelso met them at the front door with an odd assortment of weapons bristling from his bandy frame.

"I don't think you'll need the machete," Preston said to his valet as the four men and Nathan piled into the carriage. Thankfully the carriage was large, or Kelso would have been responsible for wounding more than one of them.

"You never can tell," Kelso responded. "I like to be prepared."

"So do I," Marsfield said, drawing several boxes of pistols from under the seat as the carriage got under way. He offered one to Preston, who shook his head.

"I won't need it," he said. He planned to beat the bloody little weasel to within an inch of his life.

Marsfield nodded, and they set their plans as best they could without exact knowledge of the premises.

Matty sat in the one uncovered chair in the receiving room of the grand house, her hands folded in her lap. The rest of the furniture and the paintings were draped in dustcovers.

So far Walmsley had not left her alone for a minute. When she'd claimed to need to use the facilities, he'd had his cohort Stanford fetch a chamber pot and set it in the corner of the room without even a screen for privacy. The man had leered at her with unholy glee on his skeletal face. She'd declined with an indignant huff and had sat in the chair where she had remained for the last twenty minutes.

"Let's just do it and be done with it," Stanford said.

"We'll stick to the plan," Walmsley replied, sitting on the covered arm of a nearby sofa.

"We can make it look like an accident. Just like the others."

"No. Two accidents are believable. Three would cause someone to investigate. Like bloody Bathers. How dare he stick his nose in my business? First we throw him off the track."

"We could—"

"No. My plan is brilliant."

Matty heard the front door open and two sets of footsteps.

"You're late," Walmsley said to a tall, nervous man and a blowsy woman as they entered carrying several parcels.

"Yer wanted us to get the blond wig, didn't yer? T'weren't easy to find for what yer were willing to pay." She ripped open one of the parcels and plopped the long wig over her greasy hair. "How do I look?"

"Stunning," Walmsley said with obvious disgust.

However, the other man and Stanford complimented her profusely.

"Let's get on with it," Walmsley insisted with impatience. He turned to Matty. "Hand over your garments to Dora here."

She stood and gave the woman her hat and coat.

"The dress, too," Walmsley said, waving his gun.

She crossed her arms and glared at him.

Walmsley chuckled. "Lady Matilda, let me introduce Dr. Emile DuBoche. Perhaps you've heard of him? No? Emile and I have several interests in common. His specialty is pain. He's making a fascinating study of the human body's ability to withstand tremendous pain when fear is the motivator. Would you like to get to know him better?"

"No, thank you," Matty said, maintaining her stance and expression with difficulty.

"I, of course, am interested in the application of his findings to women," Walmsley continued. He leaned closer. "Emile prefers young boys. About the age of that lad I saw at your house. What was his name?"

Matty's knees threatened to buckle.

"Not going to tell me? Not a problem. Stanford? Would you go back to—"

"What am I supposed to wear?" Matty asked, reaching for the buttons at her neck.

"Give her your dress, Dora," Walmsley directed.

The other woman stripped with practiced ease and held out the red satin and black lace garment to Matty. The smell alone caused her to recoil. She tossed her dress to Dora, but allowed the replacement to drop to the floor. Two small black bugs scrambled to regain their home.

Matty took several steps back.

"I'd rather wear this," she said, picking up the discarded cotton dustcover that had previously protected her chair, and wrapping it around her shoulders.

"Suit yourself." Walmsley turned to Dora, who now resembled Matty as she had arrived at the house. "Remember, walk nice and slow. You're a lady out for a stroll with your lover, the good doctor. We want all the nosy neighbors to see you leave."

Then Walmsley shook hands with Emile. "Don't catch a cab until you get to the end of the block, then go straight to the docks. Make sure you call her Lady Matilda several times in front of the driver so he'll remember it. The captain of the *Wanderer* is expecting you and will leave as soon as you're on board. Have a good trip, and I'll send you word when you can return."

"I don't know why we gotta go to Spain," Dora

whined. "I hate all them fore-ners; what, I can't understand a word they say. And the food gives me gas."

"Emile needs to leave London for a time and, this
way, we can kill two birds with one stone."

"Kill two birds," Stanford said with a chuckle.

"Shut up," Walmsley said. He smiled at Dora, and
handed her a fat purse. "Buy yourself something pretty
in Spain."

"Thanks. I will." She tucked the purse between her
breasts, and took the doctor's arm. "Come on, ducks."

Matty knew the woman would be fish bait before the
ship ever reached the coast of Spain. She started to say
something, but Walmsley moved to stand in front of
her.

"If you don't do exactly as you're told, Stanford will
return to Bathers's town house. I prefer women, but I
can make do with a boy if I must."

Matty turned her face away and stared at a spot over
his shoulder.

She would have her chance to escape. She prayed
she would.

Preston stuck his head out the window of the carriage to see what was holding up traffic. A dray had
upset its load, and the workmen were taking their time
restoring it to rights. He opened the door, deciding it
would be faster on foot. As he turned to tell the others
he would go ahead, Nathan stood half-in and half-out
of the door and pointed to the far end of the block.

Matty and a man hailed a hack and got inside. Preston pointed the cab out to the coachman and offered
him twenty guineas if he could catch it. The carriage
started into motion before Preston had even climbed

back in. He leaped and landed spread across the laps of his friends.

"Was that Walmsley?" Marsfield asked, pulling his head back in the other window on that side.

Preston scrambled to his seat, only to be knocked sideways as the coachman drove over something large, hopefully not a person. The carriage sped down the wrong side of the street, the coachman yelling, and people, horses, and dogs scampering out of the way.

"I don't think so," Preston said. "Too tall. Walmsley is probably no more than a head taller than Matty."

"Then who was he?" Marsfield asked.

"No idea. Was anyone else at the house?" Preston asked Nathan, and the boy shook his head. He turned to Marsfield and said, "I didn't see much of his face. Did you? Did he look familiar?"

Marsfield waved him to silence and closed his eyes, obviously trying to concentrate and place the face.

They rode in silence, hanging on to keep from falling on top of each other.

"We'll find out soon enough," Burke said, pointing out of the other window.

Preston climbed to that side of the carriage. The hack had stopped, and Matty and the man were halfway up the gangplank of a ship. Marsfield's carriage pulled to a stop, wheels screeching as the coachman leaned on the hand brake. On board the ship, the man leaned over and kissed Matty, and they went belowdecks.

The men tumbled out of the carriage as the gangplank was withdrawn. They yelled at the captain and crew, who only flipped rude hand gestures and refused to replace the gangplank.

Preston sat in the carriage with his head in his hands. Something was very wrong.

Marsfield stuck his head back in the door. "Come on, man. We'll hire a boat. A fishing scow. Anything."

Then the answer hit Preston. How could he have been so stupid? "Get back in the carriage," he said. He called for Burke, Kelso, and Nathan to get back in the carriage, too.

"I'm sorry," Marsfield said. "But despite your feelings, you can't leave her in that man's clutches. That's Dr. Emile DuBoche, and you don't want to know what he does to women."

The other men returned, and Preston directed everyone to get back in the carriage with all haste.

Marsfield refused. "You can't leave her with—"

"I'm sorry for whoever that woman is, but that was not Matty. Therefore—"

"What do you mean she wasn't Matty?" Burke asked.

The other men looked at each other, confusion obvious.

"Maybe she wasn't the woman you thought you knew," Marsfield said in a conciliatory tone, "but—"

"That was not Matty," Preston said, more sure of himself with every moment. "She would never leave her children like that."

"She seemed right friendly with that man," Burke pointed out.

For the first time in years, Preston wanted to deck his friend. "That was not Matty," he said through clenched teeth. "It was a rudimentary ruse, and I bloody fell for it. Because I underestimated Walmsley. Because I misjudged Matty. I won't make that mistake again."

Nathan climbed into the carriage and sat next to Preston, signaling his faith and support.

"Back to Harding Street," Burke said as he took the opposite seat. "We're with you."

"Same plan?" Marsfield asked as the coach lurched into motion.

"With one small difference," Preston said as Kelso climbed in and shut the door. If Walmsley had harmed Matty in any way, Preston would slit his scrawny throat.

Matty blinked her eyes open and shook the fog from her head.

"Welcome back, my dear," Walmsley said, but his voice sounded as if she were underwater. "I was afraid Stanford had used too much ether. I mean, what is the point of performing experiments if you're not awake to participate?"

She swallowed. Her mouth felt like an entire boll of cotton, seeds and all, had been stuffed inside it, and she tasted a strange sweetness. She tried to move and discovered her arms were held in place, straight out at both sides by wide leather straps wrapped around her wrists and nailed to a large wood piece of furniture. As they were now in a bedroom, she assumed she stood in front of an armoire. Across the room, Walmsley cleared off a small table and brought it to within a few feet of her.

"I apologize for the crude surroundings," he said as he set a large black leather bag on the table. "Dr. DuBoche and I have a well-equipped laboratory I'm sure you'll find quite interesting, but we can't leave until dark."

He proceeded to remove a number of wicked-looking instruments from his bag, caressing each one before laying it on a cloth marked with dark stains that looked suspiciously like dried blood.

She jerked on the leather straps, trying to free her hands.

"I wouldn't do that," he said, without looking up. "Those straps are my own design. Quite ingenious, if I do say so myself. The more you struggle, the tighter they bind."

He placed a scalpel on the cloth. "And don't bother screaming for help."

He waved around the room, and she noticed that thick wool tapestries had been hung on each wall.

"Not as efficient as my laboratory, but wool is useful for blocking sound, so I'm quite sure they will do."

Matty swallowed again, the taste of bile overpowering all else. "You'll never get away with this," she choked out.

"Really, my dear, I had expected something a bit more original from you." He sounded truly disappointed. "It's not often we get a lady of such exalted lineage, but even the commonest whore says the same thing." He looked at her, his expression a pout. "And I had so eagerly anticipated your resistance that I went to all this trouble rather than wait. Do say you're not going to let me down."

Her chances for escape had dwindled to nothing. She clung to her one hope.

"Preston will—"

"Bah! I've already outwitted that fool, Bathers," Walmsley said, throwing an arm up and stepping toward her, his face livid. Then he stopped and closed his eyes. "I must be calm in order to remember everything," he mumbled to himself. "I'm not doing this for self-gratification, but in the pursuit of knowledge. Breathe in composure. Breathe out and be in control." He opened his eyes and smiled at her. "Shall we begin?"

Chapter 22

Walmsley stepped toward Matty with two strange metal clips in one hand, a pair of scissors in the other.

"Let's cut away those restricting clothes and start with the nipple pincers, shall we?"

Matty sucked in a deep breath and grabbed the leather straps. He cut away the laces on her chemise and tossed the sharp scissors aside. As he fumbled with the whatever-he-had-called-them, she brought up her knee as hard as she could, considering she couldn't get any backswing. Apparently it was enough, because he doubled over with a keening moan.

"You bitch," he choked out, collapsing to his knees.

"You wanted resistance," she said, giving him a smile even though she was aware this might well be her last hurrah. "You're interested in pain? Remember that pain, you sick pervert."

Walmsley staggered to his feet and then to the bellpull.

"You'll pay for that," he squeaked out. He cleared his throat. "As soon as Stanford gets here to help me strap your feet."

The butler was not long responding. Although she fought as best she could, the task was soon accomplished.

Walmsley took a seat by the fireplace, one hand

cradling his injured groin. "Take these things away," he said, pointing to a tray set out nearby, and dismissing the servant. "I don't have time to eat now."

Stanford continued to ogle her bare breasts as he fumbled with the dishes on the tray. She would have liked a cup of tea from the still-steaming pot to wet her dry mouth, but she wouldn't give them the satisfaction of asking for it.

"Stop dawdling," Walmsley said. "You'll have your chance later, just as you always do."

Stanford grinned and licked his nonexistent lips. Her stomach lurched, and she spat out the bile that came to her mouth. He gave her one last leer as he exited.

Walmsley leaned back in the chair and closed his eyes. However, her hope that he had fallen asleep was quickly dashed, for within a few moments he was up and searching for the items he had dropped earlier.

Preston tapped his foot on the front stoop. The plan called for him to wait three minutes in order to give Burke and Kelso time to run around the house and get to the back door. Then he and Marsfield would go in the front. His friend would question the butler or footman while Burke and Kelso rounded up any other servants, and Preston would locate Matty.

Nathan tugged on his coat. The boy had refused to wait in the carriage. Preston understood and leaned down to explain why they were waiting. The entire plan was predicated on Marsfield's insistence they could not break into a man's house on mere suspicion. Even as he said the words, they made no sense. Nathan had said Matty was in that house, and he believed the boy.

To hell with waiting.

Preston kicked the front door open and marched in.

Stanford, the skeletal butler from the country, paused three-quarters of the way down the stairs, then turned on his heel and started back up.

Preston ran after him.

Stanford turned and threw the tray at his head.

Preston dodged the flying dishes by flattening himself against the wall. Taking the steps two at a time, he gained on the butler, and tackled him.

Reasoning the man had headed for his employer at the first sign of trouble, he climbed over the man and left the butler for Marsfield to deal with. At the top of the stairs, Preston paused. Too many doors lay to either side of the main hall. Which one was she behind? He turned back to question the butler, then noticed footprints in the dusty carpet. Two larger sets of prints made by men's shoes, and two wandering trails. It looked as if the two men had dragged something between them.

Like a body.

His heart lurched, and his stomach threatened to revolt.

Calling upon his training, he locked his emotions into someplace deep inside so they wouldn't impede what he had to do. He pulled the knife from his boot and followed the tracks, moving swiftly, yet ready in case Walmsley or any of his unknown number of cohorts had heard the disturbance below. Someone could pop out of any one of the doors with a pistol or rifle.

He heard a sound behind him and whipped around, ready to confront the canny attacker who had waited until he had passed their door before jumping out at him.

Matty bit her lip as she watched Walmsley wander about the room looking under dustcovers and behind chairs.

"Where could that other nipple pincer have got to?" he asked, scratching his head.

Matty figured she didn't have much time, and she couldn't wait for Preston. Who was she trying to fool? Herself? Preston wasn't going to rescue her. He didn't know where she was, or even that she wasn't at home. He was at his club. He probably wouldn't even remember for days that she existed.

She blinked back her tears and searched her brain for something to do. Perhaps if she fainted. He'd said he wanted her awake. She'd never fainted in her life, but she could pretend. What if she pretended to faint every time he came near her? Would he leave her alone, or did he also carry smelling salts in his bag? It wasn't much of a plan, but it was all she could come up with.

He tossed the metal device he had found. "I've never used just one before. Would a single one in rotation have any scientific interest?" He shook his head. "My thesis compares classes of women; therefore, the tests must remain exactly the same to be of any value."

Matty had just begun to relax when he cried out and dove underneath the bed.

Preston whipped around and stayed his hand. With his left arm, he caught Nathan around the waist as the boy made to run past him.

"He got away from me," Marsfield whispered, coming up behind Nathan. "Slippery little imp."

"You must wait on the stairs," Preston said to Nathan, who shook his head. "I'm counting on you and Marsfield to watch my back."

Nathan hesitated, but finally agreed, and Preston set him on his feet and shoved him toward his friend, who clamped a hand on the boy's shoulder.

"Kelso is guarding the butler," Marsfield whispered. "Burke is checking all the rooms downstairs, but so far no one is about. Do you think we're too late?"

Preston shook his head. That butler had been serving someone, and he would bet it was Walmsley. The man whose only hope for remaining alive was that he hadn't harmed Matty. Preston turned and ran down the hall, making as little noise as possible, which wasn't hard on the thick carpeting. Little puffs of dust exploded with each step as he followed the tracks, secure in the knowledge his friend would not only watch his back but would also watch out for Nathan.

He reached the door and paused. Leaning his ear against the wood, he heard no sounds through the thick planks, but the trail led to this door, and it could be no other. He hoped the silence didn't mean he was too late. He backed up to the wall and slammed into the door with his shoulder.

Matty nearly fainted for real when Preston burst through the door. In relief. In happiness. In embarrassment. Though she called out his name immediately, he barely glanced at her before he looked away.

Preston had quickly ascertained Matty was in no pressing danger, and he made taking care of Walmsley his first priority. The man had half crawled under the bed when Preston yanked him out by the ankles and flipped him to his back.

"Don't hurt me," Walmsley sniveled, cowering against the dustcover.

Disgusted, Preston sheathed his knife and hauled the poor excuse for a man up by his coat and necktie.

Holding him up with his left hand, Preston hit him with a right cross that would have made Gentleman Jim proud. Walmsley sank to the floor in a pathetic heap, unconscious after a single blow. Pity. Preston would have enjoyed pummeling him senseless.

He turned to Matty. He cut her down, gave her his greatcoat to wear, and took her in his arms; all the while she cried and kept saying she was sorry.

"There's nothing for you to apologize for, sweetheart. None of this is your fault." He smoothed back her hair and held her closer. He recognized her delayed reaction, had seen similar in other people. He would give anything to save her from reliving her ordeal, but he also recognized it was necessary if she was to get it out of her system. All he could do was hold her and reassure her everything would be all right.

Matty could not stop the tears. Big gulping sobs shook her whole body. She tried to tell Preston she was sorry she'd lost faith in him, that she'd believed he wouldn't come after her. She tried to tell him what had happened, but the words jumbled together and made no sense. She finally gave up and just enjoyed the safety of his arms.

Preston sensed something, then heard a movement behind him and turned, pushing Matty to his back. Walmsley stood across the room, facing them with a gun in each hand.

"How touching," he snarled. "The ever-popular and oh-so-bloody-noble Lord Bathers is willing to die to protect his woman. Well, I'm more than happy to oblige the obtrusive."

Suddenly, Walmsley cried out, dropped the guns, and grabbed his leg. An unfamiliar knife stuck in his thigh.

Nathan stood in the doorway, his hand outstretched

in the follow-through position. Preston was surprised and grateful for the help, and relieved Matty was all right, but most of all he was proud of Nathan. The boy stood there for a moment before he ran to Matty.

"I'm bleeding," Walmsley cried. "Somebody help. Get a doctor."

After kneeling down and hugging Nathan, Matty held him out at arm's length. "Where did you get that knife?"

"From Joseph. He s-said I would need it." The boy looked up at Preston. "I've b-been p-practicing."

"I'm bleeding to death here, in case anyone cares."

All three turned and said "We don't" in unison.

Preston did step toward Walmsley, though, but only close enough to kick the guns into the hallway far out of his reach.

"I'm calling the constable. I'll have that boy arrested," Walmsley said as he took off his tie and tried to make a tourniquet of it. "We have laws in this city against attempted murder."

Preston placed one arm around Matty's waist and one around Nathan's shoulders. "Let's go home."

Marsfield waited outside the door.

"Thanks for giving us a minute," Preston said.

Marsfield looked down at Nathan with a frown. "That's twice he got away from me." He grinned and tousled the boy's hair. "You've got potential."

Preston pushed Nathan toward the stairs. "Don't try to recruit him until after he's graduated from school."

"Hey, you out there," Walmsley hollered. "I'm bleeding. I need a doctor."

"Take my carriage," Marsfield said. "We'll clean up this mess and catch a hackney cab."

Preston nodded his thanks. "We'll see you later."

"The detectives of Scotland Yard will have some

questions for both of you. I'll try to put them off for a few days."

Again Preston thanked him, and they followed after Nathan.

Matty struggled with the greatcoat, trying to hold it so the hem wouldn't drag on the floor and trip her.

Preston swung her up into his arms and carried her down the stairs and out to the carriage.

"Recruit Nathan for what?" she asked.

"We'll discuss it later." He settled on the seat, cradled her against his chest, and leaned back to close his eyes for a moment. He just wanted to hold her close, savor her life. He could have lost her. His heart was full to bursting with things he wanted to say to her, but dash it all, Nathan's presence stilled his tongue.

Matty snuggled into Preston's warmth, drawing strength and comfort from his closeness. Even if it was only pity that motivated him, she was so needy at that moment she would take whatever comfort she could get. Thankfully, Nathan's presence gave her an excuse not to talk to Preston about the experience, because all she wanted to do was forget. Forget what had happened, forget Walmsley, and forget the way Preston had looked at her with disgust in his eyes.

Preston slouched further into the sofa. He put his feet up and crossed his arms. He had no intention of leaving his own library in his own house until he had a chance to see Matty. He'd had so little time with her in the carriage, and any conversation had been inhibited by Nathan's presence. Yet he had sensed Matty needed to talk. Then the moment they had reached home, she'd been whisked upstairs by Anne and Edith, who were cosseting and cooing over *the poor dear*.

Cordelia had finally admitted she was exhausted and allowed Burke to take her home. Marsfield had taken his children home for their governess to put to bed, and had returned for his wife. Still Matty had not come downstairs.

"Brandy?" Marsfield asked.

Preston shook his head and closed his eyes. He didn't want brandy, and he didn't want to talk; he just wanted to make sure Matty was all right.

Eventually, Anne came downstairs. Preston heard her and Marsfield talking, but he feigned sleep. He didn't want yet-another secondhand report on Matty's condition.

"The poor dear finally went to sleep after a hot bath and warm toddy," Anne said. "Her ordeal terrified her, but that monster didn't physically harm her."

"Do you think she'll sleep through the night?" Marsfield asked. "Should you stay?"

"No. That won't be necessary. She should sleep."

Ha! They didn't know Matty like he did. She would be up wandering in the middle of the night like always. And when she came looking for a book to read or some warm milk, he would be waiting.

Marsfield rang for the footman and requested his carriage.

"Thank you for your assistance," Kelso said. "I've wrapped several hot bricks for your feet and given them to Giles for your ride home. It's quite chilly outside."

There were noises to indicate Marsfield and Anne donned their outer garments.

"Shall we drop Preston at his club?" Anne asked.

"Look at the man. He's exhausted," Marsfield said. "Throw a blanket over him and let him sleep."

"But sir, he can't—"

"I do not want you to wake him, Kelso. He rode all night and has had a rough day. He can go to his club when he wakes, whatever time that is. I'm depending on you to keep everyone out of this room tomorrow morning until he calls."

"Yes, sir."

"No waking him to take off his coat, or his shoes, or for any other reason. Let him sleep. Understood?"

Preston sent Marsfield a silent thank you.

"Yes, sir," Kelso agreed, and Preston could well imagine the strained look on his valet's face at the thought of him sleeping in his clothes, especially as stained and dirty as they were.

Someone tucked a blanket around his shoulders, and he recognized Anne's perfume and her gentle touch. She kissed him on the forehead and whispered good night. Funny, he felt nothing more than simple gratitude. As if his sister had kissed him.

He listened as Kelso—he assumed it was Kelso from his step—closed the draperies, banked the fire, and blew out the lamps.

After they all left and the door closed, Preston rose and removed his coat and shoes, using only the dim light from the fireplace coals. He waited until the house grew quiet, then opened the door several inches so he could see the stairs, and settled down for a long wait.

Matty reached the end of her book and closed the cover with a sigh. But she did not get out of the comfortable chair. Although she had pretended to be asleep in order to get rid of Edith and Anne, actually trying to sleep would be a waste of time. If she kept reliving her ordeal while awake, closing her eyes would be to invite a nightmare.

She rubbed her eyes. Her mother's clock that she had brought all the way from Tennessee said half past two. She decided to check on the children, uncurled her legs, and stuck her feet into her slippers. As long as she was up, she might as well get another book. And maybe something warm to drink. She missed her little house where hot milk was only a few steps away. She'd never been afraid at home, even though the nearest neighbor was miles away. Yet with so many people nearby, people who would respond to the bellpull even in the middle of the night, she was afraid to sleep.

Walmsley may not have hurt her physically, but she had been violated, her peace of mind shattered by the intrusion of his evil. The knowledge that he was still out there disturbed her. Even though Anne had assured her he was behind bars, what if he escaped? What if he returned? And why had he singled her out? What had she done to attract his malice?

She shivered.

The only time she'd felt safe had been in Preston's arms.

Where was he right now? She stood at the window and looked across the garden to the street beyond. Was he sleeping? Was he playing cards? Dancing?

With a sigh she donned her robe. Tomorrow was going to be a hectic day. Hopefully she would be too busy to even think about what had happened. Would Preston come to the party? She hadn't even mentioned it to him, what with everything else.

She picked up the candlestick. She would check on the children and then go downstairs to the kitchen. Perhaps she should put a few drops of laudanum in her warm milk. She had refused earlier, but Edith had left the bottle on the nightstand.

Matty sipped her milk as she made her way to the library for another book to read. She set her cup on the table and slid the library door open. Unexpectedly, Preston sat sprawled in the corner of the sofa, one arm across the back, a blanket pooled around his feet. She stepped inside and eased the door closed so as not to wake him.

Moving quietly in her soft slippers, she crossed the room. Even in sleep he looked tired and unhappy; frown lines traversed his forehead as if nightmares marred his sleep, too.

She set the candlestick on the table and picked up the blanket. Yielding to impulse, she sat on the couch, leaned against him, and draped the blanket over them both.

He dropped his arm around her. "What took you so long?"

She jumped, but he snuggled her closer.

"I thought you were asleep. I didn't mean to—"

"Just resting my eyes." He tipped her chin up. "Have you slept at all?"

She ducked her head. "Of course."

"The truth."

"Some," she said into his chest.

"Not at all?"

She nodded, rubbing her cheek against his shirtfront. "I keep seeing his face leering at me. I keep wondering what I did to attract his—"

"You did nothing." He cupped her cheek and tipped her chin up to look her in the eye. "He is the one who did the wrong. Not you."

"But why me?"

He had to tell her the truth, even if it wiped the expression of trust off her face. She deserved to know.

"He chose you because of your name, because you are the Duke of Norbundshire's granddaughter."

"If that's an example of what happens to the relatives of dukes, I'm glad this whole business will soon be over. I'll be more than happy to return to being plain Matty Maxwell. Then maybe I can get some sleep."

He ran his thumb along the dark smudge under her eye. "You are the same person inside as you've always been. The name makes no difference. What he did makes no difference. You could call yourself Armethia Picklewart and you'd still be Matty inside."

She smiled, and it became a wide yawn. He pulled her head to his chest and massaged her back.

"Mmm, I could sleep here."

Rest was the best thing for her. And she felt so good, so right, in his arms. He would tell her again later, in the morning, when she was refreshed and better able to handle the truth.

"Close your eyes and rest a bit then."

She popped her head up. "Why did you turn away from me?"

"When did I . . . What are you talking about?"

"When you rescued me. You took one look at me tied up in Walmsley's bedroom and turned away in disgust."

"No, I checked first to make sure you were all right. Then I turned to take care of that weasel."

"I don't disgust you?"

"No! Never. I'm sorry if I—"

"Then why didn't you kiss me?"

"What? When?"

"In the carriage."

"Nathan was there."

"Once we got home."

"Everyone was here. And Edith and Anne wouldn't let me anywhere near you."

"Right now. Kiss me now."

"Matty, I think—"

"See."

She pulled away from him, and he tightened his grip.

"You're vulnerable right now. You've been under stress, and I can't take advantage of your defenseless state. You need rest and quiet and—"

"I need a good memory to counterbalance the bad one. In fact . . ." She threw the blanket off and sat up. Then she crawled on top of him, pulling up her nightgown and exposing her thighs, and straddled his hips with her knees.

His penis, half hard whenever she was near, sprang to attention with the pressure of her body. He ignored the insistent throbbing, subjugating his desires due to her greater need for rest and recuperation.

"Matty, I—"

"Are you telling me no?" she asked, pulling the studs from his shirt and baring his chest as she ran her hands over his skin.

He stilled her hands.

"You don't—"

"But I do know," she said, looking him in the eye. "Whenever I think of this day, I want to remember this night."

He brought her hands to his mouth and kissed each palm in turn. "I can never tell you no."

She grinned. "Then kiss me. And be quick about it."

He caught her in his arms and kissed her, softly, gently. He would wipe out the memory of her terror with tenderness. She pressed into his kiss, but he would not give into his raging needs and backed off, gently caressing her lips and stroking her back with the lightest of touches.

She pushed away from him and sat back, frowning.

A band constricted around his heart. He'd been as gentle as possible.

"If you didn't want to kiss me, you could have just said so."

She started to climb off him, and he stopped her with a hand on each thigh.

"Of course I want to kiss you. That's what I was doing."

"You were kissing me like you would kiss your grandmother."

"I was not!"

"All right, not exactly. But close."

"I was being gentle. And considerate."

"Is that what you call it?"

"Yes, and believe me, it wasn't easy."

"That's what I thought." She jerked free, stood, and started for the door.

He jumped up and caught her in an embrace, turning her to face him and refusing to let her pull away. Once she had stilled, he said, "Look at me."

She shook her head. "I don't want your pity," she said to his chest.

He cupped her face with his hands. "It was hard to be gentle because what I wanted to do was this." And he kissed her. Hard. Letting loose the searing heat of his passion, his need for her. He embraced her and held her tight against his body.

She responded with equal fervor, standing on tiptoe to wrap her arms around his neck—opening, giving, taking.

Mouths and lips and tongues. Kissing and sucking

and nipping. He tasted her passion. His passion. His or hers, one and the same. Tasted need. Tasted love.

He cupped her derriere, pressing her closer, and she ground her hips against him.

He groaned. She moaned. And they understood each other. No words were necessary when their bodies spoke so eloquently and in complete accord.

With mad abandon, they ripped off their clothes, each other's clothes. Buttons flying. Seams tearing. Awkward because he would not lose her lips. He drank her kiss like a man in the desert falling headlong into an oasis.

Flesh touching flesh. Glorious, and yet not enough.

He lifted her into his arms.

Matty wanted to tell him so many things. How wonderful he felt. How he made her feel. But words would not string together in any sensible manner. "Yes, yes," she whispered, the best she could manage.

He carried her to the sofa, kicking aside garments as he walked, giving her a minute to catch her breath. He started to set her down.

"No," she said, holding tighter around his neck.

He stopped.

"Not enough room," she explained. "We could go upstairs to my bed."

Preston shook his head. "I can't wait that long." He set her on her feet and grabbed the blanket.

She watched the play of his muscles as he spread the soft wool on the carpet in front of the fireplace and stirred the fire to life. The golden light made his skin glow, highlighting the sinewy muscles. Done with his task, he turned and looked at her.

"You are so beautiful," he said.

She shook her head and wrapped her arms around her waist. "I know what I look like." She had never been a raving beauty. Her nose was too large. Her eyebrows too pale. Her hips were broad, her waist thick. Her legs were too short. The list was endless.

"You're perfect," he said. He stepped forward and took her hands, holding her arms wide. "Don't be shy. I like looking at you."

"Preston, please, I—"

"Your skin is like the finest alabaster, smooth and silky to the touch. Only warm. And it's like golden honey where the sun has kissed it."

"Well, I hate hats and—"

"Hush, and let me finish. I want to kiss everywhere the sun has been and taste that golden sweetness. I want to taste everywhere the sun has missed. Like milk and honey."

He pulled her forward to stand on the blanket.

"You are beautiful. And it is more than the sum of your lovely features. The luminosity of your spirit shines and is my sun. Your warmth is air to me now. Your smile is sweet water. I'm not a poet—"

"You're doing pretty damn well," she said. He made her feel beautiful.

He grinned. "If I were a poet I'd write sonnets to the parts of your body I adore, and as you read them, I'd kiss those particular spots and prove my words."

She raised one eyebrow. "What parts?"

He stepped forward. "Your elbows," he said, cupping one in each hand.

"My elbows," she sputtered. Had he gone mad?

"A highly underrated body part." He leaned down and kissed the soft inner portion of her right elbow, laving it with his tongue.

"I see what you mean," she said as he switched to the other one, and her thighs quivered. She never would have thought of the elbow as an erogenous body part, but then again, her body responded anywhere he touched.

"And elbows are quite useful for this." He moved her arms upward and wrapped them around his neck.

He kissed her. A long, slow kiss.

"Knees are also unappreciated," he said, sinking to the blanket and bringing her with him.

"I can see they're quite necessary," she said.

"And hips," he said, swinging her legs around and leaning forward so she lay back on the soft pallet.

"Do you have an unusual fondness for joints?"

"Not at all," he said, unperturbed, settling next to her. "I'm simply pointing out that I adore all of you. Though admittedly, I do have favorite parts."

He stroked her breasts and her breath caught in her throat.

"Firm, and yet so soft. I will be compelled to write many sonnets to your breasts, if only to adore them in this manner as often as possible."

He kissed one, swirling the nipple with his tongue and mimicking the movement with his thumb on her other breast. She arched her back, and he supported her with one arm.

He slid his hand lower across her stomach, and then lower, lower.

"And here is yet another favorite," he said, his voice husky and his lips brushing her breast, his breath warm.

She felt a gush of wetness and stilled in embarrassment. What was happening?

"Yes, oh yes, my lovely one."

Well, if he liked it, it must be all right. Then he touched the nub that gave her so much pleasure, and she forgot everything but the glory of his touch, his magic hands.

Preston delighted in the intensity of her response, took joy in her pleasure. He sucked her nipple into his mouth and used his fingers and thumb to bring her to the brink.

She moaned and clutched him, her fingers kneading his shoulders.

He positioned himself between her legs. He drove into her in one smooth stroke, feeling as if he had come home after a long absence.

Mindful of the sparsely cushioned floor beneath her, he sat back on his heels, drawing her with him so she sat in his lap. Despite a few awkward moves, and getting the pallet in a tangle, he managed to flip them around so he was on his back and she was again astride his hips. He bent his knees and lifted his backside off the floor to pull the blanket out of the way.

As he plopped down with a bit more energy than he'd intended, her gasp of wide-eyed surprise was enough for him to repeat the motion again and again. She braced her hands on his chest, gripped his waist on either side with her knees, and rode him like a wild mustang.

Her vagina quivered around his penis, a tight sheath massaging his length, milking him. He groaned with the intense pleasure and knew he would not last as long as he would have liked. She arched and threw her head back, calling his name. And he could not control himself any longer. He clamped her hips to him and drove deeply, once, twice, finding his release as she reached her peak.

Matty collapsed boneless against his chest. He flipped the blanket over them both. Holding her close as their breathing returned to normal.

"Now what?" she asked.

Chapter 23

Matty folded her arms on his chest and propped her chin on her forearms. They were still on the floor after making love in front of the now-dying fire. "What do we do now?" she asked Preston. "It seems a bit anti-climactic to just stand up and get dressed."

He laughed, and she felt the vibrations through her body.

"We could sleep," he said.

"We could talk."

He groaned. "Why do women want to talk after making love?"

"Do all women want to talk?"

"I don't know. I haven't made love to them all. I'll have to get back to you later on that."

She punched him in the arm, and he chuckled.

"How many women have you made love with?"

"I am not going to answer that question."

"It must have been lots because you're really good at it. Not that I have anyone to compare you to, but I just know. Five women? Ten? Twenty? Stop me if I'm getting close."

"I refuse to answer. Not only because I never kept score, but because the truth is, although I may have had sex with others, I've only made love with one woman."

"Who was that?"

"You're joking?"

"No. I mean, I probably don't know her, but still a name—"

"Matty Maxwell."

"Yes? What?"

"That's her name."

"Me? I'm the one?"

"Who did you think I meant? And just to clarify the terminology, we made love together."

She closed her eyes. "Damn. I wanted you to make a memory, and you've made one helluva memory."

"What makes you think we're done?"

And he made love with her again. Slowly. Tenderly.

Kelso was up and about before dawn, as was his custom. He carried a clean shirt, a tie, and underclothes for his master in one hand, and a pitcher of hot water in the other, a towel draped over his arm.

At the door to the library, he paused and turned to look at the table. Where did that half-empty glass of milk come from? He would need to speak to Giles about his sloppiness.

Balancing the linen in the crook of his arm, he slid the door open. Moving silently in the near darkness, he placed the items on the table near the door, at the ready when Preston awoke. He bent to pick up something from the floor, assuming His Lordship had discarded his shirt in such an uncharacteristic manner due to his being half asleep at the time. Then he realized it was a woman's chemise. His gaze flew to the sofa.

Preston was still asleep, draped half on and half off the sofa as if he had fallen there in exhaustion and pulled the blanket over him. Them. Matty's head and hand rested on Preston's bare chest.

Kelso spun on his heel and scooted back to the hall.
He closed the door and cleared his throat.

He then rapped firmly on the door.

"Enter, and die," Preston called.

Kelso smiled. "Good morning, milord," he said
through the door. "I thought you might wish to retreat
to your club before the rest of the house is up and
about."

"Thank you, Kelso. You may go to the kitchen and
see about my breakfast. I should want a tray in about
twenty minutes."

"Very good, sir."

He left to perform the requested errand, sending up
a prayer that everything would turn out for the best.

Matty stretched and greeted the morning with a
smile. She barely remembered Preston carrying her up
to her room in the wee hours before dawn, but she remembered everything else about the previous night.

She smiled and jumped out of bed.

Anxious to get started on the many things she had to
do for the party, she rang the bell for Edith, washed,
and chose her old blue dress to work in.

"Good afternoon, milady," Edith said as she entered
with a breakfast tray. "Why are you wearing that old
thing when you have so many pretty frocks now?"

Matty looked at the clock. Half past noon!

"Oh, no. Why did you let me sleep so late? There's
so much to do."

"Mr. Kelso said you were not to be disturbed."

"Did he say when Preston would return?" A thrilling
shiver raced up her back at the thought of seeing Preston again.

"No, he didn't say."

Matty hid her disappointment by grabbing a piece of toast and gulping her coffee. "Where's Nathan? Bess? What are they up to today?"

"Bess is already napping, and Nathan is with Giles and Lord Burke cutting down the tree to go in the parlor. A ridiculous notion in my opinion."

Matty wiped her hands. That was all the breakfast she had time to eat. She tied on a large apron and retrieved her notebook, with her list of last minute duties, from her desk. First on the list, flower arrangements. She groaned. Anne had shown her the basics, but it took Matty an hour to achieve the same effect her friend had managed in mere minutes. And she needed four arrangements. "Have the flowers arrived?"

"In the kitchen's cool room."

Matty tucked her notebook in her pocket and set off. As she raced down the stairs, an insistent knocking sounded on the front door. Giles was gone, and Kelso was nowhere around. Matty hesitated. The last so-called guest had been Walmsley. Her heart pounded as if it would come out of her breast. An irrational panic gripped her like a giant fist squeezing the breath out of her lungs.

Damnation and dagnabbit. She would not let that man make her afraid of the simple act of answering a door. Despite her fear, she forced herself to open it.

"Good afternoon. Is this the residence of Lord Bathers?" a robust elderly man asked, removing his hat to reveal a striking shock of white hair.

Matty gave a sigh of relief. With his ruddy cheeks, his ample belly, and the friendly twinkle in his eyes, it had to be the man Anne had hired to portray Father Christmas for the children. "I must say you've been perfectly cast in the role," she said.

"I beg your pardon?"

"You quite look like Father Christmas."

The man laughed, and he turned to say something over his shoulder. She noticed two more men behind him.

"Oh, I wasn't aware Lady Anne had hired all of you."

"These are my friends—"

"We only have one costume."

The white-haired man cleared his throat. "Madam—"

She heard Bess's and Edith's voices on the upper stairs.

"Quick," Matty said. "I don't want Bess to see you." She tugged on his arm, pulling him toward the servants' stairs. "You'll have to stay out of sight until the party, but I'm sure Mrs. Donafry can find you a bite to eat in the meantime."

"Donafry of the pudding fame?" he asked, following her, and the others trailing behind him.

"Yes," she said with a laugh. "And she's been cooking nonstop for days."

She skipped ahead to let Mrs. Donafry know she should keep the three men downstairs and feed them all they wanted. The three elderly men entered the kitchen sniffing appreciatively, and with large grins on their faces.

Mrs. Donafry, a tall, imposing woman, rapped her wooden spoon on the table. "Hold out your hands. No one comes to my table with dirty fingernails."

Two of the men immediately held out their hands and turned them over and back like obedient schoolboys. The third man quickly followed suit.

The cook grunted in satisfaction. "What are your names?"

Father Christmas introduced his friends Loth and Wiggy, and himself as Shaky, short for Shakespeare. Then he said, "To quote the Earl of Lytton, 'We may live

without poetry, music, and art; We may live without conscience, and live without heart; We may live without
friends; We may live without books; But civilized man
cannot live without cooks.' And so I salute you." He
bowed in her direction.

"What a lot of rot," Mrs. Donafry said, in her gruff
voice, but she had a pleased smile. "Sit down."

They scrambled for chairs.

"And mind your manners. Make a mess on my table
and you'll be cooling your heels in the barn."

"May we have some pudding, please?" Shaky asked.

Matty retrieved her flowers and set them on a side
table with the vases while she went to fetch a sharp
knife to cut the stems. When she returned, Wiggy had
started arranging the flowers for the dining room in a
long, low container.

"That's beautiful," she said.

"He can't hear you," Shaky said. "Lost his ear horn
about a month ago, and he's stone-deaf without it."

"He's quite talented with flowers," she said.

"He used to make the arrangements for the church
altar," Loth said.

"Misses his garden, Wiggy does," Shaky added. "He'll
gladly take care of your flowers if you'll let him."

She tapped Wiggy on the shoulder and, when he
turned, she nodded to the flowers and smiled. Then she
kissed him on the cheek to thank him in a way he could
understand.

The man actually blushed, and Shaky laughed.

Mrs. Donafry banged her spoon on the table. "You'll
not be disrespectful to Lady Matilda."

Shaky turned to look at Matty with a surprised expression.

Mrs. Donafry set a bowl of unshelled peas before Shaky and a bowl of unpeeled potatoes before Loth. "You might as well earn your supper like your friend there," she said. "Do a good job, and I'll give you a double portion of pudding."

Both men set to work with determination.

"I apologize for any unintentional disrespect," Shaky said as he shelled peas with enthusiasm, if not much skill.

"None taken," Matty responded with a smile.

"We thought you were the maid or the house-keeper," Loth explained.

Mrs. Donafry cleared her throat and gave them a stern look, but Matty only laughed.

"I must leave you in Mrs. Donafry's capable hands," she said, taking out her notebook. "So much to do."

"We'll see you later," Shaky said, eyeing the fruit pies the cook had set on the windowsill to cool.

"Oh dear, what about costumes?" Matty asked. "We only have the one."

"Don't you worry about that, dearie," Mrs. Donafry said, turning her toward the stairs. "Mr. Kelso will think of something. By the time of the party he'll have these three looking fine and dandy."

Matty paused on the stairs and turned to look back. Something she couldn't put her finger on didn't seem quite right; not really wrong in a worrisome sense, just not totally right.

She shook off her strange feeling. As she climbed the stairs, she dug a small pencil out of her pocket and made a note to send Giles on an errand for some last-minute Christmas gifts.

* * *

Matty checked another item off her list. Only two more items and then all she'd have left to do would be to get dressed for the party. She came around the corner and spotted Nathan creeping toward the parlor door. With a few quick steps she grabbed him around the waist and spun him away from the closed door.

"No, you don't," she said. "You can't see the tree and presents until the party."

"I'm s-sneaking up on G-Giles." Nathan looked up at her, and he had used the art supplies to paint his face in garish stripes and designs. "We're p-playing c-cowboys and Indians. I'm the Indian."

"Really?"

"If I s-surprise him, I get a p-piece of c-candy." Nathan reached to the door. "He's in the parlor," he whispered.

"No, he's not."

"I heard him."

"Giles isn't in the parlor because I sent him on an errand."

"Aw, d-darn. We was having f-fun."

"I thought you were playing with your sister."

He made a face. "Edith is with her." He pantomimed bathing and combing long hair, swirling it into curls. He made a simpering expression into a pretend mirror.

Matty bit her lip to keep from laughing. He obviously did not share his sister's love of primping and pampering. "Sounds like a good idea. I think it's time for your bath, too."

"D-don't n-need one."

"Oh, yes, you do," she said, turning him toward the stairs. "You can't meet Father Christmas with dirt behind your ears." She reached for his ear, and he ducked away. She grabbed him and tickled him. They were soon scrambling around on the floor, laughing and giggling.

"Stop that this instant!"

Matty rolled to her back and looked up at the woman standing in the parlor doorway. She was elegantly attired in a fashionable bronze afternoon dress with abundant ecru lace trimming. Her iron-gray hair was upswept into a pompadour, and a large angular hat perched atop it at a precarious slant. She held an ebony walking stick in one hand and pounded it on the floor.

"I should have you turned out without a reference for that revolting behavior," the woman said.

Matty stood and smoothed out her apron. Nathan hid behind her skirt. Despite her first impression that the woman was tall, Matty stood nearly eye to eye.

"We were only having a bit of fun."

"Shenanigans. It's positively dreadful, but I don't know why I should have expected better. No wonder I've waited nine minutes and still have no tea."

Matty turned and motioned for Nathan to go upstairs. "Don't worry. I'll be fine," she whispered to him.

Nathan trailed upstairs, keeping an eye on the stranger.

Matty folded her hands at her waist. "Madam, I don't know who you are, but—"

"That is demonstrably obvious by your impertinent behavior."

"As you are in theory my guest—"

"*Your* guest? I should say not," the older woman said.

Matty bristled at the woman's rudeness. "In that case, I'd be pleased to show you to the door."

The woman simply raised her chin and looked down her nose. Matty walked to the door and paused as the housekeeper entered the hall carrying a loaded tray and then skidded to a halt.

"Never mind tea, Mrs. Manor," she said. "The *lady* was just leaving." She opened the door.

"Mrs. Manor, I shall return at precisely eight o'clock this evening. Tell my son I expect him to be here. And I expect that insolent chit to be gone." With that, the older woman sailed out the door.

Matty clung to the doorknob with both hands as she looked to Mrs. Manor with desperate hope. "Tell me I did not just kick Preston's mother out of his house."

"I'm afraid I can't," she said with a commiserating expression.

And she was coming back. At eight. When Matty would have a house full of party guests.

She shut the door slowly, then walked to the library, sat at the desk, and got out paper and a pen.

Mrs. Manor followed. She put the tray on the table and poured some tea. "What are you doing?" she asked as she sat the cup on the desk within Matty's reach.

"I'm canceling the party." She quickly scrawled notes to Anne, Cordelia, and Vivian, apologizing for the last-minute change in plans. "Please see these are delivered right away."

"Are you sure that's necessary?"

"I can hardly expect guests to endure an unpleasant scene."

"But you've worked so hard, and the children are so excited. Maybe she won't show. Maybe His Lordship can call on her and prevent her from coming."

"Since we're not sure when Preston will return, we can't count on his help."

Matty retrieved the note that was addressed to Anne and added a postscript. If Anne so desired, Matty would send Father Christmas over to her house to see

Andrea and Stephen either before or after he made his
appearance for Nathan and Bess. Pasting a brave smile
on her face, she gave the housekeeper back the note.

"Please tell the staff we'll still have a festive evening,
only with fewer people." She stood. "Now I should
start getting dressed."

She wanted to look her best when she saw Preston.
And gave him the bad news about his mother.

Matty rarely spent hours on her toilette, but she had
bathed and washed her hair and soothed lotion on her
skin. Then she had donned a new white lace chemise,
a corset, black silk stockings, red garters, black kid
leather dancing slippers, and a white petticoat—and
her favorite turquoise robe to sit for Edith to style her
hair. No simple coronet of braids or classic chignon
would suffice. Edith insisted the new dress deserved
something special, and fashioned Matty's hair into a
mass of ringlets caught up high on her head with red
rosebuds nestled here and there and a few curls left to
trail along one side of her neck.

When she received word that Preston waited downstairs, she rushed Edith through the rest of the process,
adding three more white lacy petticoats before donning
the magnificent dress. Made of red silk shot with
golden threads, the fitted bodice had a wide band that
crossed over her breasts and around her shoulders almost like sleeves, but it left her shoulders bare. A bit of
her lacy chemise showed, as well as more cleavage
than she'd expected. The front of the dress was plain,
allowing the beauty of the material to shine. The skirt,
a full ten yards around the bottom, was then caught
up in the back in a series of poufs, making the small

bustle and exposing the lower layer of lace on her petticoat.

Matty added golden ear bobs that had been her mother's, long white evening gloves, a gold paper fan, and a gold mesh reticule to hold her handkerchief and scent bottle.

As she walked slowly down the stairs, the appreciation in Preston's eyes was worth all the effort. He had been leaning against the newel, chatting with the servants milling about the entrance hall, when it suddenly had become quiet and he'd looked up and straightened to attention.

She smiled. He was so handsome in his black evening attire, with his snowy cravat and gold shirt studs. For the holiday, he had added a holly boutonniere.

The servants, in their best uniforms, lined up by rank in the traditional salute to the lady of the house. From Kelso, in black tails and white gloves—as he was performing the duties of butler—to Giles, in full-dress livery, everyone stood at attention. Even the temporary help was included, with Shaky in his Father Christmas mask and costume, and Loth and Wiggy in green britches the same color as the footman's livery, red coats cut like fox-hunting jackets, and jaunty peaked hats and pointy slippers. Matty had no idea from where the extra costumes could have possibly come.

"You are a vision of loveliness," Preston said, taking her hand for the last few steps.

He bowed low over her hand, and she curtsied as deep and as graceful as she had ever managed. Then they turned and returned the staff's salute in the same manner.

Matty signaled Giles to bring her the basket she'd

left under the table, and she handed the first present to Kelso, a black silk vest she had made.

"This is not necessary, milady. Lord Bathers has already given us our Christmas gratuity, and he has been quite generous."

"A mere token of my appreciation," she said.

Kelso probably understood the scam would be over in a few days, and then the household would return to what it had been before. Some of the newly hired staff would be out of a job.

She gave Mrs. Manor and Mrs. Donafry lace jabots they could wear with any dress, and thanked them for making her and the children feel welcome. She gave the two maids lace-edged handkerchiefs, thanking them for jobs well done. She gave Giles a pocketknife and thanked him for being a friend to Nathan.

Then she came to the trio of actors. She gave Wiggy a new ear horn, and Loth a bright purple handkerchief, which he immediately used a corner of to dab his eyes. And for Shaky she had a long, red, velvet scarf, to keep his neck warm and protect his voice.

"Are we ready?" Edith called from out of sight at the top of the stairs.

Matty rushed Shaky and the other two men into the library to hide, while Edith brought down Bess looking adorable in her white lace dress with the red ribbons, white stockings, and red shoes, and her head a mass of golden curls. Nathan followed, tugging at the neckline of his wide collar. He had absolutely refused to wear either velvet or short pants. Matty had finally compromised on velvet long pants. And he looked very nice.

Edith stood Bess on the floor, and Matty took her hand. Time to reveal their very-first Christmas tree to the children.

She nodded to Kelso, but it was Preston who stepped forward to fling open both panels of the parlor door.

"Surprise!"

And for the first time in her life, Matty nearly fainted.

Chapter 24

Matty could not believe her eyes. In the parlor, quietly waiting the entire time, were Preston's friends, Marsfield and Anne and their children, Burke and Cordelia, and Vivian and a portly man wearing a vividly embroidered vest, who could be none other than her husband Theo. All the people she had sent notes to canceling the party.

Preston caught her up in a searing kiss. Everyone cheered, and her cheeks flamed.

"You're standing under the mistletoe," he whispered, with that oh-so-charming melt-her-knees smile. "What else could I do?"

"That was no mistletoe kiss," she whispered back.

"Just wait until I get you alone; then we'll put this mistletoe to good use." At the same time, he put an arm around her waist and drew her into the room.

Anne stepped forward.

"I don't understand," Matty said. "Didn't you get my note?"

"Yes, of course. However, Mrs. Manor, bless her, sent word about the reason for your distress."

Matty looked over her shoulder, but the hall was miraculously devoid of servants.

"We've all faced Preston's mother at one time or another, so we decided to be here to offer you moral support," Anne said.

"And we positively refuse to miss a good party," Vivian said, and everyone cheered.

"With your permission," Anne continued, "we'll simply rearrange the schedule for the evening. The children will go off to dinner at, say, about quarter to eight. Then after the evening's *entertainment*—"

Matty groaned, and Preston, his arm still around her waist, gave her a squeeze.

"Then Father Christmas will visit—"

Everyone cheered.

"Then the children will be put to bed—"

Marsfield cheered. When his daughter Andrea gave him a sour look, he tickled her back to a smile.

"And the adults can have a late supper," Anne finished.

"I'll drink to that," Theodore said.

"Watch that you don't toast too much, or we'll have to put you to bed early like the children," Vivian said to him.

"Thank you all," Matty said, sniffing and digging in her reticule for her handkerchief. "I've never had friends like you before. This is really a Christmas to remember."

Several other handkerchiefs came out, and Cordelia bawled like a baby.

"She's very emotional right now," Burke explained, escorting his wife to a chair and handing her his large handkerchief to replace her dainty, lace, useless one.

"I thought this was a party," Theo said. "Let's have some music." He seated himself at the baby grand piano in the corner and started pounding out lively Christmas carols with enthusiasm.

Giles served champagne in fluted crystal glasses, and strawberry punch in cups to the children. The maids circulated with tasty tidbits. And Preston and

Matty made the rounds among the noisy, festive group to wish everyone a happy holiday.

Matty stepped back to take in the wonderful picture. Burke and Marsfield sat on the floor playing a game with Nathan and Stephen that seemed to involve wooden disks and sticks, and much slapping of the floor and laughing. Bess sat on Vivian's lap, examining her many beaded necklaces. Also on the sofa were Cordelia and Andrea discussing names for her babies. Anne and Theodore played a duet almost in syncopation.

"Making a memory?" Preston asked, slipping up behind her and wrapping his arms around her waist.

"Yes," she said with a smile, placing her arms over his and leaning back.

He pulled her into the dining room and around the corner out of sight, and kissed her.

"There's no mistletoe in here," she said.

"Who needs it?"

And he kissed her again.

"I've been waiting all day for this," he said. He reached into his pocket, pulled out a small box, and gave it to her.

"I thought we were giving presents later," she said.

"This isn't a Christmas gift," he said. "It's something that belongs to you."

Confused, she opened the box to reveal a ring, a large ruby surrounded by diamonds.

"It was my grandmother's engagement ring. It's now yours. I love you, Matty Maxwell. Will you marry me?"

"Oh my." He had surprised her. "Marriage?"

"That's not exactly the answer I was looking for."

But she had more to consider than herself. She had her children. Obviously Preston had done very well for himself, but even he had admitted to traveling five of the last seven years. She didn't want her children to grow up traveling from one place to another, running scams, running from the law occasionally. The way she had grown up. A flimflam man did not make the best father, did not allow for putting down roots. She could not see Preston farming. And then there was the matter of his family.

"There is a lot to think about. I love you, too, but that doesn't mean we should get married," she said.

"Say that again."

"That doesn't—"

"No, the part where you said you love me."

"I love you."

"And I love you. That's all that matters. We can work everything else out."

"The children—"

"I love your children, too. And I'd be pleased and proud to be their father."

"No more scams?"

He took a deep breath. "About that—"

"Never mind." Matty pressed her lips together. Even if he promised to give up his life, it would not last. Her father had given it up. For a while. But it hadn't lasted. Could she take whatever Preston could give? Could she survive when he left? And he would. Eventually.

Then again, how could she not grab at happiness, however long it would last?

"Matty, I should . . ." He paused and turned toward the door.

And she noticed the sudden silence in the other room.

Had his mother shown up early?

Bess started to cry, and Matty rushed into the parlor.

She stopped short and blinked in disbelief. "Reverend Henshaw?"

The man clung to the doorjamb with one hand, dragging Giles, who had his arms wrapped around Henshaw's foot, and fighting off Kelso, who plucked at his arms and hands to either loosen his grip or grab the pistol Henshaw waved about in his other hand.

"There you are," Henshaw said to her. "My love, my fiancée, my intended. I'm here to save you from a fate worse than death."

Matty swallowed and looked around. Anne was already on the move, carrying Bess out of the room and herding her children in front of her. Behind her, Burke carried Nathan, who glared at Henshaw and struggled to be free. Theodore rang the bellpull as if he were chiming midnight on Big Ben. Vivian helped Cordelia to a chair in the corner, while Marsfield moved to stand at her side with Preston.

"What are you doing here?" she asked Henshaw. She waved off Kelso and Giles.

"I followed you." Henshaw straightened his coat, and he stepped forward with a jerk of his head. "To save you from evil. Look at how you're dressed." He waved the gun in her direction. "Harlot. Jezebel. I'm here to save you from this life of sin and wickedness."

Preston bristled. "He's mad."

Marsfield laid his hand on his friend's arm. "I've sent for the constable," he said, low enough for only Matty and Preston to hear. "Let's not let anyone get hurt in the meantime."

"You!" Henshaw said, pointing at Preston. "You're the one who dragged her into the mud of depravity, into this pit of debauchery. You shall burn in hell for your decadence."

"Perhaps so, but that is not for you to decide," Preston

said, his tone even and calm. "Now I suggest you leave my house quietly."

"I am your salvation," he said to Matty. "You were chosen by God to be my wife. When we're married—"

"That will never happen," she said.

He shook the gun at her. "It will. It will." He pulled a book from his pocket. "I'll marry us myself. Right now. Dearly beloved—"

"She cannot marry without my permission," Shaky said as he entered from the hall wearing his Father Christmas costume.

"Who the hell are you supposed to be?" Henshaw asked the large man.

"No, Shaky," Matty said, afraid Henshaw would shoot him for interfering. "Stay out of this."

"I can't," he said, removing his mask. He looked Matty in the eye. "I am the Duke of Norbundshire, and you are my granddaughter."

Henshaw sank to his knees and bent over as if to kiss the man's boots. "I request her hand in marriage. God has told me her money should be used for the church."

The women's skirts billowed as they dropped gracefully into curtsies, and the men bowed.

"Your Grace," everyone said in near unison.

"Curtsy," Preston whispered out of the side of his mouth. "He really is the duke."

But Matty just stared. Her grandfather.

And she realized the crushing truth. Preston had lied to her from the beginning. He had never intended to scam the duke. She was the mark. The patsy. Preston had scammed her. He'd flimflammed her like an ignorant rube. Shame on him. Shame on her for believing him.

She turned and ran, not caring where she went, but needing some air, some space. Needing to get as far away from Preston as possible. She should have known better. What could a man like him possibly see in her? How could she have been so stupid as to believe he was attracted to her? Oh, he was attracted, all right, to her grandfather's bank account.

She ran outside, and the winter night air slapped her in the face. She breathed in the bracing cold. What was she doing? Running away was not a viable option. She would have to go back for her children. Slowing to a walk, she wrapped her arms around her waist.

Warmth settled around her shoulders, and she spun around to face Preston, his white shirt glowing in the moonlight. She shrugged out of his coat and held it out to him.

"Please," he said. "Please wear it. You don't want to catch cold."

If she got sick, she wouldn't be able to leave easily. She swirled the coat over her shoulders and jammed in her arms, realizing her mistake too late. His cologne drifted up; his warmth surrounded her.

"You lied to me from the very beginning," she said, lashing out to counteract his nearness.

"If I'd told you the truth, you wouldn't have believed me. You never would have come with me."

"So you resorted to lies. Or was that your plan all along?"

"I tried to tell you several times."

"You didn't try very hard."

"The time just never seemed right."

She snorted. Was he waiting for the right moment when they danced? When they made love? Was everything he'd said a lie?

"Matty, I love you. I want to marry you."

She couldn't trust him. "And the fact that I have a fortune is just a bonus? You're no better than Henshaw." She didn't mean that, but it had come out, and she wouldn't take it back.

"Keep your bloody money. I don't need it, never wanted it. In fact, I saw your inheritance as something I would have to overcome. A deterrent."

He seemed so sincere. But he had seemed so before.

"Nice touch. Decry the very thing you're after. And it would have worked except I've learned my lesson the hard way. I refuse to be manipulated by you again."

He held out his hands. "What can I do to convince you I love you and want to spend the rest of my life with you?"

"Nothing," she said, pushing by him to return to the house. "Absolutely nothing."

Preston stood in the snow, not feeling the cold, not feeling the wind, because the really frigid icicles speared his heart. He had hurt her, and that caused him immense pain. Surprised that his heart still beat, that his blood still coursed through his veins, he started walking toward the house and the rest of his dismal life without her. One step at a time.

Matty stood at the parlor door looking at the friends who would soon hate her. Preston's friends.

"Thank you all for coming this evening. Please excuse me for the rest of the party."

Without another word, not trusting herself to look directly at any one person, she turned and went up the stairs, managing to hold her tears until she made it to her room.

She took off Preston's coat and threw it across the room. Then she decided she didn't even want it in the room with her and would throw it out in the hall. When she picked it up, an envelope fell out, and it was addressed to her in Preston's precise hand. She didn't want to read anything that flimflamming man had to say. Marching to the fireplace, she started to toss it in the grate, but paused at the last second.

She weighed the thick, heavy envelope in her hand. Surely he could not have written that many sonnets in a single day? Cursing herself for a fool, she gave in to her curiosity and ripped open his seal.

The first sheet of the packet was Preston's personal writing paper and had his crest in the upper left corner.

My dearest love,

I searched high and low for the perfect gift. I found no silk as soft as your skin, no perfume as sweet as your scent, no lace as delicate as your hair. Mere jewels paled when compared to the sparkle in your eyes.

And yet I wanted something special, something meaningful to mark our first Christmas together. Please accept this in lieu of the moon and stars I would have given you except they would not fit into the envelope.

You have brought me so much joy; I hope this returns a small measure of it to you.

You once accused me of having no heart, and that is true. I have given it to you.

Your Preston

Matty sank to the floor, her knees no longer capable of holding her heavy heart. She flipped through the packet of papers that followed the letter. With gold seals and bits of wax and ribbons and lots of big legal-sounding words, the papers gave Matilda Maxwell complete and irrevocable guardianship of Nathan Walker Maxwell and Elizabeth "Bess" Marie Maxwell.

One set of papers was signed by the American Ambassador for President Lincoln, and the other set was signed by Queen Victoria. Thanks to Preston, no one would ever take her children from her.

He had seen into her heart and given her the one gift that meant more to her than anything else in the world, except him. She loved him as much as she loved her children.

She scrambled to her feet and ran down the hall, then pounded down the stairs, calling his name. She slid to a halt in front of the parlor doors, but the room was empty.

Norbundshire caught her arm. "Everyone just left. I guess no one was in a party mood anymore."

"Where did they go?"

"Home, I assume."

She looked around the foyer as if Preston might have stayed behind. The constable, writing in his notebook, stood over Henshaw, who was crouched on the floor muttering. Kelso and Giles, both armed, stood guard. Loth and Wiggy, seated in chairs borrowed from the library, looked on with interest. Everyone else was gone. Preston was gone.

"I have to go after him. I have to talk to him. Kelso, I need the carriage, or a horse. Or a cab. Anything."

"Now, now," Norbundshire said. "Preston has gone to his club, and you won't be allowed in there. I'm sure whatever you have to say can wait until morning," he said.

"No, it can't. He asked me to marry him, and I told him no." Desperate for his help, she grabbed his lapels. "If you're my real grandfather and care anything about my happiness, you'll get him back here. Please."

"We can send Giles after him. But, why, if you already told him no?"

She slumped into the chair beside Wiggy. What was the use? Preston would not come back to see her, and she couldn't blame him. "He probably hates me after all the terrible things I said."

"Does that mean you've changed your mind?" Norbundshire asked.

"Preston will never willingly see me or speak to me again. I was that horrid to him. I realized too late the only thing that matters is I love him. I don't care what he does, or where we have to go." She sniffed. "And now it's too late."

Norbundshire turned to the constable. "Can you catch the carriage that just left here?"

"I am a representative of the law," the indignant constable said. "I can't chase a man down because some chit is crying."

Norbundshire rose to his full height. "Do you know who I am?"

"Father Christmas?" the constable answered.

"I am the Duke of Norbundshire," he said in a booming voice that echoed off the marble floor.

Henshaw stood slowly, and he spoke to the duke. "Preston is the devil incarnate, and good riddance to him. But I'm still here and I'm willing to marry Matty even though she's ruined, utterly ruined."

"Be careful what you say about my granddaughter."

"It's true." Henshaw laid his hand on his heart. "They lived in the same house, traveled together without a proper chaperone. That Preston had carnal knowledge of her is a given. But I forgive her, for she is weak, as all women are weak in matters of the flesh. I will be her strength. When we're married, I'll ensure she never strays from the path of righteousness again."

The duke turned to face Matty. "Is this true?"

"That he's crazy? Yes. Or did you mean, am I ruined?

I suppose that depends on your interpretation of the term."

"For argument's sake, let's use the generally accepted definition. Because if you are, and Preston is the man responsible, I'll send the law after him to bring him back here to face his responsibilities." Her grandfather winked at her. "There's no way he can refuse to come."

She smiled up at him and stood to give him a hug. "In that case, I am ruined. Utterly, thoroughly, and completely ruined."

"Constable! That man who just left here is responsible for despoiling my granddaughter. Fetch him back here immediately."

The constable put his notebook away and shambled to the door. "I hate domestic cases," he mumbled.

"Hurry up, man," Norbundshire said. "Don't let the bounder get away."

"What about that one?" the lawman asked, pointing over his shoulder at Henshaw.

"We'll keep him here for you," Kelso promised.

The constable left shaking his head, and Matty soon heard whistles, and the wheels of his wagon, and the horses' hooves clattering over the cobblestones. He would bring Preston back. She had to believe that. Now she had to think of something to say to Preston when he was forcibly brought in the door.

Norbundshire held a quick, whispered conversation with Loth and Wiggy, and then he offered his arm to Matty. "Shall we have a glass of champagne to celebrate your engagement?"

"That might be premature. Preston may recant his proposal." In all likelihood he would never want to see her again, but at least she'd have a chance to tell him how she felt.

"Rubbish. He impressed me as a man with a good bit

of gray matter between his ears. What sensible man would not want to marry my granddaughter?"

She took a seat on the sofa, and he joined her.

"I can't help but wonder why my father never told me about you."

Norbundshire breathed out a long sigh. "I can't speak for your father, but I suppose in his own way he was trying to protect you. When I told Cecelia I would cut her off without a penny if she married your father, she laughed and said your father was the only man who didn't want to marry her for her portion. I thought she was wrong and he'd leave her brokenhearted. Instead, she left me. Your father made her happy, and you were the light of her life."

"How do you know this?"

"She wrote me every week, told every little detail about you." He smiled. "I had never known babies could be so fascinating until I saw you through her eyes. I saved all her letters."

"If you knew about me, why didn't you contact me?" Matty was torn between her interest in the man who had known her mother, and loyalty to her father. "Surely my father would not have prevented that."

"Not on purpose; or maybe so, I don't know. I tried to find you, to no avail. Then once, when I was rereading your mother's letters, I came across a reference to a family farm in Tennessee. I sent another detective, and found you had lived there for a while but I was too late. From then on, every time the detective got close, your father would move to a new town."

Matty nodded. That made sense. Sometimes her father would pack up and have them leave even though she couldn't see how the scam they were working could have busted.

"So finally, I stopped sending the detectives after

you and simply waited for your father to bring you back to the farm. I wrote to the local churchman—"

"You mean Henshaw?"

"Yes, I'm sorry to say. I asked Henshaw to keep an eye out for you and notify me if you returned. Paid him quite handsomely, too."

"And he didn't contact you when I came back?" More pieces of the puzzle were falling into place.

"Oh, he wrote me."

"Then why—"

"By then, my heirs had started to disappear. My nephew Chauncey Smythe was lost at sea. After Matthew and Merton Carleton were killed in a carriage accident, Walmsley became the heir, and I suspected him of having a hand in their deaths."

"Walmsley is your heir? We're related to him?"

"Quite distantly, but obviously not far enough. I feared for your safety should your whereabouts become known, so I didn't contact you. I pretended to believe you were dead; however, Henshaw and I continued to correspond."

"When I was with Walmsley, that man Stanford mentioned something about arranging accidents. He was talking about your other heirs, wasn't he?"

"I'm afraid so. Unfortunately, I can't prove it."

"Now I understand why Preston said my name was the reason Walmsley had chosen me." And she understood why he hadn't told her the truth at that time. He truly had tried, and she had prevented him. How many other times had she stopped him without her knowing she'd done it?

"I'm not sure if I can forgive him for bringing you to London and putting you in danger. In fact, I can't figure why he did it? After all—"

"The queen sent me to fetch her."

Preston! Joy surging through her, she stood and started toward the door, but faltered to a halt after a few steps. His expression was stonily bland, but his eyes burned like dark coals.

"Victoria?" Norbundshire jumped to his feet. "Blast it, I knew I shouldn't have told that interfering woman the truth."

Preston didn't move a muscle. "I was told only that Her Majesty wished to have her favorite cousin and his estranged granddaughter reconciled. I was *assigned* to bring her to London using any methods necessary."

Behind him, Marsfield and Anne stood by in stoic support of their friend, the constable took notes, and Kelso, Loth, and Wiggy watched with avid interest.

"Did that give you permission to—"

"Grandfather, please," Matty said, laying a hand on his arm. "Let me handle this." She walked and stood within a foot of Preston, close enough to smell his cologne, close enough to feel the heat of his anger. His hair was mussed, his tie askew, his coat torn and dirty. He refused to meet her gaze, staring at a spot over her left shoulder. She walked around him, looking him up and down like a prize stallion. His hands were hand-cuffed behind his back. "I see he was not thrilled to come back here," she said to the constable.

"He gave us a bit of a tussle, but I had half a dozen of my lads give me a hand." The constable consulted his notebook. "They had already let off Lord and Lady Deering, and were in the process of unloading the Marsfields here, who followed us back here in their own carriage, of their own volition, leaving behind their two children in the custody of their nanny, May-berry." He slapped his notebook shut. "Who is going to go down to the station with me to press charges?"

"Bear with me for a minute, please," Matty said. The

fact that he was working for the queen explained many things. But even if Matty accepted that Preston was not a flimflam man, she still had a few unanswered questions. She returned to her place in front of Preston. "If this matter goes to court, you will be sworn in, so let's just pretend that has already happened and tell the truth now. Did the queen authorize you to lie to me?"

"I did not get my orders directly from the queen."

"Who ordered you, and by what authority?"

Preston did not answer until Marsfield whispered, "Go ahead."

"Lord Marsfield works for the queen, and I work for him."

"As what? Not a servant or a clerk, then what?"

"I am an agent."

"And exactly what does an agent do?" Matty asked.

"Whatever I am assigned to do."

"Such as?"

"That's confidential."

"Very well. Let's concentrate on this particular assignment. Did Marsfield authorize you to lie to me?"

"Not in so many words."

"Did he authorize you to trick me into coming to London?"

"I was told not to fail in my mission regardless of the methods necessary."

"Were you authorized to purchase gifts for me?"

"Any expenses directly related to the mission will be reimbursed by the crown."

She stepped closer. "Were you authorized to make me fall in love with you?"

His gaze flicked to hers, and then away again. "I was not aware that had happened."

"Were you authorized to kiss me?" She stepped

within inches of him. "To make love with me?" she whispered.

He groaned. "Matty, I—"

She put her arms around his neck and kissed him with all the love in her heart. After a moment's resistance, he returned the kiss. His response told her all she needed to know. He still loved her. Flimflam man or an agent of the queen, Preston was the man she loved.

When she stepped away, he asked, "Why did you do that?"

She grinned up at him. "Because you're standing under the mistletoe." She turned to the constable. "Please take those handcuffs off so he can kiss me properly."

The man did as he was told, and Preston wrapped his arms around her waist. She framed his dear face with her hands and said, "Yes."

"When?"

"Now."

"Can't."

"Tomorrow?"

"What are you two talking about?" Norbundshire asked.

"Getting married," Matty and Preston said together, without looking away from each other.

And everyone applauded. Except the constable, who mumbled, "I should have known this would happen."

Preston kissed Matty with the passion he had tried to suppress since seeing her again.

"From the looks of it, we'd better get them married right away," Norbundshire said.

Preston turned to him and said, "Your Grace, I respectfully ask for your granddaughter's hand in marriage."

"That's a bit of putting the horse after the cart, but I appreciate the observance of the formality. You have my blessing. Congratulations."

"Thank you." Preston shook hands with the duke.

Matty gave her grandfather a hug and kissed him on the cheek. Then everyone wanted a chance to congratulate the couple, shake hands, or kiss the bride-to-be. Kelso served champagne, and toasts were made.

Norbundshire called for everyone's attention. "As I said earlier, I think this marriage better take place as soon as possible. How about tonight? Nothing better than a Christmas wedding."

Everyone cheered, but Preston looked glum. "I'm afraid that's impossible. I tried to get a special license, but the office was closed."

The duke laid his finger aside his nose. "It helps to know the right people," he said in a stage whisper. "Loth? Wiggy? Where are you?"

His two friends stepped forward and handed him several pieces of paper.

"These will do just fine. You can add the seals in the morning. Ladies and gentlemen, may I introduce you to Bishop Wickham, better known as Wiggy. He's retired from most of his duties, but he is still technically a bishop and authorized to perform marriage ceremonies. In addition, I have the honor of presenting Lord Latham, Chancellor emeritus, who has written out a special license and will see it's filed with yesterday's date. Now, let's have a wedding!"

Preston looked at Matty and she nodded, radiant with joy.

"Are you ready?" he asked.

"Yes."

"That's my favorite word."

"Shouldn't we wait for—"

"I don't want to wait a single minute longer than necessary. Not for anyone or anything."

"One half hour? I want to get the children, and you should at least straighten your tie."

"Agreed. One half hour." He looked at the clock. "It's seven fifteen. In thirty minutes you'd better be standing in front of that fireplace ready to say I do, or I'll come and get you. Nothing is going to stop this wedding."

Chapter 25

Preston waited, suddenly nervous. Not about marriage to Matty, but about the wedding itself. The preparations had been slapped together so fast, something was bound to go wrong.

His best friend Burke, who had been roused from sleep and hurriedly rushed back, stood by his side. Burke fussed with his tie for the umpteenth time.

"Stop," Preston said. "It's fine. You're making me jumpy."

"Cordelia and I were dressed and out the door in eight minutes flat. I do believe that is a world's record."

"Doesn't count because you could not have been totally undressed."

"True, but . . . How could you know that?"

"Because I've known you for years and years, and you always have a hot chocolate and precisely three biscuits before you get ready for bed."

"Unless I've been drinking, which I was earlier."

"Then you have a hot lemon toddy and three soda biscuits. You are a man who likes his routines."

Burke looked at his wife, sitting with her grandmother Vivian and her husband Theo, who also had been rushed back. He smiled. "This is only the first night of many my usual routine will be disrupted. Cordelia had her first labor pain and—"

"What? And she's here? She should be—"

"Don't panic. It was only a twinge, and everything is under control."

"I cannot believe how calm you are." Especially after his friend had spent the last few months hovering over her like a hen with one prize chick.

"Vivian said the babies are coming a bit early, but it will be hours and hours yet, and Cordelia absolutely refused to miss the wedding."

Then Preston's attention was caught by a movement at the parlor door. Little Bess entered and walked past the rows of chairs that had been set up for the guests and the servants. She carried a basket and tossed rose petals onto the floor, one at a time. Anne followed, the matron of honor, but Preston barely glanced at her. His gaze sought only Matty.

She entered on Nathan's arm.

Matty wore a crown of white flowers on her head. The wisp of lace netting over her face did not hide the sparkle of her sapphire-blue eyes or her luminous smile. She carried three long-stemmed roses tied in a green ribbon the color of Preston's family's livery. In the traditional language of flowers, the one yellow rose symbolized friendship, the red one stood for passion, and the white for pure and true love.

The ceremony proceeded smoothly. Nathan gave away the bride, responding proudly and without a stutter, and Bess echoed his words. But they had not even gotten to the part that asked for any objections when they heard a loud gasp from the back of the room.

"This is sacrilege," an outraged woman's voice said.

Everyone turned to face the door.

Lady Stiles, Preston's mother, stood shaking with indignation. "How dare you make a mockery of the wedding ceremony? Who is responsible for this . . . this heinous travesty?"

She marched up the aisle.

"Sit down, Mother," Preston said, thankful he sounded calmer than he felt. "You are disrupting the ceremony."

"I should hope so." She turned to Matty. "You! Wasn't I plainspoken enough earlier when I said—"

"Mother, may I present my bride—"

"You cannot marry this tramp, not even in this sham wedding."

"Now just a minute." The duke stood up. "That's my granddaughter you're speaking of."

Lady Stiles whirled on him. "Father Christmas? That is too much." She turned to the little man with the ear horn, riding jacket, and pointed shoes. "And who are you supposed to be? The Lord of Misrule?" Without waiting for an answer, she turned to Burke. "Your mother will be scandalized by your part in this, and believe me, I'll not hesitate to tell her." She nodded firmly.

Everyone seemed to recover from their shock at once and started to explain. Preston held up his hands for silence.

"Mother, do not say another word. This is not a sham wedding. It is real. I am marrying Matty and you will—"

"I will not allow it. Just look at her. The red dress—"

Preston turned to Matty, and he took her hands in his. "She is the most beautiful woman in the world, and I love her. Please proceed with the ceremony."

"I'm going to faint." Lady Stiles put her hand to her forehead. "Smelling salts. Anyone?"

"Have you ever been on the stage?" Norbundshire asked. "Nice performance."

She spared him a glare. "Listen to reason, Preston. That woman is a—"

"I suggest you stop right there." This was neither the time nor the place, but if he didn't do something, his mother would continue to disrupt the ceremony. "If you do not sit down and be quiet, or better still, leave," he whispered, "I will be forced to reveal your little indiscretion. You're not exactly qualified to judge others in the morality department."

"What are you talking about?"

"The fact that Lord Stiles is not my real father. That I am not the true heir, but a bastard."

She gasped and sat down on the nearest chair. "Where did you get such a ridiculous idea?"

"No point in lying. I heard you arguing with Stiles many a time. He would throw it in your face. *That boy is not my son.* Once I knew that, I never questioned why he didn't spend any time with me, or teach me to hunt and fish like other fathers."

"He didn't mean it. He just had a difficult time dealing with your . . . your . . ."

"The circumstances of my birth? My bastard state?"

"Stop saying that word. You are not one. Your father couldn't handle your imperfection. At the time, he was quite overwhelmed with suddenly and unexpectedly becoming the earl. He anticipated so much from a son, and couldn't face the fact you needed special help."

"Perhaps I should speak for myself."

Lord Stiles walked into the room as if he owned the house and everything in it. As he always did. Always the lord of the manor, cool and distant, unapproachable. Tall and distinguished, his silver-gray hair was an asset to his looks rather than a detriment. Preston's three sisters, who looked nothing like him but resembled his mother in their light coloring and pale blue eyes, trailed behind his father.

"Good evening, everyone," Stiles said with unflustered ease. "I was in a cab on my way home from my club expecting nothing more than a dull family supper, when I noticed my carriage parked out front, and discovered my three daughters left shivering in the cold. I logically deduced something was wrong. May I be of service?"

"Your son is marrying that—"

"Careful, Angie. As we've learned belatedly, words can leave wounds that are difficult to heal. Preston, I heard a part of your conversation with your mother, as did the rest of these people. You are my son regardless of any careless words spoken in frustration, and despite my shortcomings as a father. You have only to look at the portrait of my older brother, rest his soul, to see the striking resemblance. Now, perhaps you should introduce me to your bride so at least I can say we met before the wedding."

"But . . . but . . ." Lady Stiles sputtered. "Aren't you going to stop this—"

"No. I stand by whatever choice he makes."

"Well said." Norbundshire stepped forward and shook the earl's hand.

"Hello, Shaky. Didn't recognize you in that outfit." Stiles looked the other man up and down. "Nice coat. New fashion?"

Matty tugged on Preston's arm. She nodded toward his three sisters huddled in the back of the room and took a step in that direction. If he wasn't careful, she would want his sisters to be included in the wedding somehow, as bridesmaids or some such nonsense. And then they would need flowers, and who knew what all. It could be hours before the wedding got restarted, and then they would probably have to start over at the beginning. He grabbed her arm and brought her back to his side.

"We're getting married right now."

Cordelia cried out, and Burke rushed to her side.

"I'm fine," Cordelia said. "I was just surprised by the intensity."

Preston turned to the bishop. "You'd better get to *I do* without delay."

Wiggy rushed through *love, honor, and obey* at top speed, and then said in a breathless voice, "I now pronounce you man and wife. You may kiss the bride." Then he had to sit down.

Preston cupped Matty's face in his hands, and the rest of the world faded away. "My dear, sweet wife. I now have a heart because you have given me yours."

Matty smiled up at her new husband, her world, her happiness. "Kiss me, my love. And be quick about it."

More Regency Romance From Zebra